Shadows over Stonewycke

Books by the Phillips/Pella Writing Team

The Journals of Corrie Belle Hollister

My Father's World
Daughter of Grace
On the Trail of the Truth
A Place in the Sun
Sea to Shining Sea

The Stonewycke Trilogy

The Heather Hills of Stonewycke
Flight from Stonewycke
Lady of Stonewycke

The Stonewycke Legacy

Stranger at Stonewycke
Shadows over Stonewycke
Treasure of Stonewycke

The Highland Collection

Jamie MacLeod: Highland Lass
Robbie Taggart: Highland Sailor

The Russians

The Crown and the Crucible
A House Divided

Shadows over Stonewycke

Michael Phillips
Judith Pella

BETHANY HOUSE PUBLISHERS
MINNEAPOLIS, MINNESOTA 55438
A Division of Bethany Fellowship, Inc.

Manuscript edited by Penelope Stokes.

Cover illustration by Dan Thornberg,
Bethany House Publishers staff artist.

Published by Bethany House Publishers
A Division of Bethany Fellowship, Inc.
6820 Auto Club Road, Minneapolis, Minnesota 55438

Printed in the United States of America

Library of Congress Cataloging-in-Publication Data

Phillips, Michael R., 1946–
    Shadows over Stonewycke/Michael Phillips, Judith Pella.
        p. cm. — (The Stonewycke legacy ; 2)
        1. World War, 1939–1945—Fiction. I. Pella, Judith. II. Title.
III. Series: Phillips, Michael R., 1946–   Stonewycke legacy ; 2.
PS3566.H492S54   1988
813'.54—dc19   88–10332
ISBN 0–87123–901–9 (pbk.)   CIP

Dedication

To my father, Denver Phillips,
and his good friend, Warren Dowling,
both of whose wartime experiences
fell upon my eager boyhood ears.

The Authors

The PHILLIPS/PELLA writing team had its beginning in the longstanding friendship of Michael and Judy Phillips with Judith Pella. Michael Phillips, with a number of nonfiction books to his credit, had been writing for several years. During a Bible study at Pella's home he chanced upon a half-completed sheet of paper sticking out of a typewriter. His author's instincts aroused, he inspected it more closely, and asked their friend, "Do you write?" A discussion followed, common interests were explored, and it was not long before the Phillips invited Pella to their home for dinner to discuss collaboration on a proposed series of novels. Thus, the best-selling "Stonewycke" books were born, which led in turn to "The Highland Collection."

Judith Pella holds a nursing degree and B.A. in Social Sciences. Her background as a writer stems from her avid reading and researching in historical, adventure, and geographical venues. Pella, with her two sons, resides in Eureka, California. Michael Phillips, who holds a degree from Humboldt State University and continues his post-graduate studies in history, owns and operates Christian bookstores on the West Coast. He is the editor of the best-selling George MacDonald Classic Reprint Series and is also MacDonald's biographer. The Phillips also live in Eureka with their three sons.

Contents

Introduction

Out of conflict and crisis frequently emerge life's most significant periods of inner growth. Indeed, according to the Scriptures, from diversity are fortitude and spiritual stamina born.

Allison and Logan's story in Book 1 of The Stonewycke Legacy was a happy one. Yet their coming together cannot be viewed as an end, but rather as the beginning of an ongoing journey that, if it is to build a permanent relationship of love, will encompass more than simply living "happily ever after."

Certainly a deep joy has its part in this journey, but a truly God-divined path will be richly filled with trials as well. The long-haul character of life's most meaningful relationships and experiences is often overlooked by our short-sighted vision which views only the now. We make decisions lightly, little considering the day-by-day lifetime of dedication necessary to carry them out. Nor do we adequately foresee the unavoidable adversities which will build inner resiliency and strength of character that enables us to persevere in those aspects of life to which we have pledged ourselves.

In no two areas of life do our decisions and surface expectations run aground from lack of awareness of the long-haul than in marriage and spiritual dedication. The commitment required to transform a loving marriage into a lifetime partnership of sustained growth and mutual fulfillment parallels the commitment required to sustain one's Christian life following the one-time decision to follow Christ.

Neither commitment to marriage nor to God comes easy. The decision can be made in a moment. Living out the commitment to that decision, after the gloss fades, over the course of decades—that requires something altogether different than a burst of enthusiasm. That sort of lifetime commitment requires *daily* dedication to endure, to stick with the decision over the long-haul.

It is no surprise, then, that so often in the Bible God uses marriage as the perfect illustration or "type" of what being a Christian is really like. Entering into a marriage covenant, and giving one's life to Christ (as His "bride") are similar in a host of ways.

Little wonder, therefore, that when Logan Macintyre and his new bride Allison MacNeil begin to falter in their new lives as Christians, their marriage relationship also starts to waver. They must both learn that most fundamental of lessons: that commitment requires sacrifice, that love re-

9

quires the laying down of one's *own* preconceptions, and that only in denying one's *self* and surrendering all to the Lord will true fulfillment come.

Their story, and their struggle, is not a unique one. All husbands and wives—and all Christians—must eventually pass through the same refining process if they are to discover what true commitment is—to one another and to the Lord.

That process of growth is the soil out of which maturity is able to blossom.

Michael Phillips
Judith Pella
% 1707 E St.
Eureka, CA 95501

1 / Man in the Shadows

The shrill blast of an auto horn blared through the hushed foggy night.

A young man making his stealthy way down the empty street started involuntarily, then paused for a moment. He hugged the concrete wall to his right, keeping well within the shadows. As the car passed, he exhaled a sharp breath and continued on, his heart thudding a hard rhythm within his chest. He had told himself a thousand times there was nothing to be afraid of. No one could have any idea what he was up to. It wasn't as if he were sneaking around in enemy-occupied territory. Yet such analysis was unable to quiet the pounding of his heart.

There was no way he could have been followed! He had taken every precaution, every side street, used all the old ruses. But if someone had by chance slipped up at headquarters—enemy territory or not—it might mean his neck. There were, after all, dangers he knew nothing about. He hated to admit it, but he really knew very little about this game.

He glanced at his wristwatch, but could not make out the tiny hands in the surrounding darkness. The blackout, meant to deter the German Luftwaffe, provided excellent cover for sneaking unnoticed through the streets, even though it did make his watch impossible to read. He had to find out the time. He couldn't be late. And he had another several blocks to go before reaching the bridge.

The hour was late; the deserted streets bore clear witness to that. But you couldn't judge the hour by the activity—Londoners turned in early these days. Since war with Germany had become a reality over a year ago, the people toiled to the limits of human endurance to prepare their small island against the encroaching threat of Adolph Hitler. Seventy-hour work weeks left little physical reserve for walking at night—except for those whose work began at these nefarious hours.

This particular night crawler knew all about factory work. He had put in his own share of long, tedious hours. He'd pushed pencils and brooms. He'd sat behind cluttered, wearisome desks as well as cleaned them. So despite his frayed nerves on this night, the change from his past seven years of drudgery was welcome. Now he wondered how he'd tolerated the monotony for that long.

He had tried to stick to a routine. He'd tried to hold a "normal" job. But it had been no use. His fingers and feet and senses had never gotten over their itch. All that time he had thought he was finished with occupa-

11

tions requiring eyes in the back of his head. But now it looked as if such employment had not finished with *him*. How great that sense of exhilaration felt—just like the old days!

True, there was an added dimension to what he was doing these days: fear. A wrongly spoken word, a mistaken contact, even an overly curious neighbor, could land him squarely in a prison camp or in front of a firing squad. This was no game, as it had been before.

Yet the terror only served to heighten the challenge, the thrill. At least now he was *doing* something—something useful, he hoped.

Suddenly the roar of an automobile broke into his thoughts as it rounded a corner and sped his way. He crouched out of sight and waited. The headlamps were dimmed according to blackout regulations, but in the dull flicker of illumination it afforded, the time on his watch was clearly evident. It was three minutes to eleven.

The man jumped out of his temporary shelter the instant the car was past, and immediately quickened his pace. His rendezvous was to take place at eleven sharp. If he missed it, he could not only endanger his contact, but would almost certainly quell his superior's willingness to confer another such assignment on him.

All at once he heard footsteps. A regular beat of leather soles against the hard pavement, seemingly in perfect rhythm with his own, echoed behind him. His heart raced again, even as his feet slowed to a stop. He paused before a closed shop window, pretending to look at the wares behind the glass. It was hardly a believable ploy since he could barely make out whether he was observing shoes, teapots, or women's hose. But at least it would tell him if the time had come to start worrying again.

The footsteps continued, getting louder. A short pudgy man came indistinctly into view, strolled by, tipping a gray derby hat and breaking the intense quiet of the night with a jaunty, "Evenin', mate!"

As the innocuous little man passed into the invisible silence, the edgy night-walker shook his head and reminded himself that he had to keep his cool. That had always been his major asset. He needed it now more than ever.

Even as the man's retreating steps were swallowed up by the night, in the distance the faint sounds of a ship's horn could be heard from upriver, its deep-rumbling tone carried through the sound-dulling fog. The familiar echo reminded him of Big Ben, now strangely silent because of the war, and brought home to him more graphically than ever the fact that he was late. The man hastened on.

In four minutes he stood at the foot of London Bridge. A more fitting place could not have been chosen for such a meeting—especially at this hour! Wreaths of gray fog clung to the towering steel. The night was calm, and the fog swirled about in slow motion, weaving in and out of the pilings below and the steel columns above the bridge, obscuring the topmost spires—an eerie reminder that strange, almost cosmic forces were hurling world events toward an unknown end.

The scene was straight out of a cheap spy novel. But this was no story; there was a war on, and this kind of thing happened from the necessity born of the times. Though he had a penchant for adventure, he would have liked the place better in the sunlight, buzzing with traffic and life. It was crazy to send him alone to such a deserted place. It was too obvious, too great an invitation for foul play.

He peered into the fog, then began walking straight ahead. He had gone perhaps a hundred and fifty feet when he realized the bridge wasn't deserted at all. At first he thought it might be his contact, but as he drew closer he saw that he was approaching a young couple. A soldier and a young lady were standing arm in arm, gazing out upon the Thames.

What brought them out so late? he wondered absently, momentarily allowing his thoughts to drift away from his own concerns. No doubt the fellow had been called up and this was their last night together before he was shipped off to some distant part of the war. The scene was a melancholy one; there were probably tears in the girl's eyes.

Or perhaps the soldier was home on leave and the words being softly spoken were of blissful happiness at the reunion. The war made all of life a drama, and every man and woman occupied a private little corner of the stage on which to play out his or her personal destiny.

This man's destiny at the moment, however, was farther along the bridge. He had no time to philosophize over two young lovers, nor stew about his own unfitness to be a soldier.

Instinctively he glanced once more at his watch, forgetting it would do him little good. It had to be time for his meeting. Past time. He knew he was late. Where was his contact? This was the place—center of the span. Eleven p.m.

The man slowed his pace, walked a little farther. Behind him the romancing couple ambled away, and he was left alone. Finally he stopped altogether. He turned his eyes toward the river, of which he could catch but an occasional glimmer as the black slow-moving current glided silently through the fog and darkness. An occasional dull foghorn in the distance broke the heavy silence.

"Good evening, mein Herr," said a voice suddenly out of the empty night behind him. The accent was decidedly German. Though the tone was quiet and the words evenly spoken, he could not help nearly jumping out of his skin. He had heard no approaching steps, and thought he was completely alone. "The river is grand under the night sky, is it not?" the foreign voice went on.

What would old Skits think to see me so jumpy? he thought to himself, but to the stranger he replied, "It is grand any time of the day," making every effort to infuse his voice with a calm his heart did not feel. He could not betray that he had been startled.

The code phrases of introduction were particularly ridiculous just now, but at least they gave the two men assurance that they had each found the right person.

"I am Gunther," said the contact, a tall, lean, middle-aged man dressed in a heavy wool overcoat and slanted felt hat that shadowed an austere, pock-marked face. Had the young man been able to make out the features under the felt brim more clearly, his fear would only have been the greater. It was not a friendly face. "Who are you?"

"Macintyre—" The instant the word passed his lips, Logan Macintyre realized his foolish blunder.

"—Trinity, that is," he added hastily. They had been given code names—his was *Trinity* and his contact was *Gunther*. How could he have done something so stupid? He must be slipping, losing his touch, forgetting that whatever the cloak of solemnity over this business, it was, deep down, nothing more than a complicated con game. His error had not gone unnoticed.

"I see they send me a novice," said Gunther, shaking his head.

"Don't worry. I know what I'm doing."

"Hopefully that will not matter," replied Gunther.

Logan wrinkled his brow. He didn't like to think that he had come all the way across town, risking who could tell what hazards, only to be told that his part in this assignment was relatively unimportant.

Yet who was he trying to kid? That fact had been clear enough from the beginning. They had said, "We need a stand-in . . . a body. You won't have to know anything, do anything. We just need somebody they don't know."

Logan had desperately wanted to believe it would be more than that. He had probably even imagined all the need for secrecy and stealth in getting here. He glanced at Gunther. It was dark, but he could see it in his eyes nonetheless: it had not even mattered that he had used his real name instead of the code.

"Where are we going?" asked Logan, glad to change the subject.

"We will walk as we talk," replied his companion, ". . . to avoid eavesdroppers."

There wasn't a soul in sight, and Logan could not imagine a possible hiding place a hundred and fifty feet above the icy Thames. But he did not argue the point.

"Now, about your assignment . . ." continued Gunther, who was already a pace ahead.

Logan took a deep breath and turned to follow Gunther as he strode away. No matter what he did tonight, or how trivial his task, he was determined to prove his worth.

2 / The Hills of Stonewycke _____

The morning was especially crisp and vivid. Fresh snow had fallen during the night, covering the hills and valleys of Stonewycke and the Strathy Valley with a clean, sparkling layer of white.

Though the sky was blue and the sun shone brightly, the air was frigid as only January in northern Scotland could be. Even the faintest hint of wind would have given the air cruel fingers with which to reach in and lay hold of the very marrow of one's bones. But on this particular morning the wind was quiet, and Allison did not mind the frosty chill as she traipsed along the icy path. She had been out walking at this same early hour every morning for the last week, hoping that the barren frozen landscape of her surroundings would in some miraculous way instill a new peace into her consciousness.

She sighed, then stooped down to scoop up a handful of the snow, and her thoughts were diverted to the more pleasant paths of her childhood. How she and her brothers and sister had always delighted when the first snows had fallen! Little May, the youngest of the four, had been too small to join in to much of the winter mayhem, but occasionally their mother would bundle up the little one and Allison would take her for a wild ride down the hill on the sled.

And the snowball fights!

Her brothers were merciless as they stood behind their stockpiled cache of icy ammunition, pelting whomever chanced by, regardless of age, sex, or religion. Occasionally they grudgingly admitted that even she had a pretty good arm for a girl.

Allison smiled. Those had been happy times. Her mother and father had made Stonewycke a joyful place to grow up. But just as quickly as the involuntary movement tugged at her lips, it began to fade.

They were all grown up now. Sled rides and snowball fights and stories read by Mother and Daddy while the four of them snuggled cozily under a blanket seemed far in the past these days. And if the years themselves had fallen short in the maturing process, the war was rapidly finishing the job. Ian, the eldest, a pilot in the RAF, was stationed in Africa, and Nat was with the 51st Highland Division of Scotland. After distinguishing themselves in France at the time of the Dunkirk evacuation, Nat's division was being reassigned and Nat hoped for a place in a newly formed commando unit. Both were men now, seasoned soldiers, yet Nat was not yet even twenty-one years old.

Time was passing so quickly. Allison was now twenty-five. The war had come suddenly to dominate their lives, changing them all, forcing maturity upon them perhaps before its rightful time, pushing them onto paths they might otherwise never have chosen. Yet Allison wondered if she could truly lay the blame for her own mixed-up life on this war. If she questioned herself honestly, she had to admit that her confusion had begun long before Adolf Hitler had stormed through Poland. She couldn't pinpoint the exact moment. There was not a particular day she remembered when she could say, "Then it was when the joy began to fade . . . when things began to unravel." It had come upon her gradually, and the moments of discontent remained so mixed with alternating seasons of joy that she was still not entirely certain what was happening.

Before her thoughts progressed further, she glanced down at her palm still holding its handful of snow, now unconsciously molded by her gloved fingers into a round ball. With a swift motion she flung it into the air, watching it arch back to earth, falling with a silent puff of white spray into a snowbank. If only she could cast her tensions away so easily!

What had gone wrong? It had all started out so wonderfully!

During those weeks and months following his near-fatal wound, she and Logan had been blissfully in love. Everything had fallen perfectly into place for them—their meeting, their new spiritual priorities, their hopes for the future. The first injection of *realism*, if such it could be called, into the idyllic season of the budding of their young love came when her mother and father counseled them to wait rather than rush immediately into marriage. They were young—especially Allison, only seventeen at the time. And Logan needed time to establish a living, a legitimate one, capable of supporting a family.

They had waited, Logan perhaps more patiently than Allison. The trip to London was made as planned. Allison, Joanna, and Logan had seen much, met some of Logan's old friends, and had a pleasurable time cementing their new relationships one with another. Even Joanna and Allison seemed to have discovered each other in many respects for the first time. After their return to Stonewycke, Logan once again took up his duties as mechanic to the estate and surrounding crofts.

At length the wedding was planned for February 1933, almost a year from the day Logan had entered into their lives. Ironically, in hindsight, it also coincided closely with Hitler's rise to power in Germany. If that had any significance at the time, Allison was certainly unaware of it. The forebodings from the Continent did not become ominous for several years to come.

However, the death that previous December of her great-grandfather suddenly made a February wedding seem unthinkable. Who could possibly plan a wedding with the loss of such a beloved family patriarch so fresh? With old Dorey's passing at ninety, the whole community mourned. Yet in spite of the loss of her beloved, Lady Margaret would have them wait no longer than the summer. And so the much anticipated event finally took place in June of 1933.

It was a day long remembered in the environs of Port Strathy, rivaled only by the wedding of Joanna and Alec in the scope of its hospitality. But unlike Joanna's, which was held in the local church, Allison's took place on the estate itself, in the lovely gardens tended by Lord Duncan, in special tribute to the beloved man.

There could not have been a more perfect day. Allison cherished no more misguided notions about class distinctions, and the whole valley was present, from poorest to wealthiest, from refined to most humble. Patty Doohan was bridesmaid, along with Sarah Bramford and Olivia Fairgate. Allison wore her mother's exquisite wedding dress of sculptured lace and pearls; Logan looked even more debonair than usual in his pinstriped dark blue tuxedo and tails. Several times throughout the day he was heard to say, *If only Skittles could see me now!* But notwithstanding the absence of his old friend, he had managed to bring Molly Ludlowe north by train, as well as his mother from Glasgow. Joanna welcomed them warmly as they had her when she visited them before the wedding. She made them feel completely a part of the family and after the ceremony, both stayed on with her in the castle for a week.

Everyone commented on what a striking couple the two newlyweds made. The wait had done them good, for now Allison was sure that it was not only in appearance that they were so perfectly suited. There were many ways in which they complemented each other. Logan enjoyed Allison's independent spirit, but was not intimidated by it. Allison both admired and needed the strong masculine protection and leadership Logan gave, and at the same time could not help loving his easygoing, lighthearted nature. They had seemed so right for each other. Could it be that the very qualities that had originally drawn them together had now turned against them?

Something her great-grandfather had said to her before his death came back with increasing frequency these days: "I believe God has brought you and Logan together, my dear. I see a bond growing between the two of you that reminds me of your great-grandmother and me when we were your age. Your love will surely count for much in the Kingdom. But—" Here Dorey's ancient brown eyes deepened with intensity; Allison knew he spoke not mere words but feelings born out of his depth of experience. "But the path He has laid out for you may not be free from pain and sorrow."

Allison had been touched by the words at the time, for she loved and highly respected her great-grandfather. But, in the idealism of youth, it was easy to shrug them off as springing more from the pessimism of old age than any reality she needed concern herself with.

Yet as the words came back to her on many occasions these days, she had grown to see them as the result of his wisdom, not any misplaced elderly melancholia. The deep sensitivity that had worked its way into his nature through the years of his solitude had given him vision to perceive what lay down the road for the young couple. Dorey and Logan had also spoken privately together for an hour while Dorey lay in the bed from which he would not arise.

Allison had always wondered if that last conversation between the two men had somehow concerned the same matter. Logan had been solemn and subdued afterward, but never revealed to a soul what had transpired between them.

If Dorey had sensed trouble in the union, the logical question Allison found herself asking was: Why had he done nothing to prevent it? Allison had come to respect him more than she might at one time have cared to admit; they would have listened to his counsel.

Yet even as she debated with herself, she knew what he would have said. *Child*, she could hear his voice saying, *this love is ordained of God. It is to be. It may be a love that will know sorrow, that is true. Of that kind of love I am intimately familiar. But while we are upon this earth, it is our response to the sorrows the Lord sends that carve out the cavity within our natures to hold the joy He pours into them. The greater the sorrows, the greater the possible joys, and the greater our potential service to Him. Love your young man, and marry him, and serve the Lord with him. And when sorrows come, as they surely will, let them deepen your love and enlarge your capacity to receive God's life.*

Yes, that is what Dorey would have said.

And she could not imagine, even now, life without Logan. She had loved him then, and she loved him still.

Yet, could she be sure that love would be enough?

3 / South to London

Not long after the wedding, Logan began to grow restive.

Working as the estate mechanic had been all right for Logan Macintyre, bachelor, ne'er-do-well, and sometimes con man. But as son-in-law to nobility, he began to see the grease on his hands from a different perspective. He cared nothing at all for class distinctions; neither did the family into which he had been grafted in the tradition of Ian Duncan and Alec MacNeil apply any pressure for him to "better himself." Yet pride is a strange phenomenon, often showing neither logic nor sense, and assuming a variety of intricate disguises. Slowly Logan's self-respect began to dwindle. He felt like a leech, taking but never giving, living off the family spoils and offering nothing substantive in return. He had fended for himself all his life, and now he was reduced to taking what the lower side of his nature called "hand-outs" from his wife's family.

He did not doubt their love and their acceptance of him. Yet he could not keep from feeling less a man for being under the protective covering of Stonewycke. To keep his eroding respect for himself intact, he needed to make something of himself and his marriage on his own.

"But, Logan," Allison tried to tell him, "you work hard, and more than earn your way."

"Do you think we'd ever afford a place like this on fifteen pounds a month?" he rejoined caustically. He hadn't wanted to argue, but he was frustrated—mostly with himself.

"Well, maybe not . . . but, then, none of us could actually afford Stonewycke, if you think about it." Allison had tried to lighten the heavy atmosphere, but Logan was in no mood, especially since he had just arrived at a decision that would not make Allison happy.

"I want to move to London," he said flatly.

Allison stared into his face blankly. The greatest irony about his statement was that only a couple of years before, Allison had longed to escape the boredom—as she considered it then—of Stonewycke. She had dreamed of an exciting life in the city. Edinburgh would have suited her fine. But London! That would have been the fulfillment of all she could have desired!

But now, with new priorities, new commitments—not only to Logan, but also to family, to land, and not least of all to her faith—she had come at last to feel an intrinsic part of everything that Stonewycke represented. How could she even think about leaving at this particular moment? Lady

Margaret was ailing, and her mother feared she might not be with them much longer.

A time of tension followed. Logan was unhappy where he was, that was clear. Allison was miserable for him, but she could not bear the thought of leaving. Without anything settled, life managed to go on, but a strained silence came to characterize what had once been a relationship full of laughter and shared joys.

One day about a month later, Logan received a mysterious letter. He opened it privately and not until that evening did he show it to Allison. She bit her lip as she read it, then looked up at him, unable to speak.

"I'm going to take the job," he said with finality, leaving Allison little room for refutation.

The letter was from a friend in London who was opening a restaurant. He had offered Logan a position.

"But you have work *here*," she replied.

"Work, maybe. But no future."

"How can you say that? Someday you'll—"

"Someday I'll what? Be an even better mechanic! Don't you see, Allison? Sometime I'll have to get out on my own."

"But why, Logan? Why now? We're in the middle of a depression. We're secure here for the present. Why risk that?"

"It's just something I have to do."

"But what do you know about the restaurant business? It doesn't make sense for you to jump at the first thing to come along."

"You said it—we're in a depression. I'm lucky to have such an offer."

"But things couldn't possibly be as good for us in London as they are here."

"There's just no way I can make you understand," he said, throwing down the letter and stalking away.

Allison might have continued to rebel at the idea, but the following day her mother and great-grandmother took her aside for a long, soul-searching conversation. When she left them she knew what she must do.

"Stonewycke will still be here once he knows what he wants to do with his life," they reminded her. "Stonewycke will always be here. And we will be here for you, too."

Perhaps she had known all along what her answer to Logan must be, but the two older women had guided her in the right direction, helping her to see where her true love must lie.

Leaving Strathy had not been easy—for either Allison or Logan. Tears had flowed that day without restraint. For despite Logan's determination to stand on his own two feet, he had developed—perhaps more than he realized on the conscious level—a deep love for old Stonewycke. Not only was it the place where his dear ancestor Digory had lived, but it was also filled with recent memories. Here Logan had met his God. Here, on these lovely heather hills, his and Allison's life together had begun. And here they had pledged their lives to each other.

Logan did not carelessly walk away from all this, but he was doing what he felt he had to do. What made it the hardest on him was his certainty that he did not have the family's approval in his decision. Logan still had much to learn about the family into which he had come. Had he been able to summon the courage to reveal his hidden fears and motives openly to Alec and Joanna and Lady Margaret, he would have quickly discovered their understanding and compassion to be far-reaching and filled with tenderness. They would no doubt have supported him, perhaps even applauded his high principles, though they might well, at the same time, have cautioned him to be heedful of pride. Above all, they would have held him up in prayer while wrapping him in the understanding arms of love.

But Logan had lived too long encased in a protective shield designed to mask his innermost feelings. It went against his very nature to open his soul and reveal all. And the door seemed to shut all the more tightly when his feelings of inferiority began to harass him. God was at work, slowly peeling back one layer of his inner being at a time. But Logan was not yet ready to yield himself entirely up to the process and say, "Thy *complete* will be done with me."

Once Allison had resigned herself to the change, she and Logan settled down to their new lives and found renewed happiness in each other. They located a flat in Shoreditch, not far from Molly Ludlowe. It was no Stonewycke, and was noticeably threadbare for a girl who had grown up, if not with wealth, at least in a comfortable home, free from want. Allison made a commendable attempt to turn the tiny place into a home. She painted the dingy rooms, hung curtains, and arranged a few prints she had brought from Scotland. Here and there were scattered reminders of Strathy.

Almost to Allison's surprise, after some time had passed she began to find the city life appealing. She had always sensed that the agrarian nature had not run quite so deeply in her blood as in her mother and her ancestors. And when that truth bore in upon her even more forcibly after a couple of years in the city, she was not certain whether to be happy or sad. She hoped she was not an anomaly in the strong line of Stonewycke matriarchs that had maintained their vigilant watch over the northern valley for more than a century. Certainly the same Ramsey and Duncan blood coursed through her veins. Yet she found herself thrilled to dress up to attend a play or a concert—not a frequent occurrence, since Logan would accept very little financial help from her family—almost as happy as she knew Lady Margaret had been to walk the Scottish hills.

Even in the midst of the worldwide depression, the young couple managed to live adequately. Logan's personality insured his success in his friend's enterprise. Despite their gradual drifting apart, Allison found plenty to occupy her time. Many of her former acquaintances, having finished school or married, had come south to the social and financial hub of the world, and she began to mix with them as before.

But Allison's friends did not appeal to Logan, and he shied away, keeping more and more to himself. Not that he minded their blue blood, or so he told himself. Such things had never bothered him before. But he wanted to make something of himself. He wanted more in life than had previously been his, and he didn't want to slide into it like the Bramfords and the Fairgates and the Robertsons. He could hardly help resenting their genteel ways. His motives were not ones of greed; he simply wanted to better his lot, to stand on his own two feet. And at the same time, by virtue of his marriage, he felt compelled to provide Allison with a standard of life he thought she deserved. Mixing with her friends only seemed to emphasize his deficiencies. He would become something first; then he would be able to walk in such circles with head high.

In the meantime, just a few months after their move to the city, Lady Margaret went to join her beloved Dorey. Her death was painless and peaceful; with the confidence of one going home at last, she joyfully relinquished this life and embraced the real life of eternity. And although the family mourned, they found joy amidst their tears in the certainty that they would all, at last, be reunited.

Allison grieved for her great-grandmother's passing, then threw herself with renewed vigor into her schedule of social activities. Keeping busy seemed to alleviate the pain of her loss, but gradually her life and Logan's began to follow divergent paths. Too proud to admit his own insecurities, Logan put up a front toward the outside world, and without realizing it at first, toward Allison as well. Wrapped up in her own activities, she was unable to see the forces gnawing away at him until their communication had already broken down. When at length Allison began to sense that perhaps her husband was not as content as he seemed, she was unable to get him to open up in order to find what was bothering him.

The situation was aggravated by Logan's unstable employment status. The restaurant position, after a hopeful beginning, soon fell short of Logan's expectations for advancement. He had conceived of himself as a public relations man and head maitre d'. But when the restaurant did not grow as anticipated, he found himself nothing more than a low-paid waiter, with little hope that more would be offered. His personality and connections had little trouble landing him jobs, even in the midst of hard times, but they led nowhere. Money was scarce and talented people were out of work everywhere. He took a position in a brokerage firm, but sitting behind a desk all day hardly suited his adventurous disposition. Besides, the investment trade was in terrible straits. Then came a string of dead-end jobs—shoe salesman, cab driver, hotel desk clerk, night watchman/janitor—each one appearing better than the last, but none in the end measuring up to Logan's high hopes.

Though the first five years of their marriage followed this pattern, they were not years without occasional moments of happiness. The foundation of love begun in their first days together helped transcend the tensions of their present lives. But time ate away at their faltering relationship, and the closeness they had once shared was not sufficient in itself to bolster a sagging foundation. Involved in personal frustrations, both Allison and Logan were too preoccupied to see that the focus of their lives had dramatically shifted. No longer were they putting the other first in their considerations, and no longer were they jointly looking for guidance from the God to whom they had committed their lives. Thus they were unable to see that He alone could deliver their marriage from the pitfalls toward which it was certainly bound.

Letters back to Stonewycke veiled the problems. But during the two or three visits Joanna and Alec made during the time, the hidden frustrations could not help surfacing. Allison's parents tried to intercede, but both Logan and Allison had so slipped back into their former tendencies that they were unable to listen humbly enough and let go of pride and selfishness enough to see the true nature of their need.

4 / The Coming of War

Curiously, in spite of the difficulties she and Logan had had, Allison found herself longing for a child. A baby, she hoped, would pull the two of them together, give them a common focus in life and perhaps renew their love. But for over four years this gift was denied them.

Then in 1938, coinciding frighteningly with what Churchill called Hitler's rape of Austria and later invasion of Czechoslovakia, Allison found that her prayers were answered. She could have wished for happier times to bring her new daughter, Joanna, into the world. But despite the tensions throughout Europe from Germany's aggressive movements, Allison could not have been happier to welcome her mother into their simple London flat. Joanna would be staying to share the Christmas season with Allison and Logan and her new granddaughter.

The child for a time drew her parents together again, but the change was temporary at best. Only a year later, in the fall of 1939, war finally came to France and Britain. By now the mask of their love had worn so thin that they had to admit all was not well. For Logan, the war only deepened his feelings of having failed—himself, his wife, and now his growing family. The moment hostilities were declared, he tried to enlist. His prison record, however, came back to haunt him. Though by most standards his offenses were minor ones, the mere hint of his having been involved in counterfeiting, coupled with his unexplained four months in Germany in 1929, placed Logan in what British Recruitment considered a "high risk" category. Logan could not divulge the details of the con he had been working on in Germany for fear of repercussions to friends; so, while his peers marched proudly off to fight the Germans, he had to bear the shame of remaining behind. No matter what he turned his hand to, it seemed he failed. He began to look back with longing to his pre-marriage days with Skittles and Billy. True, what he was doing then was not a virtuous pursuit. But he had been good at it—and enjoyed it.

At least the financial worries of the depression years were now past since jobs were plenteous in wartime Britain. The war immediately spawned whole new industries, and now Logan took a low-level position in a munitions factory, hoping in time to move up. If he couldn't join the war effort as a soldier, then he might as well do what he could behind the lines, and profit from it as well. However, the hoped-for advancement never came, and after nearly a year the assembly-line job had become pure drudgery. Allison had begun to think that perhaps he had settled down, though deep inside she knew him too well to believe he could be happy at such employment for long.

In the spring of 1940, he came home early one day, casually planted a kiss on Allison's cheek, and began to play with little Joanna, now a toddler, as if there were nothing unusual in his appearance in midafternoon.

"Logan," the inquisitive Allison asked, "you're never home before six or six-thirty." She tried to sound casual, but feared her voice betrayed her concern. "Is . . . anything wrong?"

"I've got a new job."

"They've moved you to a new department?"

Logan understood the thrust of her questioning well enough. They had been through the process enough times for him to sense her dissatisfaction with his unstable job situation without her having to say a word. But not inclined to argue just now, he too attempted to strike a casual attitude, as if they had never spoken of such things before.

"No," he answered, "that factory job wasn't for me. I have a friend who's found me something . . . more interesting. It's perfect. No more job changes for a long time."

"Logan—" Allison began, her voice thinning in frustration. Then she stopped herself. "What is it?" she asked.

"It's in an office . . ." He hesitated a moment; Allison sensed immediately that he was holding something back.

"You've never liked office work."

"This is different. I'll be working for the government." There was a slight defensiveness in his tone.

"The government? But I thought—"

"What's the matter, don't you believe me?" he snapped. "Why the third degree? I'll be doing something to help the country!"

"Of course I believe you. It's just—"

"Don't worry. I'm making more money than at the factory."

"How could you say such a thing? You know your happiness means more than money to me."

"Your trips to Harrods would not seem to indicate that. Even with rationing, you've managed to run up a sizable bill."

"Logan—!" she protested, then turned away, biting her lip.

Logan immediately regretted his harsh, defensive words. Haltingly he reached out to lay his hand on her shoulder, but she tensed beneath his touch.

"I'm sorry," he said.

"I'm only interested in you, Logan," she replied in a trembling voice. "I just want so badly for you to be happy, and for us—to be . . ."

"My dear Ali," he replied gently, gathering her into his arms, "that's all I want, too—for you—for us both."

Thus the brief argument over Logan's job ended, heated words giving way to the love for one another still struggling to surface. Yet notwithstanding, no lasting understanding between them was to be found. Allison's specific questions with regard to Logan's new position were forgotten in the immediacy of one brief moment of blissful togetherness. But he never did open to her further. And desiring no renewal of the tension, Allison swallowed her hurt and did not ask again, though with the passage of every new day she longed more than ever to know, to share his life. As still more time passed, a deep-set fear began to gnaw away at the edges of Allison's consciousness—the dread that perhaps he had returned to his old ways. He occasionally spoke of his new "job," but always in the most vague and general of terms. And what governmental position, she thought, would require such odd and irregular hours, and seemingly so much secrecy? Yet she steadfastly refused to believe he had reverted back to his life on the streets, and made a concerted effort to push such possibilities from her mind.

In the summer of 1940, England began to gear up for the expected German invasion of the tiny island, essentially all that stood in Hitler's way of a total conquest of Europe. With many in like circumstances, Allison made plans to leave London with their daughter, intending to return to the safety of Stonewycke until the danger of enemy attack had passed. In vain she tried to convince Logan to join her. But he insisted that his job responsibilities were too important to leave now. Again she questioned him without success as to the nature of what he did. His sudden loyalty, she said, hardly seemed characteristic of the man who had had no fewer than a dozen jobs in five years and had had little qualms about leaving any of them. Still he would reveal nothing, leaving Allison to make the journey north alone, and fearing the worst.

"Well, I should at least have your office number in case I need to reach you," she said at length with resignation in her voice. Such was not, however, her only reason for making that request.

"I'll be sure to call you two or three times a week," he answered evasively.

"But what if there's an emergency? How will I get hold of you?"

"Nothing's likely to happen," he replied, then paused. "Well . . . here's a number, then. But only for an emergency, nothing else." He quickly jotted a phone number down on a slip of paper and handed it to her.

"Maybe I shouldn't go, Logan," Allison sighed as she took the paper. "I don't want to leave you here alone. All this talk of invasion is probably just an overreaction. Last year everyone left the cities so worried, and nothing ever came of it."

"It's different now that France has fallen," said Logan. "The Nazis are only forty miles away, and they have no reason to hold back. Everyone knows Hitler's only waiting for the right time to attack."

Allison sighed again. "I suppose you're right. And you'd no doubt be happier if I went away," she said, voicing the fear that was more real to her than any Nazi invasion.

Logan turned away, shaking his head in frustration. "It has nothing to do with that!" he said angrily. Yet even as he spoke the words, he could not honestly say there was no truth in the accusation. Instead, he lamely added, "This is wartime, Allison. We both have things we have to do. Everyone is making sacrifices. Your father and brothers are in the army. You and your mother volunteer your time. Why can't you let me have the chance to do my part, too?"

"I didn't know your job had anything to do with the war," said Allison, trying to be sympathetic.

"I didn't say it did—exactly. But at least here in London I might have the opportunity to do something."

"You *were* doing something at the munitions factory—"

"Are you going to start on that again?"

Allison sighed. "I guess it is best I go. We can't seem to talk about much of anything these days."

"We might be able to if you could only trust me a little."

Allison said nothing.

"Besides, the fact is, it's just not safe in London right now."

At that moment a waking cry came from the next room. Allison turned to go, and thus the conversation was kept from escalating further.

Allison tarried in London another week, hoping somehow to convince Logan to leave with her. But in this effort she met with no success, and as the days passed she knew it would be foolhardy to expose their daughter any longer to the terrible German air raids. They had begun in early July and mounted in severity as the summer progressed.

So in the end Allison returned north to Stonewycke. She arrived at her beloved home and fell into her mother's arms hurt, confused, and even a bit lonely. But she dried the tears of her first day, by the second was able to breathe deeply again of the fragrant sea air, and on the third took baby Jo out for a walk. Inside, however, she remained silently afraid, wondering what her husband was doing during her absence, and what she would find upon her return.

5 / Mother and Daughter ⸺

Joanna saw her daughter in the distance as she crested the top of the snow-covered hill. Even from here Joanna could see the pensive, troubled expression—not at all like her usual confident self. Times had changed. Her daughter was a woman now, with all the cares of adulthood pressing upon her.

It had been almost six months since her daughter and granddaughter had come to Stonewycke to escape the bombing in London. The year 1940 had been difficult, not only for their family, but for all of Britain. London had nearly been lost under the assault of the German air attack, and the threat of invasion remained ever present.

It had been an especially hard time for Allison. Not only had the distance separated her from her husband, but their parting had not been on the best of terms. Of course it was wartime, and many women were having to deal with such anxieties. There were thousands who had lost their husbands. Unfortunately, such knowledge made it no easier for Allison. At least when I had kissed Alec farewell, thought Joanna; the embrace was tender, and each of us was sure of our abiding love. If only Allison possessed such a memory to carry her through!

Logan had spent two weeks at Strathy during Christmastime. But Joanna sensed the awkwardness he felt, acutely feeling the absence of the other men, away at war while he comfortably celebrated a holiday with the women. Had that been his only discomfort, of course, the atmosphere might have been better. But the sensitive mother could tell there was still tension between Allison and Logan and if anything, it had worsened.

If only they could shed their insecurities and self-centered motives, thought Joanna. Yet how much better would she have done at their age? Their faith may have cooled, but Joanna was certain it was not completely cold. They only needed something to remind them of life's real priorities, and then to nudge them back along the right path. Hopefully something would come out of this difficult time to accomplish that. Joanna regretted that she could not be that instrument. But as respectful as the young people were, they did not always heed her words of wisdom.

Dear Lord, Joanna silently prayed, *I know they both have hearts for you. Do what you must to mature them out of themselves. Refocus their eyes, Lord, onto the needs of each other, and onto you.*

How often Joanna wished she possessed the compelling wisdom of her grandmother! But Lady Margaret was gone, and even after many years, sometimes when stumbling upon a familiar object or a dearly loved place, Joanna would often find herself in tears. There was nothing about the estate that had not in some way been touched by dear Maggie. Joanna doubted she would ever cease to feel her loss.

Then Joanna smiled softly to herself. *Grandma left her wisdom, too*, she thought. *As her presence and the memory of her smile linger in places and things so does her spirit linger through all the grounds of Stonewycke. Perhaps her wisdom, too, passed down from God through her, lingers in those of us whom she loved.*

"Oh, Lord," whispered Joanna, "I know she left me with a spiritual heritage that is not dependent on my own strength or insight. Through her I learned that my strength is in you. When I call on you, you are there. Continue her legacy, Lord. If it be your will, transfer the cloak of her wisdom to me, as she prayed on the very day of her death. And, like your servant Elisha, let me be faithful to serve you with it. Give me your wisdom, Lord God. And make me your faithful and obedient daughter."

Even as she voiced the prayer, as she had done on numerous occasions previously, Joanna's thoughts went back to that day eight years earlier. No doubt sensing that her time was short and desiring her final moments to be spent with her dear granddaughter, Lady Margaret had called Joanna to her bedside. She smiled, for there was no fear in her, and took Joanna's hand in hers.

"I remember," the peaceful old woman had said in a faint voice, "another time I thought I was dying. Even in my delirium back then I knew I could not die without passing on to you the heritage of Stonewycke, though I was nearly too late. But God spared me, and it was as though He had given me a second life. How many times since then have I given Him thanks for allowing me to live these later years of my life with you, and with my Ian!"

"He must have known that I still had much to learn from you," said Joanna lovingly.

"You have learned well, my dear child. You have been an inspiration to me as well. I can go in peace to my rest."

"Oh, Grandma!" Joanna closed her eyes as they filled with tears.

"You will no doubt cry much in the next days, Joanna. How I wish I could be there to comfort you! But you will have our Lord to rely on. Remember His words, 'I must go away, that the Comforter can come.' Let Him comfort you, my dear, for it is now my time to go away. You will not begrudge me going to my Ian?"

"No, Grandma," said Joanna, with a smile through her tears. "Tell dear Dorey I love him more than ever."

"I will, child. I think he knows!"

"I will miss the two of you," said Joanna, weeping afresh.

"I have asked myself what final words I would leave you with. But I think I have given you all I have to give. If not, I suppose it is too late now."

She chuckled softly. "Twenty-two years ago I gave you the heritage of my family, though you hardly knew what it meant at the time. You had to come to Scotland to discover it for yourself."

Margaret paused. The lengthy speech was clearly taking its toll, but she struggled to continue. "But now, Joanna," she went on, "I leave you with the most important gift of all—the very sustenance and lifeblood of Stonewycke—the one inheritance that can never leave you: the love and hope of our Lord. I pray our heavenly Father will pass on to you a hundredfold whatever I might have. I think what you will face in this modern twentieth-century world will far surpass anything we of previous generations could imagine. But I know His strength will be equal to it, and He will remain faithful to you."

By now Margaret's eyes were flashing with the fire of her younger years, and tears streamed down Joanna's face. The fire, however, was not of youth but rather the final swelling glow of a dying ember, as the light from this life faded into the light of the life to come. When Joanna looked up through her glistening eyes a moment later, the dear lady's eyes were closed and she slept peacefully. Joanna bent down and kissed the wrinkled cheek, then rose to leave the room.

When she returned in two hours to bring her tea, Maggie had breathed her last breath and her peacefulness was not of this world.

Joanna fell upon her knees and quietly wept. For so many generations the continuation of the Stonewycke bloodline had lain with the woman. Alec was a strong, godly, man, worthy to head a great house. Yet in that moment Joanna knew that, as the next woman in the Ramsey/Duncan lineage, a heavy responsibility now rested on her shoulders. Thus at forty-three, she became matriarch of the proud and ancient family. From that moment she was always conscious of the memory of both Atlanta and Margaret, seeking not only to follow the guidance of their God and hers, but aware of their spirit, their love for Stonewycke, and their legacy living on through her.

Now, at fifty-one, the gray had taken over more of her hair. She was a grandmother herself. Her husband and two of her sons were out of the country fighting in a fearful war. And her eldest daughter's marriage, begun with such high hopes, was charting a dangerous course through rocky water, and she seemed powerless to help.

She looked up, saw Allison drawing near, raised her hand in a wave, and smiled warmly.

"Good morning, dear," said Joanna. "Do you mind some company?"

"Of course not. I was just out . . . you know, thinking."

"It is a beautiful day for that," replied Joanna.

"But the more I think, and even try to pray, the more confusing it all becomes," said Allison in frustration.

Joanna reached around her daughter's shoulder and gave her a hug as they continued to walk slowly.

Allison sighed deeply, glancing away into the distance. In her heart she knew her words to be, though true, only a shadow of the whole truth. She realized that she had offered no more than perfunctory prayers, having somehow convinced herself that God expected her to work everything out for herself. She had drifted from her Father, she knew that. How to recapture the intimacy she had once known was another matter. That was a path she had never walked. And admitting to her mother the void that had crept into her heart would have been more difficult still.

But Joanna was not Maggie's granddaughter for nothing.

"He will speak," she said at length, "but you must be open to hear Him. God's guidance always involves both His speaking and our listening."

Allison did not reply for a moment. "Mother," she said abruptly, as if she had not heard Joanna's words, "what do you think will happen if Logan and I can't . . . well, work things out?"

"There is always a solution, Allison."

"I . . . I'm just not sure that's true—marriages do break up, you know."

Joanna winced inwardly. She tried hard to mask the stab of pain at the thought.

"I really hoped the months apart would improve things. But Christmas showed me nothing has changed. I really don't think he loves me anymore."

"Oh, Allison, dear! That can't be true!"

"He barely talks to me," said Allison, her eyes filling with tears.

"He's been through many changes in the last few years," said Joanna. "A whole new lifestyle, both spiritually and socially. Perhaps we've expected too much of him too quickly."

"Are you defending him, Mother?" Allison shot back, a hint of anger surfacing through her tears of hurt.

"I'm only saying there are always two sides to every problem. It always helps to try to look at things from the other person's perspective. I know he's been under a great deal of pressure, both from the war and trying to find a job he's happy with. But I'm sure his motives still spring from his love for you."

"I tried to believe that for a while. But you don't know what it's been like, Mother. And his job! That's part of his problem!"

"You mean his not finding anything lucrative? Times have been—"

"I don't care how much money we have. I just want him—like it used to be. But I'm afraid he's gone back to his old life."

"You don't really think so!"

"Why else has he been so mysterious about it?"

"Have you asked him?"

"Every time I so much as hint at trying to find out what he does, he explodes with his usual evasiveness. I just can't trust anything he says."

"I know it may be especially difficult just now," said Joanna slowly. "But once you begin to doubt someone you love, a close relationship can fall apart quickly. Perhaps if you *could* trust him and—"

"How can I? He lied to me, Mother!" Allison burst out. "When I left London, months ago, he gave me a phone number. He said never to use it except for an emergency. So I never did. It was supposed to be his office number."

"And?"

"All during the time he was here at Christmas I tried to drag out of him some of the details about his job, but he was more evasive than ever. So last week I called the number. I just had to know! Mother, the number he gave me was for Billy Cochran's shop!"

"Is that so terrible?" asked Joanna.

"Don't you see? He lied! He told me he was working for the government, but he's just back into the old life—I know it."

"There may be some other explanation. Maybe he wasn't allowed to give out the office number and knew Billy would be able to reach him."

"Oh, Mother, if only that were true! But there's more! After the call to Billy's, I decided to try the apartment. Ever since he told me he had a position with the government, I couldn't help wondering. There was something in his tone that didn't ring true. I found myself—well, I didn't know what to think. I didn't want to think the worst. But when I called, someone I didn't know answered—in our apartment! Someone with a distinct German accent!"

"Allison, what are you saying?"

"I don't know, Mother. But if he is working for the government, I can't help wondering just *what* government. He's been acting more and more strange . . . distant—upset about not being able to get into the army. He's said some things—"

Allison paused and took a deep breath, then exhaled slowly and thoughtfully. "Well," she said at length, "I suppose what he's doing doesn't matter all that much anyway. Our problems began long before now."

Joanna kept further thoughts to herself. For all she knew, her daughter's assessment could be right. Yet from the very beginning she had seen a core of rectitude in Logan. Lady Margaret had seen it too, even when he had first come to Stonewycke with fraudulent intentions. She had sensed something amiss in his motives back then, but she had not failed to sense the heart of honor that beat within him—the heritage of Digory's blood, her grandmother had always maintained.

Whatever secret Logan now possessed, Joanna knew he would never use it to intentionally hurt his family or those he loved, especially Allison.

Yet it was possible, she had to admit to herself, that his perception of honor could have become confused and distorted amid the pressures and struggles of his present situation. Some men even convince themselves their wives will be better off without them, and use such wrong rationalizations for their own self-centered ends. She prayed such would not happen with Logan.

Could he possibly return to his old life? His turnabout had been so complete. He even made financial restitution wherever possible, and was still faithfully repaying a loan he had obtained from her and Alec in order to clear off one sizable old debt. His initial faith may have cooled, but had it gone so far? Was he trying to right his past wrongs by allowing himself to become involved in new present ones?

No! She would not believe it! She had talked to Allison about trust, and now here she herself was starting to doubt her son-in-law. She would not believe it! He was a good man, an honorable man, a faithful man to his wife and young daughter! She *would* believe that! She had to!

Allison's last words had been spoken with such finality that Joanna could not find an easy response.

Perhaps the time for words was past. She gave her daughter another hug, then released her. The women parted in silence. Allison continued along the crusty path toward their home. Joanna watched her go for a moment, then turned in the opposite direction.

Ten minutes later she stood before a simple marker, her warm breath sending white clouds into the frosty morning air. The words on the stone were simple—Maggie had wanted it that way, to match her husband's. No frills, no quotations, not even *Lady*. The stone read: Margaret Ramsey Duncan 1846–1933.

How could future generations, from that humble inscription, know all that she had meant—first as Maggie, later as Lady Margaret—to this valley? *I must be faithful to my journal*, Joanna thought to herself. *Maggie and what she had stood for must not be forgotten.*

Joanna glanced at the small family plot. To the right of Maggie and Ian lay James and Atlanta Duncan. Toward the rear of the fenced, well-kept grounds, with a larger stone than the rest, lay the grave of Anson Ramsey, flanked by his wife and two sons. But this was not the time to dwell on the past; the present contained cares enough. *Oh, Grandmother!* thought Joanna, glancing down at Maggie's grave again, *what would you do for Allison and Logan if you were alive?*

Joanna sighed. She knew the answer. Maggie would tell her to trust God, just as she herself gave that same advice to Allison. Who else but God was capable to heal and restore her daughter's marriage, and most important of all, to revive both Allison's and Logan's waning faith? He had worked mightily in Maggie's life. He had reunited her and Ian. He had saved Ian from the turmoil of his middle years. He had brought her to

Scotland against all odds. How could she doubt that the same God who had been so repeatedly faithful in the past would not work in this new generation as He had in those of the past?

Silently Joanna prayed the prayer that could only be born out of one's deep relationship with the Lord through the years:

Oh, God, do whatever you must to bring them back to each other . . . and back to you. Take them where you must, take them through what you must, bring to them whatever joys and sufferings you must, so that in the end, Lord, their eyes are fully opened to your love for them.

And even as Joanna turned and slowly followed Allison back to the ancient family castle known for centuries simply as Stonewycke, she had done what Maggie herself would have done. Even in what she considered her own weakness, she had performed the one vital act, the most important single thing she could have done for her daughter and son-in-law: she had given them in prayer into the hands of God.

The granite walls of Stonewycke gave her comfort when she entered them a few moments later; she sensed once again that the Spirit of the living God dwelt here still. He who had profoundly touched and changed so many lives in the past would not fail to touch the lives of future generations through the prayers of those who had come before, through her own prayers, and through prayers yet to be prayed. God's ways were beyond finding out. But of one thing she could be certain: the prayers of His people would never go unheeded.

6 / Recruitment

The telephone's insistent ringing echoed through the cold London flat.

Logan paused at the open front door, hesitating. He was running late and couldn't afford a delay. He started to close the door, then thought, What if it's headquarters? Could there have been a change in plans?

Still the phone rang, and again.

"Blast!" he said with a frustrated sigh, slamming the door behind him and reentering the apartment.

He reached the phone and picked up the receiver on the sixth ring. His heart sank when he heard the voice on the other end.

"Logan, dear? Hello! It's me—Allison!"

"Ali," replied Logan, doing his best to instill enthusiasm into his tone. But this was the worst possible time for a call. He was too keyed up about his meeting with Gunther coming up to give her the kind of attention she would expect.

"Are you okay, Logan?"

"Sure, of course . . . fine."

"You sound . . . funny, just now."

"It's just a surprise, that's all. I didn't expect to hear from you."

"I miss you so much, Logan."

"I miss you too . . . of course," Logan replied. The words were true, in spite of their troubles.

"Do you?"

"You know I do! How could you—?" He stopped himself. He couldn't get into an argument about it now.

"Logan, why don't you come to Scotland?"

"I can't just leave. You know that. Especially now. There are important things going on." His words made him remember his pressing appointment. He glanced at his watch.

"What could be more important than your own family? Your daughter is growing so fast, and you have hardly seen her in—"

"Don't start on me, Ali—" interrupted Logan. How could he make her understand what he hardly understood himself? He loved her. He loved them both. Yet at the same time maybe it was easier to be away, not reminded every time they tried to talk of the tensions which so easily sprang up between them. As he hesitated, searching for the right words, the clock on the mantel chimed the quarter hour.

35

"Allison, let's not talk about it right now," he continued lamely.

"When is there ever going to come a time when you will talk about it?" she retorted. The bitterness in her voice was not even disguised.

The line was silent a moment. He attempted to pacify her.

"Sometime when we're together," he said, his tone hinting at past tenderness. "Talking by phone when we're four hundred miles apart is hardly the best way."

"But there'll *never* come a good time. Even when we're together you won't talk. You were here just three weeks ago. But you might as well have been a thousand miles away!"

The accusation sent Logan back behind his wall of self-preservation. "I have to go," he said flatly. "I've got an appointment. We'll talk about it sometime later."

"By then it may be too late!" she said stiffly, and before he could utter another word, a loud click was heard on the other end of the line.

The knot in Logan's stomach grew tighter as he approached Euston station and his rendezvous with Gunther.

He should have let the phone ring; now was no time to be beset with personal problems! He had to concentrate on the business at hand! But try as he might, he could not erase from his mind the mental picture of Allison slamming down the phone, and probably bursting into tears of mingled anguish and anger.

Why did she have to call right then? She certainly managed to make things difficult for him! At last he had found a job he was suited for, and one he liked. If he had to keep it secret from his wife, thousands of other men did no less, and their wives didn't fly into an uproar over it. Why couldn't she be proud of him for once, instead of always badgering him to "talk things over"? There was nothing to talk over if she wouldn't trust him!

Who was he trying to kid? Skits would have seen right through his facade in a second. For the first time he found himself glad his old mentor wasn't there. He would have had no kind words for Logan, trying to pass off tight security as an excuse to avoid communication with his wife. He wouldn't have believed it any more than Allison did.

But why couldn't she just trust him! His past life made his need for her confidence more imperative than for other men. He had to sense that she believed in him, that she wanted him to succeed.

But sometimes he had the feeling she was just waiting for him to slip up, to backslide, to drift into his old "techniques" for raising cash—especially between jobs when money was tight. Not that he wasn't tempted. How many times had he strolled past an old hangout, only to feel his heart race at the thought of how easy it would be to strike up a card game and bring home a nice thick bankroll to tide them over?

If the years of frustration had dulled his relationship with God, they had not negated the moral commitments that had sprung from that commitment. Moreover, his morality seemed about the only thing he had left to offer Allison.

If he was going to work so hard to keep straight, he thought, the least she can do is keep her suspicions in check every time some tiny questionable uncertainty arises in her mind.

Well, he stubbornly said to himself, *I'm not going to quit the only job I seem cut out for just to please her*.

He'd been waiting too long for this chance. It had taken two months since that first meeting with Gunther on London Bridge in November. There'd been two failed attempts. He had almost begun to fear that the whole thing would fizzle out. And if this assignment went, so would his new job. This deal with Gunther was his one chance to make good, to convince them to keep him on. He hoped he wasn't placing too much hope in one assignment. But he couldn't help thinking that some of the higher-ups were watching him, and that if he showed well and displayed some pluck, well—it would lead to bigger things.

It had been pure luck he'd landed in the midst of all this in the first place. After being rejected twice by the army, he had resigned himself to sitting out the war in some wretched factory with women and men too old to make a difference anywhere else.

Then came the phone call from Arnie Kramer.

He had known Arnie in the old days, and, though a public-school boy, he was a decent enough fellow and a fair hand around a card table. Now Kramer was no longer Arnie, but *Arnold*, and a major at that. He worked for the Intelligence Corps. The years had been good to him, he said. He'd settled down, moved up quickly, and now was having more fun *in* the system than he'd ever dreamed of when trying to fleece it with all his penny-ante games. The stakes were higher, and the game sometimes got dangerous. But the thrill was there, and sometimes there could be money in it. He was doing a bit of recruiting, he said, and could they possibly meet? Logan agreed.

"But the army won't have me," said Logan after he had listened to the opening gambit of his friend's proposal, certain that he must have been misinformed about his availability for active service.

"The *regular* army—bah!" said Kramer with the usual disdain of one corps for another. "If *they* rejected you, that's as good a recommendation as you could get!"

"What exactly is it you want me to do?" asked Logan, his interest piqued.

Kramer leaned his hefty frame forward, and lowered his voice to a conspiratorial whisper, a sparkle of merriment in his small dark eyes. It was just like the old days, only now Logan was the prey. And now Logan had no idea he was being reeled in by one who had grown just as shrewd in the ancient game as he. "Just a bit of cloak and dagger, Logan, m' lad!"

"Spying?"

Arnie nodded.

"You've got to be kidding! What do I know about that?"

Kramer threw his head back and laughed heartily. "Why, man, you've been doing it all your life!"

"Cons, maybe. But hardly spying!"

"Same thing. Only now you won't have to worry about ending up in an English prison for it."

Logan touched his moustache thoughtfully. "I don't know . . ." he said hesitantly, though his heart was racing with excitement. "I've got a family now, Arnie."

"Believe me," answered Kramer in his buoyant style, "you'll be in far less danger than all the blokes out on the battlefield. And you'll work in London—no separation from your family. Of course, you won't be able to tell your wife what it's about. But you'll be doing your country a great service, and she'll forgive you in the end."

"What'll I tell her?"

"We'll arrange a cover story, naturally. No problem. We do it all the time. Security and all that, you know."

"I hate to lie to her."

Kramer laughed again. "That hardly sounds like the Logan Macintyre I used to know. Reformed, eh?"

"I suppose I have changed a bit . . ." Logan replied, stumbling over the words. He wished he had the guts to say more. But in a moment the opportunity was past. After all, this was hardly the time or place to start talking about God.

"Very commendable," said Kramer. "I've changed too, Logan, my man. But look at it this way—the secrecy is for your family's protection as well as for yours and ours." Kramer tried to keep his tone lighthearted, but from under his thick brown eyebrows he was eyeing his quarry. The only reason they wanted Logan was because he was sure never to be recognized by any of the opposing agents. They didn't need *him* in the strict sense of the word. Anyone would do. But Arnie had always liked Logan, had seen him cool under fire, even if only during card game hustles, and had made up his mind that Logan was his man. Therefore, he eyed him carefully, not wanting to bring him in too quickly. Logan had to *want* it— the essence of a good con. So Arnie waited. "Don't turn me down, Logan. You'll be perfect for this work."

Logan didn't turn Major Arnold Kramer down. He wasn't about to miss out on a chance like this! He knew he'd be perfect for the work. He hardly needed Arnie to tell him that! At least, the work would be perfect for *him*.

How could he refuse when he'd been hoping for an opportunity like this for the last six years?

Allison would, or *should*, understand. If she loved him, she would be able to accept him and what he did—no questions asked.

The impasse was a classic one, each expecting the other to make the move that would right the relationship and settle the rocking boat of their marriage. Allison expected confidence and open sharing; Logan expected blind trust.

The love which had drawn them together was still there, but was buried beneath so many layers of selfishness and stubbornness that it surfaced upon rarer and rarer occasions. Yet as Logan sat silently next to the tall, sinister-looking Gunther on the speeding train, his thoughts focused on Allison rather than on what lay ahead. This did happen to be one of those infrequent moments when he fell into self-reflection, and he found himself wondering if he had done all he should have to make the marriage work.

She was probably right—he was a louse. He didn't deserve someone like her. But he'd make it up. He'd tell her everything. As soon as this assignment was over, he'd dash up to Scotland. Maybe even stay awhile. They had always been happy there. He was certain they'd be able to patch everything up.

Just as quickly as the contemplative mood had come, it passed. With his marriage satisfactorily resolved in his mind for the moment, he could now turn his concentration upon the task at hand.

7 / The Assignment

Gunther was a German agent now controlled by British intelligence, MI5. His double agency was, of course, unknown to the Germans—one of a number of similar closely guarded secrets.

Once Gunther had been enlisted to the British side, MI5 began to develop an intricate plan to use him to infiltrate Germany's spy network. If Gunther's defection could be kept secret from Berlin long enough to plant up to a half-dozen experienced Britons throughout mainland Europe, the benefits to the Allied cause could conceivably shorten the war considerably.

The German had represented to his superiors in the Abwehr, the intelligence branch of the German military, that he had recruited several subagents. When, two months ago, they had radioed that they wanted to meet one of these recruits, British intelligence had to produce someone to fit the bill without risking any of their knowledgeable experienced men. Until the legitimacy of Gunther's position was absolutely assured, MI5 had to play cat-and-mouse, insuring that the setup was sound. They could not risk putting a man who had vital information into the hands of the Abwehr. What if, after all, Gunther's defection was nothing more than an elaborate trick to lure a couple of ranking British spies into German hands?

Then Arnie Kramer had thought of Logan. His criminal record would make him an ideal recruit for the Germans. Kramer had his *own* little private network of eyes and ears throughout London, and had done his homework well on Logan. He knew Logan was down on his luck—marriage going sour, rejected by the army, unable to hold a job. He was the perfectly believable candidate for jumping ship. All MI5 would have to do would be to alter the name on Logan's record, and everything else about his past should suit the Germans fine.

Of course, Kramer didn't think it would do to reveal the entire scope of the plan to Logan. No need for him to know that he was nothing more than a decoy, so that if Gunther's loyalties were still to the east of the Channel, they could torture Logan all they wanted to and never get anything vital out of him. If Gunther was for real, and the plan held up, Logan would be in no danger, and they could easily substitute experienced men for the infiltration of the Abwehr later on. If there was danger . . . well, better one like Logan be sacrificed for the good of the cause than any vital information be lost.

So Kramer made his devious offer to his old friend, played out his role of offering Logan a favor most believably, and suddenly Logan was a British spy—or at least so he chose to think. He didn't much like the name Kramer handed him. But *Lawrence MacVey* suited his Scottish accent, and he went along with it.

"You won't need to know a word of German, mate!" said Kramer. "Old Gunther'll have them krauts so anxious to have you they won't care about details like that. Everything's so topsy-turvy anyway, you can't tell who's who anymore by what language they're using. France is where most of the action is, and the French and English and German all mix up there so much—blimey! The tongue in a man's mouth means nothing!"

It'll be a lark, thought Logan, and he wasn't getting paid badly either. The first meeting on London Bridge with the German had instilled in him the seriousness of the situation. But he was still game to play out his hand. Gunther had briefed him thoroughly on what he was to do at the meeting with the Germans—which essentially amounted to nothing—and now they just had to carry it out. The Germans would be watching Logan, Kramer would be watching Gunther, and Gunther would no doubt be watching for the safety of his own backside. Little did Logan realize that he had been "brought in" for nothing more than this simple "one-act play" being staged for the Germans. But just as little did Kramer realize that when the time came to drop the curtain to end Logan's brief performance, plans would change, and the single act would become a complex drama involving many actors, dozens of curtain calls—all carried out with inexperienced Logan Macintyre occupying center stage.

Two meetings subsequent to London Bridge had aborted. The first had been blown, of all things, by Scotland Yard, who had not been informed that the trawler was in the hire of MI5. Contrary to Arnie's steadfast assurances, Logan nearly wound up back in jail. The second time a heavy fog had prevented their making contact with the German sub.

Now he and Gunther were about to make a third attempt. Their train was within minutes of Cleethorpes, a fishing village on the northeast coast of England, where MI5 had another trawler ready to carry them to a rendezvous with a German U-boat in the North Sea.

As the train jerked to a stop at the tiny coastal station, Logan stole a glance at his associate. *He is a cool number*, thought Logan with mingled admiration and intimidation. He knew very well that Logan was a complete novice. Yet the fact seemed not to bother him. It was almost as if—

No, that is too crazy even to consider! Logan argued with himself. Arnie would never have sold me out! He guaranteed that Gunther was completely dependable.

Logan's mind went back to his second meeting with his old friend, as if trying to reassure himself now that it was too late to back out. Kramer had laid out the plan to him. "Dependable," he'd said; ". . . all ours. Nothing to worry about, Logan!" Gunther had proved himself on several missions, Arnie had added. "There's no question he's with us . . . no question!" According to the major, Gunther had gone to work for the Germans in the first place under some duress and had been very cooperative right from the beginning when British intelligence had captured him within two hours of his parachute landing.

Might his cooperative spirit been just a bit too convenient? Logan found himself wondering. But he dismissed the thought from his mind. He didn't even want to think what might happen if, once they were aboard the sub, Gunther decided to betray him to the Nazis.

That was the trouble with this business—you could never really trust anyone.

Gunther rose from his seat, gathering his belongings from the upper compartment. Logan followed him down the aisle, and soon they stepped out into the chill evening air. He looked around and was at least relieved that it was a clear night. No fog would abort this meeting.

"It's the *Anna Marie*, isn't it?" said Gunther, glancing furtively about.

"What?"

"The trawler," said Gunther tersely, as if the failure to read his mind was a serious flaw. "The trawler is the *Anna Marie*?"

"Yes, that's it," replied Logan. *What is this?* he thought. Surely Gunther wasn't quizzing him at this late hour! But just as surely he didn't need to be reminded of the name of the trawler.

The two walked silently on. Logan drew his overcoat tightly around him. The streets were deserted, but Logan knew it was more than the January cold that kept them in. The east coast of England had been hit hard by the Luftwaffe. Not as dramatically this far north as farther south, but the fear of attack was always present. What would these simple townsfolk think if they knew that but a few miles away, in their placid fishing waters, a Nazi submarine lay awaiting reports from two supposed spies?

What would they do if they thought *he* was one of them? No doubt, shoot first, and ask questions later.

A brisk ten-minute walk brought them to the dock. It reminded Logan of Port Strathy. Fifteen or twenty boats of varying sizes bobbed up and down at their moorings. No human being was in sight; the only sounds were the creakings and groanings and bumpings and scrapings from the docks, boats, and ropes—all accompanying the gentle slap-slap-slap of the water against the sides of the rocking vessels. A single boat pulling out to sea at this hour was certain to arouse suspicion, and no doubt MI5, with their intense mistrust of all other agencies, had informed none of the locals of what was about to transpire.

The *Anna Marie* sat silently waiting in the seventh slip down, an innocent-enough looking forty-foot trawler. Though MI5 had procured the ship, Gunther had hired the crew, which consisted of two sailors. They had been kept in the dark about the purpose of the mission, but were Nazi sympathizers quite willing, for the right price, to carry out a mission of dubious intent with sealed lips. Logan would have preferred an Admiralty man at the helm, but Gunther had convinced Kramer that the Germans would too easily spot a Navy man. "Perhaps," Logan told Kramer at the time, "but would they have any more difficulty spotting an MI5 man?"

"You, my boy," Kramer had replied, "that's the difference! I've seen you hob-nob with society one minute, and the next pass yourself off as a coal miner. The Germans will be plum pudding for you, putty in your hand, as it were. Why else do you think I recommended you for the job?"

Logan tried to catch hold of Arnie's confidence in him. He wished Gunther would do the same.

Gunther approached the boat, making no apparent effort to muffle the echoing of his boots as they walked out to the slip. He stopped, leaned forward, and called out in a low but clear voice, "Is there anyone aboard?"

Logan cringed. That German accent—it was going to get them all strung up if he blurted out something in the wrong crowd.

Before he had a chance to worry further, a figure appeared from below. In the darkness Logan could make out a man shorter than himself, small and wiry. An electric torch suddenly flashed on its beam, seemingly aimed directly for Logan's eyes. It blinded him momentarily.

"What's yer business?" came a harsh voice in a gravelly whisper.

"If the fishing is good—especially the herring—we'd like to engage your boat." It was the prearranged code phrase. Any Cleethorpes fisherman worth his salt knew there to be no herring off the coast at this time of year.

"Oh yeah—that is, ah . . . the fishing is good, especially at night," came the nearly muffed reply.

Gunther grimaced with disgust at another incompetent. Even though he had already spoken twice with the man, he liked to play the little game with code phrases carried off to perfection.

He said nothing further, but swung aboard the trawler. Logan followed. In a moment his feet were planted firmly on the deck. He glanced about to take in his surroundings. He had had no formal training in the spy business, but Arnie had done his best to instill in him some practical tricks of the trade. The foremost principle was to examine your surroundings so that you had at least two possible plans of retreat and escape in mind at all times. You could never tell when a setup would turn on you. When that happened, a second or two delay could be the difference between getting away and landing in prison camp.

What Logan saw was a typical fishing vessel, not unlike Jesse Cameron's, though a little smaller, complete with all the nets, ropes, and other gear essential to earning one's livelihood at sea. The reek of fish was everywhere; there could certainly be no doubt as to the authenticity of this craft! Vessels such as these had made a success of the evacuation of Dunkirk the year before, and since then the British had commandeered several for use in patrolling the coast. There was no way to tell, from a quick look about, whether this was a permanent MI5 craft, or was being used just for the night.

The three men headed for the cabin, located aft. Logan could not help being reminded of his first experience aboard Jesse Cameron's boat, on that crisp northern morning when she had shanghaied him aboard her trawler. It had turned out one of the most memorable days of his life. He had learned a great deal that day, about more than fishing. The fact that he had almost drowned did not in the least diminish the value of the experience.

But though the *Anna Marie* evoked such pleasant memories, it had little else in common with the *Little Stevie* on this chill and sinister night. On that day years ago he had been disappointed to have the cruise off Strathy's harbor come to an end. Tonight, however, he was praying for the hours to pass quickly and to get the whole thing safely over with.

At the same time, he was looking for an escape route should the whole operation blow apart.

8 / Interview at Sea

"So, Herr MacVey," began Colonel von Graff. "You do not mind if I use your real name? I find code names so tedious."

They had located the German submarine without difficulty, had been taken below, and Logan at last found himself face-to-face with the stern German officer who could well determine his fate. The man spoke perfect English, but with a thick accent.

"You're the boss," replied Logan, striking a cocky, halfway belligerent attitude. Arnie had told him not to grovel; they would buy his story more readily if he didn't make it too easy for them, and maybe respect him more in the process. "No one respects a weakling!" he had added.

"As I was saying," continued the colonel, "I have noted in your file—"

"File! You blokes have a file on me?" exclaimed Logan in angry offense. He knew perfectly well they would check his record, but he was warming up to the game.

"Do not be offended, Herr MacVey. It is standard procedure—merely routine. The Abwehr trusts no one, even its own."

"So I've heard," said Logan caustically.

"You do not approve?" said the colonel, raising one eyebrow.

"One does what one has to do," replied Logan. "I suppose you Germans are no different."

"Indeed. And it would seem doing what might be considered somewhat—how do you say, irregular?—is something you are familiar with."

"Just what's that supposed to mean?" snapped Logan.

"Only that I took note of your prison record with interest," replied the colonel.

Logan leaned against the bulkhead, folded his arms across his chest, and sent his gaze directly toward the colonel's, as if challenging him to make an issue of his record. Logan and von Graff were in a tiny cabin, alone. Gunther had departed to some other part of the sub while the colonel carried out his interrogation. Logan had refused the chair that had been offered when the interview began five minutes earlier and merely stood with his back to the wall. The colonel sat at a small wooden table bolted to the floor.

Colonel Martin von Graff, an average-sized but imposing man in his late forties, carried a physique primed to military fitness, more than an equal match to most men regardless of size. His brown, close-cut hair was graying slightly at the temples, adding an element of venerability to his square, taut, clean-shaven face. His clear, precisely clipped speech accentuated his confident nature. He was accustomed to issuing orders and being obeyed. He was clearly a man not easily crossed or lied to.

"The dirty Crown," said Logan, pointedly slurring his last word with disgust; "tossed me into the chokey—half the charges were trumped up, and I didn't have a fancy title to get me off."

"The son of a Glasgow laborer," added von Graff, "himself in jail several times for petty theft."

How much information did Arnie let them have? wondered Logan. They just better have left out all mention of Allison and Stonewycke.

"It's the only way a poor blighter can get ahead in this rotten country," said Logan.

"You hope to find something better in Germany?"

"There's something to be said for a place where a house painter can rise to power."

Von Graff winced. The Germans did not like to be reminded that their Führer had once been a common laborer. Even as the words were past his lips, Logan realized this was not to be the best approach. The Nazis weren't like the Communists, proud of a working man's heritage.

"Hitler also has a prison record," Logan added smugly.

"And so you feel your crimes were of a *political* nature?"

"In Britain only Jews and noblemen get anywhere." The words nearly choked Logan, but he had to move the interview toward ground to which this Nazi could relate. He had to try to appeal to the man's Teutonic prejudice so as to take the attention off himself. "The only crime is that a man with white skin and pure breeding has to rob and steal to keep starvation from killing him, while the *Jews* control all the money."

"I see," said the colonel, without affect.

This man gives the word cool *new meaning*, thought Logan. Either he indulged in no political or racial fancies, or he had them as precisely under control as he did everything else about him.

"Look," said Logan impatiently, "did you call me here to discuss anything besides my prison record?"

"Indeed I did," answered von Graff. "But what I have in mind will involve some sensitive areas that a man without scruples—"

"I get your drift," interrupted Logan.

"You have reformed of your life of crime, I take it, Herr MacVey?"

"I have no intention of stealing from the Reich, if that's what you mean."

"What exactly brought about this reform—your marriage, perhaps?"

"My marriage?"

"My report indicates you were married in 1933 to an Allison Bently of Yorkshire, after which you desisted from your criminal activities."

What is this? thought Logan. He and Arnie had never discussed this aspect of his life and past in relation to what would be placed in his record. Somehow he had assumed that all mention of his marriage had been eliminated. Well, if Arnie had falsified the records, at least he had had the foresight to alter the names and places. That is, *if* he had indeed changed them. What if von Graff was baiting him, throwing out misinformation to catch him up? To see how far Logan was willing to carry the truth?

"Listen," answered Logan at length, "I want my family left out of this. They have nothing whatever to do with my political viewpoints. Besides, my wife and I haven't been together in months."

"A divorce. . . ?"

"Not yet—but my wife had nothing to do with any of this, see? And I want it kept that way—or I don't deal."

"There is no reason for her to be involved," replied von Graff.

A rap came on the door; and an aide entered with a tray containing a coffeepot and cups. "Will that be all, mein Colonel?" he asked. The colonel dismissed him briskly, and he turned and exited.

"I wish I could offer you something stronger, but it is best we keep our heads about us," said the colonel as he poured out the coffee from an antique silver urn that could not have looked more out of place aboard a German war sub. "Do you take anything?" he asked Logan.

"Cream and sugar," answered Logan.

"Two lumps?"

Logan nodded.

Suddenly the whole tenor of the meeting had changed. This was no longer a confab of spies, but a tea party. Von Graff had ceased for the moment being a military man, and instead was carrying out the role of host at an elegant dinner party. Logan recalled that the title "von" indicated nobility, and he wondered if in the colonel's case it was more than merely an inherited appellation. Yes, the man's nature was honed sharp, like a deadly weapon. But he had risen to his position without forgetting to bring along his silver coffee service and fine china. His wit and savoir-faire were perhaps restrained in these austere surroundings, but as he was served, Logan could easily picture von Graff moving gracefully about at an elite cocktail reception.

Still, through it all there remained something unchanged in his eyes, a raw chill that belonged to the battlefield, and it was visible even as he spoke in an apparently social vein.

"You British will never learn how to drink coffee properly," he said, handing Logan the Wedgewood cup and saucer.

"We've always been resistant to change," replied Logan noncommittally.

"You hope that by adding cream and sugar you will make the coffee taste like tea?"

"Maybe."

"But alas, the two drinks are as different as . . ."

The colonel's sentence was completed by the knowing glance in his eyes.

"You're right. Nothing can turn coffee into tea."

"So it is with life," von Graff went on in a philosophical tone. Logan smiled at how deftly the colonel had maneuvered the conversation back to cases. "I was going to say a moment ago, as different as the Germans and the British. Throw in a pinch of this ideology or a dash of that doctrine and you still have what you began with—in your case an Englishman, born and bred. You can't alter a man's heritage any more than cream and sugar will alter the basic flavor of coffee."

"Hardly an Englishman!" corrected Logan. "A Scot, to be specific. And no true Scotsman would ever consider himself an *Englishman*. All true Scots would agree—the union of 1707 be hanged!"

"So the Scots, the Irish, and the Welsh would align themselves with fascism as a means to an end?"

"Why not?"

"They are hardly fascist."

"I can't believe that ideology would matter a fig to Hitler if he could get any of the Commonwealth countries to turn on England."

"And is nationalism *your* motivation, Herr MacVey?" asked von Graff.

"Does it matter?"

"You spoke earlier of poverty and Jews," said the colonel. "I wonder if you are a zealot."

Logan leaned forward, peering intently into his interviewer's eyes to give added emphasis to his words.

"To tell you the truth, von Graff," he said, "I have only one ideology, and that's Lawrence MacVey!"

Logan had slipped very comfortably into his role, and hardly balked at such an outright lie, and did not even stumble over the use of the strange name. "I figure that deep down you Germans are just like me, and that's why I'm here."

Von Graff laughed—not a merry laugh, but a dry response to a droll witticism.

"Hitler wrote in *Mein Kampf*," he said, " 'The conviction of the justification of using even the most brutal weapons is always dependent on the presence of *fanatical* belief in the necessity of the victory of a revolutionary new order on this globe.' The Third Reich is such a new order, and the extent of the Führer's fanatical belief has only begun to be seen."

"Are you saying, then, that my observation regarding the Reich's motivations is incorrect?"

"It is correct," answered the colonel. "But I would hasten to suggest that if you should ever meet the Führer, you not put it quite so succinctly."

He rose, refilled the coffee cups, then began again.

"I must say, I am relieved, Herr MacVey. An opportunist is so much easier to work with than a zealot. However, opportunists do possess one serious drawback."

"Which is?" asked Logan.

"Since they have no loyalties, it is forever difficult to predict when—and if—a sweeter opportunity will lure them away."

"Not in my case," Logan assured the colonel coolly. "I'm no zealot, but I'll die before I sleep in the same bed with Britain. It has nothing to do with ideology. It has everything to do with *me*, and what they did to me. There are only two sides in this war—Britain and her cronies against your Fatherland. That leaves me with only one choice. It helps, though, that I expect to be well-compensated for my services."

"The Reich expects such compensation to be well-earned."

"And that brings us back to the beginning," said Logan, "which is why I've been asked here. Certainly not for the stimulating conversation I've provided. You could have had that in Berlin."

"You'd be surprised, mein Herr," replied von Graff pensively. "You'd be surprised . . ."

He raised his cup of black coffee to his lips and drained off the remainder of its contents. "I believe this is a superb time to come to the point of our little meeting," he added, changing back into his brisk military voice.

"Then I pass muster?"

"Time will tell, Herr MacVey. But for now, as you might say, Why not?"

Logan could think of a hundred reasons why he should not have passed his interviewer's scrutiny, but none of them mattered as long as von Graff bought his act. He restrained a relieved sigh. Everything was going well enough; Arnie would be proud of him.

Taking advantage of the brief pause in the conversation, von Graff bent over and shuffled through some papers in a briefcase that sat on the floor next to him. In a moment he withdrew a large-sized folded sheet, pushed aside the coffee things, and opened it out on the table. It was a map of England.

"This is where I want you to begin," said the colonel, his slim, neatly manicured finger pressed against the southeast coast of England. "Sussex, Kent, and Essex," he continued. "I want everything you can get on coastal defenses. Specifically the location of anti-aircraft guns and the status of the electrically controlled land mines. Also, detailed damage reports after bombings. Finally, I want you to take a copy of this map and update it for us. As you can see, it is a few years old."

"Sounds as if you haven't given up hopes of invasion," Logan prompted coyly.

"Keep in mind, MacVey," replied von Graff, "that yours is the task of reporter, not interpreter. Many a good spy has failed because he has tried to second-guess his superiors."

"I'll keep that in mind," Logan answered. But if von Graff expected humility to accompany such a reply, he got none from Logan.

"Entrench yourself in that region," continued the colonel. "I'm certain you'll have no problem establishing a cover. When you leave here tonight, you will take with you a wireless transmitter—you do know how to operate a wireless, I take it?"

"Of course," Logan lied. Actually he had never seen one at close quarters before. But Arnie would handle all that.

"Here is your code and its key," von Graff said, handing him a thick folder along with the map. "Continue to use the same code name—Trinity, wasn't it?"

Logan nodded.

"An interesting choice. A covert reference to the *Third* Reich, perhaps?"

"Pretty clever, wouldn't you agree?" replied Logan. But even as he spoke he was thinking of how the name really had come about. Von Graff would have been surprised, and probably appalled.

One Sunday morning Logan and Allison had attended a little church not far from their Shoreditch flat. He had already encountered Arnie Kramer, and his thoughts were full of the major's offer. He could hardly remember a thing about the service itself. But as he sat there silently with Allison at his side, he found himself thinking that if he wanted to do this spy thing right, he ought to come up with a code name for himself. "You'll be taking on many names and characters from here on out," Arnie had told him. Then he chuckled reassuringly. "But don't worry, the same old Logan Macintyre will always be there somewhere!"

While Logan sat in church, unable to focus his mind on the sermon, his eye fell upon the word *Trinity* engraved in ornate script upon a window. Since his thoughts of late had never been far from his potential new occupation, he immediately perceived the parallel between Arnie's statement and the spiritual manifestation represented by the window. He chided himself at his cheek in comparing what he was doing with anything spiritual. Yet when he had to give a code name, *Trinity* was the name that came to his lips.

So now, here he was telling lies to a Nazi colonel, using a name he had stolen from a stained-glass window. None of it made much sense. But maybe somehow the name, which had nothing whatever to do with the Third Reich, would force some sanity or meaning into the topsy-turvy world in which Logan Macintyre now found himself entangled.

9 / Unexpected Twist

"He had what!" exploded Kramer.

"A box . . . a transmitter, I told you."

"You were supposed to stick close. I told you not to let MacVey be alone with the krauts!"

"They took me away," replied Gunther defensively. "I had no choice."

Kramer looked away, thinking for a moment. Then he went on.

"So you heard nothing of what went on?"

"No. Only what Trinity told me on the way back."

"Trinity . . . MacVey . . . Mac—!" burst out Kramer again, but caught himself. "This was only supposed to be a one-time operation. What am I supposed to do with a novice in the middle of a cauldron of Nazis?"

"It might not be a completely lost cause," said Gunther.

Kramer rose from his chair, eyeing his companion momentarily, then ambled slowly to the window, his back to Gunther, and looked out on the street below. There was something else about this new twist he didn't like. He was further than ever from being able to assess Gunther's true loyalties. For all he could tell, *he* was the one who had been set up, and now Gunther had him just where he wanted him. That's what he hated about this bloody business—you never really *knew*, at bottom, where people's loyalties lay! Double agents, triple agents, quadruple agents! And there was Logan, the unsuspecting amateur, right in the middle of it as the wild card!

Blast! If he only had one of his own men in it! He should probably pull the plug on Logan, get him out of it, cover his tracks, and hang Gunther out to dry. It was just too risky. If this German wasn't on the level, there was too much at stake, especially if they were now able to manipulate Logan.

He didn't like it! He wasn't tightly in control, and that made him nervous. But on the other hand, what if Gunther *was* solidly in their camp? He could ill afford to blow such a perfect defection. Maybe they could still pull out Logan as planned with Arnie's boys operating the radio. But Gunther had said he had the impression the Abwehr was going to want to deal directly with Trinity, which would get sticky if they insisted on more face-to-face meetings. They had to get Logan out; he didn't know anything of these affairs, con man that he was. He just hadn't counted on it going so far. Logan had been supposed to keep quiet, let Gunther handle it. Now, here he was all signed up as a German agent, coming back to England with

51

a wireless and a full set of orders, for heaven's sake! The thing was ridiculous!

"So, what makes you so optimistic?" asked Arnie, turning. His face revealed little of his doubt to the German.

"I see no problem with keeping Trinity in," replied Gunther.

"Keep him in! Why, that would mean—"

Kramer stopped. He had to keep his wits about him. He still wasn't completely sure whom he was talking to. If Gunther still belonged to the Germans, it could be to his advantage to have a novice as his protege.

"He doesn't have the experience for this kind of thing," he said finally.

"But he has conquered the biggest obstacle already. They trust him."

"Ha! You believe that? Then you are more of an idiot than I thought, mein lieber Freund."

"They gave him a wireless and instructions."

"It's a setup, I tell you. How long have you been in this business, Gunther?"

"Long enough!" snapped the German.

"Long enough to recognize a checkup, an audition, when you see one?"

Kramer stopped. Perhaps he had already said too much. After all, Gunther was riding high in his own trial balloon at this very moment. Kramer didn't want to push him too hard and blow him back across the Channel if he truly was theirs.

Gunther did not reply, and was left to his own reflections. He too was thinking what a complex and subtle business this was.

Kramer turned his back again, thought for a couple minutes, then opened his mouth to speak. When he spun back around, however, Gunther was gone. He had left the room silently; Kramer had not even heard the door.

He sighed deeply. Who could tell, though? Maybe Gunther was right. Logan *had* handled himself pretty well. If the Abwehr contact had at least thought him worth testing, that might be a good sign. Perhaps his old friend Logan might prove more useful than he had first anticipated.

Keep him in—a novel idea! Maybe a good one. They could manage Gunther.

No one could say Major Arnold Kramer had advanced to his present position by being afraid to go out on a limb occasionally.

10 / Short Furlough

It was one of those crisp days of April when the chill in the air is a sufficient reminder that the last snow has only recently thawed. But accompanying the brisk temperature was a bright persistent sun, and had he been on land, better yet in the countryside, there would have been a fragrance of flowers in the air, speaking with conviction that spring had arrived.

As he leaned against the rail, sucking in the tangy salt breezes, Logan recalled another spring nine years ago when he had sailed northward on this very schooner. Then he had come bearing lies and deception, and a plan to swindle the most prominent family in town. As the schooner slid into its slip in Port Strathy's harbor, on this spring day of 1941, Logan somehow felt that very little had changed.

He found himself almost wishing Arnie hadn't so willingly granted permission for this brief leave. But things had been going so well, he was probably glad to reward Logan in this way. Logan had contacted von Graff upon several occasions by wireless, had fed him what information Arnie had supplied, and on the whole Kramer seemed pleased with the way things were developing. He had had Gunther reassigned farther north temporarily so as to remove at least one element of chance from Logan's activities. He'd let some of the other boys keep an eye on him for a while; Kramer himself would have his hands full keeping tabs on Logan and von Graff, at least until Logan knew how to handle himself in the spy game.

As he was handing Logan his official papers for the trip north, Kramer had rather off-handedly mentioned that he had had an ulterior motive, aside from all else, for giving Logan a brief respite.

"What's up?" asked Logan, curious.

"You never told me you could speak French," said the major.

"You never asked."

"It's a good thing I was looking over your personnel file." Kramer absently tapped a manila folder lying on his desk. "How good are you?"

"Not bad, I suppose," said Logan modestly.

"Level with me, Logan."

"They always said I had a knack for it."

"By which they meant what?"

"That I didn't have an English accent, I suppose. It came natural to me."

"And where did you pick it up?"

"I was there for a couple years in '29 and '30."

"On what business?"

"You know how it was back then, Arnie. Things had begun to get a little touchy for me. So in order to promote my continued freedom, I decided to see what the Continent had to offer. A friend and I had a pretty decent setup in Le Mans in the racing game until the gendarmes got onto us. Then I drifted down to the Riviera. I didn't make my fortune, but I did pick up the language."

"Well, I mentioned you to the boys in *SOE*."

"Sorry—I haven't got all your initials down yet."

"Special Operations Executive," replied Kramer. "They specialize in overseas espionage, sabotage, that sort of thing. They need operatives who speak French, especially now with the Continent totally in the hands of the Germans and the role of the underground so crucial."

He paused and glanced at Logan.

"What are you suggesting, Arnie?" Logan asked.

"I don't know, but it made sense to me. You've done well so far. But the training's rather stiff, and only a fraction of those who can speak the language manage to pass. It's an elitist outfit."

"You can't seriously be considering *me!*"

"Why not? You've shown some guts recently. You might be good at it. So I had them put your name on the roster for the next training session. It's coming up in a month."

Logan knew only a little about the SOE, but since that conversation with Arnie Kramer, he had tried to remember everything he'd heard. They operated behind enemy lines, constantly walking the tightrope between a hazardous freedom and capture. In case of the latter, torture was certain, death probable. The missions were of the highest importance, yet at the same time were as close to suicide assignments as the British could offer. Few operatives returned without having at least flirted with death. It was a long way from petty con games, or even posing as a German spy in a quiet English port town.

As Logan looked up at the harbor of Port Strathy, he recalled that his first thought after hearing Arnie's proposal about the SOE was of his family. He would be seeing them soon. And as difficult as his marriage had been over the last few years, down inside he still wanted it to work. He couldn't keep lying to Allison. In a few minutes he would again be holding her in his arms. He'd been thinking about what Kramer had said during the whole of his voyage north, and finally he knew what his answer had to be.

No, Arnie Kramer, he thought to himself, *this is one assignment I cannot accept.*

The schooner's crew was already busy casting the ropes out to catch the dock's moorings. Out on the wharf Logan saw several familiar faces. He returned their friendly greetings, gradually warming to the idea of his return, realizing that perhaps it was not like the first time at all. He was no stranger coming to Stonewycke this time. These people were his friends; he was part of this little community, and he held nothing but goodwill in his heart for these people.

Where was Allison? Civilian communications were so haywire since the war. He wondered if she'd even received his telegram. He probably should have telephoned. But as much as he hated to admit it, he'd been just a bit afraid to talk to her. Their last conversation still haunted his memory.

He quickly scanned the faces lining the shore again, but then suddenly his eyes were diverted to the street running adjacent to the Bluster N' Blow. Allison's dark golden hair seemed to reflect the crimson of the sun itself, and her cheeks held a rosy glow from her hurried pace. The moment her blue eyes spotted him on the deck of the waiting boat, her lips broke into a warm, lively smile and her step quickened still further.

"Ali!" he shouted, running down the barely situated gangway. All his earlier ambivalence dissolved at the sight of his wife, nor was he embarrassed at the good-natured cheer that rose from the crowd of onlookers as he rushed forward and took her into his arms.

"Oh, Logan!" she exclaimed.

He could find no immediate words. He wrapped his arms tightly around her and held her close, then bent down to kiss her. But as his lips met hers, there were tears in her eyes. He felt tears rising in his own as well.

"We must look like a couple of ninnies," he said at last.

"It'll give all the people something to talk about for the next week," replied Allison. "We're improving the morale of the neighborhood!"

Logan laughed.

As they stood together for a lingering moment, forgotten were the tensions, the doubts, the harsh words, and the pain of recent meetings. Seemingly for a few brief careless minutes they were once again newlyweds, jubilant in their love and in the sheer joy of being together. They turned, and hand-in-hand walked back along the street to the car.

Logan jumped behind the wheel of the old Austin. It started right up, another reminder that this day was different than that on which he and Allison had first met, when the old car had stubbornly coughed and sputtered until Logan appeared with his timely mixture of expertise and good luck.

As he wheeled the car around, he reflected back to that earlier time. Like that finicky Austin, their first encounters had been but sputtering attempts toward relationship, each antagonizing the stubborn pride of the other. When the day of the flood came, it was as if the water itself had begun a cleansing process within them. They were soon to learn, however, that such inner cleansing had nothing to do with the flood. Rather, it was God himself who was washing them clean, and drawing them together in the process, as He drew their spirits toward His heart of love. He who would become their Lord was tearing down the walls that each had erected, though in the years since that time, without knowing it, they had both built them back up again.

But for the moment, as they flew out of Port Strathy and up the hill toward the ancient estate, their thoughts were filled with the good times of their youth.

"Tell me—" began Allison, but at the same moment Logan had also tried to speak. They laughed.

"You go ahead," said Allison. "What were you going to say, Logan?"

"It's not that important."

"I want to hear," she insisted. "I've waited so long just to hear your voice since . . ."

She hesitated, and Logan said nothing.

"Oh, Logan, I'm so sorry about what I did on the phone!" she added.

"Forget it. Everything's forgiven," replied Logan. "Let's both just forget the past and start out new."

"Logan, how I wish . . ." But even as she spoke, Allison paused, as if some sudden assurance had stolen upon her. "Yes, we can, can't we? Oh, it's so good to see you . . . I'm so glad you're home!"

The word *home* stung Logan with an odd sensation. Yes, there was a part of him that had felt like he was coming home as the schooner rounded the head and pointed its bow into the bay. Yet another part of him . . .

Even as the thought darted into his mind he silently cursed himself for spoiling the sweet mood of their reunion.

"I'm glad too, Ali," he said, and left it at that.

Then followed a silence. Logan could not shake the cloud that had suddenly showed itself on his horizon. The quiet would have become awkward had they allowed it to linger on, but Allison interceded in time.

"You should see little Joanna," she said. "You won't recognize her. She's so big, and talks all the time. She'll soon be two—just imagine!"

"I've thought of nothing else," he answered, "except you."

She slipped her arm through his and snuggled closer.

"We had a letter from Dad yesterday," she said, trying to fill him in on family news.

"How is he?"

"He says he's healthy and all. But he hasn't seen Ian, which is a disappointment to him—they're both in North Africa, you know, and he was hoping they'd see more of each other. He can't say much about the war, but Mother sensed some discouragement. About all he had to say on the bright side was that he'd been studying camels and was fascinated."

Logan laughed. "Always the vet! Your dad is really quite a guy."

"Yes," sighed Allison, thinking of how long it took her to discover that fact. She now knew what a wonderful man her father was—even more so now that he was absent from her.

"Things haven't gone so well in Africa," continued Logan, "since the Germans sent in Rommel a couple of months ago. He's pushed the British troops back nearly all the way to the Egyptian border."

"Do you think . . . is Dad in any danger?"

"Of course not!" Logan replied with all the confidence he could muster. "That was stupid of me to say."

"No! I want to know what's going on. I hate it when the government and newspapers try to whitewash everything. How do you have such current information? We have to struggle for every tidbit we get up here."

"Oh . . . well." Logan quickly sought in his head for a plausible explanation other than that he'd heard it at MI5. "I met a talkative soldier on the train," he lied, hating himself for it.

"Well I wish I'd meet a talkative soldier some time." She hadn't seemed to notice his momentary hesitation. "But he probably wouldn't have told *me* anything—no one will say anything to a woman about the war."

"It can't be as bad as all that. This is a new age. Women are in all kinds of vital positions." *Even intelligence*, he was about to say, but thought better of it.

"Probably not. I'm sure I just imagined it. But it's so frustrating! Sometimes I wish I were a man, Logan, so I could *do* something. I'd rather be part of the fight than sitting around rolling bandages and collecting tin."

"That's important too, you know. Keeps the morale high, for the boys to know the women are waiting for them at home—so I've been told."

"That's so old-fashioned, Logan! We'd rather be part of it all."

As Allison spoke, they drove through the open iron gates of Stonewycke. Logan chuckled as he braked the car in front of the courtyard fountain. The image of Allison dressed in army fatigues, hefting a rifle over her shoulder, was an amusing one indeed.

But the passionate words of his young wife also touched Logan's heart. She had so much spirit, such vitality and energy! Yes, she no doubt *would* make a good soldier—strong and courageous, even daring.

As they climbed out of the car, the large front door opened and Joanna walked out and hurried toward Logan.

He turned and faced her.

"Logan!" she said, "it's so good to see you! Welcome back!"

He paused a moment, then bowed deeply, and rose. "Charming, as always, Lady MacNeil!" he said, with exaggerated tone and a twinkle in his eye.

The women both eyed each other with a grin. Each then took an arm, and Logan, as if exulting in his triumphant return, led the way toward the house, all three laughing in the joy of his irrepressibly buoyant spirit.

11 / Like Old Times

In her desperation to have everything right again between them, Allison forgot a principle she knew only too well—that wounds do not often heal so readily. Seeing Logan again, with the old lilt in his step and sparkle in his eye and wisecrack on his tongue convinced her that she could lay aside all the fears and doubts about their marriage that had been plaguing her. They were together now, and that was all that mattered. He had come to her. He had known she needed him, and had left London and all that had been so important to him—for her.

Alas, the next few days only aided Allison in her blissful misconception. Patience had never been one of her greatest assets, and she could not wait for the depth of discernment which might have allowed her to see that the ground under her feet was not as smooth as she wanted it to be. But for the blessed present, spring had come to the land, and to the soul of young Allison Macintyre.

As the coming of growth and green, planting and blossoms, warmth and rain gradually took over the Strathy countryside, so did joy and apparent happiness surround the young couple. As if reacquainting themselves with one another, as well as old haunts and old memories together, they walked for miles, both visiting old friends and simply enjoying the glorious coastline and inland beauty. On horseback they rode upon the surrounding hills and along the sandy beach, just as Maggie and Ian had done some seventy-five years before. Though all upon it had changed, the land had not, still possessing a power to move, a power to invoke reflection, a power to open the spirit to the heart of its Creator.

Once again talk flowed easily between them. Neither seemed to notice, or care, that amid all the profusion of conversation, they subconsciously avoided anything that hinted at the deep or the personal. Neither wanted to threaten the precarious balance of relationship that seemed to be growing once more between them. Instinctively they realized it too tender a thing yet to be examined directly without endangering its frail life. Therefore they kept in constant motion. Joanna commented one evening that she had hardly seen Logan again since the day of his arrival, and had not had the chance to sit down and talk with him about anything.

He laughed it off.

"Ah, my dear mother-in-law," he said flippantly, "these are not the days for serious conversation. The world is at war, and darkness surrounds us on all sides. These are the times, rather, when we must laugh and make merry. For tomorrow we may, as the saying goes—well, perhaps the remainder of said proverb had best remain unspoken. Nevertheless, I do not choose to add to the world's gloom with serious reflection, introspection, and pontification. My calling has always been to bring a little levity to the world!"

He lifted his glass, to Allison's delight, and Joanna joined in the laughter at his speech. However, as it subsided, neither of the two young people noted the deep anxious furrow of concern that remained in her brow.

One day the sun rose especially warm. A cool breeze would no doubt later come blowing in off the ocean as a reminder of recently departed winter. A few clouds dotted the sky, but Logan, undaunted, walked into the kitchen about ten to see if he could cajole the cook into preparing a basket for an outdoor feast.

Twenty minutes later, he emerged with the basket over his arm and a carefree smile on his face. He found Allison in the family parlor sewing while listening to the radio. She looked up as he entered, and her look of concentration immediately brightened.

"What have we here?" she asked cheerfully.

"This, *mon chèri*," replied Logan with a humble bow and tip of his cap, "is a *celebration de vivre*—a celebration of life! Come join me, fair maiden!"

"Logan . . . what?" exclaimed Allison, delighted, yet still puzzled.

"An old-fashioned Scottish picnic, what else!"

He reached out, took her hand, and pulled her from her seat up to his side.

"Did you prepare that all by yourself?" asked Allison, peeking into the basket.

"I had some help. Now come, before the weather changes."

"We'll still need coats."

"What else were coats invented for?" he answered playfully. "I remember reading all about it. *Voila!* The coat has been invented; now the world can picnic!"

"Logan, you *are* crazy!" exclaimed Allison, dropping her sewing and jumping up. "I'll get the baby ready."

In ten minutes they were all three in the Austin bumping along a back road that ran south behind the estate. Though rutted and unpaved, the road traversed mostly flat terrain with acres of crop land spreading out to the right and left. Already the farmers were out in the fields plowing and preparing the earth for spring planting. Allison and Logan waved at old Fergie, the estate's factor, as he huffed and puffed, carrying his jelly-like frame across the newly made furrows back to his truck.

After some distance the road veered toward the west, and the cultivated land gave way to low-lying hills covered with now dormant heather. The

Austin groaned and labored its way up and down one incline after another, and at the top of one Logan stopped for a few minutes to let it cool down a bit.

"Where are we going?" asked Allison, finally able to contain her curiosity no longer.

"A secret place," answered Logan, grinning as he started up the engine and pulled back onto the road.

"I grew up here, Logan. How can you have a secret spot that I know nothing about?"

"Just you wait, my dear."

Allison sat back expectantly as the familiar countryside of her home rolled past. The day was going to be a magical one; she sensed it in the very air around them. In the four days since Logan had returned to Stonewycke, her confidence in their relationship had grown tremendously. She was more sure of Logan than she had been for some time, and knew that this afternoon would be the perfect time to bring up a subject she now felt certain he would be enthusiastic about. It had been on her mind constantly ever since she had received his telegram, and now the time was right. Perhaps God had at last arranged everything perfectly for the plan that had been in the back of her mind for months.

All at once the car came to a stop. Deep in thought, Allison had scarcely noticed that they had slowed and pulled off the road. Glancing around, she realized that the place was indeed unfamiliar to her. The ground had turned rocky, and the road, which had been gradually disintegrating, now disappeared altogether.

"All ashore!" declared Logan. "We've a wee hike before we reach our destination."

He hopped out of the car and in a moment was lifting the sleeping baby off Allison's lap with one hand, while he helped Allison out with the other.

"I'll get the basket," said Allison.

Logan hoisted his daughter, waking now to the activity around her, onto his shoulders, the child giggling with glee. "Daddy!" she squealed happily.

The sight brought tears to Allison's eyes. It was so right, so perfect. She had waited so long for this reunion, this rekindling of their love, for the old Logan to surface once again. This was where they belonged. Why had they fought so much . . . why had they even gone to London? This was their life. God had given them a wonderful family and a beautiful home in Scotland. There was no reason for them not to be content. And as she observed her husband and daughter together, Allison sighed, never doubting that they would be together like this from now on.

She followed Logan through a small wood, and after about ten minutes the densely packed pine trees opened out into a secluded little meadow. Three sides remained walled by the wood, and on the fourth, below a steep bank, the icy cold Lindow River splashed and danced on its way to the sea.

"How on earth did you find this place?" asked Allison when they paused in the middle of the lush green grass of the meadow. "It's beautiful!"

Logan smiled, feeling quite pleased with himself. "Your mother told me about it last night when I asked her where a good spot for a picnic might be. I wish I could say it was my own discovery. But honesty forces me to fess up!"

Allison laughed. "You always were a shrewd one, Logan. But I wonder why she never told us about it, or brought us here."

"I asked her that myself," replied Logan. "She told me she always thought it would bring more pleasure to the one who made the discovery on his own. She said she and Alec used to bring you children near here all the time, hoping that one day you would make the discovery. But so far Ian is the only one to have found it."

"But she told you?"

Logan laughed. "I suppose she figured with my ignorance of the country life and my city ways, I would never find it on my own. Besides, I told her I wanted someplace special."

"So that's it," said Allison. She put her arms around Logan and lightly kissed his cheek. "Thank you."

But the youngster, still perched atop her daddy, had no patience for tender love scenes, and called out, "Daddy, down!"

Logan swung her gently into his arms, and then with a great fatherly hug and kiss set her on the ground where she immediately took off gleefully through the grass. Logan turned to assist Allison with the picnic things.

"Your mother said some old folks she knew by the name of Cuttahay first showed her this spot," said Logan as he shook out the blanket and spread it on the grass.

"Oh yes. The Cuttahays were the first friends Mother had here in Port Strathy," said Allison.

"Well, apparently they used to come here when they were courting. Old Mr. Cuttahay used to strip off his shirt, dive into the water, then swim to the other side and back, just to impress his sweetheart," said Logan. As he spoke he stood up and sauntered toward the riverbank.

Allison giggled. "I can hardly imagine old Nathaniel diving into the Lindow." Then she gasped, "Logan, what are you doing?"

As Allison spoke, Logan had dramatically begun to tear off his coat and shirt.

"I can impress my lassie, too!"

Allison burst into disbelieving laughter.

"But the water's freezing. You'll catch your death of cold!"

"I'm a rugged fellow," said Logan, making ready to dive.

"But you don't need to impress me, Logan," she said, with as much earnestness as her mirth would allow.

"I don't?" he replied. Though his face continued to smile as he glanced back at her, his voice momentarily sounded as if a small part of him truly was surprised with her statement.

Had Allison been more secure within herself concerning their relationship, his simple question might have slipped by almost unnoticed. She might even have continued the lighthearted banter in kind. However, his tone stung her, and before she even realized what was happening, she had blurted out words she quickly regretted.

"Logan, I don't think you've ever really known me!" Her lip trembled as she spoke, as she fought back tears.

Logan stepped back from the edge of the bank, his merry mood suddenly gone. He gathered up his things, hurried to Allison's side and knelt down on the blanket, facing her.

"I was only joking," he said. The fib came so easily to his lips. His inner self excused it on the grounds that lying was better at the moment than strife.

"Oh, never mind about it," replied Allison, forcing a bright smile to her face, and hastily wiping her eyes dry. "I'd better get the baby."

She jumped up and went off after their daughter, spending some time helping the child pick flowers and chase a butterfly. Allison prolonged the diversion long enough to regain her self-control.

When she returned Logan had laid out lunch, and the three ate while Logan and Allison chatted about things inconsequential, using the antics of their daughter as a protective shield to keep the conversation light. But a stilted air settled over the remainder of the afternoon, as if each saw that despite the surface merriment, the hurts and stresses continued to simmer as though in a covered pot. Yet both Allison and Logan clung determinedly to the surface appearance of cordiality, not wanting the cover to blow off again, desperate to avoid a confrontation.

Had Allison considered it carefully, she would have altogether forgotten about what she had hoped to discuss with Logan. However, the peaceful meadow, filled with pleasant ghosts from the past, and the reassuring roar of the river, along with the semblance of congeniality between them, all combined to lull her into a forgetful state of security. I won't let my own emotions out, she thought; only mention the thing and then let it drop.

The three finished lunch, walked about the meadow, hiked through a portion of the wood, and then returned to the blanket to partake of the sweet shortbread the cook had baked the day before. Logan stretched himself out, leaning lazily against an old stump, while little Joanna climbed sleepily into his lap.

"You are a dear thing, my sweet little lass," he said, lovingly stroking her mass of amber-colored curls. "I often wonder how I could have deserved such a blessing."

"Lady Margaret would have said that we don't deserve God's blessings," replied Allison, "but we receive them only because He loves us so."

"Or would she perhaps quote my old progenitor Digory to say it?" laughed Logan. "She did like to tell me about him. I suppose she thought it would make me more receptive to know that spiritual blood flowed in my veins. The dear old lady—I still miss her."

"Don't we all!"

"I can just hear her say it, like you said. And the words were never truer than in my case." Logan reached out and took Allison's hand. "Why am I not more thankful, more receptive to His blessings to me?"

"I know," said Allison. "Since I've come back home, though I've grumbled and complained more than I should, I now see I have everything anyone could want."

"And you're happy, Ali?" Logan, too, had forgotten to take care of dangerous ground.

"Now that you're here with me, Logan, I'm more than happy—I'm ecstatic!"

Logan sighed, then reached out his arm and drew her close. Allison laid her head peacefully against him, and the next several minutes were spent just quietly listening to the lovely sounds of spring.

"For the first time in a long time, Logan," said Allison at length, "I feel we can begin to think of the future."

"Not many want to do that during wartime," replied Logan. "It's dangerous to make plans when everything is so uncertain."

"But it's different for us," answered Allison confidently. "I know you've felt bad about not getting into the army, about not having a job you liked, about not doing anything you felt was important, but now I see that maybe God planned it that way for us."

"Oh?"

"I can't say why, but I really believe we've been given something special, something better than jobs or wealth or anything, and we'd be foolish not to accept it and take advantage of it."

"How do you mean 'take advantage of it'?" asked Logan, unable to restrain the caution creeping into his tone. "Accept what?"

"Accept who we are, where we are, and then try to have the very best family we can have."

"I see . . ."

"Like it's been these last few days, Logan."

"They have been wonderful."

"And now that you're going to stay—"

"Allison—"

But she hurried on, unable, or unwilling, to hear her hopes contradicted.

"Logan," she said excitedly, "I've found the perfect job for you—right here in Port Strathy. I've been dying to tell you, but it wasn't confirmed until yesterday."

"You went out and *found* me a job?"

"It wasn't exactly like that," she hurriedly replied. "But I heard that Mr. Thomas, who manages the fish plant, was retiring. I just knew you'd be right for the job, so I spoke to—"

"I already *have* a job, Allison."

"Yes, but this is here, and now that you're staying—"

"That's another thing. Whoever said I was staying?"

"But it only makes sense to—"

"I'll tell you what makes sense," interrupted Logan, the measured calm of his voice finally breaking and giving way to the simmering anger rising within him. "It makes sense that a man finds his own jobs, and that he has some say in where he lives!"

"But I thought—"

"Allison," he said slowly and calmly. He closed his eyes and tried to force the anger from his tone. When he continued, a certain forced gentleness had returned to his voice. He deeply wanted to make her able to understand. "I'm sorry if I let you think that. But I never said we were going to live here. I'm not sure myself what the future holds. But right now I'm doing something I enjoy and I'm not ready to make a change."

"You're never sure! And while you're trying to decide what to do with your life, your daughter and I bounce about never knowing what tomorrow will bring. What kind of life do you think it's been for us?"

"Is that really how it's been for you?"

"Yes."

"But we've been in the same flat in London for years."

"With no sense of permanency. We never could feel settled, for at the drop of a hat you might take a job in South America. We are always on the edge, Logan. I'm always wondering what you're going to be doing next. All I want is a real home."

"No, Allison. All you want is to live here at Stonewycke!"

"Is that so terrible?"

"But don't you see—this is *your* home. It's not mine—or *ours*."

"Why can't it be yours?"

"Because it's *not* mine! You're the heir, the daughter. I'm nothing but the distant offshoot of a hired hand. I've got to make something of myself— on my own! Don't you see? How else can I stand on my own two feet? I thought you understood that when you married me!"

"I thought I understood a lot of things when we got married."

"What's that supposed to mean?"

"Just that I thought I knew you, that's all."

"Oh, fine! So you wouldn't have married me in the first place if you'd known that someday I wanted to be a man in my own right, on my own terms! You wanted me to be satisfied tinkering with farm equipment all my life?"

"I didn't say I wouldn't have married you, Logan."

"You just as well as said it! I may not know where everything fits, or exactly what I want to spend the rest of my life doing. But I would certainly expect more loyalty than that from a wife!"

"So it's my fault you can't hold a job?"

"I've held my jobs! And been good at them, too! No thanks to you, always out gallivanting around with your society friends."

"You leave my friends out of it! If it weren't for them, I'd have gone crazy in London, thanks to you!"

"You see what I mean? That's some loyalty from a wife!"

"What do you expect when you never talk, don't even tell me what you do?"

"You never showed any interest! Then whenever I did try to say anything about my work, all you did was criticize it and tell me I ought to go back to Stonewycke. Is it any wonder I couldn't find anything that seemed right?"

"If you'd stick to something, maybe it would become right."

"How can I do that when I don't know what it is I want to stick to?"

"Logan, you're thirty-two years old. Don't you think it's time you decided?"

The words tore painfully into Logan, for they exposed a part of him he desperately sought to avoid. Were he to face the full implication of Allison's words honestly, he feared he might have to admit that their problems truly were his fault, stemming from his inability to accept the responsibilities that life had given him. Therefore, he lashed angrily out at her instead.

"And if I don't, if it takes me some time to find the right thing, then you are going to do it for me, is that it? You can't wait for me to make my own way?"

"Oh, Logan, sometimes you can be so immature!"

Had he not been holding baby Joanna in his arms, Logan would at that moment have jumped up and stalked away. But though his entire body was taut, he remained where he was. The child stirred and whimpered restlessly, even though he had fought to keep his voice low. Logan stroked her hair and tried to quiet her; the muscles in his jaw twitched as he clenched his teeth, but he remained silent.

"It's an excellent job, Logan," Allison continued, trying to sound calm, as if to make up for her cruel outburst. "Very well-paying, and not without prestige in this town."

"But I don't *want* it!"

"You just said you don't know what you want," pleaded Allison.

"When are you going to realize that I can't live by the patterns you devise? A man has got to live his own life!"

"I don't understand you!" replied Allison, growing tearful. "Aren't we supposed to want the same things?"

"But you seem to think you're in a better position to determine my future than I am."

"I was just trying to help."

"Don't kid yourself, Allison! You were trying to get me to do what *you* thought would be best—what would be best for *you*. How many times have you stopped to ask yourself what might be best for *me*?"

"I thought it would be best for you."

"I think you're deceiving yourself. Just because I'm unsure of my future doesn't mean I have to jump to your side of the fence and take anything that's offered."

"I didn't know we were on different sides!"

"Well, the way you treat me like a little child who can't even make his own decision, I don't know what else you'd call it!"

He deposited the baby in her arms, jumped up, and started to walk away. If they hadn't had to drive home together, he would have kept going.

"We can't talk anymore, can we, Logan?" said Allison. Silent tears dropped from her eyes.

"We were doing fine until you started trying to maneuver and manipulate my life." As he spoke he did not turn to face her. He knew his words were only half the truth. Even in the midst of his anger, he knew she was right about two things. She *had* only been trying to help, and he *was* immature. But why couldn't she just accept him like he was and let him find his own help? He was as good a husband as a lot of men. Why couldn't she just lay off?

In the meantime, the child had awakened fully, whining and crying, as if sensing the element of strife that surrounded her.

The once-peaceful afternoon was over. The picnic was packed away in silence, and they departed Letty and Nathaniel Cuttahay's lovely little meadow.

A sense of defeat and loss pervaded the ride home. Not a word was spoken, though neither Allison nor Logan yet fully realized just what they had lost.

12 / A Time for Reflection _____

Logan and Allison entered the great old house together, but as soon as Allison had gone upstairs and disappeared round a corner, probably to have a good cry in some private place, Logan swung around and exited the house.

He left the Austin parked in front—after all, it wasn't *his* car to take at will—and set off on foot. The notion of walking and thinking did not exactly appeal to him, but it beat hanging idly about the old castle. And unfortunately he couldn't stop the flow of whatever might come into his mind. Hopefully if he kept on the go, the thoughts wouldn't get too deep. He'd had enough of that for one day!

He headed off in the general direction of town, though he didn't really care to run into anyone he knew. But maybe after the two-and-a-half-mile trek, he'd be ready for some distractions. He might even check out the action at the Bluster N' Blow, or down at Hamilton's.

The fine spring day had grown blustery, and an edge of chill accompanied the northeasterly breezes. Only patches of blue could be found in the sky now. Logan hitched his collar up around his neck, remembering as he did so his playful attempt to "impress" Allison earlier at the Lindow. That water would have been cold!

The gesture may have been a foolish one. But Logan had to face it— he did want to impress Allison; he had been trying to do so for the last nine years. She may *say* he didn't have to, but it looked otherwise to him. Why else had she used her influence to get him a job? What other reason was there for her always hounding him about moving back to Stonewycke? His own choices weren't good enough for her.

But were they even good enough for him?

Was his own insecurity about who he was coming back to haunt him? He'd always walked with a cocky step and a confident word on his tongue. But down inside, didn't he really know that he would never measure up alongside this family? He'd been stupid to think he could change, adapt, become one of them. He was a man of the streets, an ex-crook, a card sharp, nothing more than a common confidence man.

Could it ever be different? He had tried. Maybe he could be more respectable, more able to fit into Allison's world, if he could just settle on some definite course for his life. But in all this time he hadn't found anything that "clicked."

Many reasons why flooded his mind. He didn't want to think that they were nothing more than cheap excuses. He had no education, for one thing, and no capital with which to start anything. He could borrow from his in-laws, but that had its drawbacks, especially for one trying to stand on his own. His prison record was terribly limiting, for eight out of ten potential employers wouldn't think of hiring an ex-convict.

Was it his fault he had only one talent, and that that talent happened to function best in areas of somewhat disputable legality? What could a man do? Wasn't God supposed to take care of all that, make him fit in somewhere else?

There must be something out there that could satisfy him as much as his old life had. He had been happy in the old days, happier than he had been at any recent time, that was for sure.

A smile crept onto his face as he thought of some of the antics he and Skittles had carried out. As if it were yesterday, he could still clearly see his dear old friend perched upon a pub stool playing the part of the drunken braggart, challenging any who dared contradict his profound scriptural knowledge. The old Adam and Eve gag had truly been one of the best! Like taking candy from a baby! And with him playing his part of the innocent bystander with cool aplomb, together they had made quite a financial killing.

And there was the ever-faithful accident victim routine, in which Skittles would collapse in front of a car in slow-moving traffic, convincing the unsuspecting driver that he had nearly killed a helpless old man. At the most opportune moment Logan would appear as an eyewitness. After fifteen minutes of Skittles' moaning, the driver was more than willing to make an on-the-spot cash settlement rather than risking a possible lawsuit.

It was not the most original ploy, and used at one time or another by every street hustler worth his salt. But he and Skittles had been one of the best duos around; they had raised the con to the level of an art form.

And there were many others. There was hardly a gambler in London who could match Logan's flair and nimble fingers with a deck of cards. He'd been good, and it had been fun. He couldn't help that.

Intellectually, he knew his old ways were inconsistent with the new life God had given him, and with the life of integrity he had tried to establish since. Yet he couldn't keep from smiling as he recalled those days, nor hold back a sense of disappointment from stealing over his heart as he realized what a failure his supposed "new" life was by comparison. Had it all been an illusion? Had God for some reason not come through for him as He seemed to for others? Was he himself somehow to blame for this failure?

Of course, right now he *did* like what he was doing. It was legitimate, and it even had something of the same thrill as his old lifestyle. Arnie was right; he *was* good at it, tailormade for the job. But what would happen after the war was over? What then? He'd be right back where he began.

Logan came to a small wooden bridge and paused in the middle to watch the tiny stream rush toward the west where it would deposit its winter runoff into the Lindow. The bridge was still fairly new; the flood ten years ago had washed the old one away. He had been so sure of himself back then when he and Allison fell in love, so certain everything would work out perfectly for them.

Was it now time at last to admit that it hadn't, maybe that it couldn't, and cut his losses?

He let out a dry, bitter laugh. *Still the gambler, eh, Logan?* he silently rebuked himself. *Know when to raise, when to hold steady, when to fold.* His strategies worked around the gaming tables; could they be applied to life as well? Was it time to fold, to throw in his cards, admit that it had all been a gigantic mistake?

It seemed that he and Allison had done all they could. Maybe it would be different if they could communicate. But today only proved once again that any attempt to talk about things that mattered only led them back along the same bitter paths of discord. Perhaps it was true, after all, that they both wanted different things in life. How could a man and woman possibly stick together and make a go of it if they had opposite goals? They had struggled for over seven years trying to hang on to the thrill of their initial love, but it had long since worn too thin to sustain them anymore. And if they were going different directions in life, how could they ever hope to regain it?

By now Logan had reached the environs of Port Strathy. He tried to focus his attention on his surroundings. He *had* to get his thoughts going in another direction, for they only seemed to be leading him into a dark abyss, and he dreaded to think what might lie at the end. But the town was quiet at this hour and offered little hope of distraction. The farmers had not yet returned home from the fields, and the fishers were inside resting before their night runs. Many of the men were gone, off to fight in the war, or to lend their services to the more lucrative factories in the south. The war had even changed Port Strathy. When it was over, no doubt many of those very men would not want to return to this slow-paced, poverty-bound northern valley. Others would have no choice but be forever separated from their earthly home. He had heard that the Peters clan had already lost two sons. Jimmy MacMillan, his old fishing and poker cronie, had been killed at Dunkirk. They said he had dragged ten wounded men to safety during the mass evacuation and was going back for more when a mortar struck him down. How many more would die before it ended?

But at least they died honorably, thought Logan morosely. Maybe Jimmy was even a little to be envied. He went off to war and died a hero. His life meant something. And though his loved ones left behind would mourn his passing, they could also swell with pride at the mention of his name. The only use he himself could be was to skulk around in dark alleys. Even if a stray bullet chanced his way and killed him, the military and MI5 and all official agencies would disavow any connection with him in order to protect other agents in the field. He would be a nothing, a nonentity, not a hero. All Allison would get was a letter from some magistrate stating that her husband's body had been discovered, the apparent victim of a street mugging. Everything would fit in her mind too: once a street hoodlum, always a street hoodlum.

"So much for diversion," mumbled Logan glumly.

Unconsciously he struck out on the path leading to the harbor. Maybe a visit with Jesse Cameron would help. But even as the thought came to him and her animated face rose in his mind's eye, he wondered to himself if he really wanted to see the feisty fisherwoman. She certainly would not let him get away with mere superficial chitchat.

No, he couldn't deal with that just now. Instead, he took the street westward. He'd go out on the beach and sit on a lonely sand dune for a while till he got his thoughts straightened out. Right now he didn't want to see anybody!

Passing the harbor and then crossing the wide stretch of flat sandy beach that rose gradually fifty yards inland to rolling dunes, Logan caught the heavy odor of fish from the processing plant. Suddenly the sounds of the machinery inside and the squawking of the perpetual gathering of gulls around the refuse bins invaded his consciousness as well.

Just what he needed! A not-so-subtle reminder of today's blow-up with Allison. A reminder that he didn't *have* to die some inglorious death on a dirty back street in Northhampton or Brighton. A reminder that if he would just give in and be what they all expected of him, he could make everyone happy. A reminder that a whole new life awaited him as manager of Port Strathy's major industry. A reminder that if he would only—

But it wasn't what *he* wanted. He shook his head in frustration.

And from his self-centeredness, anger arose to join his feelings of being abused and misunderstood. Did Allison really know him so little that she could think he'd be happy there? *She is the selfish one*, he thought. Her husband couldn't be a war hero, so at least she could make him into a prestigious pillar of the community. *Her* community! To make *her* look good! To give *her* security and contentment.

But what about *him*? What about what *he* wanted? What about his own happiness and sense of worth?

Yet, who could blame her? Everyone would agree that she deserved so much better than what she got, and Logan would be the first to concur. She would have made any of her public school friends proud as their wife. She had been courted by the cream of the crop before he came along. Today, she could have been the wife of a lord or a financier. But instead she was stuck with a nobody, a hoodlum, and worse. She wanted more for him because *she* deserved more. Yet the truth would always be that she would never have more than a second-rate loser for a husband. And there was nothing he could do about it. He was what he was. He couldn't change his past, his common blood, his street-wise ways. He was not one of *them*, never would be, never could be. He was a hustler. He would never be able to fit into Allison's mold, even if he wanted to. Right now he wasn't sure he *did* want to. But even if he did, even if he took the job, even if he became utterly respectable on the outside, it would never change the person he was inside.

Again came the conviction—Allison deserved better. She would be better off without him. Then she could be free. And he could follow his own life without having to carry around the guilt of knowing he didn't measure up to what she needed.

Logan came to an impasse in his thoughts. What to do? They both wanted the other to be happy. There still flowed love between them. Yet each was unable to sacrifice personal goals and personal contentment toward that end. Happiness for the other, yes—but while preserving their own individual goals for life. Was such a thing possible? Probably not.

Why couldn't marriage be that way? Why couldn't *both* people be happy? Why did *one* have to give everything up, lose his identity, in order for the other to be content? It *must* be possible for a marriage to work so that both husband and wife were satisfied. Molly and Skits had certainly enjoyed that kind of marriage. And he had known others too. What was the secret?

Maybe it all boiled down to whether the marriage was meant to be in the first place. And if not . . . then probably all the scheming in the world wouldn't make it work.

Was that where he and Allison stood at this moment—in a marriage that had never been meant to be in the first place, and was therefore doomed to fail no matter what either of them did? Not a pleasant thought!

Logan sighed, stood slowly, and headed back down the hill of sand the way he had come. Again he avoided the harbor. He couldn't see Jesse right now, or anyone for that matter. He almost wished he had the guts to go down to Roy's in Old Town and get plastered. But he hadn't yet sunk so low as to go out on a drunken binge.

He supposed he should pray. But he couldn't make his mind focus enough for that. All he could see was his pitiful self, his failure as a husband, and the terrible thing he knew he was going to have to do before many more hours had passed.

13 / A Mother's Advice

When she and Logan had parted, Allison rushed upstairs. She gave the child to the nurse, then sought the silence of the library where she could unburden her pain behind stacks of silent, unseeing books.

By the time she emerged some time later, it had grown dark and stormy outside. She heard the steady pelting of rain against the windows, but all throughout the house was quiet. She hadn't been aware of the passage of time and was now unsure how late it was. Had everyone gone to bed? She found herself wondering where Logan was, or if he was still there at all.

Her heart ached at that final thought. She knew she had been wrong to make him angry. But it was such a little thing! Why did he have to be so stubborn, so proud? Allison knew they could be happy here at Stonewycke. Why couldn't he see that! What difference did a job make? Why did he always fly off the handle at any mention of it? Especially when all she was ever trying to do was help! *Being together*—that's what was important. Loving each other. Why couldn't he see that? Why couldn't he—?

She couldn't finish the thought. She had felt certain of his love when he had stepped off the schooner four days ago. But now . . .

Suddenly Allison heard the floor creak behind her. She started and spun around, her heart pounding. But the disappointment was clearly evident on her face when she saw it was not Logan at all.

"There you are, Allison."

"Mother."

"I saw the car in front, but I didn't see you and Logan return," said Joanna. "Dinner will be ready soon."

"I—we . . ." Allison began, but the tears, which had only been checked on the surface, rushed forth again. She bit her lip and screwed her eyes shut, but nothing could stop them from flowing afresh as if the well-springs of her sadness had not abated a drop from the last hour's crying.

"Dear, what is it?" said Joanna, approaching. But she hardly needed to ask the question. She had sensed that her daughter and son-in-law had all along been running from their problems and that sooner or later a painful confrontation must occur. For the moment, however, she said nothing more. She placed an arm around Allison, led her to one of the library chairs, and sat down quietly next to her, comforting her with the nearness of motherly love.

Gradually Allison managed a tearful account of the afternoon. She told her mother everything, from the joyful discovery of the secluded meadow to the final angry outburst of emotion. She ended with the question she had already posed to herself many times.

"Mother, why can't we work things out?"

Joanna knew the reason. But was her daughter ready to hear it?

"Allison," she began, "there has to be some self-sacrifice in a marriage. If you both stubbornly try to hang on to your own personal desires, you might never work things out. People so often mistake what marriage really is all about. It's not *getting*. It's *laying down* your life for the other."

"Well, I've sacrificed plenty!" exclaimed Allison. "I willingly left home and went to London. I've lived in that crummy flat, where my friends are embarrassed to visit me. I've put up with his starting a new job practically every week, and when he's between jobs, living on a budget that makes rationing look like wealth. What has Logan ever sacrificed?"

"Is it truly sacrifice, dear, when you expect something in return?"

"There you go sticking up for him again!" retorted Allison.

"I'm not sticking up for either of you," returned Joanna, her calm, soft-spoken voice rising slightly. "You both just have a lot to learn about marriage, that's all. And about what sacrifice *really* means. You say you love him and he loves you, yet I haven't seen either of you demonstrate the kind of love for each other that Paul says is to characterize a marriage, the kind of love Jesus had for the Church, the kind of love that lays down its life for the other. That's what marriage is—laying down your life, not having things comfortable and how you want them."

"But I've tried so hard, Mother!" replied Allison, breaking into fresh tears.

"Oh, my dear child," said Joanna, taking her weeping daughter into her arms, gently stroking her head. After a few moments she said, "You can't make a marriage work without facing that simple fact of what sacrifice really means. And then you have to ask God to help you do it. It's not easy, Allison—for anyone. It hasn't been easy for me. But God can and will help, once you reach that point of being willing to lay everything down. Only He can give you the strength to do what it might take to heal your relationship. True loving sacrifice goes so against our human grain that it is impossible for us to do alone."

"I've prayed and prayed, Mother." Allison sniffed and wiped her reddened eyes with a handkerchief provided by her mother. "But what's the use, when Logan doesn't care and won't talk about it? I'm sure he doesn't pray about any of it. I'm afraid he's gotten away from his faith. I thought it would only make things worse if I hounded him about it, so I just let it go—maybe I let mine slip too, I don't know. But we are still Christians, Mother. Shouldn't that mean something?"

"Being a Christian is no magic cure-all," answered Joanna. "Especially in a marriage. Belief counts for far less than a willingness to put the other person first. When things happen within us, and the lines of communication break down, God is still there, but we get out of tune to the sound of His voice. Then we give ourselves preeminence over others, and before you know it, some deep problems have set into our lives."

"So then what are you supposed to do?"

"Two things. You have to try to start listening for the quiet sound of God's voice, and be sure to do what He says. And then you have to look for opportunities to put others first, in your case, Logan."

"Oh, but what does it matter, unless Logan is listening to God also? I can't force him to make our marriage work if he doesn't care!"

"It has to start with someone, Allison."

"But why does it always have to be me?"

"I'm sure Logan would think *he's* the one holding it together."

"That's crazy!"

"Maybe to you. But we all think we're being more unselfish than perhaps in reality we are—including Logan, *and* including you. Besides, I believe he still does care, dear. But regardless, it doesn't mean *you* should stop caring."

"Why does it have to be so hard?" said Allison, shaking her head hopelessly. She rose slowly. "I better check on the baby. I don't even know how long it's been since I left her with the nurse."

"Allison," Joanna called hurriedly after her daughter, before she had completely disappeared out the door. "Would it help for the three of us to talk together?"

"I doubt Logan would ever agree to such a thing," Allison replied, and then was gone.

Joanna sat alone in the library for several more moments. It is all so clear! she pondered. How can they be so blind to such an elemental scriptural principle? They were both afraid to admit their own personal responsibility for contributing to their problems and lack of communication. Why was taking responsibility such a fearsome thing? Why was the first instinct always self-defense, followed by laying blame on another?

Yet, what could be worse than watching their marriage destroyed?

Joanna felt the frustration of one who knows that the time for words might well be over. Nevertheless, with deep faith she bowed her head, knowing that time for prayer was never past.

14 / A Season for Parting

Slowly Logan retraced his steps along the sandy shore back toward town.

It was seven-thirty in the morning, and already he had been up for well over two hours. Hardly knowing where else to go, he walked to town in the darkness of pre-dawn, and was on the beach, slowly sauntering along alone with his thoughts as the sun gradually crept up in the east.

In the obscure distance, indistinct through the settled fog, the vague outlines of fishing boats in the harbor could be seen as he approached. High in the sky the fog was thin, showing every promise of burning off as the day advanced. But it clung to the water thickly, lending an eerie quietude to the early morning. The partially visible masts of Port Strathy's fleet resembled some ancient ghostlike wraiths whose bodily mass had mostly vaporized from the face of the earth. All around, the water was still. Not a breath of wind remained from the short-lived storm of the previous night, and through the mist the surface of the sea was almost glasslike until it reached the very shore, where it suddenly curled into activity as the sand came up from underneath to meet it.

Logan observed these things as one unable to focus on their ethereal and yet common beauty. With his eyes he beheld, while his mind was elsewhere.

His future was before him; his past had faded from his memory almost as the boats had faded through the fog. Everything was now, and his decision was a heavy weight, which, sadly, he took it upon himself to bear alone.

Allison had not seen Logan since they parted after returning from their picnic. He had been absent at both dinner and breakfast, and from the look of him one might easily have supposed he had neither eaten nor slept in all that time. His hair was rumpled, his face sported a two-day growth of beard, and the white shirt he wore under a navy sweater vest was creased and wrinkled, as were his slacks. If he had slept, he must have been fully clothed at the time. Dark circles ringed his eyes.

She sat in the family room, making a poor pretense of sewing again. It was an eternal job these days, for no one dared throw out old clothes when new things were so hard to come by. But Allison's thoughts were far too occupied to make much good of her fingers, wartime necessities notwithstanding. She had been alternately mad and worried over Logan, and still,

75

when she looked up and saw him standing there, couldn't quite resolve which of the two emotions to give the upper hand.

It might have eased her anger a little had she known he had passed the night in the stable in his uncle Digory's old room. The thought had never occurred to her, hardly surprising since Logan did not talk much about how deeply special that place had remained to him. From the very beginning, even when he had come as a confidence man out to swindle this family, it had always represented an element of simplicity and purity toward which he might turn—qualities in which he knew he was seriously lacking. Always when he entered that room, he seemed to feel some of the gentle spirit of the old groom, hoping that it might somehow touch him and jar him back to those things that were important and meaningful in life.

It would no doubt have fanned the flames of her anger to have known some of the paths of his thoughts as he sat there alone, however.

The spirit of Digory's old home had done little for him last night. All he had for his efforts was a pounding head, a sore back, and an empty ache in his heart, which his early-morning walk to town and back had done nothing to resolve. Despite his awareness of his own personal shortcomings, he could not keep from blaming Allison for her independent attitude and her lack of support. His was not a healthy mind-set for reconciliation.

Allison could see from his face that he had come seeking her.

For a moment neither said a word. Unconsciously both seemed to know what was coming next, but neither could open their mouths to speak. It was, after all, Logan who had arrived at the decision and made the effort to come find her, and it was he, therefore, who first broke the silence.

"Allison," he said, "there is no way I can take that job." His mouth had gone dry as cold ashes. That wasn't what he had planned to say, but the other words stuck in his throat.

"It was wrong of me to try to force it on you. I'm sorry."

"I understand. There are things you want, and that you ought to have, and it's not possible for me—"

"I only want us to be happy again."

"Do you really think that's possible anymore?"

"Yes, it is!" she insisted in an imploring tone. "It doesn't matter where—here or in London. You'll find the right job. You don't need my help."

"But you're forgetting, I already have a job."

"What kind of job must it be that you can't even tell me what it is?" said Allison, her irritation gaining the upper hand at the prick of an old wound.

"I thought it didn't matter to you as long as we were happy," he rejoined, sharply poking at a sore spot within him.

"How can I be happy when I know you don't trust me enough to tell me what you're doing—when I live in fear that it's so bad you are ashamed to tell me?"

"I've told you over and over that it's nothing like that," he answered. "You're the one without any trust!"

"No trust!" exclaimed Allison, incredulous. "I left my home and went to London with you, didn't I?"

"Ha! Left your home, but you remind me of the fact every week. And even so, you keep doubting me. Because I was once a con, you will always doubt me."

"And you blame me, when you hide from me what you're doing? What else am I supposed to think?"

"I don't know what you're supposed to think. All I know is that trust has got to start with you."

"Me! Why does it always have to start with me?"

"Because a wife has got to trust her husband."

"And a husband doesn't have to trust his wife? What kind of a partnership is that?"

"I never said marriage was a partnership."

"Oh, I see! So it's a dictatorship, where the husband rules the roost, is that it?"

"I didn't say that, either! You know me better than that."

"Do I? Sometimes I wonder!"

"What's that supposed to mean?"

"It means I just don't think I know you anymore, Logan. You don't trust me, but don't think there's anything wrong with it. Yet you expect blind trust out of me. Hardly a fair arrangement, if you ask me!"

"All I know is that if a wife doesn't trust her husband, there's nothing left between them. Trust has got to start with the wife. Maybe my past makes that impossible for you. But I just know I can't live with it anymore."

Allison was silent, fuming, angry, hurt, wanting to yell at him and hold him all at once. In her confusion she sat speechless. Logan stood before her stiff and awkward, wanting also to hold her, but knowing the time for that had passed.

"It's more than just a lack of trust," he finally went on, painfully forcing each word from his lips. "I realized it for the first time yesterday, though it's been there all along. We want different things. We're going different directions in life. We have different goals, different needs, different expectations. I suppose I was just never meant to be the kind of family man you want and need. I'm sorry for all that. I wanted to be. I tried to be. But it's just not working—"

"Logan, no."

"Please, Allison, let me finish."

"No, I won't! I know what you're going to say, and it's not right!" She jumped up and looked directly into his eyes. "I still love you, and I know you still love me, Logan. And that's all that is important."

"I'm not even sure of that anymore."

"I don't believe it!"

"Sure, maybe part of us still has that love, but if neither of us can trust each other, if we can't talk about anything without arguing, then what does it matter? Love or not, it's falling apart. You must see that."

"We can make it work," said Allison. "If you could only see that I want so badly to trust you."

"There we are again," replied Logan. "If only *I* could see. You *want* to trust me. But admit it—you don't." He turned and walked to the stone hearth where a fire sent rays of warmth into the room. He could face her no longer. "I think we need some time apart," he finally added.

"We've already been separated for months," Allison protested lamely, "and what good has it done?"

"That was different. For this past year we've been deceiving ourselves into thinking it was nothing but the inconvenience of wartime. It's time we faced reality. We're no good for each other. Not now. We're cut out of different cloth. Reality—do you understand me? No fairy tale romances, but reality. This time there may be no passionate dockside reunion."

"How can I understand what you are saying? This is all so ridiculous. I love you and you still love me. There *has* to be some other way."

"Allison, you have to start looking at things as they really are, not how you *want* them to be. You want to think that a kiss and hug and a few apologies will cure everything. But then what happens the next time I come home with a new job, or the next time you get irritated at me because you can't stand our flat? What then? To make this work, a lot of changes would have to happen. And I haven't heard you say a word about changing. I'm not sure you're willing to change that much. I know I've got lots of problems in this relationship. Probably most of them, for all I know. I realize I'm not as communicative about my work as you'd like. I'm aware of a lot I've done wrong. But right now I don't know if I can change who I am. And I'm at the point that I know when to quit kidding myself. Allison, it's just not going to work, don't you see?"

"Logan, I know we have problems—"

"Until last night, I never thought I'd be saying this," he interrupted. He closed his eyes. Each word was an agony of effort. "Allison," he continued, "I'm leaving . . ."

He forced his eyes open. It was too cowardly to say such a thing without looking directly at her. "I pray it won't be forever, but we both have to face that possibility."

"I won't let you do this!" she cried.

"Allison, don't. You have to believe me when I say that I truly consider this the best thing I could do for you."

"How could it be?"

"You'll be free of me, free of the heartache, free of the problems. You'll finally be able to be the person you should be."

He dropped his gaze, turned, and walked from the room.

With each step he took, Allison wanted to run after him, grab him, somehow force him to stay. But she stood still as stone, huge tears of grief silently welling up from within her and overflowing her eyes.

Was it pride that kept her rooted to the floor? Or was it the awful certainty that he meant what he said, and that nothing she could do would be able to stop him in the end?

15 / Final Interview _____

Joanna reread her letter from Alec.

This was not the first time they had been parted. There had been an earlier war. But they had a granddaughter now, and Alec was too old for this sort of thing. She wished he'd never volunteered.

Somehow it seemed she should be immune, but the pains of war were to be borne not only by the young. The old, perhaps, carried even more than their share. Especially mothers and fathers. She wished Alec were here, yet she was proud that he had not fallen back on his age as an excuse to exempt him from serving his country. When his old regiment had been called up, desperate for veteran officers, he had jumped to the call immediately. A few months ago he had been promoted to full colonel for his heroism while in Libya during the taking of Bardia and Tobruk, notable British victories in North Africa. Maybe she didn't wish he hadn't volunteered; he was a man to be proud of. Unfortunately, Bardia and Tobruk were to be among the last British victories in Africa for some time. She couldn't help being anxious.

Alec said nothing in his letter about his heroism or exploits. Joanna could sense immediately that his normal robust optimism was missing. He was a natural leader of men. But it was not in his nature to lead them to their deaths. The weight of the burden was bearing down upon him.

He asked Joanna, as he always did, for her prayers. But now even the scrawl of his handwriting seemed to bear the signs of desperate entreaty. He had made an obvious attempt to lighten the letter with a humorous account of his attempt to purchase a gift for Joanna in an Arab bazaar in Cairo. It had been a wild farce in two languages, each at top pitch. Alec had been more than willing to pay the original asking price until his guide reminded him not to offend the seller by doing thus. Even at the end, once all the dust had settled and he found himself walking away from the booth with the desired item in hand, he was not sure whether he had come away with a bargain, or had himself been taken. But it hardly mattered; he had offended the man anyway, for as he walked away he heard the Egyptian spit at his back. He was sure, however, that it had nothing to do with the sale.

"Joanna," he wrote, "these people hate the British as much, probably more, than they do the Germans. I guess they *know* what we are like— they have had a hundred years of our tyranny—and they can't believe the

Nazis could be worse. It's all so ironic, yet we fight on here. But I doubt the British Empire will survive this war, even if we somehow are able to win. And that seems so doubtful as I write.''

He went on to say, for the tenth or twentieth time, that he missed her, that he longed for a time to sit and talk over with her all the experiences and sensations he was encountering daily. ''This land is so foreign,'' he added at the end. ''The people are indeed mysterious, but no less so than I must appear to them. Yet I also feel a strange kinship with these Arabs. Is it because it was here, in this ancient part of the world, that God chose to live out His human existence? I think I am coming to understand so much better many things I read in His Word. Oh, I have so much to share with you, but how can I possibly write it all on paper? I need you, and yet I can't say how much longer it will be until we are together. This war is far from over, my dearest. Sometimes I fear it has only begun. But God sustains me. In the words of Paul, *I am troubled on every side, yet not distressed; perplexed, but not in despair; persecuted, but not forsaken; cast down, but not destroyed!*''

A tear fell from Joanna's eye onto the paper. She quickly brushed it away so as not spoil the ink. Who knew when the next precious letter might come? These little pieces of paper with the familiar writing on them were now the most treasured of her possessions.

She wiped at the stubborn flow from her eyes, picked up her own pen, and took a clean sheet from the desk at which she sat in her great-grand-mother Atlanta's own dayroom. A bright, crackling fire blazed warmth upon her, almost making her forget the chill that had come over the land outside.

She wrote in the fine hand her husband had always admired, and for which he would scan each day's bag of envelopes as if ten thousand pounds were waiting in the one addressed in the proper hand.

My dearest Alec,

I have read your letter a dozen times and more in the week since I received it. Each word is almost as precious to me as the memory of your own dear face. Your final words have given me so much encouragement. Isn't that typical? Here you are at war, facing who knows what dangers, while I am safe in our dear old Stonewycke. Yet it is you who are encouraging me. It is cold outside, but a cheery fire helps me to keep my spirits up. We have had rain, then warm sun, then a chilling, all in twenty-four hours. Our beloved Scotland's weather, you know! What you wouldn't probably give for some of our cold! Oh, Alec, I love this old place, this dear Stonewycke! Sitting here brings me such peace sometimes. There is a heritage . . . a legacy to this place that makes me feel part of ancient truths, ancient people, roots and strengths that extend far beyond my own vision.

I feel something of the same thing being married to you. For you, dear Alec, are like Stonewycke in so many ways—strong, solid, immovable.

You bring me strength, you have loved me so, you have helped make me who I am by believing in me, loving me, trusting me, and giving yourself for me. *You* are my Stonewycke—my peace, my heritage. Though I forget all else, I will never cease to thank God for you, my dear! I cannot imagine life without you.

Events of late have made me more aware than ever of the special gift He has given us, and especially of the sacrifices of love you have made for me. You know of the struggles of Allison and Logan. I fear their floundering relationship is not improving. I pray there is some truth to the adage that things are always darkest just before the dawn. I know that God must have brought them together for a purpose—

Joanna glanced up from her desk at the soft tap on the dayroom door. She laid down her pen and turned.

"Come in," she said.

Logan's appearance was considerably improved since his encounter with Allison several hours earlier. He had bathed, combed his hair, and shaved. He wore a tweed suit, fresh white shirt and necktie. In his hand he held the checkered cap that had once belonged to his old friend Skittles, and over his arm was slung a woolen overcoat. Joanna realized immediately that he was dressed for travel, though even without the clothes she would have been able to read in his eyes and by his demeanor that he had come to say goodbye.

"I hope I'm not disturbing you, Lady Joanna," he began formally.

"Not at all," answered Joanna. "Would you care to sit down?"

"I think I'll stand, if you don't mind." He paused, shifting his hat to his other hand and took a deep breath before continuing. "I did not want to leave without seeing you first."

"You are leaving, then?"

"Yes, I'm afraid so."

"I'm sorry your visit must be so short. I sense this wasn't in your plan."

"No, it wasn't, Lady Joanna. You see, Allison and I—"

He stopped, raising his eyes momentarily to the high-vaulted ceiling. Joanna could tell he was on the very edge of self-control, desperately fighting to retain his grasp on his emotions.

"It's not working out between us," he went on, blurting out the words and forgetting his formality. "I came to you today because I want you to understand that the last thing I would ever want to do is hurt Allison. I don't take lightly—"

He stopped, unable to continue. Sensing his emotion, Joanna rose and went to him. She took his arm and gently led him to the sofa where she urged him to sit. She took the place beside him and laid her hands on his, which were cold and trembling.

"You don't plan to come back, do you, Logan?" she said at length.

"I don't know." He closed his eyes, squeezing back tears. "I would still like to believe in miracles, Joanna. But I doubt one is possible in this case. Our wants and needs are so different, and we can't even talk civilly about it. I'm sure the fault is mine, but what can I do? I've tried to change, to be the kind of husband she wants. But she deserves something more, and it would have been better for me never to have married her in the first place."

"But you *did* marry, Logan," said Joanna. "You have a child. You opened yourself to those responsibilities. This isn't a game of cards where you can throw in your hand if things fail to go your way." She saw him visibly wince at her apt analogy. "The last thing I want to do is speak harshly to you when you are hurting. Believe me, I feel for the pain you are going through. And it's hardly in my nature to criticize. But since it seems that for now I'm the only one left, then I must speak clearly to you."

"I deserve everything you have to say," Logan replied contritely. "I can't help it if I'm not made for the kind of life Allison wants. And because of my mistake, it's making us both miserable."

"There are no mistakes with God. Marriage is a unity, Logan, a symbol of the unity that is to exist between believers and their Lord. Do you know what unity is? It's not like and like. It's a joining of opposites. It's not unity unless there is diversity coming together. That's what marriage is meant to be—diversity, differences that come together and join as one."

"But we're *too* different!"

"There's no such thing as *too* different. The greater the differences, the greater the unity, therefore the greater the love."

"It's no use, Joanna. What you say may be right. But we're *not* unified."

"That's true, but not because the marriage was a mistake but because the two of you aren't committed to making it work, to achieving the unity God intended in the face of your very diverse personalities."

"But how long are we supposed to go on being miserable?"

"You think being unhappy is a valid excuse for breaking a sacred vow?"

"That's not fair, Joanna," replied Logan. "You make it sound like I'm slapping God in the face because I'm admitting that Allison and I can't get along."

"That's exactly what you're doing. *He's* the one who brought you together, and now you're turning your back on something that was clearly His doing."

"But I can't believe God expects us to go through the rest of our lives in misery just because we made the mistake of getting married in the first place."

"I told you, there are no mistakes with God. You both gave your future to Him, and your marriage was the result. But even if it was a mistake, once married, your marriage then became part of God's perfect plan for each of you. You can't go back and undo it. He has already taken up your marriage, drawn it into His plan. It is now the same as if He had intended it all along. So even if I admit to its being a mistake back then—which I don't—it is still a more serious mistake to turn your back on it now. Logan, maybe there are times when dissolving a marriage seems to be a tragic necessity. Only God knows. But I do know that, contrary to how freely men and women—even Christians—allow their marriages to break up, God's plan is for reconciliation, not separation. He ordained marriage, and He intends for husbands and wives to stay together. Don't make the mistake of disobeying God's command for the sake of a little temporal happiness.''

"So you think God expects people to be miserable just to stick together even if they no longer love each other?''

"I don't know what God expects,'' replied Joanna. "But I do know that His people are not free to choose the kind of life they think best suits them. Your life is no longer your own. As a Christian you are no more at the center of the decision-making process. God's instructions must take preeminence. Then we must put others ahead of ourselves. That is always God's way. I would say the very same thing to Allison. The life of the Christian is a life of denying yourself—there can be no true happiness without that.

"To answer your question, no, I don't think God wants us miserable. But love has far less to do with marriage than most people think. People say they no longer love each other and use that as an excuse for walking away from a marriage. But love has nothing to do with it. It's a matter of obedience. Are they going to obey the Lord, or not? Are they going to commit themselves to the marriage, in obedience to God, or not? People were making a go of ordinary—even dull—marriages for centuries before this modern notion of *being in love* became such a part of it. People back then understood commitment. They understood that every marriage relationship has its problems and you make the best of it. People nowadays understand so little about what marriage really means at its core. And I'm afraid so do you, Logan. Every marriage is hard. Every two people are incompatible in many ways. A happy marriage is not one that doesn't have those things, but one where you learn to put the other first and thus use those incompatibilities as opportunities for serving your mate. That's what makes a marriage work.''

"Well maybe I'm just not cut out for that,'' said Logan. "You might be right. But maybe I don't have what it takes either for marriage *or* for being a Christian. I only know I can't be happy until I figure out just where Logan Macintyre belongs!''

"But don't you see? You'll *never* be happy while putting yourself first. That's not the way happiness works. The world is upside-down from God's way. The only path to happiness, Logan, is by giving yourself, sacrificing yourself, for others—even for Allison. There just is no happiness apart from that. There's only more misery with yourself as ruler of your own life."

"But what about Allison? She's unhappy, too. She can't be content while I'm trying to figure out what I'm supposed to do. I'm doing this for her as much as myself."

"Oh, Logan, don't fool yourself. The best thing for Allison is for you to be by her side. If you're going to do this, then at least be man enough to take responsibility for it on your own shoulders. That's nonsense about it being for Allison's best. There is only one best for a couple, and that's for each to lay down his life for the other."

"Okay! It's selfish of me. It's my decision. I hate myself for it, but right now I can't see any other way!" As he spoke, he pulled himself to his feet.

Joanna knew the conversation was over. She rose also after a brief awkward pause, then put her arms around him in a loving, motherly hug.

"Logan, I will always love you as a son. But in that love I must honestly tell you that God will not let you off so easily. His love is too great to do that. You can turn your back on it now, but because of His loving grace, He *will* one day bring you back to face this again."

Tears had gathered in the corners of Logan's eyes, but he walked to the door in silence and did not allow them to overwhelm him. Once there, he paused, and turned back to his mother-in-law.

"Goodbye, Joanna."

She could see the struggle within him. He turned again, and hurried out the door, as though he might lose his resolve if he hesitated any longer. But when the door clicked shut, it seemed to announce that, for now at least, the time for reflection, for self-evaluation, and for repentance was past.

Tearfully Joanna returned to her desk. But she could not bring herself to write the kind of letter due a struggling soldier at war. Then she recalled the words of hope that Alec had quoted: *Perplexed, but not in despair . . . cast down, but not destroyed.*

Was I too hard on Logan? she wondered. She had certainly not said what he wanted to hear. Yet he had to be told the truth, hard or not. No good could come of glossing over it. Perhaps the day would come when her words would come back to his mind, and perhaps then they would penetrate deep enough to have impact. For now, there was but one thing she could do.

Joanna fell to her knees beside the sofa. To the Source of hopeful promises she would turn in prayer. Her Lord would sustain her, and more, He would not allow Logan to be destroyed by his own self-will. Her prophetic final statement to her son-in-law was more than mere words. She had spoken the truth. God would not let go of His dear child.

16 / Training

The dark room suddenly blazed with light.

Logan had been sleeping heavily, and in the first moments, seemed only able to respond in slow motion. He lifted his head from his pillow. Men were pushing their way into his room. To his groggy senses they sounded like an army. Well-armed as the intruders were, however, there were but three of them.

"Get up!" one of them shouted.

Clumsily Logan swung his feet out of bed.

"Qu'est-ce que c'est? What is this?" he asked in French, his voice still thick with sleep.

"Who are you?" demanded the man who had spoken before, belligerently ignoring Logan's question.

Logan propped his elbows on his knees and rubbed his face with shaky hands. "Maurice Baudot . . ." he said sluggishly. "Je m'appelle Maurice Baudot," he repeated, as if with more certainty.

"D'où venez-vous?"

"Avignon . . . I'm from Avignon." Logan rubbed his eyes and tried to shake the sleep from his head.

"What is your business here?"

"I am a wine merchant . . ."

All at once his interrogator's cruel look faded into a smile. He handed his rifle to one of his companions and drew up a chair, which he proceeded to straddle comfortably.

"You forgot that we changed your occupation last night," said the man, now in a friendly voice. "Otherwise, not a bad show. You even remembered to reply in French, which is not easy for a Britisher waking from a dead sleep."

"Thanks," said Logan indifferently. "Now can I go back to sleep?" He was already halfway to his pillow.

"And I loved your groggy act," chuckled the man. "Sometimes the quickest tip-off is a steady flow of answers that are *too* well rehearsed."

"You call that an *act*!" said Logan, "after you had me traipsing over twenty-five miles of mountains yesterday followed by four hours of deciphering instructions?"

The early morning intruder was one of Logan's Special Operations instructors, and their exchange one of many such mock-up exercises. In the intelligence training course that Logan had begun three months earlier, he could never tell from which direction his readiness was to be assaulted next. The course was nearly at its conclusion, and he had been made proficient in a variety of activities, from blowing up bridges to walking down a street looking as inconspicuous as possible. He was nearly ready to set out on the path he had chosen.

It was odd. He had never actually made a conscious decision to take Arnie up on his offer. When he had left Allison at Stonewycke, he had headed aimlessly south. He spent a few days in Glasgow, and, though his mother was undemanding, requiring of him no tedious explanations, he soon could not bear the quiet, pensive atmosphere the visit seemed to thrust upon him. He didn't want to think of anything. At least not so soon. He had to keep moving, and so before many days had elapsed he had said farewell to his childhood home, and was on the road again.

It took him two drifting weeks to reach London, and the first stop he made was at Arnie's office. He had never said to himself, "I'm going to London and take that job." But perhaps he knew all along that that's what he was eventually going to do. For one thing, the danger of the assignment no longer troubled him. Perhaps he felt, without knowing it, that he had less to live for now. When he walked into Arnie's office, all he wanted to do was get away, to forget. What better way to do so than in the shadowy, unreal world of the espionage game?

As soon as his visitors departed, Logan fell quickly back to sleep. If nothing else, during the last months he had been kept too exhausted to think of anything beyond the rigors of the training. Some time soon he would turn his attentions back toward his problems with Allison. But for now, he was just too tired.

When Logan completed his training a week later, he was entitled to a leave before entering the field. He wanted none of that, however, and requested an immediate assignment. Thus, before the week was out, he found himself standing before one Major Rayburn Atkinson on a secret RAF air base in the south of England.

Atkinson, a career man in the regular army, was the consummate military personality. He had received three field promotions during the Great War, and the Victoria Cross for heroism during the second Battle of the Marne in 1918. It seemed as though the second "war to end all wars" would prove his swan song, however, for at its very beginning at Dunkirk, Atkinson received wounds resulting in a left arm amputation and a blinded left eye. But he was not the kind of man to be easily placed out of the action on some dusty shelf. He fought the military bureaucracy as valiantly as he did the Germans, and it was not long after his recovery that a place was found in this vital department of Intelligence. He was now the key liaison between agents and their government. It was his responsibility to apprise agents of their assignments, and see to it that they were properly equipped for their tasks. In short, a good many of the agents sent on dangerous missions into enemy territory depended on Major Atkinson for their very lives.

It would not have been difficult for Logan to find himself intimidated by this iron-willed man, and Atkinson seemed determined to do just that. He sat, stiff-backed, behind his desk, his pinned-up sleeve seeming more a badge of honor than of shame. The black patch over his left eye said as much as the steel-gray right eye, which spoke of boldness, courage, and not a little defiance.

"I see you finished training only less than a week ago," he said in a voice that was no less commanding despite its low volume.

"Yes, sir," Logan replied, standing at attention in front of the desk, with all the respect this old soldier deserved.

"You refused the leave to which you were entitled?"

"Yes, sir. I had just had a lengthy leave three months earlier."

"Your record indicates you have a wife."

"Yes, sir."

"Yet you turned down a leave prior to embarking on a dangerous assignment from which no one can be certain you will return."

"I've waited a long time to get actively involved in the war," said Logan somewhat defensively. "I doubt that it will wait for me forever."

"I've seen many an eager soldier in my day, lad, and none who were healthy and red-blooded as you appear to be were ever known to miss a chance to be with their wives or lovers before shipping out unless something was amiss at home."

Logan did not reply. He had no desire to elaborate on his marital problems with this officer whom he barely knew.

"It is one thing for a regular soldier to hit the battlefield with problems on the home front occupying his mind," said the major. "But for one in your position, it could prove nothing less than suicide."

"I assure you, Major, I know where my duty lies, and I am fully able to keep my concentration on my job."

"Well it is *my* duty to insure that any escaping is done from the other end," Atkinson said firmly, though his voice never rose above its original soft tone. "That's not what this unit is about. Do you understand?"

"I understand, sir."

Atkinson leaned back in his swivel chair, and for a long moment allowed his eye to move up and down in a thorough examination of this would-be agent standing before him.

"I seriously wonder if you do, Macintyre."

"Sir?"

"I'm going to be frank with you, young man," he said, then paused.

He leaned forward, his eye still focused on Logan, though now it rested only on his face, intently probing Logan's eyes. Logan did not flinch, though he desperately wanted to look away. He didn't want to betray the anger rising within him.

"I have my doubts about you, Macintyre," continued the major. "To put it succinctly, I don't think you have what it takes for this job."

"Meaning no disrespect, sir," answered Logan, "but it would have been nice if someone would have mentioned that before I *successfully* completed three months of training."

"For one thing, Macintyre, screening volunteers is not my job. If it were, you can be certain I would have voiced my doubts. For another thing, as far as your success during training is concerned, I believe it would be a small enough matter for a man of your diverse talents and background to succeed in such a situation. I think you would understand my meaning if I used the old expression 'bluff your way through.' But I don't believe you are tough enough to succeed in a *real* situation."

"I had to survive on the streets before I was ten years old."

"You lack discipline," countered Atkinson. "And you lack staying power. According to your record, the only thing you've ever done that's lasted longer than a year is your marriage—and now it appears as if that is failing also. How can we be certain that you won't get out there where it can be rough, and decide it's too much for you? Or worse, what if you get captured? How long could you hold up under torture?"

"Can any man truly answer those questions, Major?"

"It helps to have a sound track record."

"Does this mean you're going to blackball me?"

"If Major Kramer hadn't so highly recommended you, yes. I'd tell you to go back to I-Corps and continue with the work you were doing for them. But I've known Arnold a long time, and I respect his opinion."

Atkinson opened a folder that had been lying in front of him and leafed quickly through several pages. "It says here you were classified as a sharp-shooter during training."

"I guess I did something right," replied Logan, forgetting himself in the relief of apparently being accepted—though reluctantly—by this hard-nosed army major.

Atkinson opened his desk drawer and took out a small automatic pistol. Before Logan even had a chance to wonder what was coming next, the major tossed the weapon in Logan's direction. Logan reacted swiftly and caught it in one smooth motion.

"Tell me something, Macintyre—have you ever *killed* anyone?"

Logan's mind froze in place for a moment as he stared down at the major's gun. He was thinking of the last time—besides his training—when he had held a similar weapon. He had been sitting in a deserted cottage holding a pistol on one of Chase Morgan's men. He had to keep the man prisoner long enough to allow Allison to get safely away. The only problem was that he was himself slowly succumbing to a serious wound. But he had threatened Lombardi that he would kill him if he tried anything. Logan's threat, however, was never to be proven, for he passed out and the hoodlum escaped, fortunately not in time to overtake Allison. Logan had never touched a gun either before or after that moment. He had never physically harmed anyone in his life. He'd never even been involved in a common fistfight. He'd always used his mouth, and had managed to talk his way out of many jams. He'd recently been exposed to hand-to-hand combat techniques during his training, but that was different, and the major knew it. Steadily he returned the man's gaze, then said, "No, I haven't."

"You probably think I'm a real hard case, don't you, Macintyre?"

Logan pointedly did not respond.

"There's a reason for that," the major went on. "I'm responsible for the men I send out. I don't like to lose any—even cocky con men. Unfortunately, I lose too many just from the natural hazard of the job. But as much care as I try to take, I still have trouble sleeping at night. There's no way I could send out an incompetent."

"Will you allow *me* to be frank with you, Major?" asked Logan steadily.

Atkinson nodded solemnly.

"I have spent more than half my life defying the law," Logan began resolutely, "and more time in jail for it than I care to admit. There used to be a noble character or two in my family—at least on one side of it. I have one ancestor who was held in rather high esteem by some pretty grand people. But in less than half a lifetime I've managed to disgrace the whole lot. And when I tried to establish some kind of honest life, I royally botched the job. Now I've got a chance to change all that. Well, Major, you were right when you said that it would have been easy for me to bluff my way through SOE training. But I'm not bluffing about this—"

Logan's gaze momentarily turned hard and serious. "I don't plan to disgrace my family again. I intend to bring some honor to the name of Logan Macintyre or—"

"Die trying?" interjected Atkinson.

"If that's what it takes."

There followed a long, heavy silence.

Logan could say no more. It was up to the major now. If only he could read that steely gray eye.

At length the major lifted a thick brown paper packet from his desk. He hefted it in his hand, apparently in thought, for a few seconds, then handed it out to Logan.

"This is your assignment," he said.

Logan reached across the table and took the packet in his hand and began to open it.

"You will commit the contents to memory," said Atkinson. "We will be sending one million francs with you to be distributed to various contacts as indicated in the papers you are now holding. You will be dropped by parachute some forty miles north of Paris. Your contact is Henri Renouvin in the city. His address and code identification phrases are all in there." He cocked his head to indicate the packet. "Renouvin's network just lost its radio operator, so, since you fared well enough in that area during training, one of your duties will be to train a new one for them. Their radioman was captured, so we are also sending new codes—it's far too much to memorize; you'll have to carry them. But you don't want to be caught with them on you. The organization there has taken quite a bit of battering lately, so we'll be looking for you to pull them back together."

Atkinson paused to hand Logan another smaller envelope. "In here you'll find your French identity card, travel permit, ration book, and one hundred thousand francs for your personal use. Your cover name is Michel Tanant. From here on out you are to erase Logan Macintyre from memory. He no longer exists. You are now a bookseller from Lyon. Your cover is convenient in that Renouvin owns a bookstore in Paris, and thus your contact with him will not arouse undue suspicion. You will have a day or two to completely familiarize yourself with Tanant's background. I've instructed your training officer to devise some drills and tests for you so that by the time your life is on the line, his identity will be ground into you deeper than your own. From now on, your final training is to be taken with the utmost seriousness. No more bluffs, Macintyre. It's deadly serious. Do I make myself clear?"

Logan nodded.

"There is one other item in that envelope you ought to be aware of— a cyanide tablet. I believe you know what to do with that, though I pray you'll never have to use it. Oh, this is for you also."

He took something from his desk drawer, and when he held his hand out, Logan saw a lieutenant's star. "You can't wear this, or even take it with you, but the title is official nonetheless. You're hardly regular army, but you'll no doubt be dealing from time to time with escaped British POW's and other personnel, and we felt some rank would serve you well— not to mention its usefulness should you ever be captured."

Logan stared quietly at the gold star before taking it. Until this moment he had not wanted to believe he was officially in His Majesty's Armed Services. Suddenly he was an officer.

"Have you any questions?" asked the major.

"Dozens," replied Logan, "but probably none that you need answer, or would care to."

"Well, read through and memorize your material first. It ought to fill in the gaps. Then report back here day after tomorrow. I'm afraid I can't give you more time than that. We'll have our final briefing then. There will be a Whitley bomber ready for you that evening."

"I'll be ready by then."

Atkinson leveled his gaze once more on Logan. "Yes . . . I think you just might be." He paused a moment, still riveting his single eye straight ahead.

"I don't know whether to like you or not, Macintyre," he finally added. "But in either case, I wish you the best. You just might make it, after all."

He stood and extended his hand.

The gesture, preceded as it had been by the softly spoken words, were the only acquiescence he gave that perhaps he was slowly gaining faith in this untried, unproven would-be spy.

17 / The Drop

Bright stars dotted the clear night sky.

It was a perfect night for flying, but Logan secretly wished for a few more clouds to cover the lone parachute that would soon be floating down from the heavens to the earth below. Not a few agents more experienced than he were captured the instant their feet touched the ground. Logan did not want to be one of them.

Crouched over the opening of the Whitley's fuselage, at about six hundred feet in the air, Logan could just barely make out some of the distinct features of the landscape below. He caught a glimpse of one or two farmhouses, but because of the blackout and the fact that it was three a.m., he couldn't tell whether they were occupied or deserted. He hoped he would not have need of them, for a small reception committee was to meet him at the drop site to see that he got safely on his way to Paris. Beyond the farmhouses, Logan saw a stretch of open countryside, fringed with a belt of trees.

"We're goin' t' try an' land ye close t' that clump o' trees, so ye willna be far frae cover," came the voice of the plane's navigator from behind where Logan sat.

"Not *too* close, I hope," said Logan. He could not keep his knees from trembling a bit at the thought of the jump that lay ahead, but the warmly familiar burr of the navigator's Scottish accent helped soothe his natural fear. The fact that the navigator happened to be a fellow countryman was perhaps a small blessing, but a blessing nonetheless. "By the way," added Logan, "I'm from Scotland too."

"I thought I heard a wee bit o' the Glaswegian in yer tone, but no enocht, t' be sure. Ye been awa too lang, laddie!"

"Yes, perhaps I have," mused Logan.

"Noo," continued the navigator good-naturedly, "ye needna worry aboot oor pilot's aim. He's one o' the best, an' he'll see that ye land as gently as if ye were one o' his ain bairns—an' Joe's got three o' them, so he kens what he's aboot!"

Logan smiled. "I've a child of my own back home," he said. It felt good to get his mind momentarily off what he was about to do.

"Do ye noo?" The navigator's ruddy face spread into a warm grin. "Weel, he'll have good reason t' be prood o' ye when he sees ye next."

"It's a she . . . my daughter."

With each word, Logan's tone grew with pride. Perhaps he did not think of himself as a father often enough.

"Weel, in that case, ye better make good an' certain ye jump clear o' them trees!"

Then came the pilot's shout: "Get ready!"

Logan had made four practice jumps in training. But they had not become easier with repetition. The supreme moment of terror when he had to leap out into thin air, certain each time that he would meet his death, was a fear far beyond any he had ever known on the ground. It was a totally unnatural thing for a man to do. Those practice jumps had been the most paralyzing experiences of his life, no matter that each lasted only about fifteen seconds from the moment he left the plane to the instant his body hit the ground. And they had been done on lighted, well-secured fields in England. His reception committee of French resistance fighters couldn't guarantee that they'd be able to use any lights, and from the dark look of the ground below, Logan had to assume he was going to have to jump blind. Not knowing where the ground was in a fall of twenty feet per second could result in two broken legs—or worse.

Logan sat on the edge of the bomb port, his legs dangling outside the plane. He double-checked his rubber helmet and body pads, and made sure his small suitcase was firmly attached to his pack. Then the navigator attached his parachute strap to the static line. If all went well, the weight of his body would automatically open the chute. If it didn't, he'd have to grab the cord himself and hope for the best.

"She's in tiptop shape," assured the navigator, as if he had read Logan's thoughts.

"Go!" cried the pilot from the cockpit.

Logan could not hesitate a moment now, for even a delay of two or three seconds could carry him miles off course and most likely into the trees.

"I hate this . . ." he breathed, as he let his body slip through the port.

"God bless ye, laddie!" shouted the navigator, but Logan only heard the words fading quickly away from him as if in a dream.

The draft of the plane threw him violently back, and that jolting was followed almost immediately by a hard jerk on his armpits. The chute had opened safely—as they usually did.

If jumping from the plane had been terrifying, then those next few seconds made up for it slightly. With the deafening racket of the plane's engines quickly fading into the distance, suddenly Logan was surrounded by a deep ethereal silence. The overwhelming sense of peace and well-being was almost so great as to make the terror of jumping worth it. Unfortunately, it was all too brief.

As much as he would have liked the silent sensation of floating weightless to go on and on, time was ticking rapidly away in unforgiving seconds, not eons, and he had to force his attention to the earth, slanted away below him. He thought he caught a brief glimpse of figures on the edge of the wood, but he couldn't be certain. All was black below him, but he thought he saw a deeper blackness, which must be the ground. Closer and closer it loomed, rushing at him like a giant speeding train. He bent his knees in readiness, trying with all the intensity he could muster to judge the moment of impact.

Suddenly his feet slammed against the solid ground at fifteen mph.

He let his knees buckle to absorb the blow, and in the same motion rolled to his side.

His body rolled over itself, distorting his perceptions, and in another instant he felt the silky parachute floating down upon him. Instead of the soft earth, his shoulder hit a rock and he cried out in pain. At least it wasn't my head, he thought with indistinct gratitude.

In a couple of seconds he lay still, trying to right his senses. But before he had a chance to settle back into a normal state of awareness and determine "up" from "down," he heard shouts.

"Dear Lord," he murmured, "please be with me." It was the first prayer he had uttered in a long time, and though it had popped out without forethought, never had he meant a prayer more sincerely.

The approaching voices were near now—and they were speaking French.

He felt hands untangling him from his chute and the lines.

"Bonsoir! Bonsoir, mon ami! Michel Tanant, n'est-ce pas? You made it!"

In his relief and exhilaration at seeing friendly, smiling faces, Logan forgot his recognition code. He jumped to his feet and grasped the fellow's hand, shaking it fervently.

"Oui, monsieur!" answered Logan. "Yes, I'm Michel Tanant!"

Logan could hardly contain his ebullience at having successfully completed this hazardous and enervating stage of his mission. He was safely in France! But the better part of his adventures still lay ahead.

18 / Allison's Resolution

Spring had come and gone at Stonewycke, and now autumn was nipping impatiently at the heels of summer. And while Logan was taking his first steps on French soil, Allison strolled pensively along paths lined with brilliant purple heather.

In the months since she and Logan had parted, Allison had experienced a wide gamut of emotional changes, ranging from self-pity to sympathy for Logan, to anger, to despair, to renewed love for her husband. They came and went in no particular order, returning at will, one following another in unpredictable fashion.

At this particular moment, walking with a gentle warm breeze at her back, Allison's present state was one of something akin to a gloomy hopelessness. For four months she had not heard a single word from Logan. Perhaps that was partly her own fault, she reasoned while in a more tender mood. For at first she had stubbornly refused to make any attempt to correspond. *He* had left her. She wasn't about to demean herself by begging him to return, and she felt that even a neutral newsy letter might be construed as such.

But three weeks ago, in one of her sympathetic frames of mind, she had decided to write him, ostensibly to inform him that their daughter had caught cold and had been ill for two weeks. An angry mood followed when she received absolutely no reply from Logan. A while later that was replaced by worry: what if something had happened to him?

She tried another letter, this one studiously devoid of anything approaching the personal.

Still no answer.

It had now been a week since her third letter, and she knew there would be no answer to that one, either.

Pausing in her walk at the crest of a small knoll, she surveyed the view. She had come west of the castle about a mile, taking no road but rather traipsing across open fields of heather and gorse. She had descended a bit from where the walls of Stonewycke stood, yet she still stood high enough to see some sparkle from the sea off to the north. Allison thought of how much she had grown to love this place. Why couldn't Logan feel the same way about it?

But he had to have his busy city and flashy jobs! He didn't care about anyone's happiness but his own. The day he left he'd said he realized he wasn't cut out to be a family man. And so, that was it—it was too much effort for him to try, and so much easier just to forget the whole thing. What did it matter to him if *she* was miserable, and that their child was abandoned to a broken home? Oh no, it was perfectly all right as long as Logan Macintyre was happy!

Suddenly, in the midst of her thoughts, it dawned on Allison how quickly her despair had turned into anger. It was the first time she had seen the transformation so clearly. How could she feel sorry for him one moment and despise him the next?

It was not right of her. Even in the midst of her irritation with Logan, she suddenly realized her own attitude was not all it should be either.

But then, how could it be? Nothing about this whole mess was right. Everything was so cockeyed, so mixed up. How could she possibly figure anything out if she couldn't even decide whose fault it was?

At that moment, her eye caught an especially vibrant clump of heather. Taking a few steps to reach it, she bent down and plucked off a twig.

"I should pick a bunch to take home," she murmured under her breath, as she immediately began to break off more branches and fashion them into a little rustic bouquet.

She had several in her hand when all at once she stopped. She had been thinking of something before she spotted the heather. It had seemed important. What was it? . . .

Oh yes—blame . . . fault.

No wonder she had allowed her attention to be diverted!

Why was the laying of blame so important to her? What was it her mother had said? *You both have a lot to learn about marriage.* If Allison was going to lay blame, it was on both of them. Could she trust her mother's perceptions? All this time she had blamed Logan for everything. Was it possible she was just as much at fault? Did she truly have as much to do with their problems as he? Did she really understand marriage that little? Was Logan right—she did not let herself *see* things as they really were?

She wanted so desperately for things to be ideal, perfect, problem-free. Maybe she had let herself be blinded to realities. If that was true, then she would have to face that fact squarely.

Oh, God, she prayed silently, *help me to see . . . help me to understand. Show me what to do!*

Allison paused in her anguished prayer. She had prayed many times before. She had poured out her heart to God over the course of the last eight years upon many occasions. And she believed that He heard. But something happened to Allison in that moment following her heart's cry which had never happened before.

For the first time, she paused to listen . . . to *hear* the voice of God in response. Rather than continuing her *own* petitions, she waited, silencing her mind, her heart, her voice—and listened. Her heart was at last ready to receive the truths He had been waiting to give. The first answer came through the words of Allison's mother.

Allison, there has to be some self-sacrifice in a marriage, she had said. At the time Allison had argued, defending herself on the grounds of what she thought she had given up. All at once now she saw that she had completely misunderstood her mother's words. Joanna had not been speaking of externals at all, but of heart attitude, of having her mind and heart fixed in an orientation of submissive and loving sacrifice. What a far different thing that was than giving up this or that while maintaining a resistant and self-centered posture!

If you both stubbornly try to hang on to your own personal desires, you might never work things out.

How right her mother had been! *People so often mistake what marriage really is all about*. That was certainly true of her! She had wanted to get out of it what was best for *her*. Laying down her life for Logan, in loving and sacrificial service to him, whether she ever received anything in return, had *not* been her idea of marriage! She had expected Logan to go at least halfway—maybe even just a little more. After all, the husband was to be the leader, the provider. Wasn't it *his* responsibility to care for the wife, and make the marriage pleasant for her?

Oh, she had had it all backward! She *had* been placing false expectations on him—expecting him to serve her! Both her mother and Logan had been right! Her eyes had been blinded. But now in response to the cry of her heart, God was beginning to open them at last.

There was something else her mother had said, only the other day. She had scarcely been paying attention at the time, had not even wanted to hear. But now the words came ringing back:

"You are responsible only for yourself, your own reactions, your own responses. You cannot expect Logan to do his part. Your eyes must be focused only on your self-sacrifice to him, not his to you. Nor can you gauge what you give by what you expect to receive in return, nor by what you think you deserve.

"Marriage is not a fifty-fifty proposition as so many modern thinkers would have us believe, Allison. Each partner must give everything, expecting nothing in return, to make a marriage work. The standard has got to be one hundred percent-zero percent—from each person's vantage point. The moment you say, "I'll only go ninety-nine percent of the way and I'll expect the other to do his fair one percent share," the false and selfish expectations begin to creep in, and the whole marriage begins to be undermined. That one percent you place on the other is the open door to every problem in every marriage. You've got to sacrifice, lay down, give, and love the full one hundred percent. God established marriage, and in His economy, that's the only way it can work. Whenever man tries to make it work using a different formula, it can only end in self-centeredness, disappointment, and misery."

As bits and pieces of her mother's passionate plea came back to her, Allison's eyes gradually filled with tears. She had, indeed, been guilty of expecting Logan to go not one percent, not ten or twenty percent, but fifty percent of the way—probably even more! She had expected him to meet *her* needs, to love *her*, to sacrifice for *her*. And what small so-called sacrifices she had thought she had made had all come grudgingly from within her, and she had held them against him. Everything she had done had been self-motivated!

Well, now it was time to turn it around. God had spoken to her. And now He was indeed showing her what to do. He had given no easy answer. But then she had not asked for one.

Oh, but how hard it would be to go back, to humbly have to admit defeat, to admit wrong attitudes! How easy it would be to expect Logan to share in the blame! How easy it would be to become angry with him all over again if he listened to her words of contrition and then turned upon her a haughty reply! How could she possibly keep from expecting from him at least a fifty percent response, or ten, or even one?

She didn't know if she could face him with apology in her mouth and renewed commitment to laying down of self in her heart. Especially if his response was hostile or skeptical, as perhaps he had every right to be.

Then, as if she were struck by some heavenly bolt, a kind of revelation dawned upon her. God had not told her to succeed. He had only said to take the first step!

That's all she had to do! What became of it, Logan's response, what she would do next—that was all God's concern.

She had to go back to London. That much was clear. She had to find Logan; she had to talk to him; she had to make herself vulnerable even to his possible rejection, and she had to tell him of her commitment to be to him at last a wife after God's fashion.

What he would say, what she would do then, she did not know. For one of the first times in her life, she truly felt in God's hands. He would guide her steps. She was sure that somehow He would restore their marriage.

But the first step had to be her obedience.

19 / Back to London

World events appeared in perfect accord with the direction Allison believed God wanted her to take. In June of 1941, Hitler shifted the force of his interest away from Britain. His mighty Wehrmacht and stunning Luftwaffe suddenly did an about-face and turned upon Russia. It would be for historians to debate why he made such a move, and perhaps for the Third Reich to lament. But with the fifteen-thousand-mile Russian front to occupy his troops, Hitler could not now hope to win the tiny island forty miles across the sea west of France, one of the few bastions of freedom now left in Europe. Thus, Britain was granted a respite after nearly a year of relentless blitzkrieg. And for Allison, it meant that she could return to London that autumn to make an attempt to heal the wounds of her marriage.

As Allison waited for her cab in front of Victoria Station, she was horrified at what met her gaze.

Yes, the Battle of Britain had been won, but it had been a victory for which the brave British people had paid dearly. In many places heaps of brick and stone lay where familiar buildings had once stood. She had heard that the civilian death toll ranged in the multiple thousands. Huge portions of old Londontown lay in rubble. Ancient cathedrals had been gutted, parts of St. Paul's and the House of Commons were destroyed, and bombs had even fallen dangerously close to Buckingham Palace.

Yet amid all the destruction it was evident that the British people themselves were largely untouched, at least in their undaunted spirits, which, under the leadership of Winston Churchill, remained typically stoic and courageous. Perhaps it was because they knew there was no time for despair—the hedonist enemy may have been turned from their door, but he was by no means defeated.

"Where to, mum?" asked the cabby as Allison ducked inside the black automobile.

"To 314 Clemments Street," said Allison.

"Right-o!" replied the cabby. "Been away long, mum?"

"Throughout most of the bombing, I'm afraid."

"Oh, I wouldn't be ashamed of that, wot with the little one and all." He cocked his head toward little Joanna, who inched a little closer to her mother while under the scrutiny of this stranger. "Many's the wife wot got out of the city last year."

"I never imagined it would be so bad," said Allison while the cab maneuvered into the traffic.

"It were a livin' inferno at times," replied the cabby, "but we'll kick the tar out o' them krauts yet! I 'spect yer 'usband's out doin' jist that, eh, mum?"

Allison did not answer, pretending not to hear. Yet she had to ask herself: was the reason for her silence that she was ashamed of Logan? She didn't know, but at least she finally had the courage to face the question. Or was her reluctance a further reminder that she didn't even *know* what Logan was doing?

No, she was not ashamed. She knew Logan had anguished over being perceived as a coward for not being able to get into the army. But *she* knew he was a brave man.

She had to remember to tell him that. There was so much more he must know. Since leaving Scotland, it seemed she was growing and changing minute by minute. With every humbling she was able to bring to bear upon herself, God seemed to give her more insight concerning Logan and their relationship. She was coming to understand how self-sacrifice and humility went hand-in-hand, and thus she could see how her pride had been a terrible barrier in their marriage. And when some of her old thinking tried to creep in, telling her that Logan was a proud and stubborn man too, she could remind herself that she was only responsible for *her* responses.

And with these changes within herself, Allison's love for Logan was restoring itself as well.

She could hardly wait to see him! She cautioned herself, saying she couldn't expect overnight changes. But it would be good just to be with him again, and she held an assurance in her heart that she would be able to accept things as they were. As silent and uncommunicative as he wanted to be was fine with her. She just longed to be his wife again!

All at once the cab jerked to a stop. Her heart raced within her and her stomach fluttered. She couldn't help it—she was nervous.

" 'Ere you go, mum," said the cabby, opening the door. Allison climbed out, while he rushed around to the boot of the car for her suitcases. "Please, 'low me to carry these up fer ye, mum."

At the door of her apartment she paid him and thanked him for his kindness.

She waited until he had gone before raising her hand to knock. When no answer came, she pulled out her key and glanced at her watch.

"Daddy here, Mummy?" asked her daughter.

"I don't know, honey," replied Allison. She hadn't wanted to barge in unannounced. But it was only four-thirty in the afternoon. He was no doubt still at work.

She inserted the key, but the door did not open. A panic seized her. But there was their name, still on the door! She tried it again, gave the key half a twist to the right, then jammed it forward, twisting it to the left. The lock clicked and the door opened. It had been so long she had forgotten about the trick to the lock. Still, it seemed a little tighter than usual.

A dank chill greeted her the moment she stepped across the threshold, and a mildewy odor permeated the air. A more objective visitor would immediately have realized she was stepping into a place that had not been occupied for some time—months perhaps, or more. There had been no heat turned on to dry out the dampness, nor had the windows been opened to air out the stale odors. Yet Allison clicked on the lights and wandered half through the place before the truth dawned on her that Logan was gone.

From all appearances he might have never been here after leaving Stonewycke in April. Or if he had been back, his stay had been brief, for it had been weeks and weeks since anyone had been here. He must have paid the rent up in advance, and then left. Slowly, painfully, the reality began to settle in upon Allison—he had gone away, and not even bothered to tell her.

For once she didn't care for her own sake—it didn't matter how he wanted to treat her. She could cope with it, even love him in spite of it now. But he had a child. Didn't he feel any responsibility for their daughter? That was the painful question.

She had been receiving regular checks from him all along—at least she always assumed they were from Logan, though they had always been cashier's checks, with no name upon them but her own, accompanied by nothing, not even a note. Yet was there no duty laid to his charge beyond money? What if something happened—an emergency? The recent illness had proved minor. But what if it had been something worse? Had he stopped caring for *everything*?

Already, without even noticing what she was doing, Allison had slipped back into the old pattern of casting blame onto Logan. Suddenly she realized what she'd been doing. This was not going to be easy—changing all her old ways and habits of thinking!

"Where Daddy?" Jo's pleading voice interrupted Allison's thoughts. She sank down onto the sofa, then looked full into the sweet blue eyes that were reminding her more and more of her great-grandmother Maggie's.

"Oh, dear little pumpkin," she said, "your daddy loves you . . . and me. But he's not here right now. It's only that he's a little confused—"

She had to stop, for tears had begun to rise to the surface of her eyes, accompanied by a thick knot in her throat. "Oh, my little darling, what are we going to do?"

She sat, taking the child onto her lap, and held her tight while she wept softly. It was not many minutes before she awoke to the selfish element in her tears. No one would have blamed her for crying at that moment, but she had not given a single thought to Logan.

Where was *Logan*? What was *he* going through? He was no cold, unfeeling man without human emotions and compassion as her old self tried to tell her. He needed her love, her prayers, not her accusations. Yet even as she tried to lift him up before his Father and hers, some deep inner resistance prevented her from saying the words. The struggles would be many before she would be able to completely forget the hurts of the past, the seeming unfairnesses. She wanted to pray for him, but the thoughts and words would not focus.

In the midst of her mental tussle, a noise outside the apartment door distracted her.

Her ears perked up at the sound. She jumped to her feet, hoping against everything her rational mind told her that it might be Logan. The doorknob was rattling, as if someone were fitting a key into the lock. Her heart leapt into her throat. She stood staring at the door.

The next moment it swung open, and there stood the bent and wizened figure of Billy Cochran. He stopped short in his tracks, looking every bit as surprised as Allison did disappointed.

"Well, I'm blowed!" he exclaimed when he found his voice. "I sure didn't mean t' barge right in on you, Miz Macintyre." His normally irascible tone was noticeably softened, almost deferential. Lady Allison Macintyre was the only member of the nobility he had ever known personally, and notwithstanding that most people in the twentieth century gave not a fig for such distinctions, Billy could still remember a time when it was not thought comical for a man to bow in such a presence. Though his hunched back seemed to give the appearance of that action, in fact he merely afforded to Allison what respect the tone of his voice could command.

"That's all right, Mr. Cochran," answered Allison kindly. She had always considered him a sweet old man, no matter that her perception had often amused Logan. In point of fact, Cochran's heart was made of gold, though, except in the presence of the wife of his friend Logan, he seemed bent on giving exactly the opposite impression with his surly manner. "Do come in," she added with a smile, hoping her reddened, puffy eyes were not too noticeable.

Billy shuffled rather awkwardly into the room, removed his hat, and stood fingering its rim for some moments before speaking.

" 'Tis right nice t' see you agin, Miz Macintyre," he said, managing a smile that to anyone else would have looked even more alarming than his usual scowl. "If I'd —"

"I don't mind," replied Allison. "Are you . . . looking in on the place for Logan?"

"That's right, mum. 'Course, now as yer back, I'll be leavin' you t' yer privacy."

"I appreciate what you've been doing. Tell me, Mr. Cochran, how long has it been since—"

Allison paused. It was hard to admit to a relative stranger that she had no knowledge of her husband's recent activities. But she had to know.

"—since you started coming by?"

"Now, lemme see . . ." He screwed up his face in deep thought and silently counted his fingers. "April, it would of been when I came the first time. That'd be—"

"Four months," sighed Allison, at last accepting the reality of the situation. Their apartment had not seen Logan for almost as long as she. "Please sit down, Mr. Cochran," she went on; "that is, if you have a moment."

"Don't mind if I do, mum. Them stairs is mighty steep." He lowered his small frame into a chair adjacent to Allison's. Then, as if the act of sitting down next to this gentlewoman brought them into, if not equal status, then at least closer proximity, he appeared to relax, and said in a more personal tone, "Miz Macintyre, there hain't nothin' wrong, is there?"

For a brief moment Allison attempted to put on her secure and self-assured mask. But there was something in the old man's eyes—a deep, almost fatherly concern—that made her suddenly blurt out the fears from the depths of her heart.

"Oh, Mr. Cochran, I haven't seen or heard from Logan in four months! I don't know what to think. Can you tell me anything? What is he doing? Where is he?"

Billy frowned, and thoughtfully scratched his large nose. "I didn't think it were so bad," he mused, mostly to himself. "If ye're beggin' me pardon, mum, I don't mean t' be so forward, but you see, Logan did talk a mite t' me afore 'e left. Didn't give me no details, but 'e said there was some problems, that is, atween you an' him, mum."

"What did he say?" she asked anxiously. "Do you know where he went?"

"Didn't say much, I'm feared t' say. Just that 'e was goin' away fer a bit, an' would I check in on things every now an' then." Billy took a long slow breath. "But 'e was real mysterious 'bout it. Wouldn't give me so much as a clue."

"Don't you have any idea, Mr. Cochran?" pleaded Allison. "Was he—has he been involved, you know . . . with his old life?"

"No!" answered the ex-counterfeiter emphatically. "I'd swear on it with me life!"

"Have you noticed anything unusual when you've been here?"

"Only stumblin' in on you today, Miz Macintyre," he replied. " 'Cept that 'e ast me t' pick up 'is mail, but there hain't been a stitch of it."

"None?"

Cochran shook his head.

"But I've written," Allison went on. "Surely my letters have arrived."

"Not so's I seen them."

Allison leaned forward excitedly as a new idea came to her. "Mr. Cochran, is it possible Logan could be in the city—coming here only to pick up the mail?"

" 'Tis a wild notion, if I may say so, mum. Not that Logan hain't experienced at layin' low. But I doubt 'e could do it 'thout *me* findin' out. 'Sides, 'e gave me the distinct impression as 'e was leavin' town fer a spell."

"But it *is* possible he's still in London?"

Slowly, somewhat regretfully, Billy cocked his head to indicate doubt.

"Now, mum, would you be permittin' me to speak openly?"

"Yes, of course." Despite her affirmation, Allison's voice contained a trace of hesitancy, as her old self sought to hide from the truth.

" 'Tis like this, mum," Billy began. "This 'ere world is pretty crazy these days, an' anythin's liable t' happen. An' I hain't sayin' you ought not t' hope fer the best. I know Logan'll be back. I'd wage me last bob on it. But I'm thinkin' you'll be only 'urtin' yerself if you don't accept things as they are right now, an' that's that he's long gone, who knows where. I mean, you'd not be doin' you or that dear wee girl there no good if you go beside yerself at every sound you hear, or every distant face that might resemble Logan."

"You're saying to give up on him?"

"No, mum. The bloke'll be back. You can count on that. I'm only sayin' there's no tellin' how much longer he's bound t' be gone. In the meantime, you gots t' go on with your life. You gots t' let things 'appen as they may."

"You're probably right, Mr. Cochran."

"But Logan's comin' back, you don't 'ave to worry none about that!"

"How can you be so certain?"

" 'Cause I *know* the blighter. Oh, he's got 'is problems t' be sure, jist like the rest of us. But there hain't a finer, more honorable man aroun'— what'd give 'is life fer a friend if he had t'—than Logan Macintyre. An' he loves you too, an' that's a fact!"

When the conversation waned, Allison rose, asked Billy to stay for some tea, which the small, unstocked kitchen was still able to supply, to which he heartily agreed. When he left an hour later, Allison embraced him warmly. Never before, at least within the old man's memory, had anyone expressed such a feeling toward him, and the act of affection flustered and pleased the dear man more than he cared to show. He forced out his stammered goodbyes, insisting that Allison call on him if she needed anything at all.

He would have been further embarrassed, and perhaps pleased, had he known that he had come as an answer to Allison's prayers. Hours after he had departed, while she lay upon her bed in the dark, she played over again his words of encouragement in her mind.

Perhaps tomorrow, or next week, she would despair again. But for now, God had sent, through her husband's old friend, a sustaining message of hope.

20 / Rue de Varennes

The gusty breeze rising off the Seine was unable to dispel the summer warmth of the city. Logan had long since removed his jacket and tucked it into his knapsack, which he had slung French-style over one shoulder. As he walked down the Champs-Elysees, he could not shake a deep oppression that came not from the heat but from the sights his eyes beheld.

Along the historic avenue the German occupation forces were playing out their daily noontime ritual. The garrison of the Kommandant von Gross-Paris, with colors flying in the air and a band beating out victorious notes, marched in arrogant affirmation of their rule. It was one of those sights that would not soon fade from Logan's memory. To him it looked as if the Nazi jackboots would literally tramp out the spirit of the mighty French capital. He remembered the grand City of Lights in the late twenties when he had been there. They had called it "Gay Paree" then, and it had certainly been just that. Of course back then the French were still cocky with *their* victory over the Germans. How could they know that within a score of years *they* would be the vanquished, or that their hated oppressors would march unopposed in the very shadow of the Arc de Triomphe?

It hardly mattered that few passers-by stopped to watch the spectacle. The grim looks he saw upon so many of the faces said all there was to say. Marshall Pétain, leader of the so-called government, now exiled to Vichy, had said shortly after the Germans marched into Paris: "Is it not enough that France is defeated? Must she be dishonored as well?" Yet it had largely been the apathy of the French people that had made for such an easy victory for Hitler. A peculiar and unpredictable nation politically, perched precariously through the centuries between England and Spain or between England and Germany, she was ill-suited temperamentally to step into the role of ally to her longtime adversary. The French were much later than the English to see the evil of the Third Reich, and on the day France fell, Frenchmen cheered and toasted Pétain's armistice.

Yet by this time Logan could see a pervading shadow of shame on many of the faces around him. The truth was now clear; but now it was too late. They were a nation vanquished, and their pride was trampled underfoot. They could not believe with their exiled leader that it was wisdom rather than cowardice "to come to terms with yesterday's enemy." Yet what could they do against this foe when even their most honored military hero had capitulated? There were Frenchmen, however, who did believe there was something they could do. Feeling that old Pétain had betrayed them, though their numbers were yet few, these would never cease to fight for the freedom of their Paris, their France. "Liberty, equality, fraternity" were no shallow words to them, but a slogan that ignited the inner fires of their nationalistic fervor. Charles de Gaulle, an obscure but patriotic general, had fled to Britain, now the home of Free France, where he slowly was being joined by those of his countrymen determined to keep up the fight. Other patriots had chosen to remain in France. Whether by choice or necessity, theirs was the task to which de Gaulle had called them in the wake of the fall of France in 1940: "Whatever happens, the flame of French resistance must not die, and will not die."

It was a small group of such Frenchmen Logan now sought. He turned his back on the parading soldiers, and pointed his steps toward the bank of the Seine.

One twenty-four, rue de Varennes. The address had been pressed permanently into his memory during the hours of memorization in England. Behind that unassuming door lay the headquarters of a resistance operation that had sprung up nearly a year ago. Their numbers were unknown, but they had been effective enough to warrant a good portion of the money Logan now carried securely in a money belt beneath his shirt.

They had recently come on hard times. Two weeks ago their radio operator, along with a handful of others, had been captured. As far as London could tell no one had talked, but a lot of damage could be done in a short time, especially where German interrogators were concerned. If the bookstore on the rue de Varennes had been compromised, Logan could be walking into a dangerous situation. Of course, I am only a bookseller from Lyon, he reminded himself. How could I know this place has ties to the Resistance?

When he came within two blocks of the bookstore, he grew vigilant. The narrow street appeared innocent enough, with four or five casual strollers stopping now and then at the various shops—a grocer, a chemist, a cafe—all typically Parisian. A woman leaned out from her second-floor apartment window, exchanging a few words with the grocer's wife about the new ration regulations. Some children were skipping rope in an alleyway singing a pleasant, childish ditty. For a moment Logan began to question his original impression of the occupation. But life did go on, after all. What else could people do? Children had to play, and women had to discuss the price of bread, even if the Nazis roamed the streets.

Logan could see nothing suspicious about. Slowly he approached the bookstore, nestled between the cafe and the chemist. There was no name, merely the words *La Librairie* printed in plain roman lettering across the door.

Logan opened the door and walked in. Immediately a bell clanged overhead. Stepping inside, he saw that no one, not even the proprietor, was present. He took a moment to appraise his surroundings—a tiny room where barely five persons could browse comfortably among the stacks and shelves of hundreds of volumes. There appeared little order to the categories of books, or at least it gave such an impression because there was so much crammed into the small available space. The musty smell of old books and dust heightened the assurance that it was, indeed, a bookstore.

Logan had no time to reflect further, for in but a second or two the proprietor himself appeared. Logan had well learned the name Henri Renouvin, though he had been given no description or history of the man. In all his attempts to visualize him in his mind, he had never come even close to this small, compact bookseller in his mid-forties who stood before him. Logan had been looking for a tough embattled soldier of the night, not a simple shopkeeper, which was exactly what this man appeared to be. His thinning blond hair, dimpled chin, and wire-rimmed glasses, which framed sensitive blue eyes, all gave the impression of an intellectual.

"Puis-je vous aider? May I help you?" he asked in a friendly, unassuming tone, as if the encounter were nothing more out of the way than a businessman greeting a potential customer.

"Oui," answered Logan, "that is, if you are Henri Renouvin."

"I am."

"Then you will be pleased to hear the messages I bear," continued Logan in perfect idiomatic French, using the recognition phrase he had learned from the file back at headquarters: "My Aunt Emily from Lyon wanted you to know she has recovered from her illness."

"Ah, oui!" answered Renouvin, his quiet features suddenly animating into life. "It is good news. She is a fine woman like her daughter Marie!"

"Marie, too, sends her greetings and is sorry she was unable to write."

Renouvin stepped up to Logan and gave him a firm welcoming pat on the shoulder as they exchanged handshakes.

"We were not even certain our message got through," Renouvin went on. "The radio has been nearly useless since we lost Jacques, though we must try to communicate. You cannot imagine how welcome you are! But come into the back—it is not good to talk out here."

"Is it safe for me to remain?"

"Oui, oui, most certainly," replied Renouvin, leading Logan as he spoke through a curtained doorway into a dimly lit room that was as dominated with rows and piles of books as was the store itself. In addition to the books were stacks of crates and cardboard boxes, a roll-top desk nestled between more books against one wall, and a small table that had three of the wooden crates situated around it, apparently to be used in lieu of chairs.

Renouvin motioned Logan to one of these crates, and while he seated himself, the bookseller took two heavy pottery cups from a shelf nailed haphazardly on the wall over the table. "Would you like a bowl of coffee?" he asked. "It is actually only ersatz, that horrible brew they expect us to drink these days, while no doubt the real coffee goes to Berlin. But it is freshly brewed at least."

"Merci," replied Logan. "You seem pretty certain there is no danger here."

Renouvin sat on a crate opposite Logan's. "There is always danger in Paris these days, my friend. But we are very careful, and it helps that the Boche* are not too smart. That must sound ridiculous from a man who has just lost four valuable workers."

Renouvin sighed heavily. "But it was not carelessness or stupidity that brought about their demise."

"They were betrayed?"

"It is a strong possibility. But fortunately, only Jacques knew about *La Librairie* and other incriminating locations where we conduct our business. He died before the Boche got anything out of him." Renouvin paused reflectively. "But," he began again in a lighter tone, "tell me about yourself."

"I am Michel Tanant," said Logan, "bookseller from Lyon."

"Clever touch! Do you know anything of the book trade?"

"Very little."

"No matter, as long as your skills in, shall we say, *other areas* are adequate."

"I hope they are," said Logan. But his inner confidence was still struggling to match the apparent importance this man was placing in him.

"You are British?"

"My accent is that bad?"

"Non, non!" said Renouvin apologetically. "It is quite good, in fact. It will fool the Germans easily, and many Frenchmen will not give you a second look. Whoever placed you from Lyon knew his business. Your accent resembles that usually found in the Alpine region of the south."

Logan drained off the last of his ersatz coffee, grimacing in spite of himself.

"Please forgive me, Michel, mon ami, for serving you such a dreadful brew," said Renouvin. "When the war is over and we are free again, you will come to my house and I will offer you the best French coffee you have ever had."

Logan smiled. It was going to be easy to like this man who spoke with the good-natured congeniality of one without a care in the world. How could anyone guess that he was daily but a breath away from death, and that he held in his brain enough information to bring down hundreds of others also? Yet perhaps it was the very aura of angelic innocence surrounding him that had kept him alive these many months. Logan knew he would long for the time he could visit this man without guile and enjoy pleasant, even trivial conver-

---

*Boche—French slang for Germans.

sation. But now, such notions were out of the question. This cup of coffee was not a luxury at all. There was much to be done, and much danger hanging over them despite the innocent look of things.

The urgency of their business must also have been pressing itself upon Renouvin, for he leaned intently forward and began to give Logan a brief synopsis of the operation at *La Librairie*.

"Now that poor Jacques is gone," he began, "there are only five of us who know of the bookstore. Each of us has a circuit of agents that operate blind, for the most part. If any is captured, he knows only one or two names at most, and the identities of the five of us are known only among ourselves. My network, for example, knows me as *L'Oiselet*, little bird, and can contact me only through a post office box. None of them know anything about the bookstore or that I am involved with others like myself. The five of us who operate our little networks out of *La Librairie* are something like the hub of a wheel, from which many, many spokes go out. If the Nazis have any knowledge of L'Oiselet, which they do not, there is no way they can connect him to Henri Renouvin, bookseller. All the pieces are separate. That is why Jacques's capture and death did not compromise *La Librairie*. As for myself, I act mostly as a collector and disseminator of information. My four associates do more of the footwork of the organization, and are thus more exposed than I. You will meet each of them in due time. But for now, mon ami, we must get you settled. You are tired and hungry, non?"

Logan was certainly that, and more, though it was only then, with the concerned words of this kindly gentleman, that he realized just how taxing his two-day journey to Paris had been. He had eaten but scantily since his drop. Though he had a pocketful of perfectly good, however forged, ration coupons, he had not mastered the local idiosyncrasies well enough to use them with confidence, despite his training in current regulations. He had nearly blown his cover in his fumbling novice attempt last night at dinner, and had ended up with nothing more than bread and coffee. Since then he had managed only a few turnips plucked from the fields this morning on his way into the city. Sleep had posed an additional problem; even for a city lad like himself, Paris was an intimidating place, and it was hardly worth the effort to try to locate a hole to curl up in for a while.

Renouvin set Logan up in a hotel a few blocks from the bookstore, with effusive regrets that he could not open up his own small flat to him. Such a plan would have been to court danger needlessly, however, and they both realized it. He then saw to it that Logan had a nourishing meal, while filling him in on more details of his organization. And while Renouvin had been genuinely concerned about Logan's rest, he talked with him far into the evening.

When Logan at last finally did lie down on his cheap hotel bed, he hardly noticed how hard and coarse it was. He fell soundly asleep within minutes, and it is doubtful even a Gestapo raid could have wakened him.

21 / The Resistors

Though the bright morning sun shone with a particular brilliance outside, Henri Renouvin's back room remained dim. But the figures gathered around his little table more than preferred their present business to remain ensconced in shadows.

"It's not like Jean Pierre to be late." The voice seemed to echo through the small room. It was an animated voice, full of vigor and haste, medium-pitched, though its owner's massive build gave him the appearance of a *basso profundo*.

"Keep your voice down, Antoine!" said Henri, looking over toward the table from where he stood at the sink filling a coffeepot with water.

Though a bear of a man, towering over six feet and weighing in excess of two hundred pounds, the speaker Antoine jumped up agilely from where he sat on a rickety crate barely able to sustain his weight, and began pacing nervously on the tiny floor space the cluttered room allowed. Every ounce of the man seemed a powerhouse of energy in constant motion, whether sitting or standing. His lively manner belied his fifty years, as did his thick, unruly black hair and beard, which held not a trace of gray. Even his eyes were alive and vibrant, emanating a love of life that seemed impervious to his present agitation. He appeared to be a man who both laughed and wept easily and without shame.

"I tell you, I don't like this," said Antoine, making a supreme effort to quell the natural booming timbre of his voice. "And where is Lise? Something must be wrong! Claude, you were the last to see her. She said nothing about being late for today's gathering?"

"Non," answered the third man in the room.

"Is that all you have to say?" exclaimed Antoine, as if he had been somehow cheated by the brevity of Claude's reply.

"Oui, Antoine," answered Claude quietly, apparently unaffected by his companion's anxiety. He was of about Henri's diminutive stature. However, at that point any resemblance ended. At thirty, the man was sinewy and muscular, and, but for several deep scars about his face, might have been handsome. One scar, in particular, situated over his left eye and causing it to droop slightly, gave him an especially sinister air. This impression of lurking evil was compounded by a crooked nose and dark eyes that flashed hatred just as Antoine's sparkled with life. Claude had received his scars, if not his hatred also, at the hands of the Gestapo when he had been captured

111

with Antoine's wife and daughter. He had been severely tortured before finally getting away in the escape plot which had killed Antoine's daughter.

"You talk too much, Claude," snapped Antoine sarcastically. "Are you not even worried for our comrades?"

"I am more concerned about this Anglais we will soon be forced to entertain," replied Claude. His every word was uttered with effort, as if speaking wasted energy that could better be used for more lethal tasks.

"*Forced*," rejoined Antoine. "He brings us a million francs! For that I will kiss his feet."

"You don't think his money comes without strings?" returned Claude darkly. "In return he will expect to control our operation."

"He did not strike me as that sort," put in Henri.

"Who cares?" said Antoine extravagantly. "With that kind of money we will be able to do much damage to the Boche. Tell me that bothers you, Claude."

In response, Claude just shook his head grimly, with the barest hint of a smile on his face.

"Ha, ha!" laughed Antoine. "There is nothing you like better than killing our enemy, eh, mon ami?"

"I think perhaps he likes it *too* much," muttered Henri under his breath.

Claude bristled. "What do you know, Monsieur Mouse?" he sneered. "You sit here all day safe in your little bookstore—"

"Claude!" remonstrated Antoine, ominously halting his pacing.

"Never mind!" said Henri, with a self-deprecating wave of his hand. "Maybe he is right. Who knows?"

"None of us risks more or less than the others," Antoine replied firmly with a pointed look toward Claude.

"So be it," said Claude in a tone that made it uncertain if his words represented apology or condescension. "But I won't do the bidding of this Anglais," he continued resolutely, "no matter how much money he brings."

As if Claude had planned the timing of his last word, the discussion ended abruptly when the bell over the outer door clanged loudly. The three men started, then went rigid, none moving for some time, as if fearing this intruder might validate their earlier fears.

At last Henri stirred into motion. As the proprietor, he must greet everyone who came through his door. He set the coffeepot on the hot plate, then strode through the curtain to the front of the store.

In less than a moment he reappeared, beaming with relief. He was followed by a priest, who entered the dingy room with an air of practiced grace and aplomb, like a man well accustomed to socializing.

Antoine fairly leaped from his chair and took the newcomer in a huge embrace. "Jean Pierre!" he exclaimed.

"What a reception!" the man replied, breathless from the zeal of Antoine's greeting. "And I am only half an hour late."

"What kept you, mon père?" said Henri. "You know ordinarily we set our clocks by you."

"The Boche can sometimes be just as punctual," said the priest. "They were at my door at seven a.m. sharp." He wore a cool composure even as he delivered what could be none other than shocking news.

"Mon Dieu!" exclaimed Antoine. "What happened?"

The priest gathered his black cassock around him and lowered his trim, stately frame onto one of the crates. Everything about the man spoke of a noble breeding, a *savoir-faire* that seemed to stand in sharp contrast with his priestly calling. Even his handsome, Patrician features were smooth and unlined, refuting on the surface the venerability that one might automatically associate with his holy robes. Only his gray hair, though thick, hinted at his forty-nine years.

"Ah, merci," said Jean Pierre as Henri set a steaming cup of ersatz coffee before him. "You really must not be so concerned for me," he added, noting Henri's pained expression of concern. "Once or twice a month the Gestapo try to make life difficult for me, rousting me out for questioning, occasionally arresting me. It has become almost a ritual I depend on. They put me through their ridiculous little barrage of interrogation, then release me because they never have enough evidence to hold me. I think they are naturally skeptical of anyone whose business it is to do good in the world."

"Someday they may get lucky," warned Antoine.

"But I have more than mere luck on my behalf, eh, mon ami?"

"Those collaborators in your congregation will not stick their necks out for you indefinitely, mon père," cautioned Henri.

"It was not collaborators of whom I spoke, Henri," said Jean Pierre. "There is a heavenly Protector who will never fail me."

"And what about the rest of us?" challenged Claude, disgruntled as always by Jean Pierre's composure, as well as his irritating habit of making absurd references to a higher power.

"He will protect even you, Claude," smiled the priest, with more fondness than disdain.

"Nevertheless, Jean Pierre," said Antoine, "and I mean no disrespect, but do you think it wise for you to have come directly here? How can you be certain you were not followed?"

"You know I am always followed," answered the priest. "But the last thing the Gestapo suspect is a priest visiting his favorite bookstore."

"Mon Dieu!" exploded Claude rising. "Do you mean you led them here, and they are watching us? They may have seen the rest of—"

"Relax, my friend," assured the priest, scarcely raising the volume of his voice despite the other man's angry outburst. "You may rest assured that in honor of today's special significance, I gave my shadow the slip long before I came anywhere near the rue de Varennes."

He paused and glanced around the room, as if noticing for the first time that something was out of place. "Where is Lise?" he asked.

Henri merely shook his head and sighed. Antoine continued with his pacing, and Claude, who had reluctantly resumed his seat, only grunted, as if the priest's question was in itself proof of some point he had just made.

Before anyone had the opportunity to answer, the bell clanged again. All movement in the back room stopped once more as Henri made his way to the front, with only slightly less trepidation than before.

Logan had overslept on his first night in Paris.

It was little wonder, for he had not slept soundly in days. Even prior to leaving England, he had been so steeped in his preparatory efforts and so keyed up in anticipation of this mission that he had slept little. But though he might be justified in sleeping so long, to sleep so soundly in the midst of this Gestapo-infested city was nothing short of pure folly, or so he told himself as he hastened out of bed. He would have to be more careful of that in the future.

He had hoped to have time to unpack and study the layout of the hotel, but that would have to wait. He was already late for his scheduled appointment with Renouvin. He dressed quickly, found he was too late for the stale roll and coffee provided to guests on the premises, ate a hurried breakfast in a cafe across from the hotel, then headed toward the rue de Varennes. Knowing he was a good thirty minutes late, his most difficult task was to walk casually and take a sufficiently roundabout route; to run or even rush his walk could mean death to an agent. Any appearance of haste could do nothing but draw attention to him, and that was the last thing any agent wanted behind foreign lines, where all eyes were suspicious.

When he pushed open the door of the bookstore, setting off the overhead bell, he had only a moment to wait before Renouvin emerged to greet him. Henri's face was tense, missing its usual affable smile.

"I'm sorry to be late, Henri," said Logan, assuming his tardiness the cause of the man's anxiety.

"Think nothing of it," replied Renouvin, attempting a smile for his guest's benefit. "It appears everyone is late this morning. Come back and meet my compatriots."

That morning in Renouvin's storeroom Logan met the oddest-matched aggregate of men he could possibly imagine. He studied each in turn as he was introduced to them, wondering how the suave, urbane priest, the dark, dangerous Claude, and the vibrant, boisterous Antoine could have come to be associated with the mild-mannered bookseller, Henri Renouvin. If it was true that politics bred strange bedfellows, then perhaps the politics of resistance carried the old adage to the extreme. Common cause, common hatreds, common fears were enough to bring both villains and saints together against a universal enemy.

He immediately noted the air of tension in the room. Henri told him that the fifth member of their group was also late, and they were growing concerned. Henri poured out coffee for everyone, and they took up again the debate they had begun before Logan's arrival: whether they should do anything about their comrade's absence.

"If she isn't here in ten minutes," declared Antoine, "I'm going to look for her."

"You must use discretion," cautioned Henri. "Haste in our business can always lead to danger."

Jean Pierre smiled. The idea of the big emotional man using discretion seemed altogether incongruous. But he said nothing.

"Lise knows how to take care of herself," said Claude bluntly.

"Which means we should ignore the fact that she might be in danger?" shot back Antoine.

"Which means that if she can't cover her tracks, there's nothing we can do to help her anyway," replied Claude. "Like I said, she can take care of herself."

"You're not going to have much of an organization if you all don't try to take care of one another," said Logan, but he regretted his words almost before they were out of his mouth.

"Who are you to judge us, Anglais?" sneered Claude.

"For once I agree with Claude," boomed Antoine, forgetting Henri's previous injunction to be quiet. "We *do* take care of each other, and we are a good organization!"

"I didn't mean—" began Logan, but Claude quickly cut him off.

"We know what you mean, Anglais!" he seethed. "You think your English money gives you the right to tell us what to do."

"You're all wrong," returned Logan. For a brief moment his eyes locked with Claude's in what was nothing less than a power struggle between two proud men who had never seen each other five minutes before.

"For heaven's sake!" exclaimed Henri. "This gets us nowhere!"

"And certainly does not help Lise," added Jean Pierre, "whom I believe is our main concern at the moment."

"You're right, mon père," said Logan, calming. "But I think at the outset I should make one thing clear. What Claude said is not true. The last thing I want to do is tell any of you what to do. That's not what I was sent here to do. I want to help—that's all."

"C'est bien, Monsieur Tanant," said the priest diplomatically. "And help is exactly what we need at the moment. We would be fools not to accept it."

The heated atmosphere relaxed, and Henri opened his mouth to make another suggestion regarding their absent member, when the bell in front again arrested their attention.

Henri jumped to his feet, but before he could enter the store, the curtain swept aside. From the relieved exclamations on the part of the men in the storeroom, Logan surmised it to be Lise, who now hurriedly entered the room.

A petite woman of no more than thirty years of age, on first glance she appeared rather plain. She had, in fact, arranged herself to achieve exactly that effect. She wore a simple gray wool skirt and cardigan sweater over a white cotton blouse, with thick, serviceable shoes on her feet. Her brown hair was pulled haphazardly back into a pony tail that reached midway down her back, and she wore no makeup, not even a trace of lipstick. But before the war, when she had dressed for an evening at the theater or the opera, the beauty she so carefully downplayed, now that her city was crawling with Germans, had been clearly evident. Even then, however, it was not immediately discernible in her high cheekbones or perfectly chiseled nose or her intriguing widow's peak. Nor was it her eyes, black and shimmering as onyx, which first drew attention. Rather, her first attraction was her quiet, unaffected charm, her sensitivity, and chiefly the intense fervor in her contralto voice when she spoke of things that mattered.

Everyone except Logan spoke at once with their relieved greetings. Antoine embraced her in a hug that nearly swallowed her small frame, while Jean Pierre took her hands in his and squeezed them tenderly.

"Mon cher," said the priest when the others had quieted. "You are in trouble, non?"

"Not I so much, mon père," she answered, "but there is trouble."

"Sit down," said Henri, ever the thoughtful host. "Have some coffee and tell us about it."

She let Henri guide her to a chair, but all the while her eyes rested on Logan. She had known there would be a stranger in their midst this morning; that was the purpose of the meeting. But still she studied Logan, as if, despite what anyone else said, she must draw her own conclusions regarding his merit. Logan found himself squirming under her scrutinizing gaze. Instinctively he knew it was important to be accepted by her, not so much because she held any particular power in the group, but rather because he immediately sensed that she was the kind of person whose opinion was worthwhile.

"You can speak in front of Monsieur Tanant, Lise," prompted Henri.

She gave Logan a final glance, as if to say, *I still haven't decided, but I must speak anyway.*

"Madame Guillaume is being watched," she began, then paused to take a sip of Henri's coffee. "She took in two escaped British airmen yesterday, and now she is beside herself with anxiety. She called me this morning when she thought she saw the Gestapo again prowling about the neighborhood."

"Why didn't you get the airmen out immediately?" asked Henri.

"They refused to go."

"What!" cried Antoine, jumping up from the seat he had only a moment before taken. "The idiots! Don't they know they endanger her life? It has always been understood that the protection of the safe-house proprietors comes first. The airmen could only be arrested again—*she* could be shot!"

"They must understand," said Lise, "though they do not speak a word of French, and Mme. Guillaume knows no English. My own is so limited I could do nothing to remedy the situation. They are very agitated and ill. I think they have spent many very difficult weeks getting this far from Germany. Their uniforms were filthy and torn when they arrived, and Madame took them and burned them. Now they seem to think that if they go out wearing the civilian clothes she gave them, especially while the place is under surveillance, they will be arrested as spies. It's obvious they have been through a terrible ordeal. I believe they would be more reasonable otherwise. But they are so desperate for the rest and so reluctant to go out on the run again."

"It is still no excuse," Antoine said staunchly.

"I have nearly convinced them to leave," continued Lise, "but now I have no more available safe houses. I spent the last hour trying to contact everyone I knew, and no one can squeeze in even two more. Henri, I was hoping you or one of the others might have something."

Henri did not waste even the moment necessary to answer her. He was on the phone by the roll-top desk almost before her request was completed. He asked the operator for several numbers while everyone watched expectantly.

"Allô!" he said at last into the receiver. "M. Leprous? I thought you might want to know that my friend M. L'Oiselet brought by two books for you. Shall I drop them by your house?" There was a pause while Henri listened. He nodded his head slowly, his mouth spreading into a grin. "Merci . . . and au revoir," he said. He hung up the phone and turned back to the group with a satisfied smile on his face. "Voilà!" he said. "It is arranged."

He jotted down the address on a slip of paper and handed it to Lise.

"Oh, Henri! You are a savior," exclaimed Lise, and the intensity of her dark eyes lightened a moment. Her gravity it appeared might also contain room for some laughter under the right conditions. "Now I only have to get the men out of there," she added, as if it were a small matter.

"Why don't you take M. Tanant with you," suggested Jean Pierre offhandedly. "As an Englishman, perhaps he could be of some help with them."

"Merci, but I can take care of it, mon père."

Logan couldn't tell if it was defensiveness or mistrust in her tone. Then she added, "There is no need to involve anyone unnecessarily." If there was apology in her voice, it was more than likely directed at the priest.

"He has come to help us, Lise," replied Jean Pierre firmly, but at the same time gently. "I think we should let him do that, don't you?"

She hesitated for a second, though it seemed much longer, as the entire room waited in silence.

In the meantime, Logan found himself growing steadily more perturbed with this bunch. He had risked his neck to come here for their sakes, and now three out of five of them were treating him as if he were but one step removed from the Germans. He was not yet sure of the priest, whom he thought might simply be testing him, however civilly he chose to do it. Logan was just about to tell this woman, who was so arrogantly assessing him with her critical eyes, that she need not do him any favors, when she spoke.

"If he is willing . . ." she said.

It might have been nice to hear, "Merci, it would be helpful to have him come," instead of the grudging consent she finally gave. But he had not come here for thanks or appreciation. If he could help, that would be the best way to prove his loyalty and good intentions. So he swallowed his annoyance and merely nodded his assent.

A few minutes later, he found himself walking down the rue de Varennes with a very silent resistance agent at his side.

23 / First Assignment_____

They walked for ten minutes before Lise finally turned toward Logan and spoke.

"I bear you no grudges, M. Tanant."

"You're not afraid I have come to impose my will on your organization?"

A corner of her mouth curved upward, amused. It was not a smile, but was as close as she had yet come.

"I see Claude has accosted you already," she said. "He is forever thinking someone is trying to take over our operation. He imagines bogeymen everywhere. But I have no such fear. Even if it were your intention, you won't get far with Claude and Antoine."

"Then, what are you afraid of?" asked Logan. "From me, that is?"

"It has more to do with trust than fear."

"You don't trust me?"

"Trust is a commodity I have learned to dole out skeptically and scantily this last year."

She paused as a bicycle-powered velo-taxi came into sight. She waved a hand and it stopped. After she gave their destination to the driver and she and Logan had settled themselves into the rickshaw-like seat, she took up her speech again. "I don't like it, M. Tenant. I despise this world in which I must exist. I despise what it forces us to become. But it is the only world I have left. I must live in it and still keep my honor. Someday I hope things will be different . . ." She said no more, leaving whatever else there may have been of the thought unfinished. She was not accustomed to revealing her heart to many.

"I think I understand," replied Logan, saying no more. He allowed the sincerity in his voice and eyes to say the rest.

In another twenty minutes they had reached the building in which Madame Guillaume occupied a small flat. They had departed the cab a block away and walked the rest of the way to the building so they could reconnoiter the area. Lise feared that if the Gestapo did indeed have the place under watch, it might look suspicious for her to return so soon after her last visit. But a thorough examination of the street revealed that either Mme. Guillaume was mistaken or else the Gestapo had given up. Logan unwillingly reminded himself that there was one other possibility—that the Nazis had already raided the place. But he said nothing.

Inside the building, all appeared peaceful and normal. They climbed the stairs to the second floor, and Lise led the way to the door, where she knocked using a prearranged signal—two knocks, a pause of two seconds, and two more quick knocks. Only a minute passed before there was a response from inside, but to Logan it seemed inordinately long.

At last the door opened a crack. The woman on the other side smiled broadly when her eyes lighted on Lise. She opened the door the rest of the way and hurriedly ushered them in.

She was a gentle old soul, plump and wrinkled, with eyes that drooped slightly at the corners, giving her a sorrowful look like a woebegone basset hound. Yet whenever she smiled, the expression of her face was warm enough to make up for the eyes, and if there was indeed sorrow in her life, it seemed to make up for that too.

"Ah, Lise! I did not think you were ever coming back," said the woman as she placed a chubby arm around Lise and propelled her into the living room.

"Have you seen any more of the Gestapo?"

"Non, thank goodness!" she replied. "I think it was a neighbor. I heard rumors that he was a collaborator, but I could not believe it. He has lived next to me for twenty years. We made too much noise last night getting the Anglais gentlemen in here. He must have reported me."

"But they are not watching you now," said Lise. "If that is so, why have they not yet made a move against you?"

"It is most peculiar."

"Where are your men?" asked Logan. Whatever the Germans were up to, he doubted there was time to sit around analyzing it.

"This is M. Tanant," said Lise, in response to the other woman's questioning look. "He is here to help us."

"Welcome to my house, Monsieur," said the lady. "Please come this way."

They followed her down a short hall and into a dimly lit bedroom. There were two beds in the room, and on each a man was lying. A youth of about eighteen years was bent over one of the beds holding a cup for its occupant.

"That is my nephew, Paul," explained Mme. Guillaume, motioning toward the boy. "I was afraid to be here alone if the Boche should come, so I asked him if he would stay with me."

Logan marveled at the woman. She appeared so fainthearted; what could have prompted her to take on such a harrowing task? No doubt she was like so many of her courageous countrymen and women who saw a need and did not stop to wonder whether she had the heart for it before offering her aid.

Logan did not have the chance to ponder this long, for the men on the beds required his attention. One had already started up to a sitting position at the unexpected intrusion. His eyes darted nervously toward these new-comers, and did not rest until he realized he recognized one of them. The other man simply lifted his head off the pillow and let it fall back in fatigue.

"Tisna the Germans, is it noo, Bob?" he said in a voice that sounded as if he hardly cared anymore.

"I'm definitely no German!" answered Logan in English, striding up to the man's bedside. "An' what else cud I be but a muckle Scotsman just like yersel', lad!" he added, in the thickest brogue he could muster.

"Hoots!" exclaimed the man. "I must hae deed an' gone to haeven! Whaur be ye frae? I'm a MacGregor mysel' o' Balquhidder." As he spoke the sallow Scottish face spread into a huge grin, perhaps the first in many weeks.

"Logan Macintyre o' Glasgow," said Logan, not even realizing his error in revealing his real name. The Highland airman stretched out to take Logan's extended hand, then, thinking better of it, instead threw his arms all the way around Logan in an emotional embrace.

There were tears in MacGregor's eyes as he fell back on his pillow. "I'm thinkin' ye're as close as I'll be coming t' me bonny Highland fer some spell, laddie!"

" 'Tis muckle nonsense, man!" exclaimed Logan. "We're here t' get ye back on yer way. Are ye up fer it?"

MacGregor glanced over at his companion. "What do ye say, Bob?"

The one whom MacGregor addressed as Bob rose and extended his hand toward Logan. He was as worn and emaciated as his companion, and his clothing was the same coarse garb that Mme. Guillaume had provided. There was, however, a certain cool refinement about him that the Scotsman had lacked.

"I'm Robert Wainborough," he said in a genteel Eaton voice.

Logan knew the name. The elder Wainborough was an M.P. and a baronet. But Robert had carried the name to new heights as an ace R.A.F. pilot and hero of the Battle of Britain.

"Well, Wainborough," said Logan, too hurried and anxious to be impressed by this celebrity before him, "shall we be on our way?" His words were half statement, half question.

"Look, old man," he replied, then paused as he sat back tiredly on the bed and reached for a pack of cigarettes, "we don't want to endanger these people. We're ready to go. But this is the first real roof we've had over our heads since we flew that German coop two months ago. We thought here was a place where we could rest a bit, and start to feel like human beings again. We've been dodging patrols, living in ditches, stealing food—Lord, it's been miserable!"

He paused and lit his cigarette with a shaky hand. "When they told us we had to leave here before we'd even had a full night's sleep—it was more than we could bear!"

"I understand," said Logan solemnly, but he wasn't sure he actually did any more than he had really understood Lise earlier. He had been through his own trials and doubts, it is true, but he wondered if it was possible that he would ever understand either Wainborough or Lise in the way their words were truly meant. But before he had the chance to reflect further on what his future might hold, he was jolted back to reality; Wainborough was speaking again.

"Would you please explain it to them?" he said. "I flunked French at Eaton—never had much of an aptitude for languages."

"I'm sure they know, Wainborough," replied Logan. But he turned back to Lise and briefly related all that had passed between them. Then to his countryman he said, "I wish you could stay and recuperate longer, but we better start thinking about being on our way."

"Mac is in rotten shape," said Wainborough, "though he'd never admit it."

"Can you walk, Mac?"

"Point me in the direction o' me bonny Balquhidder, an' then try t' stop me, lad!" he replied with more spirit than energy. With the words he gathered his remaining strength and, with the help of Paul and Wainborough, got himself into a sitting position.

Logan turned to Lise. They spent a few moments discussing details of a plan that was beginning to form in Logan's mind. It was several miles to the new safe house, but a tram ran about four blocks from the Guillaume place that would take them almost to the doorstep of their destination. They had merely to get the soldiers safely those four blocks. Logan wished they could move under the cover of darkness, but there was no time to wait for nightfall. Besides, roaming the city at night presented its own hazards. At length Logan turned back to the R.A.F. boys.

"Have you lads seen *Gone with the Wind* yet?"

"What?" exclaimed Wainborough. "Have you gone daft, man? What do we care about movies for now?"

Logan smiled. "Have you seen it?"

Both men nodded, but cast each other puzzled looks as they did.

"Well, you two are about to play Ashley Wilkes, and I'll assume the role of Rhett Butler after a questionable evening at Belle Watling's place."

Yet another moment longer the airmen remained confused, until the light dawned on MacGregor as he remembered the scene where Rhett saved Ashley from the Union soldiers by claiming he and Ashley had just spent a drunken evening at a house of ill repute.

"I got ye!" said Mac.

"Then why don't you explain it to our bemused war hero?" said Logan with good-natured sarcasm, "while I attend to a few other details."

24 / Deja Vu

The morning was well-advanced when three drunken rousters, well doused with Mme. Guillaume's last bottle of sherry, made their wobbly way down the stairs to the first floor and out onto the sunlit street. They could not have made a better job of it had several bottles of the sherry been inside them rather than merely splashed about their head and clothes. Even Wainborough got into character and could have passed an audition for the part with ease.

They had no sooner exited the building, squinting painfully from the blast of light, when a French policeman loomed up before them. Logan did not falter a moment, but he dared not look at his companions' faces to see their reactions.

"Bonjour, Monsieur Le Gendarme!" said Logan, affecting an extravagant bow, nearly stumbling into the man's arms.

The policeman looked disdainfully down his long nose at the three. "It is early for such behavior, non?" he said sternly.

"Oui . . ." answered Logan, "unless you have been at it all night, eh?" he chuckled, hoping to appeal to this man's natural French love of a good time.

"You are fortunate I am in a generous mood," said the policeman. "But get yourselves home quickly—the Germans are not so benevolent."

"Merci beau coup! Vous êtes très bien . . . You are a good man, most kind," Logan rattled on. Then he thrust out the bottle of sherry he was holding. "Please share a drink with us."

"Get on your way before I lose my patience!"

Logan bowed again with a sickening grin; then he and his companions staggered on their way.

"You've got nerve, old chap," said Wainborough, beginning to re-evaluate his opinion of this Scotsman who had come to rescue him. "I just aged ten years, but you didn't even flinch."

"What'd ye expect?" exclaimed MacGregor. "He's a Scot, isn't he?" He didn't bother to admit that his own heart had nearly stopped at first sight of the gendarme.

Glancing in a shop window, Logan saw that Lise and Paul were behind them at some distance in case they happened to need someone to run interference for them. But he did not kid himself about the danger. He knew too much was at stake for them to risk their organization for the three of

124

them. If serious trouble came, they would be on their own. The loss of three Britons was a small price to pay to keep their network functional. He knew they would help if they could, but they could not compromise their larger work.

By now they had turned down another street, a wider avenue with more midday traffic—mostly bicycles and pedestrians, though there were also a few automobiles. Logan scrutinized their surroundings, thinking that the tram line should not be too much farther, when part way down the street he spied some commotion. A German van had pulled to a stop in the middle of the thoroughfare. His stomach lurched as he saw the S.S. soldiers barricading the street.

"We're finished!" moaned Wainborough.

Just as they passed a narrow alley, Logan nudged his companions into it, even though he saw immediately it was a dead-end.

"Wait here," he said, then stepped back onto the sidewalk and ambled to an adjacent shop window, where he paused as if shopping. In a moment Lise and Paul were at his side, feigning the same activity.

"What's going on?" asked Logan.

"Looks like a snap check," answered Lise. "I doubt it has anything to do with us. It's just a rotten coincidence. The tram stops around the corner *beyond* the barricade."

"Then we have to get past it," said Logan. Not only did they want the tram, but he now saw that a similar barricade was being installed at the other end of the street from where they had just come. They were trapped between the two groups of soldiers. "Those Germans are thorough!" he said.

"And our friends have no papers!"

"I know," said Logan grimly. He rubbed his chin thoughtfully, as if the action might magically prompt some solution to their fix. "We need a diversion," he said at length.

"What do you suggest?" said Lise.

Logan had expected some opposition, or at least some hesitation on her part in going along with him. But she seemed perfectly willing to follow his lead, perhaps because she was wise enough to know this was no place for a debate, or because she had no idea of her own to suggest.

Logan thought a moment more, then said, "How are you at being hit by a car?"

She cocked a questioning eyebrow toward him, perhaps already regretting her decision to allow Logan to play out his hand.

"I have never had the experience, so I do not know," she replied.

"You'll do fine. I'd do it myself, but since I know the dodge, I'll have to play the eyewitness."

He glanced once more up and down the street. There were few cars, so the timing would be even more crucial, and the chances of having their deception seen all the more dangerous.

"Okay," he said finally, "we'll all amble slowly toward the barricade as if we don't know one another. When a likely vehicle pulls up to the barricade, just step out and drop in front of it. But *please* make certain it's already almost at a stop. You'll also have to try to gauge a moment when the soldiers are absorbed with someone else and not noticing the car as it approaches."

"Oui," replied Lise. "I see what you are getting at. It's crazy, but it just might work."

Then Logan turned to Paul. "You must get into the line, Paul, and get the people stirred up. A discreet word here and there ought to do it, and keep moving so no one can pinpoint the trouble to you. Can you handle that?"

The boy nodded, warming to the excitement of being thus used to outwit the Boche.

Logan then returned to the alley, briefed his countrymen on their part in the ploy, and verbally gave them the address of the safe house should they become separated.

Paul moved into place in the line where already thirty or forty pedestrians were shuffling about, along with two cars. Logan judged it would not take much to incite them, for they were already cross and surly at this bothersome inconvenience. Soon Lise crossed the street, hoping that by doing thus she would divert attention from the side where the airmen would be making their escape.

A shiny black sedan pulled up to the roadblock. It would be the perfect pigeon. Out of the corner of his eye, Logan watched Lise. She was making no move. Why was she waiting?

The glare on the windshield shifted and Logan saw that the car was occupied by a German officer—nothing less than a general!

Good girl! thought Logan. She had her head about her!

The general's car pulled around the crowd, up to the barricade, and was allowed to pass. As the soldiers, four of them in all, were replacing the barricade, an older gray Renault pulled up. Logan held his breath. Lise stepped off the sidewalk.

In a moment she was down in such a commotion of squealing breaks, agonized screams, and crowd noise that Logan feared she might have actually been hit. He berated himself for coming up with the fool plan, but no matter what happened he couldn't fold now. Back in England, he and Skittles only faced a few days in jail if their scam failed. But now five lives depended on success, and there was no place to bolt to even if he wanted to.

"Someone's been killed!" came a cry from the crowd; Logan thought he recognized Paul's tenor voice.

"Mon Dieu! she's been hit!"

"There's blood! Someone help her—the girl's dead!"

"No, she's still breathing, she needs a doctor."

The voices were from many different quarters now, as the throng pressed in around the scene.

"Hey, don't push . . . someone took my wallet!"

"It's the Germans' fault!"

Curses and accusations and commotion grew, leveled both toward the Boche and between the volatile Frenchmen themselves. Pushing and shoving gave way to an occasional outbreak that looked as though it could turn the scene into an ugly mob, enough to draw two of the S.S. men from their posts into the disorderly fray. A third stepped well away from the barricade to better view the melee. A quick glance to his right showed that Wainborough and MacGregor were inching their way closer to the roadblock. Just as he was about to make his move, Logan remembered his jacket, still reeking of sherry. Tearing it off and dropping it on the ground, he rushed up to the fourth soldier, who was still firmly planted at his post.

"Please," he said, his face and tone filled with frantic entreaty, "I'm a doctor. I must get to the girl, but I can't get through the crowd. Help me!"

"Folge ihm!" the soldier grunted, pointing to the third S.S. man.

Logan shook his head, pretending not to understand, and grabbing the man's arm. "Please help me!" he said, and managed to get the man a few steps away from his position.

"Hans!" called the German to his comrade. But the third soldier was too engrossed in the noisy spectacle to hear.

"Stupid Französisch!" he said, swearing an oath vehemently at Logan, then striding hotly up to the man he had called Hans. "Take this doctor and see what he can do."

A surreptitious glance showed Logan that he had given his airmen enough time to get past the barricade. But they still had to get the few yards to the next street and around the corner out of sight.

"Oh, merci . . . merci!" exclaimed Logan effusively. He put an arm around the man, plying him with what hollow praise he could dream up.

Mac and Wainborough had broken into a trot, and Logan caught a glimpse of pain etched onto Mac's homely countenance. But the Scot hadn't made it this close to home to give up so easily. If they were spotted now, running, they would be dead ducks. Logan had to keep the German's attention another twenty or thirty seconds, yet his experience told him he had already carried the con beyond its natural limits. The soldiers would get suspicious before long.

"If you want to help," shouted the German in broken French, "then go *help*!"

Logan could stall no longer. The third soldier had taken him in tow and was shoving him through the crowd. He couldn't even chance a look over his shoulder. He breathed a quick prayer that he had bought his charges sufficient time. When he heard no outbursts at the barricade, he realized he had—the flyboys had make it! He also saw that Paul had made his exit too, sneaking to the head of the line, and passing through the quick inspection; perhaps he would be able to help the Anglais.

Now Logan could turn his energy to getting himself and Lise out of there.

Scarcely a minute or two had elapsed since the gray sedan had slammed on its brakes. As Logan elbowed his way through the crowd with the aid of his S.S. escort, he saw that Lise was only just then pulling herself to a sitting position. She shook her head groggily, while rubbing her face with her hands. Her nose was smudged, and a scrape across her cheek looked real enough, with genuine blood oozing from it. *She is definitely no amateur*, thought Logan to himself.

"Mademoiselle," he said, kneeling down beside her, "I am a doctor. Where are you hurt?"

"I will call an ambulance," said the German, seeming to be genuinely concerned.

"Non . . . non!" replied Lise. "I will be fine. I only had the wind knocked from me."

"Can you walk?" asked Logan.

"Oui. Just give me a hand." She began to pull herself unsteadily to her feet as a cheer rose from the crowd. Then she winced sharply in pain as her left knee buckled. "I think it is my hip," she said.

"I should examine you in my office," said Logan, the conscientious medical man. "It is not far—only around the corner."

"I'll call a car," offered the helpful German.

"Do not trouble yourself," said Lise, rising again on her feet. "I can manage to walk that far." She bravely smiled her thanks, then limped off with Logan's steadying arm around her. The barricade was parted for them and no one even bothered to look at their papers.

The half-block past the barricade and around the corner seemed to take hours. The urge to make a run for it was almost overpowering. But Lise and Logan kept up the ruse of doctor and patient until they were well on their way down the next street. They hoped they would be in time to catch Paul and the two refugees, but speed was always a sure way of arousing attention. They did not break into a jog until they were well out of sight, when they saw the tram coming to a stop a hundred yards ahead.

Two minutes later Logan sank gratefully onto a back seat of one of the vehicles. MacGregor, Wainborough, Paul, and Lise were all safely aboard as well, scattered throughout the car.

Barring any further interference from the Germans, they were home free, at least for this particular episode.

25 / New Compatriots_____

Logan stirred the saccharin into his coffee.

The adventure of the day was successfully over. MacGregor and Wainborough were settled into their new safe house. They could now look forward to several days of recuperation before they were moved along to the next stage of the escape line—probably Marseille in unoccupied France—and then, with the help of a guide, over the Pyrenees into Spain. Their trek was far from over, but if they were lucky they'd be home for Christmas. The snow would be piled high in the glens of MacGregor's Balquhidder, and icy wind wafting down from the mountains. His little cottage would be filled with the warm, sweet, comforting smell of peat, while his mother tended a bubbling pot of tatties and neeps. . . .

"You are deep in thought, M. Tanant," said Lise, setting a plate of bread and cheese on the table.

They had come to her flat after leaving the airmen. It was closer than the bookstore, and she thought Logan might want to see the wireless that was secreted there. He glanced up absently, hardly realizing his mind had wandered so far from the present.

"Oh, I was just thinking of home," he said. "Scotland, you know," he added with a light ironical laugh. "I suppose I was thinking more of MacGregor's home than of any home I have ever known. You know, country kitchens, peat fires, heather blooming on the hills, a cow mooing softly in the byre—the poverty-stricken but romantic Scottish highlands which everyone since Robbie Burns has loved to write and sing about?"

"What was *your* home like?" asked Lise.

"More along the line of soot-covered brick buildings for miles on end, air filled with the sharp metallic sounds of industry, smokestacks spewing out black smoke, and that singular odor only a seaport slum can produce," replied Logan. "I'm a city fellow, born and bred. Glasgow. But I'm not complaining. The city was good to me, and I rather liked it. Maybe I would have been better off in the open air and barren hills and fields; who knows?"

He paused and lifted his eyes to Lise, who had been listening with great intensity. "What about you? Are you from Paris?"

"I too am a city girl," she replied, then paused. She looked as if she was about to say more, but instead rose to refill their coffee cups.

"And. . . ?" said Logan.

She took the coffeepot from the stove and began pouring into the cups, appearing not to have heard him.

"What is there to say?" she sighed at length. "What there is of my life is all too apparent—intrigue and death, killing, deception . . . a hell of uncertainty. As for my past life, what good does it do to remember when I was alive and my days were filled with laughter? Those times are gone, and it seems they will never return."

She had spoken with such sorrow and pain; Logan had not expected the emotion it roused within him. Yet her voice contained courage too, consistent with the tough shell he had begun to associate with her.

"You are so sure the past will never come again?"

"The old France is dead, M. Tanant," she replied with sadness. "And I died a year ago when the Germans marched beneath the Arc de Triomphe," she replied, "and the fragrance of the chestnuts along the Champs-Elysees was replaced with the stench of Nazis. I died when they took my family to a concentration camp."

"I'm sorry. I didn't know."

"Do you want to know about my life now, M. Tanant?"

"You are Jewish?"

"Perhaps you object to helping us?"

"Why should I?"

"Many people do, even fellow Frenchmen."

"I am not one of them."

"Jewish educators were among the first to be 'purged,' " she went on, apparently satisfied. "Naturally the Nazis fear the intelligentsia, for it is the thinking man who can see their vile propaganda for what it is. My father was a professor of Talmud—a very subversive threat, that! He cared only for his Torah and keeping the Sabbath."

She paused and shook her head. "My poor parents—I haven't kept the Sabbath since their death, and somehow I think that fact grieves them as much as all these atrocities in the world." She set down the coffeepot and sat down in a chair across the table from Logan. "Even after they removed him from the university, he said we must forbear in peace. Then two or three of his colleagues disappeared, men who had spoken out against the Reich. He made the mistake of trying to intervene. He believed, right to the end, that all men were basically good, and he tried to deal with the Nazis as if they were reasonable men. A neighbor who watched the Gestapo carry them off said my father wore an incredible look of surprise on his face."

"How did you manage to keep out of their clutches?"

"Pure chance, I suppose. I was away when they raided our home. When I returned, it was over and my parents were gone. I would have waited for them to return, except that a neighbor told me what happened. She said the Gestapo would surely come back for me. I called Henri—he and my father grew up together. He made inquiries for me and learned that my parents and sister had been taken to Drancy, a camp just outside Paris.

After that we heard no more until the letter came to Henri informing him that my parents had died in what they called an influenza epidemic. Nothing was said about my sister. I still don't know if she is alive or dead—"

She broke off suddenly, her voice faltering, but she tightened her jaw and did not let her emotions take control.

"I would like to change the subject," she said after a brief pause.

"I'm sorry," said Logan again.

Lise attempted to smile, but the action was by no means a bright one; it did not even reach up into her eyes, but was filled with gentleness and sincerity.

"Do you mind if I call you Michel?" she finally asked. "After what we have been through today, formalities seem ridiculous."

"I don't mind," he replied, "especially since I only know your first name."

"Some life, oui?" said Lise. "And *that* is not even my real one. I cannot tell you my name, and I must forget yours."

"Forget mine?" said Logan, puzzled.

"You surely are not unaware of your error today at Mme. Guillaume's. You were so intent on giving courage to your countrymen—"

"I'd already forgotten!" exclaimed Logan, chuckling as he recalled his slip up.

"I did not want to say anything and draw further attention to it. But do not worry, I have already forgotten it also."

"I won't worry," he replied playfully. "I think I can trust you."

"You British!" she scolded. "You are so naive! But you will learn your lessons soon enough if you remain long in Paris. You should have left your *trust* back in England. It is too heavy a burden to carry here in France. Even the best intentioned comrade could spill his guts under the tortuous thumb of the Gestapo. Trust your companions only as far as you must—for your sake and theirs."

"That's what they mean when they call this a lonely life?" said Logan. "Though it has not seemed such to me yet."

"It will, Michel, it will. Then it will begin to eat away at you."

She stopped, trying to shake off the gloom that had begun to settle about her.

"So tell me about *La Librairie*," said Logan in a lighter tone. "How did such a menagerie manage to come together under one roof?"

Again Lise's lips twitched into a smile, this time accompanied by a soft chuckle.

"If you did that more often, maybe things would not appear so grim," Logan commented.

"Perhaps . . ." She seemed to meditate a moment on Logan's reference to her hidden emotions, then shook away the reflective mood to answer his question. "You think us an odd assortment? It's all quite logical, actually.

Of course, you already know of my connection to Henri. Antoine is Henri's brother-in-law, married to Henri's sister before she was killed by the Gestapo. They are not as different as it appears on the surface. Henri is the mild and gentle one; Antoine is boisterous and gentle. But both have soft hearts and nerves of steel. I would trust my life to either of them."

"Quite a statement coming from one who trusts nobody."

She cocked an eyebrow at his friendly jibe. "There are no consistencies in this business," she said smugly. "That is another thing you will have to learn."

"Speaking of inconsistencies, tell me about Claude."

"He is a shadow that stands out, even in a world of shadows," replied Lise. "The only thing I know of him is that he turned up one day with Antoine's daughter. He was with Antoine's wife and daughter when they were all three captured, and Claude was the only one to escape. I think he is a survivor, and manages to do so by keeping to himself."

"Was he in love with the girl?"

"She was most certainly in love with him. But I find it difficult to imagine such an emotion as love with the heart of one such as Claude. Though, who can say what may lie under that stone wall of his? And who am I to talk, you would perhaps say?"

"There is something immensely different between his wall and yours," said Logan. "At least that is how I perceive it. I can't quite describe it yet, but ask me when I know each of you better."

"Don't count on knowing Claude better—you, of all people. He despises the British."

"For letting France fall?"

"Nothing so pragmatic."

"What did we ever do to him?"

"Perhaps a simple difference in ideology," answered Lise. "Claude is a Communist."

"They are a wild and dangerous lot, especially now that Hitler has invaded Russia. Why do you people keep him around?"

"Antoine feels a loyalty toward him, for his daughter's sake, no doubt. But perhaps in the case of a man like Claude, it is sometimes wise to have him where you can keep an eye on him, non?"

"I hope you're right," said Logan with some skepticism. "Now, what about the most fascinating member of your secret little enclave?"

"Jean Pierre?" As she said the priest's name, Lise's taut features momentarily softened. "An incredible man. His father was Baron Olivier de Beauvoir of Belgium. Jean Pierre, for better or worse, is the only one of us whose life is an open book. Before entering the priesthood, his face appeared on the pages of every society paper in Europe. He was present at all the social events, and even considered to be something of a philanderer. I must say," she added with a smile of affection, "he still manages to be in attendance at as many parties as possible. 'For the cause,' he always says with a coy grin. His family has been in Paris for two generations, accumulating their vast wealth in the textile industry. His brother Arthur, now head of the family, is in quite tight with von Stülpnagel, the military governor of France. Jean Pierre is truly cut out of a different *cloth* than the rest of his family, in more ways than one.''

"Is his brother a collaborator, or is it some kind of front?''

"How Jean Pierre wishes it were a front! But Arthur de Beauvoir is making a fortune off the German occupation—a true profiteer. Poor Jean Pierre! I suppose he will die one day trying to atone for his brother's sins.''

"The Germans have arrested him several times, have they not?''

"Merely a show,'' replied Lise. "They hope eventually to break him down, and bring him over to their side with his brother. But they do not know Jean Pierre! He could never be one of them but he is too well-connected for them to hold him. It drives the Germans crazy! They know he is involved in the escape route, but they can do nothing about it—unless they apprehend him in the very act.''

"I appear to have fallen into quite an assemblage!'' said Logan.

"And despite what anyone says, it will be for you to take the reins and lead us.''

"What!'' protested Logan immediately. "That's not my game.''

"Quelle bêtise! Nonsense!'' replied Lise. "I saw you in action, Michel. You are the man for the job.''

"The man for what job?''

"Leading our small group.''

"I came here merely to deliver some money and teach someone how to operate a wireless, not to join your band permanently.''

"Perhaps your commander did not tell you all.''

"I was sent on assignment to help you however I could, but—''

"The help we need, Michel, is leadership.''

"I didn't know the job was vacant.''

"Henri is the closest we have to a *leader*. But he would be the first to admit that he is not capable of making *La Librairie* a truly far-reaching and effective weapon against the Nazis. He lacks the audacity, the *élan* necessary—qualities, I might add, you seem to possess in abundance.''

"What about Jean Pierre?''

"He is too visible.''

"Claude and Antoine would have something to say against your views.''

"Claude would submit to no one, that is true. But he himself could not garner the loyalty of an ant,'' Lise replied with conviction. "And Antoine, though he has the heart of a hundred patriots, knows he is no leader.''

"That is exactly how I feel about myself. I've always worked with one or two others only. I'm not your man.'' Logan knew that the sort of leadership Lise spoke of demanded more than he was willing to give. The thrill and excitement of this work were appealing enough, but not the responsibility for others. Had he looked more deeply into himself, he might have quickly seen a connection between his refusal to entertain thoughts of responsibility in this situation, and his failure in his marriage. Instead, he offered Lise another suggestion.

"What about you?" he asked.

"Face it, Michel. Whether it's here or in some other circumstance, you were meant to lead. Even if you try to hide from the inevitable, the day will come when it will find you."

The words had a strange ring of familiarity to them. Into his mind darted a fragment of something Joanna had said as he was leaving Stonewycke.

Now it was Logan's turn to change the subject.

"I'd better start instructing you on this wireless, as long as you're the one who's going to be taking it over."

She nodded her consent, and for the next hour he gave her some initial instruction, ending with the words, "I'm scheduled to transmit to London tomorrow. I'll give you your first actual experience in being *La Librairie's* new radio operator."

By the time he returned to his hotel that evening, Logan was exhausted. He stopped on the way for a quick dinner, then took a moment to call Henri from the hotel phone. It was nine o'clock by the time he dragged himself up the stairs to his room.

He kicked off his shoes and literally fell into bed. Almost immediately the moment his head hit the pillow, however, it seemed as if his mind suddenly came awake, though his body screamed out for sleep. For half an hour he fought with himself, turning back and forth, then finally swung out of bed, hoping a few paces around the room would help. All he managed to do was stub his toe against his suitcase in the darkness.

To kill time, he switched on a light, flung open the suitcase lid, and began to unpack his few things. His hand fell upon two shirts and he lifted them out.

They were French made, as were the trousers and handkerchiefs that followed. These were not really *his* things. They belonged to Michel Tanant. Razor, soap, socks—all of French origin. In addition there were several book catalogues Henri had provided him with last evening to further validate his Lyon identity. And if all this was not sufficient, his wallet was stuffed full of additional reminders—the name and number of Tanant's unit in the French army were stamped on his demobilization papers. His work permit stated that his occupation was bookseller and that he was employed at *La Ecrit Nouvelle* in Lyon. With this was the ticket he had supposedly used to travel from Lyon to Paris, officially stamped. London missed no details. He even carried a much-worn photo of Tanant's parents, now dead, whose graves the Gestapo could find in a churchyard outside Lyon—if they chose to check so closely.

Logan smiled mordantly. Taking everything together, Michel Tanant's life appeared to be on more solid ground than Logan Macintyre's. How nice it would be to be able to wrap himself up so completely in the person of this exemplary Frenchman that, as Atkinson had said, he could erase his own name from his mind.

But that was easier fantasized than carried out in reality.

To forget who he really was would mean forgetting Allison too. Could he ever do that? Did he *want* to? He had been successful over the last several months of pushing her toward the most obscure corners of his mind. He could have spoken of her to Lise, but he hadn't, though he had thought of her once or twice during the conversation. But he hadn't even mentioned that he was married.

He had told Allison that he needed time to think about their relationship. Yet he had run off to an environment where he did not even have to be himself, much less meditate on the problems of one Logan Macintyre, distant Scotsman from out of his past. It would be so easy just to let Logan die a slow and silent death. Everything he needed for his new life was right in this bag.

Oh, Allison, Allison! he thought. *This war has made everything so easy for me, easy to forget the past, easy to run away. I wonder if you'll ever understand why I must continue with what I am doing, even though it might tear us apart. You may hate me when I return—I wouldn't blame you if you already despised me. But that's a chance I guess I'll have to take.*

Suddenly he shoved aside the suitcase, only half empty. He *had* to sleep. He wouldn't be thinking such stupid, morbid, defeating thoughts if he wasn't so bloody tired!

He lay back again on the bed more determinedly than before. But he was able to find only fitful rest throughout the rest of the night, until the light of dawn pierced through the blackout shades. What sleep he did get was filled with ghoulish images and nightmares, featuring alternately Claude's sneering countenance, S.S. soldiers gunning Logan down while he was trying to run a roadblock, and Allison's lovely face—but only her face, floating as in a fog above him, crying out to him, but he could not answer.

And in her eyes were the tears of endless weeping.

26 / Face in the Crowd

Allison looked across the table at her old friend Sarah Bramford, now Sarah Fielding, wife of a well-to-do shipping magnate. The years had been kind to Sarah, though she had never been a particularly pretty girl. Today she was strikingly attractive in her exquisite Dior silk suit and rich fox stole, obviously selected from the season's new collection and priced well beyond the limits of clothing rations.

Allison tried not to think of the fact that her own dress was two years old, and had hardly been in style even then, notwithstanding that the lovely silk print did possess stylish lines and was the nicest dress she owned. If everything else in her life had been right, she would probably not even have noticed, because clothes, after all, had very little to do with her present frame of mind.

"You should have seen my Wally's face when the sheik asked him if *I* could be part of his harem!" Sarah paused to giggle in the midst of her story about her adventures on one of her husband's recent trips to the Middle East. "Oh, but those Arabs are charming," she added with a coy wink.

"My father is in Egypt," said Allison, attempting to keep her focus on the luncheon conversation as the two women sat in the plush dining room of London's Green Velvet Restaurant. "He is fascinated with the Arabs, but doesn't think they like the British much."

"They like our money, though," replied Sarah knowingly.

"They'd just as soon have German marks as British pounds."

"But as long as we still control the canal at Suez," said Sarah, "they'll be our friends. My Wally says that's why the fighting in North Africa is so crucial—keeping the sea lanes open."

"At the rate that Rommel is going, all the fighting might not matter much longer."

"What defeatest talk!" exclaimed Sarah, with more emphasis than she felt. "Don't let old Winnie Churchill hear you. Now, no more politics or war talk. It's positively depressing." She took a dainty sip of tea as if to emphasize the more vital things in life. "You haven't said a word about my dress, Allison—isn't it scrumptious?"

"It certainly is," answered Allison with proper enthusiasm. "How on earth do you manage it these days?"

"Oh, Allison, don't be so naive. If you know the right people, you can manage anything."

At that moment a waiter came to replenish their pot of tea. "Will there be anything else, ladies?" he asked.

Sarah shook her head and the man departed.

"I wore this to the Fairgate's for tea last week," she continued, as if the announcement were tantamount to the capture of the German high command. "Olivia and her mother practically drooled all over it. Have you been to their new city place over by Hyde Park? It's on Portland Place."

"No, I haven't," replied Allison.

"Oh, well, you must. By the way, did you hear that Charles was wounded recently?"

"No. How serious is it?"

"He's being sent home, but it's not terribly dreadful. Of course he *will* be decorated, so I hear." Sarah sipped again at her tea. "I can't tell you how thankful I am that Wally's back has kept him out of the military. You must feel the same way about Logan."

Allison did not reply immediately.

This was only the second time she had seen Sarah since her return to London, and she had not yet found the opportunity to bring up the subject of Logan. Actually, there had probably been any number of opportunities; she had just not found the courage.

By all appearances, it seemed that Sarah Bramford Fielding had everything—clothes, status, a happy marriage, and was even a reasonably nice person to boot, if you could overlook the superficiality of her interests, and a slightly oversized ego. But she was pleasant enough to be around.

Allison had never spoken of her marital problems to her friends, always choked by her own version of ego, better labeled pride. Yet over the last months Allison had been taking strides toward new levels of maturity. Bit by bit that very pride was being beaten down by the hammer of difficulties, and the reality of true personhood was slowly being built within her. She was learning the folly of living in a manufactured world of shallow whimsy. That world of empty priorities had blinded her to Logan's need until it was too late, and now she was about to let it supersede her own need. She couldn't let that happen. She couldn't let one more acquaintance drift off into trivialities because she lacked the courage to speak out the concerns of her heart. She needed a friend just now—a real friend. If they could but pierce the surface of their relationship, it was possible Sarah could be such a friend. They had known each other for years, but they had never attained any depth with one another. Dresses and parties and school and men and fashions had dominated their conversations, but nothing beyond. Was it possible there could be more between them? *Should* be more?

With the question Allison found herself wondering if she had purposely avoided substance in her friendships in order to keep from having to look too deeply within herself. Did she even know how to share her heart with

Sarah? What about her faith in God? Was that something she could talk about to another?

These were suddenly new questions for Allison. But they were questions whose answers she did not want to postpone any longer. Reality could only emerge between them one way. And all at once it seemed imperative to Allison that she be a *real* person, with *real* emotions, rather than trying to cover up the hurts she was struggling with inside.

"You know, Sarah," she said, "Logan and I have been having some problems."

"What is it?" asked Sarah, her high forehead creased with concern.

"It's been going on for some time, I guess," Allison went on, hesitantly, but gaining in confidence as she saw genuine feeling etched on her friend's face. "We've been separated for the last few months."

Uttering the statement was perhaps the hardest thing she had ever done in her life. Yet once it was out, she felt oddly relieved. Perhaps sitting opposite her was a friend to help her shoulder some of the burden.

"Allison, I'm so sorry," said Sarah. "Why have you waited so long to say anything?"

"It's not an easy thing to admit. I didn't know what—you know, what you might think of me."

"Nonsense. It changes nothing between us."

"Everyone wouldn't agree. A broken marriage is the kiss of death to some people. You're different in their eyes from that moment on."

"Well, I won't tell a soul if that's how you want it."

"Thank you. It's hard to admit one's failings. I guess I want people to think well of me."

"I suppose I know what you mean," sympathized Sarah. "Everyone gets together and *talks*, but nobody says what they're really thinking, what's really hurting them inside."

"For so long I've tried to keep anyone from seeing deep inside me, but lately I've been so alone. I think what I really just need is a friend—someone to confide in. We've known each other for so long that—"

"That it's about time we started to act like it," Sarah finished Allison's sentence for her. "If I let myself admit it, I need that kind of friend too."

"You?"

"I suppose my marriage itself is fine—most of the time," said Sarah. "But believe me, the London social set is the most shallow mob you ever want to see, and sometimes I'm no better."

"Remember, this is me, Sarah. I used to be a part of all that—or at least wanted to be."

"You never did quite fit in though, as much as you tried. Especially in recent years. And I mean that as a compliment!" Sarah smiled again, then added, "I always thought it had something to do with Logan."

"Not at first," replied Allison. "The focus of my life changed when I really tried to give my life to the Lord. It happened with Logan and me together about the same time, just before we were married. God began to teach me new priorities and attitudes, and before I knew it I began to feel out of place with all the gossip and backbiting and petty jealousies and flaunting of wealth that went on among us. I was the worst of the lot!"

"I did see a change in you, Allison, but I guess I was too stupid to say anything."

"We all try to put on a front of self-sufficiency. Just because I was taking being a Christian seriously doesn't mean I changed overnight, either."

"You'll never know how many times when I was with your family that I wanted to ask what made them all so . . . I don't know—different . . . complete, I suppose is the best way to describe it."

"You really felt that way?"

"Your great-grandmother always made me feel so special and loved. I knew she was a religious lady and I couldn't help wondering if that had anything to do with it. But I was always too embarrassed to ask. You know how it's embarrassing to talk about spiritual things. It shouldn't be, I suppose, but it is. You think people will laugh at you for being interested in religion. So many people think it's only for old people."

"I know. That's what I always thought, before I really knew what living closely with the Lord could mean in my life."

"But even though Lady Margaret *was* old," Sarah continued, "I always wished I could have that sparkle in my life that she had."

"So did I," said Allison with a tender smile as she recalled her many struggles over that very thing, and her eventual reunion on a deeper level with her great-grandmother. "But she would say there was no reason why we couldn't have what she did. It was simply a matter of making a choice about one's priorities and attitudes."

"It hardly seems *that* simple."

"It was her choice to let the Spirit of Christ fill her with a new outlook on life that made her who she was," replied Allison. "And that same thing happened to me nine years ago. I gave my life to God too, and for a time, things were different. I had new values and perspectives, and it really did change my attitude toward everything. Unfortunately, I allowed too many external pressures to rob that original dedication from me. I guess it happened so slowly I didn't notice. Then as things started going sour between Logan and me, I began looking in other directions for help. It took Logan's leaving to shake me up enough to begin looking in the right direction again. I'm trying to bring the Lord back into my life, but I don't know what He is planning to do with my marriage—I haven't seen or heard from Logan in five months."

"Dear, you must be miserable!"

"I'd be lying if I tried to say I wasn't. But God is giving me strength to face it, a little bit at a time. I wish I could describe it better so you could understand."

"I would like to hear more," replied Sarah.

"You would?"

"Who wouldn't want the kind of contentment Lady Margaret had? But let's talk more on the way."

"On the way where?"

"I want to surprise you."

"But the nurse is expecting me back."

"Give her a call and tell her you'll be a little late," said Sarah firmly. "You don't want to miss this."

"I feel as if I'm being kidnapped," laughed Allison.

"I didn't think I'd have to kidnap you to get you to my designer."

"What's this all about, Sarah?"

"I know a new dress won't solve your problems, Allison. And maybe it's silly to worry about what you look like. But sometimes a woman needs something new, just to feel good about herself. What do you say—it couldn't hurt, could it?" She winked and smiled.

"I could never afford—"

"Ta, ta, dear girl! This one is on my Arabian sheik!"

The next couple of hours proved a heaven-sent boon for Allison. The new dress proved the least of her delight. Rather, it was the transformation of her friendship with Sarah brought on by the newfound honesty that had flowed between them.

Late in the afternoon they left the elegant offices where Allison had been fitted for her new outfit, diligently searching the street for a taxi—not a frequent sight in those days of petrol rationing. They had walked halfway down the block when Allison stopped suddenly, her gaze focused intently on a newspaper stand across the street.

"Allison, what is it?" asked Sarah.

"That man over there—I've seen him before."

"Oh. . . ?" The revelation hardly seemed startling to Sarah.

"I saw him once with Logan."

Allison hadn't given the incident a single thought since before the blitz. It had taken place long before she had returned to Stonewycke, but now it all came back to her clearly. She and Logan were to meet for lunch at a west-end restaurant. She'd arrived a few minutes early and was speaking to the maitre d' about a table, when she spotted Logan already seated at the far end of the room. With him was a man whose austere, pock-marked face was not easy to forget. Even had the face been of more ordinary features, she could hardly have erased from her mind the reaction on the countenances of both men when they saw her approach. The stranger cut off his speech immediately and made his departure with only a curt tip of his hat for Allison's benefit. When she questioned Logan about him, his response was evasive and vague. She knew that the meeting must have something to do with his mysterious job, but Logan would say nothing, and there the matter dropped. She had hardly thought of it again until the same man should suddenly appear out of the past, bringing it all vividly back to her.

Without thinking, she stepped suddenly out into the street toward the newsstand, causing several passing autos to slam on their brakes. Hardly taking a notice, she hurried on across.

"Sir!" she called out as she approached.

The man made no response.

"I say, there at the newsstand!" she called again, reaching the other side of the street and hurrying up to where he stood.

He glanced up, a cloud of uncertainty passing over his face for an instant. As it did, Allison could see the split-second hesitation as he debated within himself what he should do. At last it appeared as if it was more compulsion than decision that forced his eyes to acknowledge her.

"Sir," she said when their eyes met, "may I please speak with you?"

But in the next instant, another cloud passed over his countenance, this time one of sudden recognition. The magazine he had been browsing fell from his hands, he turned on his heel, and quickly rushed away.

"Please—I must talk to you!" cried Allison after him.

She had taken little notice of the gathering afternoon crowd till that moment. But now suddenly it seemed as though the sidewalk was swarming with people—all bent on preventing her from catching up with the elusive stranger. Weaving her way in and out, she managed to keep him in sight for about half a block. Then suddenly he was gone.

27 / Billy's Assistance_____

"Ye're talkin' craziness, Miz Macintyre—if I might be so blunt," said Billy Cochran.

"But you might be able to find out who he was."

"An' just how do y' propose I'd be doin' that?"

"Logan used to tell me some of the things you and he'd done together," said Allison, "when he was in a good mood and wanted to make me laugh. The way he tells it, *you* could do anything!"

"Pshaw!" said Billy, but not without a flicker of pride in his eye at the compliment from an old friend.

"But I just *can't* let it go, Billy—even if it's just one chance in a hundred. Aren't long shots in the nature of your business?" she added demurely.

Billy smiled. Here was Logan's wife trying to con *him*!

The incident at the newsstand had been plaguing Allison for a whole day; now she could stand it no longer. Until that afternoon with Sarah she had resigned herself to simply biding her time until Logan saw fit to contact her. But now suddenly she realized she might be able to take steps to contact him! Billy had once cautioned her against the futility of trying to get a lead on Logan's well-cooled trail. But now everything was changed. This would be no aimless poking about—there was now something concrete to go on. She had seen a man who knew Logan, and probably knew what work he was involved in. If she could only talk to him!

Billy, however, had been none too optimistic, and had done his best to convince her against it when the next day she ventured into his list shop.

"Even allowin' fer the possibility—" said the grizzled old man.

"Then you admit, it *is* possible!"

"I admit to nothin', young lady. I'm just saying that a quick glimpse of a face in a crowd, disappearin' as fast as it showed itself, is 'ardly much evidence to lay a bet on, even for a 'undred-to-one nag."

"He knows where Logan is," pleaded Allison. "I'm sure of it. I could see it in his eyes."

"Even if it were possible to locate Logan through an old acquaintance, this 'ere bloke hain't likely the man to help you. You don't know 'is name, where he lives—nothin'! And you said yerself, he didn't appear none too friendly."

"But you could do it, Billy! I know you could, even without all that

142

information. The police do it all the time, and Logan always says you were two or three steps ahead of the law."

"I'm not so sure ye're graspin' his meanin'," said Billy with a chuckle.

"However he meant it," insisted Allison, "you're the man for the job. You care about Logan. That's more than the police would do."

"Maybe 'tis them wot ought t' help you."

"You know I can't go to them."

Before Billy could answer her, the phone rang and took his attention for a few moments.

"First call I've 'ad all day," he said, hanging up. "With the race tracks closed on account of the war, I don't get much action—'cept a cricket or rugby match now and then." He paused, jotted down something in a notebook, then turned back to the problem at hand. "I suppose ye're right; the police hain't the ones t' help you, for more reasons than one."

"But *you* can help me, Billy."

He raised his eyebrows as if the idea were too outlandish to consider.

"Miz Macintyre . . . I'm thinkin' that maybe the strain of the last few weeks has been too 'ard on you. You hain't thinkin' straight."

"You know more about this city's underworld than anyone—at least anyone *I* know."

"You hain't still thinkin' Logan's gone back t' the old life?"

"No. I believe you when you say he's not. But he still might be in some kind of trouble, and that's the logical place to start. Besides, the man I saw Logan with, and saw again at the newsstand today, did not look like he came from Chelsea."

Billy rubbed the stubbly beard on his chin for a moment. In his mind Lady Allison MacNeil Macintyre was as sweet and gentle—and innocent— as any lady he had ever known. Yet more than once Logan had hinted at the presence of a wide stubborn streak that could surface in her. And now Billy could see it more than clearly in her determined blue eyes. She was not about to be moved, now that her mind was set. But perhaps with his experience he might be able to interject some practicality into her wild scheme.

All at once he recalled a similar time when it was Logan who had approached him with a crazy idea of a sting to swindle Chase Morgan. Now it was his wife taking up where he left off. Maybe she wasn't as innocent as he made her out to be. *Both them young folks gots a stiff-necked streak in them*, he said to himself. *'Tis hardly no wonder they're havin' problems.* Logan had not listened to Billy's voice of reason ten years ago, though he had submitted enough to Billy's instruction to keep him clear of disaster.

Billy glanced up at Allison. Yes, he could tell she was going to go ahead with her hunt for her husband with or without his help. Perhaps he owed it to Logan to try to keep her out of trouble, too.

Billy removed his spectacles, which he wore constantly now, and wiped the lenses off on his sleeve. Methodically he rubbed the grime on them around in a circle, then placed them again on his nose and peered once more at his friend's wife, as if somehow his little delay might have changed things. It had not. Her eyes were just as determined as ever.

"Ye're askin' for trouble, missy," he finally replied, but there was an air of defeat clearly in his tone. "If this feller is as crooked as you think, he hain't goin' t' take kindly t' bein' dogged about London. An' even if you do find 'im, you'll probably end up regrettin' it in the end. But wot'll be more likely is you'll find 'im an' then he won't know any more about Logan's whereabouts as I do."

"You'll help me, though, won't you, Billy?"

"I'm an old fool is wot I am," he replied. But how could he refuse her pleading eyes? And he would never be able to face Logan again if he left her to her own resources, and something was to happen to her.

They began back at the newsstand. The vendor, however, was no more communicative with Billy than he had been with Allison when she had questioned him the day before. But at least they could surmise that if the stranger frequented the newsstand, then he must have reason to be often in this part of the city. If they were lucky, either his work or residence might be close by. They spent the better part of the next two days methodically visiting shops, hotels, and taverns in the nearby precincts hoping something would turn up.

By the end of the second day, Allison's voice was hoarse with repeating the man's description, and poor Billy's old arthritic limbs ached as they seldom did these days. At four o'clock they came to the door of a tobacconist shop. Billy declared that this would be his last stop for the day, and Allison gave him no argument. She was footsore, tired, and discouraged, and wanted nothing more just then but to go home, soak her feet, and play with her little girl, whom she feared she had been neglecting of late.

The pungent odor of rich blends of tobacco filled the air inside the shop, and for the hundredth time Allison forced out a description of the man she had almost begun to think was only a figment of her imagination.

"Tall, ye say?" said the stocky, balding proprietor.

"Yes," replied Allison hopefully, "and rather thin, too—bony, actually."

"Spoke with a German accent, did he?"

Allison paused. Had she ever heard them speak? No—but she recalled several phone calls Logan had received from a man whose accent was unmistakable.

"It's possible," she replied.

"Well, I reported him."

"Reported him?"

"I didn't like the looks of him, so I turned him in to the War Office," said the tobacconist. "They said as how they couldn't pick up every bloke who didn't *look* right on account of the tens of thousands of innocent refugees who came here before the war fleeing from that madman Hitler. They needed more to go on to arrest a bloke than a man's looks, they said. Well, *I* say round 'em all up, and then there'll be no doubts!"

"So, you have the man's name?" said Allison, too impatient to listen to the man's biased political ramblings.

"I do that; he had his own particular blend he ordered. He'd call me up and say, 'Prepare me so-and-so's a blend, I'll pick it up this afternoon.' No one's willin' to wait around these days and have a nice bit of conversation. Everything's done on the phone—no waiting."

"What was the man's name?" asked Allison, whose throat had suddenly gone very dry.

"I can remember without even looking in my ledger, on account of having reported him, you know. Smith was the name, a Mr. Hedley Smith."

Allison cast a woeful look at Billy. The new-found information hardly increased the chances of locating a man with a phony name.

Now it was Billy's turn to step forward.

"And 'ave you gots an address in your records, by any chance?" he asked.

" 'Course I do! What kind of businessman do you think I am?" the tobacconist replied, flipping through the pages of his ledger, while Billy craned his head to try to see for himself. "Like I said, no one wants to wait. Some blokes even call and tell me to deliver the stuff. 'Send a pound of Mr. Smith's Carolina blend over to such-and-such a place.' "

"An' where did you send our Mr. Smith's when he called?"

The man hesitated, suddenly growing wary. "Say, I don't know as I should be giving out that information."

"Look 'ere," said Billy, pulling himself up to every inch of his diminutive stature, "this young woman and I are from Immigration an' we 'ave reason t' believe yer first suspicions about this man could be correct."

"You don't *look* much like Immigration officials."

" 'Course we don't!" exclaimed Billy at the silly notion. "You don't expect us t' be walkin' around tippin' off the blokes we's after with fine duds an' a nice gov'mental accent, now do ye?"

"Let me see your identification."

Without a second's hesitation, the old confidence man pulled out his worn leather wallet and flashed it quickly before the stubborn shopkeeper's eyes. Skittles' old list-shop license, which Billy carried around with him for luck, looked official enough for most similar purposes if not scrutinized too closely.

The man behind the counter appeared satisfied, and wrote the address on a slip of paper.

All Allison's fatigue was gone when they exited the shop. "How far is it?" she asked excitedly. "Shall I call a taxi?"

"I thought we was done for the day!"

"Oh, Billy, we can't quit now! I wouldn't be able to rest knowing we are this close."

"Just funnin' you, Miz Macintyre," said Billy with a crooked but warm smile. "But the address may prove just as phony as the *Smith*. But let's take the tube t' Charing Cross. Cheaper and just as quick, an' puts us close t' where we wants t' go."

Bunker Street, it turned out, looked none too respectable, presenting a string of seedy hotels and seedier-looking pubs, broken here and there with grimy shops and dirty tenement buildings. They followed the street numbers until they came to the one the tobacconist had written down. They stopped, then glanced puzzled at one another. The chipped, worn number was painted on the bricks above the door of The Blue Crow Pub. Had the shopkeeper made a mistake, or was the address as false as the man's name?

"You best wait out 'ere, mum, whilst I goes in an' 'ave a look about," said Billy protectively.

Allison scanned the area; across the street a couple of men as rundown and seedy as the neighborhood were leering at her.

"I'll go in with you," she replied.

The Blue Crow was practically vacant. The few men present could not have been of the sturdiest caliber, and the room reeked of stale odors. Allison willingly hung back while Billy approached a man whose stained and dingy apron gave indication that he was the one in charge. They exchanged a few quiet words; then Billy thanked him and led Allison back out into the fresh air.

"No luck?" asked Allison.

"I gots me a feelin' the bloke knows the man, but he sure hain't goin' t' talk t' *us* about it. I've a bad feeling about that place."

They had started on their way once more, but Allison grabbed Billy's arm. "We can't leave it at that," she implored.

"There's no suckin' blood from a turnip."

"Offer him money—anything!"

"I tried that, mum."

"There must be a way."

"Let's be gettin' home," suggested Billy wearily. "Mebbe after a good rest, we'll come up with somethin'."

They started off, but after another few steps, Allison stopped suddenly again.

"Oh drat!" she exclaimed.

"Mum?"

"I lost my earring. I'm sure I had it when I went into that place. I'd best go back and check. I must have dropped it."

"Ye sure, mum?" said Billy, who had not seen her hand quickly snatching away the earring only a moment before.

"I'll only be a moment," said Allison, running off, not giving Billy the opportunity either to argue or to accompany her.

"Let me go," he protested.

But it was too late. She was already at the door of the place she had entered so reluctantly only five minutes earlier.

"Here it is!" she said triumphantly, exiting a few moments later, just as Billy was about to go in after her.

Billy never realized he had been taken in by the sweet Mrs. Macintyre. Had he known, he might have stayed in the next few evenings, anxiously awaiting whatever might develop from Allison's return dash into the pub. As it was, he was out and not to be reached when Allison needed him most.

She knew leaving her phone number with the pubkeeper was foolhardy at best, as was telling him she had vital information for the man they were seeking, Mr. *Smith*—which she spoke with sufficient emphasis to let him know that they both knew more than they were letting on. If the man was German, which she by now had every reason to suspect, she hoped her bait might be enough to bring him out of hiding.

Her little scheme worked. The next evening her phone rang. A man with a decidedly German accent wanted to meet her at nine p.m. In no position to argue, she scribbled down the location. Her heart was pounding when she hung up the phone. Thankfully, the rendezvous would not take place on Bunker Street. The man had instead given her the name of a different pub, The Silver Stallion, down by the river—not far from the docks. The man must like odd colored animals, thought Allison to herself. Her attempt at humor, however, was but a thin mask over her rising fear that she had gotten herself into more than she bargained for.

She tried to call Billy several times, but to no avail. Finally, as eight o'clock drew near, she had no choice but to leave the baby with her neighbor and strike out alone.

The night was dark and misty with a light fog. An evening wind had begun to blow in from the mouth of the Thames, swirling the gathering mist about the deserted streets.

Allison would be able to take the tube only part of the way. The dimly lit underground station proved just slightly less portentous than the somber open air. During the blitz these stations had been a thriving beehive of activity as thousands of Londoners sought shelter from the incessant German bombs. Many had slept regularly in whatever corner of a tube station they could find. Even now Allison observed several men dozing off on benches or in out-of-the-way corners, but now they were more likely homeless drunks than citizens fearful for their lives.

Allison got off at Tower Hill. Slowly she walked up a long flight of stairs and into the dark night. Billingsgate Market to her right was by now long deserted, but she suspected The Silver Stallion to be in that direction. There was no one about as she began walking south toward the river. It was not far; already she could hear sounds of an occasional ship or barge passing by, sounding their muted horns in warning.

She reached the river at eight-thirty. To her right, just past the Billingsgate, was London Bridge. On her left, in the vague distance through the fog, she could make out the imposing spires and turrets of Tower Bridge. Everything looked so silent and sinister in the fog and dark. Why had the man asked her to come here? *Why had she agreed?* What a fool she must be! The whole idea was stupid. She should never be here by herself. The man could be dangerous, whether or not he was a friend of Logan's. But she had come too far to turn around now. If only Billy were here!

"Dear Lord," she prayed, hardly realizing that she had not taken the time to pray about finding Logan since first spotting the stranger while with Sarah, "forgive me if I am being foolish. But please help me to learn something of Logan. Protect me, Lord."

Some ten minutes' walk more brought her alongside the Billingsgate. At least now there were a few people about here—mostly seamen, none of whom, to her relief, bothered her. None of the pubs displayed the sign she sought. At last she walked inside one to ask if she was anywhere near The Silver Stallion.

The pubkeeper gave her a peculiar smile, then laughed.

"Sure, lady," he said. "You's near it all right. Though what you'd want there I can't think!" He laughed again.

"Where is it, please?" asked Allison.

"Straight on down, miss," replied the man, still chuckling to himself.

Allison hurried out. At the next cross-street, all activity seemed to cease. Slowly she walked across. In the distance she could see nothing but dark, silent, run-down buildings. *Surely there's no pub down there*, she thought. Yet this was in the direction the man had pointed.

Slowly she continued on, her eyes scanning the buildings through the mist. They looked more like warehouses than anything, although there were signs of bomb damage all about, so it was difficult to tell. Everything had grown ominously silent around her.

Allison stopped. This was absurd. There couldn't possibly be any pub around here. She looked around one last time, walking slowly back and forth. What was that just ahead? It looked like it could be a sign. She approached. Yes—there was an old sign above the door. But the place was dark, its windows and doors boarded up. She reached the door. In the darkness she could barely make out a few letters on the old and dilapidated marker that must have at one time invited patrons to enter: *Si— Stal—* was all she could read. But that was enough! She had been led here under false pretenses. She'd been an idiot—she had to get out of here!

Allison turned to retrace her steps.

She had not even seen the black figure step out from between two buildings just beyond where she stood.

The moment she began to run an arm shot out from behind and caught her in a vise-like grip. Allison screamed.

"There's no one to hear you, Frauline," said a sinister gravelly voice. Notwithstanding his words, he clamped his hand tightly across her mouth. "I will do the talking for the moment," the accented voice went on, "but when you are required to speak, remember that I have a weapon pressed into your back."

He jabbed his pistol fiercely into her ribs to emphasize the veracity of his words. "Now, who are you, and why are you following me?"

"I'm Allison Macintyre," said Allison when the man released his fingers. She said no more, not only because her lips were trembling, but also because she hoped the mention of her name would signify her interest to the man.

"Is that supposed to mean something to me?" he snapped. It obviously did not.

"I'm only trying to find my husband," she managed to say.

"What's that to me?"

"You know him."

"Says who?"

"I've seen the two of you together. I had hoped you might be able to tell me where he is."

"His name?"

"Logan Macintyre."

"The name means nothing to me."

"But I saw you together in a restaurant, several months ago," she said in desperation. "You were talking at a table, but when I came, you stopped, and then left quickly."

An agonizing moment of silence passed. Allison could not tell if he was trying to recall the meeting or contemplating the best method for her demise.

"Ah, so that is why I recognized you at the newsstand," he said finally. "Trinity is your husband."

There was a faint hint of would-be laughter in Gunther's voice, as if the incident might be comical if the stakes weren't so deadly serious.

"Trinity? I don't understand," said Allison.

"You don't need to understand. You need only forget you ever saw me."

"Where is my husband?"

"I don't know, and I don't care."

"How do you know him?"

"We had business together once."

"What is he doing?"

"You ask too many questions."

"I have to know."

"You have to know nothing! These are dangerous times, made all the more dangerous by interfering fools."

"I am his wife!"

"If you persist in your questioning and idiotic sleuthing," said Gunther, "you will endanger the lives of many people, your husband included."

"Why? Why can't you tell me?"

"Listen to me, Frau Macintyre, you are treading upon dangerous ground. Stop, or you will find yourself with more trouble than you know what to do with. I would not like to see you dead, but I myself would kill you in order to save my own neck. Don't make me do that!"

"I will go, then!" answered Allison. "I have only one more question. Is my husband safe?"

"No one is *safe* in this dark world," Gunther replied shortly. "What is *safe*? Everything is, how do you say it here, topsyturvy? To my knowledge, no ill has come to your Trinity. But I have not seen him for months, and he is in a dangerous game." He paused. "Now, I want you to start walking," he said, slowly releasing his arm from around her neck. "You will go back the way you came—I will be watching you. Do not turn around. For you to see my face again could someday mean your death."

His tone left no doubt that his surveillance would not end with her departure from this riverfront street that night. "You will forget my face

. . . you will forget this meeting. You will forget all about me, for that matter, and about your husband also. We will all live much longer if you do so."

Allison's heart had climbed up into her throat and her legs felt like rubber. Yet they somehow managed to propel her slowly away from the awful deserted place, and from the man who might be either friend or enemy—she could not guess which. Of only one thing she was fairly certain, that he honestly knew no more of Logan's whereabouts than he had told her. The entire ordeal of this search had been a dangerous dead-end. She was no closer to finding Logan now than when she had begun. Only now she knew he was involved in something secretive, and that danger might now come to her as well.

Despite Gunther's stern injunction, she could never forget what had happened. To forget Logan altogether was unthinkable! What kind of man would suggest such a thing to a wife?

But if she could not find him or help him, there was one thing she *could* do on Logan's behalf. Something she should have thought of much sooner.

Later that night, back in the safety of her own home, Allison knelt down at her bedside and began a ritual that would continue daily for many, many months.

"Father," she prayed, "I don't know where Logan is or what he is involved in. Neither do I know where his heart is. But as you have always cared for us while we were straying through dark and shadowy valleys, care for him, Lord. As you watched over Lady Margaret and Dorey during the long years of their separation, watch over Logan. Don't let him wander far from you. Bring him continually into contact with your presence, even if at times he is unable to recognize your hand in his life. Protect him, God. Strengthen his faith again. And strengthen my own! Help me to be faithful in this commitment to prayer, and to selflessly give myself to the rebuilding of our marriage."

"And you say there's no way either of them could have seen you?"

"How many times 'ave I got to say it, mate? What kind of fool blighter does you take me for! The lady was scared clean out her skin. And as for that kraut—"

"Watch your mouth, you old fool! Don't forget you're not in England now. Over here even the walls have ears. I don't pay you what I pay you and then bring you all the way over here to have you shoot your mouth off and get us both thrown in some stalag. I pay you to keep me informed of the movements of that family and otherwise to keep silent."

"My apologies," replied the old lackey, just a hint of sarcasm underlying the respectful tone of his voice.

The man to whom he was reporting was in reality just past seventy and several years the senior of his cockney underling. But he bore himself with such peremptory authority, and the mere sound of his voice was so commanding, that few dared to cross him. To all appearances he was a man confident of always getting what he wanted.

"As I was sayin'," the man went on, "I'd been keepin' my eye on the girl like you said. Still nary a word on her man, but she's takin' up livin' in his old flat. Then she met that German fellow."

"Hmmm . . . most interesting," said the other with a wave of the hand, speaking almost to himself. He leaned back from his desk and thought for a minute or two. This was an interesting business! What could *she* possibly have to do with a German? They were the most intriguing lot! Ever since reading about the marriage in the papers, he'd been curious as to what new possibilities might open up to him. Might there be something in this he could use? Even as he thought to himself, his intense black eyes glowed with a fire deeper than any human flame. *I will bide my time*, he concluded. *As I always do.* He had spent thousands of pounds over the years, in the hopes of ultimately satisfying the demon that still tormented him and fed the fires which looked out of his eyes. Yet ultimate victory had always eluded him.

At length he exhaled sharply and looked up at the man still standing in front of his desk. From a drawer he pulled out a thick envelope.

"Here is your fare back, and a little extra for your trouble," he said. "Now you keep her under watch. I want to be able to get to her any time I want her. Is that clear?"

"All clear, mate."

"And one more thing. You ever call me *mate* again, and I'll have your throat slit. Is *that* clear?"

"Clear enough . . . sir."

A raw wind beat mercilessly upon the streets of Paris that chill November afternoon.

The porter pushing his cart of beef down the avenue Foch hitched his frayed woolen coat more tightly about him. That was his only acquiescence to the icy cold, however, and he continued to shuffle along in the same sluggish, unhurried manner that he apparently used every day, no matter what the weather. He gave every indication of being both bored and worn out, whether from life's hardships or the German occupation, it was impossible to tell.

But why should he have hurried? His meat consignment was designated for S.S. headquarters—who else ate meat in Paris these days but the Germans? And it wouldn't kill them to wait.

An especially forceful rush of wind struck him at that moment, nearly tearing his beret from the thick gray hair underneath. He grabbed at the beret with more speed than any of his other movements would have indicated was possible, and firmly clamped it back in place. Then, hunching his shoulders up and lowering his head, like a ram, into the wind, he continued on.

In another several minutes he came to the first checkpoint for the main building, which housed both a small facility for holding certain of their more important prisoners and the administration offices for the German S.S.—Schutz Staffeln, the elite police force organized by Heinrich Himmler.

"Bonjour, Monsieur Sergeant," he said in a gravelly mumble as he tipped his beret slightly.

"What have you there, old man?" barked one of the three guards standing closest by, who was in truth only a corporal.

The porter raised his bushy eyebrows as if he didn't know what to make of a question with such an obvious answer, for large shanks of meat were in plain view under the haphazardly placed canvas tarp. He stared at the guard with a deadpan expression; then finally a slow grin appeared between the tufts of his tangled gray beard, as a deep guffaw began to rumble from somewhere deep in his throat.

The guard stepped brusquely forward. "You imbecile!" he spat. "Lift some of that up—let me see under it!"

"Ah," said the porter, brightening with understanding. He pulled the

154

flap back and proceeded to shove several of the shanks this way and that. "Eh, bien?" he said when the procedure was over, wiping his hands on the grimy blood-stained apron that hung beneath his coat. "Fine cuts, non? Very lean!"

"Get on your way!" ordered the guard. "Dummkopf Französischer!"

"Merci," replied the porter, summoning the energy to continue on, shoving his cumbersome burden ahead of him.

He crossed the large cobbled courtyard, pausing once to let a squad of marching soldiers pass. He then shoved on, going around to the service entrance with his load. There the supply clerk checked his clipboard for the delivery authorization, apparently unconcerned that he was an hour and a half late according to the regular schedule, put a mark on the page, and let the porter pass inside the building.

"No wonder the old fool's so much later than the usual man," thought the guard as he watched the door close behind him. "Never seen a delivery man move so slow!"

Still ambling along at his snail's pace as if the only thing that mattered in life was placing one foot in front of the other, the porter moved down the length of one corridor, then another, pausing now and then to let soldiers pass, but meeting very few. Apparently his information had been correct, that the place would be nearly deserted during this precise time when the serving of dinner overlapped with the rotation of personnel on and off duty. Since they had to check in and out in the front of the building, the service and prison areas toward the rear were, for about a twenty-minute period, devoid of activity except for a skeleton maintenance crew. A silent observer might have questioned why he seemed to be moving away from the kitchen area where food deliveries were normally taken.

His twists and turns soon brought him to an altogether silent wing of the building, and at length he arrived at an intersection of two corridors, where he stopped, glanced furtively over his shoulder, then to his right and left.

Apparently satisfied that he was alone, he suddenly seemed to spring to life, as if his veins had just been pumped with blood from a man thirty years younger. Quickly he pushed his cart into a dark alcove, unloaded about half its contents, which he stashed in a corner on the floor, then lifted a large bundle that had been stowed beneath the meat in a hidden compartment. In the seclusion of the alcove he began to remove the outer layers of his porter's attire, including the gray wig and beard.

Logan was especially glad to get rid of the uncomfortable beard, though he laid it neatly with the other items, for he would have need of it again. From the bundle, he took the uniform of an S.S. sergeant, which he hurriedly put on. Within moments the old porter was transformed into a member of Hitler's elitist corps of protectors of the Third Reich. He placed the porter's things into the bundle, tying all together securely. At the very last he strapped on his sidearm.

Finally, taking up the bundle under his arm and inhaling a deep breath, he stepped back out into the dimly lit corridor. With stiff military bearing and purposeful stride, though no one was nearby to witness them, he walked about ten yards to a flight of stairs, which he descended into the detention area of the building. At the bottom of the steps stood a locked door with a small barred window placed at eye level, and a single buzzer on the doorpost.

Logan set the bundle down out of sight, then withdrew a handkerchief and small vial from his pocket. He saturated the cloth with a few drops from the vial, then, keeping the handkerchief out of view, stepped up and pressed the buzzer. He only hoped the German he had learned in training and had been practicing so diligently in his spare time would pass the ultimate test.

In a moment a face appeared at the window.

"Ja?" said the guard from inside. "Was wollen Sie?"

"Ich bin hier für die Gefangene Übertragung gekommen," replied Logan.

"No one told me of a transfer of prisoners."

"I've got the order right here." Logan took a folded paper from his breast pocket and held it up to the window.

The guard opened the door and Logan stepped inside.

"Immer Sicherheit! Jeden Tag Sicherheit!" complained the guard. "Every day they preach to me about security. Then they don't tell me what's going on. So what am I supposed to do?"

"Why don't you call upstairs?" said Logan, manifesting considerable impatience at this guard who displayed fewer stripes on his shoulder than he. "But be quick about it. I haven't got all day!"

The guard turned to the wall behind him where the phone hung. But he progressed no farther, for the instant his back was turned Logan stepped forward and, grasping his body with one arm, with his free hand jammed the handkerchief over his nose. In three seconds the guard went limp and slumped to the floor.

Quickly Logan dragged his unconscious body out of sight, then returned to the guard desk, grabbed up the keys, and scanned the pages of the roster. Finding the information he sought, he retrieved his bundle from outside, firmly closed the outer door, and went into the prison cell block.

Here he encountered the long hallway he had been told to expect, with locked doors running down each side, similar to the one through which he had just passed. He resisted the temptation to look into each tiny window; from the groans and whimpers he heard, he knew what kind of sight would greet his eyes. Unfortunately, he could not now help all these poor men to escape. He had come for three in particular, and so must harden himself to the pitiful sounds, trying to assure himself that one day he would see them all free.

Three-quarters of the way down the corridor he paused. He stepped up to the window of the door and saw a man sitting on his bunk, huddled against the wall with his legs pulled up to his chest, a single blanket wrapped around his shivering body. For the first time it suddenly dawned on Logan how icy cold these dark dungeons were; his own adrenaline had been pumping so hard he was almost in a sweat. Hearing a sound at his door, the man looked up.

He was Reuven Poletski, a Jew, one of the driving forces of the Warsaw resistance movement. He was a man of average size and undistinguishing features. However, his dark hair and thick brown eyebrows appeared especially vivid against the prison pallor of his skin. But he did not appear the fierce leader of men his reputation had made of him—that is, until he glanced up and his eyes met those of the man he supposed to be an S.S guard. They were filled with such contempt and defiance that Logan almost forgot who he really was and hesitated for a moment opening the door.

But the silent exchange lasted less than a second before Logan swung into action, unlocking the door and thrusting it open.

"Reuven Poletski?" he said.

"I am," replied the prisoner in what Logan took for Polish. He proudly squared his shoulders and stood courageously to meet whatever fate was in store for him.

"I'm with the Resistance," said Logan in French. "I've come to get you out of here."

"This is some trick," said Poletski, also in French, eyeing Logan warily.

"We haven't time for a cross-examination."

"I will not go without my wife and son," answered the Pole resolutely.

"Don't worry. We will get them out, too. That's my business."

"I can't believe this."

"You're a very important man, Monsieur Poletski. We certainly cannot let the Nazis have you without a fight. Now hurry."

Reuven Poletski and his family had been in the process of escaping Poland after an enormous price tag had been placed on Poletski's head. They had made it as far as Paris, and had been staying with friends until false papers and a guide out of the city could be arranged for them. But a suspicious neighbor, a collaborator, had turned them in. They had been in Gestapo hands only three days before *La Librairie*, which since Logan's arrival had been steadily gaining a reputation for successful escape operations, had been called in. Poletski had to be freed, for he knew enough to bring down the entire Warsaw resistance structure. And now with his family also in custody, there was no telling how long he could hold out. Even three days was pushing it.

"I want you to know," said Poletski, as he gathered what meager items of clothing he had, and speaking with a proud edge to his voice, "that were it only myself, I would never have left Poland—and as soon as they are safe in London, I will return."

"That's fine, Poletski," replied Logan. "But first we have to get you out of here. Come on, we haven't much time. This thing was planned for the only twenty-minute gap we could discover in this place. In another ten, these corridors will be crawling with Germans again."

Quickly they located Poletski's wife and sixteen-year-old son. Logan unlocked their door, Poletski explained excitedly, and in three or four minutes the small party was assembled once more at the guard's station. Hastily Logan changed back into his porter's clothes, while the three Polish refugees put on the Nazi uniforms Logan had smuggled into the building in his bundle.

"We hardly look like S.S. men," said Poletski, surveying the illfitting uniforms on the diminutive frames of his wife and son.

Logan took a second look. The son was nearly as tall as he was himself, and Madame Poletski filled out the uniform admirably, better than he had expected.

"Don't worry. You look fine. By the time you get to the outside gate, they won't give you a second thought. It'll be me they'll be after."

Notwithstanding Logan's assurances, Poletski was clearly nervous, though for his wife and son, not himself. How could he not be? It was insanity to attempt an escape right from under the noses of the S.S.; certain torture and death awaited them if they failed.

When they were ready to leave the detention area on the final leg of their journey to freedom, Logan paused by the unconscious guard, stooped down, and gave him another dose of chloroform from the handkerchief.

"That should hold him until we're away from here," he said.

"We would be safer if he were dead," said Poletski.

"I don't operate that way," replied Logan, rising from the floor. He opened the door and led the three escapees out of the detention block, up the stairs, and to the alcove where Logan retrieved his meat cart.

Moving quickly, they kept to the same service corridors by which Logan had come. As Logan led the way, he filled Poletski in on what to do the moment they exited the building and made for the guardhouse.

As they rounded a tight corner, Logan took the lead, and suddenly found himself face-to-face with a German officer. Immediately slapping on a toothy ingratiating grin, he tipped his beret and said in his gravelly porter's voice, "Bonjour, mon Captain." He only hoped Poletski, who had not yet come around the corner, had heard him and taken his cue.

Almost the same instant from behind him Logan heard a sharp German command:

"Move aside, Porter!"

It was Poletski, getting admirably into his character.

"Pardonnez-moi, Monsieur!" Logan replied, with profound humility, making an overdone attempt to move the cart aside. But he seemed to catch one of the wheels on one of the floor stones, causing the cart nearly to overturn. He righted it before catastrophe struck; but during the entire several seconds the captain, now pinned against the wall, was forced to attend to the errant cart, while the three other soldiers passed by on the other. Logan's smile at his discomfort was fortunately hidden beneath the tufts of his beard. Poletski and his family had marched past Logan and cart and the captain with all the precision and hauteur of the German conquerors they were dressed up to be. In the meantime, the S.S. captain hurried on down the hall in the opposite direction, just thankful to have made it by the maniac of a meatporter without breaking his neck.

At last they reached the final door. Poletski shook his head doubtfully.

"We can't possibly get out of the compound," he said. "It was pure luck we made it this far."

"Have faith, Monsieur Poletski."

"Do you plan to hide us in that thing?" he asked, cocking his head dubiously toward the meat cart.

"I have something a bit more creative in mind," said Logan. "Now, as I was starting to tell you when we were interrupted by that captain in the hallway, you let me get about fifty meters beyond the gate—three minutes should do it . . ."

Two minutes later the guards at the main gate looked up to see the old porter once more shuffling across the courtyard, pushing his now empty cart at his unhurried, sluggish pace. He paused, and nodded his head toward the corporal.

"You want to check again, non?" he said, fumbling at the ties on the tarp.

The guard looked under one edge of the canvas, then gave the cart a harsh shove.

"Get on with you, crazy old man!"

Logan said nothing, just lumbered past the gate.

For the first time he was painfully conscious of each slow, methodical step, as he listened intently behind him. But he knew that if he even picked up his pace imperceptibly, he might raise the suspicions of whatever guards were still eyeing him.

He was almost to the corner of the adjacent building when his cue came.

From inside the courtyard he heard the sound of urgent commanding shouts and the sound of running feet on the pavement.

Logan started to walk faster, but he dared not turn around. If he had, he would have seen a tall S.S. officer, followed by two shorter ones, run breathlessly up to the guardhouse and ask in frantic German, "Did a porter just come by here . . . pushing a meatcart?"

"Ja, mein Herr," answered the corporal.

Logan was now out of sight and breaking into a run.

"And you let him pass? Imbecile!" shouted Poletski. "He is a Resistance agent. We will have to go after him."

"What do you want us to do, mein Herr?"

"You have done enough already! Call inside and have them check the prison compound. We will soon be back with the agent. Come, men!"

The two others with him silently obeyed, and all three ran out of the compound and down the street in the direction Logan had gone.

When the corporal emerged from the guardhouse after making his call a minute later, the evening was once again silent. There was no sign either of the porter or the three officers in pursuit of him.

31 / Arnaud Soustelle

The closing months of 1941 were turbulent ones in Paris. If the German occupation had turned France upside-down, these months turned it inside-out.

Hitler's invasion of Russia had stirred new fervor among French Communists. A demonstration protesting the German breach of faith with Russia, a former ally, turned into a riot in August. Two Communists were executed for their part in the protest. Then followed what, in a world fraught with perfidy, seemed to be the height of betrayal to French patriots, whether they were Communist or Gaullist—hundreds of Frenchmen enlisted, forming a military division to *join* the German army in the fighting on the Russian front.

When a German soldier was gunned down in a back alley, apparently by a communist, the Nazi's reacted by taking a number of hostages. But when still another soldier was murdered, the S.S. retaliated with savage recriminations, including the execution of a dozen of these innocent French hostages. Paris became a powder keg, ready to explode on many fronts at once. The hit-and-run tactics of the French resistance fighters only angered the Germans all the more. For every French prisoner they took or hostage they executed, however, it seemed two were miraculously set free. Each time the scenario was different, but the Resistance agents seemed able to penetrate the most secure of their installations. Always there was a disguise, always a diversion. Yet the diversity made it impossible to detect ahead of time what was about to happen. Eventually talk began to circulate among S.S. and Gestapo headquarters that the escapes were all the work of a single man. A dedication began to grow to discover his identity and put a stop to his sabotage of the Third Reich's attempt to consolidate its stranglehold on Paris.

Attacks on both sides continued sporadically through the fall and winter. Controversy and discord were everywhere. The indifference of the general public was one of the most disheartening factors for those involved in the Resistance. While a handful of patriots were sacrificing their lives toward the hope of liberation, a much greater majority of Frenchmen were going on with their lives under the German occupation as if nothing had happened. And an alarming number actually fell in with the Nazis. The patriots did not know whom to hate more—the Nazis or their collaborators. How, they asked themselves, can watching the deaths of their innocent countrymen not turn the hearts of such vile traitors—if such opportunists even have hearts?

Arnaud Soustelle was among the worst of this ignoble breed.

Prior to the war he had already begun to acquire a reputation as an inspector of police with a total lack of moral scruples. For even a small bribe he would turn in a trusting friend, he could beat information out of the most stubborn of suspects, and he took special delight in devising ever more inhumane ways to torment Jews.

When the Germans came in 1940, Soustelle lost no time in hitching his loyalties to the Nazi wagon. Hitler's racism suited him well, and armed with his particular talents and a loyal retinue of informants and connections who would do anything for a price, Soustelle found himself openly welcomed by the German occupiers. He was soon serving in the Sicherheitsdienst, or simply the S.D. This security agency for the Nazi party operated in the same ignominious capacity as the Gestapo, though the S.D. more willingly welcomed civilian nationals within its ranks. Arnaud had thus far proved an extremely valuable agent for his native knowledge of the city, and his policeman's savvy served him well.

Today, however, walking down the avenue Foch with a light snowfall dusting the shoulders of his new overcoat, Soustelle felt a slight twinge of a very uncharacteristic emotion: trepidation. It was not a feeling the tough forty-five-year-old Frenchman was used to, or liked. At six feet tall, broad of chest with icy gray eyes and hawk-like nose, it was ordinarily *he* who instilled fear in others.

But it was no small matter to be summoned to S.S. headquarters, especially when he was well aware of recent failures having to do with leads he had given them. These Nazis were an unforgiving lot. Forgetting all his successes, they would probably boot him out (no doubt to some labor camp in Germany) if he wasn't careful. But, he reminded himself, as he would his superiors, he had not yet exactly failed. He had merely not yet completely succeeded. But he would. Of that they could be certain.

Thoughtful, he slipped his hand into his pocket, took out a chunk of black licorice, and popped it into his mouth. It was a habit he had acquired many years earlier, and now almost continually he had a thick wad of the stuff churning about inside his mouth. Where most men smelled of tobacco, Soustelle perennially reeked of the bitter-sweet odor of licorice.

Chewing on the candy, he continued to wonder what was in store for him as he walked. He passed the main gate unimpeded, crossed the courtyard, and entered the building. This particular part of the compound had once been a fine townhouse occupied by a wealthy Parisian. He proceeded directly up a wide stairway, paying no attention to the intricate balustrade or the expensive flocked wallpaper. In another few moments he paused before a large oak door, and, before knocking, tossed another licorice drop into his mouth. He would have argued vehemently that it was not a nervous habit, but however coincidental it was, he seemed to devour many more during times of stress.

"Herein!" came a feminine voice from inside.

"I have an appointment with the general," said Soustelle upon entering.

"Yes, Herr Soustelle," said the secretary. "General von Graff is expecting you. Go right in."

Soustelle neither paused nor hesitated. He opened the door to the inner office and stepped smartly inside the spacious room, clicking his heels sharply together while stiffly raising his right hand in the air.

"Heil Hitler!"

"Heil Hitler," replied von Graff in the more casual tone of one who does not have to try so hard to prove his loyalty.

The fortunes of Martin von Graff had altered dramatically in the last several months. He had never been completely content in the Abwehr. For one thing, he could never tolerate Admiral Canaris, that perpetual intriguer who ruled military intelligence, regardless of the fact that they were both Navy men. One never knew where one stood with the old man and, moreover, one never quite knew where the old man stood. However, lately the vacillating Canaris was leaning too dangerously toward anti-Nazism to suit von Graff. Not that he was a fanatic himself, but he was not about to risk being in the wrong camp when the Führer's designs reached their victorious climax—as they certainly must. Thus, taking masterful advantage of the constant in-fighting between the Abwehr and the Gestapo, von Graff had secured his present position in the S.S. hierarchy, upon recommendation of Heinrich Himmler himself.

Landing the Paris assignment had been a coup far beyond his hopes as a relatively new S.S. recruit. Here in the cultural hub of the world, he felt as if there might be life beyond the war, after all. Hitler was adamant that the reputation of Paris should not decline during his wartime regime—hoping, no doubt, to make it a showcase of Third Reich "culture" later. Thus the arts continued to flourish. Von Graff attended the theater or opera nearly every night, and considered himself treated to fine performances each time.

Yes, things were going well for him. He was not about to let recent setbacks destroy everything.

He leaned back in his chair and focused his cold, unrelenting gaze upon the unscrupulous French collaborator before him.

"Well, Herr Soustelle," said von Graff, "I hope it is *good* news you have for me today."

"These things take time, mon General," hedged Soustelle.

"Time, Soustelle. . . ?" Von Graff let his words trail off with an ominous impression. "In the *time* since we borrowed you from the S.D., we have lost three more major prisoners, which does *not* include last night's loss of that Jew Poletski and his family. That makes six in two months,

Herr Soustelle. I need not tell you how bad that looks.''

He was thinking as much about his own reputation as Soustelle's. To have these escapes coincide so inconveniently with his own arrival in Paris was most unfortunate.

"So you see,'' he went on, "your talk of time does not put me at ease. Time is going by and you seem to be getting nowhere.''

"I assure you, mon General, I have my best people on it,'' replied Soustelle. "I have one reliable informer in the Resistance who is almost certain these particular escapes are originating with one network, masterminded by one certain crafty man.''

"Exactly as we have suspected!'' von Graff burst out—whether in pleasure or frustration, it was hard to tell.

"Yes, mon General.''

"And who is this one crafty individual?''

"If I knew that, you and I would not be standing here sweating today, now would we?''

"You have a great deal of nerve *for a Frenchman*,'' said von Graff caustically—he did not like how close to the mark Soustelle's jibe had been.

"My nerve is what makes me good at what I do,'' said Soustelle, his boldness rising once more. He had been foolish to fear this man. "And why I seldom fail.''

"So *you* say! Thus far I have witnessed none of your reputed ingenuity.''

Von Graff rose from his chair and walked to the window behind his desk. Snow had begun to pile up in the gutters; the busy late afternoon traffic, mostly bicycles and pedestrians, hurried along to homes or cafes where they might find some warmth.

"You know nothing about this man?'' asked the general at length. It galled him that anyone, even one of the crowd below, could be the culprit, perhaps spying on him at this very moment, and yet he was no closer to finding him than if he were on another planet.

"Very little,'' answered Soustelle. "But there are already whisperings of him circulating in the streets. It seems your six are only the most famous of his escapees. Many others have benefited from his aid—especially Jews, escaped prisoners of war, foreigners who could not get out when the city was first occupied.''

"He is mocking us!'' shouted von Graff, slamming his hand down upon the desk.

"He will be ours in time, I assure you.''

"Time! Time! Meanwhile, he sets people free, and we look like fools!''

"We are already laying a trap for this traitor the people consider a folk hero. His own cleverness will be his downfall.''

"Folk hero! Bah!''

"I have heard the code name *L'Escroc* used.''

"L'Escroc. . . ?" repeated von Graff thoughtfully. "The swindler."

"Oui. They say it is the Germans he is swindling—out of their prize prisoners."

Von Graff glanced out the window at the people below once more, then spun around and flashed his piercing glint upon the Frenchman. "I want him, Soustelle; do you understand?"

"I understand perfectly. And you shall have him. I want him, too."

"I am glad we agree on that," he said with a touch of sarcasm in his tone. "I understand there is great need for S.D. units on the Eastern Front—they may soon have to draw them from Paris itself, or so I understand."

"So I have heard," replied Soustelle, returning the general's piercing gaze. He would play the man's subtle little war of nerves. He was not afraid.

"It is very cold in Russia this time of year."

"So my Russian acquaintances have said," replied Soustelle, still calmly. As he spoke a tremendous urge came upon him to dig into his pocket. But another piece of licorice would have to wait. He comforted himself with the knowledge that this new S.S. general might just have the Russian front looming in *his* future as well.

Once he was again outside, Soustelle strode down the avenue doggedly, with large determined strides, arms swinging widely. His cheeks bulged with licorice.

He would find this *L'Escroc*! He would ferret him out of whatever resistance hole he was hiding in. He would find him, or . . .

There was no *or*! He *would* find him! This fool had gone too far when he threatened the comfort and advancement of Arnaud Soustelle.

Logan glanced across the table at Henri, who was thoughtfully buttering a slice of bread.

They were enjoying a light lunch at Chez Lorainne, the cafe across from Logan's hotel, where he had become something of a regular customer of late. The conversation between the two men, however, was not as light as the meal. This had been their first major dispute since joining forces nearly four months ago.

Henri took a bite of bread with frustrating deliberation, chewing carefully, thoroughly, as he just as methodically considered his response to the current problem that faced them.

"No matter what has been done, Michel," he said at length, "he is one of us and we must help him."

"I disagree, Henri," Logan replied flatly. "This resistance business brings many strange birds together. But we must draw the line somewhere. And I draw it when it comes to aiding a cold-blooded and merciless killer."

"There are many among us who would take issue with you. A war necessitates the letting of blood."

"Are you one of them, mon ami?"

Henri sighed and stared at the bread on his plate as if he might escape to the solace of food once more. But instead he turned his gaze back to Logan.

"Boche are Boche," he said. "What difference does it make how they die?"

"You don't honestly believe that."

"Last week we blew up a train carrying German soldiers," returned Henri. "What is the difference between that and killing one in the Metro?"

Logan leaned heavily against the hard wooden back of the booth where he sat. He scrutinized Henri for a moment. *Here is a sensitive man, a feeling and compassionate man*, he thought, *caught in the ugly net of war, forced to say and do things he would never say and do under any other circumstances*. In peacetime, Logan doubted he would so much as speak harshly to a dog. He was probably the sort of man who would alter his footfall at the last moment to avoid stepping on a beetle on the sidewalk. He was a gentle man . . . a good man. Yet here he was talking about killing a trainload of men as if it were scarcely more out of the ordinary than an afternoon's walk down to the market.

"What a business!" sighed Logan at length.

"Acts of sabotage . . . acts of murder—it gets very mixed up, Michel. And to be truthful," Henri went on in a faraway voice that almost made it sound as though he wished he could say the same about himself, "I do not say you are wrong to question it."

"There is something intrinsically inhuman and atrocious about stabbing a lone man in the back, a man who is unsuspecting and probably doing nothing more sinister than enjoying a few days leave in Paris. That is murder, and I'll have no part in it. That is worlds away from helping condemned men and women to their freedom."

Logan did not like to be faced with the more glaring inconsistencies of his present vocation. He had steadfastly refused to use or carry a weapon, though perhaps he had not examined his moral code thoroughly. Probably it amounted to nothing more than a carry-over from the old days when avoiding the seamier side of his "profession" had somehow assuaged his conscience. He had never been a street fighter, though he knew he could fight. But to go beyond that . . . he didn't know, and was perhaps afraid of placing himself in the position where he'd find out.

He had avoided looking at the wider implications of what he was doing—that he was fighting in a cruel war, and that death was an intrinsic part of the process. If the axiom of guilt by association was true, then was he not equally culpable as this friend of Claude's whom they were now discussing?

He should have known that eventually he would face such an impasse, especially when dealing with such a vicious character as Claude. They had not found so much as an inch of common ground in four months, and had only avoided a blow-out because they studiously stayed out of each other's way. But the uneasy peace could not last forever, especially once Logan began to suspect Claude's part in the street killings of German soldiers. He had hinted to one or two of the others about getting rid of him, but he had never actively pursued such a notion because deep down Logan knew Claude served a vital function in the *La Librairie* network. Claude was the sabotage expert, and if he were not around to lay the bombs that blew up trains, they might try to enlist Logan for the job.

For now, however, Logan could not let himself wade through the overall moral questions of what he was involved in. Somehow he had to keep as much as possible black and white, and, failing that, he would just have to focus on the vile enemy they were all, Claude included, fighting.

"Bien entendu," Logan finally conceded with a ragged sigh. "Tell me about Claude's companion."

"He calls himself Louis," said Henri. "He was an officer in the French army and served courageously with the defenders of the Maginot Line in '40. He eluded capture when the defense finally broke, and made his way to the mountains, where he fought with the Marquis until about six months ago, when he came to Paris in an attempt to enlist support for the guerrilla fighters."

"Why don't his Communist friends help him?"

"One of his Communist friends *is* helping him," replied Henri pointedly. "He came to Claude, and Claude has come to us. Do you think this resistance will get anywhere if we maintain all these petty differences?"

"I suppose you're right."

"Besides, Louis' regular contacts are being too closely watched right now," added Henri.

"What does he want?"

"A new identity and all the falsified documents to go along with it. He wants to get to the unoccupied zone where he won't be such a hot property. I think Jean Pierre's man can accommodate us with the printing."

"No," interjected Logan quickly. "I don't want to risk Jean Pierre in this—in fact, I'm still not sure we ought to risk *anyone*."

"Look at it this way, mon ami," said Henri, his quiet voice taking on a shrewd yet fatherly quality. "Louis is a marked man and, if he remains in Paris, is sure to be caught eventually. He knows a great deal, even more about *La Librairie* than is safe. So unless you are willing to put a bullet through his head, our only recourse is to do what we can to get him out of here."

"Adroitly phrased! Beneath all that genteel facade, you are a cagey old fox, Henri." Logan shook his head in defeat, but let his lips turn up in an affectionate smile.

"You are L'Escroc. Perhaps I should be Le Renard, eh?" He winked and sent Logan a knowing grin in reply. "The fox; what do you think?"

Judging from his response, Logan did not join in the amusement. "You do not like your new-found fame, do you, Michel?" said Henri more seriously.

"Fame is not very healthy in this work," replied Logan. "Even a back table in a deserted cafe is too risky a place to be discussing such things."

"I am sorry, Michel. I would have said nothing if I thought there was the slightest chance—"

"I know, Henri," said Logan apologetically. "I suppose the whole thing isn't setting altogether well with me. It is not only the notoriety and the danger that accompanies it, but also being thought too highly of. We all work together and take the same risks. I deserve no special honor."

"If glory were all you had to worry about, then your problems would indeed be small ones."

"What do you mean?"

"L'Escroc is bound to be something of a scapegoat too," said Henri gravely. "Don't be fooled. Those who whisper the name about the streets after there has been a particularly notable escape—whether it was your doing or not—care less for your glory than to have the attention of the

Germans focused on someone besides themselves."

"Wonderful comrades we have out there," said Logan dryly.

"To most of them L'Escroc is an idea, a symbol. I think a good many of them would watch their tongues a little more closely if they really thought of him as a real person."

"I suppose this being a symbol wouldn't be so bad if some good could come of it, like bringing together some of the factions."

Henri contemplated his food once more in thought, then looked up. "Yes," he said slowly, almost regretfully. "But believe me, a symbol *is* a benefit in work such as this. I can't say it would heal all the wounds and unite the French people. But it does provide a rallying point, a symbol of hope. And that is the last thing the Germans want here in Paris. They will do everything in their power to crush it."

Saying nothing, Logan merely raised his eyes at Henri's words as their full implication settled in upon him.

"The very thing that could sustain us," said Henri, "could also destroy us. 'Entertaining hope means recognizing fear,'" he added, then paused and smiled, as if recalling a pleasant memory. "My wife is a bit 'touched in the head' over Browning, but I never thought I'd be quoting him in the midst of my present circumstances."

"You've never mentioned being married," said Logan in some astonishment.

"That is perhaps the greatest shame of this life—that we are not able to be together. Every day I pray that I will be spared long enough to see her again."

"Where is she?"

"Just before the Boche came, I was able to get Marcelle and our children south, where a friend ran a fishing boat out of Cannes. He got them to England."

"Why didn't you go with them?"

"What! And leave my precious books to the Nazis?" His eye twinkled mischievously.

"I think you and our friend Poletski are cut from the same cloth," said Logan.

"Once my family was safe," Henri went on, "how could I turn my back on my country? I was too old for the army but knew there would be many other tasks to be done, and a battlefield of sorts upon which to serve right here in Paris."

"Your wife must love you very much."

"Of course! She is my wife."

"It does not necessarily follow that she must love you. Many wives stop loving their husbands."

"Ah, Michel, that shows how little you truly understand marriage. No wife ever stopped loving her husband, when he was truly loving *her* as a man was intended to love a woman."

"Are you saying people do not fall in love, and then out of it again?"

"Michel! Michel! What has falling in love to do with marriage? Nothing! You are not married, n'est-ce pas?"

"Actually, I am married," replied Logan.

"Then for your sake—and your wife's—I hope that someday soon you leave behind this foolishness about being 'in love.' No marriage can survive unless it gets past that and to the love of sacrifice. Ah, but you are young!"

"But you said your wife loved you. I assume you love her?"

"Of course! of course! We are in love now because we first learned how to sacrifice ourselves one to the other. We have learned to serve, to lay down our lives, to wash each other's feet, so to speak. You don't do those kinds of things year after year unless you are determined to love. Not *in* love, but *determined* to love."

"Hmm," mused Logan. "I guess I always thought love had to come first in a marriage."

"Non, mon ami. Love—that comes second! First comes commitment, sacrifice. Then, and *only* then, comes *true* and lasting love. That is why my wife and I *are* now in love."

Logan said no more. He had certainly been given plenty to think about.

33 / A Quiet Supper

When Henri and Logan parted, Logan set out on his bicycle to make necessary contacts to begin arranging things for Louis. A printer was his first stop. The man on the left bank was not as good as Jean Pierre's man, but his work would be adequate, and Logan was firm about not involving the priest. He had never discussed the moral complexities of such matters with him, but Logan didn't think it would be fair to place a priest in such a compromising position. He wasn't altogether comfortable with the decision he had just made regarding the fugitive Louis, but now that he had made it, he would handle everything on his own.

Since the printing of the identity papers would take three days, Logan next set about locating a safe house for Claude's friend while he waited. It was five o'clock in the afternoon when he finally trudged up the stairs of Lise's building on his last task of the day. He had a pocketful of messages to be radioed to London that evening.

She looked down with some dismay at the sheaf of papers Logan held out to her once he had stepped inside her apartment.

"I'm sorry," he apologized. He knew the longer the radio was transmitting at one time, the greater the risk of detection.

"It's not that," said Lise. "But there were detector vans out last night and I had to shut off. I still have a good deal from yesterday to send."

"Do you think they're onto you?" asked Logan.

"No. I think it was just a general sweep of the area."

"Well, I'll stick around as lookout while you send."

"It's still some time before I can transmit."

"Then why don't we go have some dinner while we wait—I'm starved."

She smiled. "It's a long time since I ate in a restaurant for pleasure, without it being for some kind of rendezvous."

"Let's make a point of forgetting all about the underground."

"We can try," she replied.

They walked down the stairs and to a cafe about two blocks away. Since it was Friday, the place was quite busy, and Logan found himself enjoying the festive activity around him. By all appearances he and Lise were just two friends relaxing after a hard week, not a British agent and a Resistance radio operator. The concierge welcomed them warmly and did not even notice their sudden consternation when several German officers entered shortly afterward and sat down only two tables away.

But they were innocents tonight and had no reason to fear the Germans. At least not for another hour. Besides, the presence of the officers only reinforced their determination to avoid mention of their underground existence.

In the months since Logan had come to Paris, he and Lise had worked frequently together, spending countless hours over the wireless, not to mention a wide variety of other missions. Though Lise had softened her original attitude toward Logan considerably, not since that first evening in her apartment had she revealed any more of her heart to him. It was as though she was embarrassed at having exposed a chink in her armor, and now wanted to make up for that lapse by proving such incidents were rare.

She was a complex woman, indeed, and Logan was intrigued by her.

But if Lise had not opened up to Logan, it was not for his lack of trying. The very mystery surrounding this young Frenchwoman compelled him to probe deeper. He was curious to know what thoughts hovered behind those keenly sensitive dark eyes. What did she think about L'Escroc? What were her deeper motives for what she did? Had she ever been in love? What were her political leanings? What did she think about *him*?

Intuitively Logan sensed that her perceptions would be wise and valuable, as well as interesting. If only she could be induced to express them more freely!

When the meal was finished and the coffee served, Logan leaned contentedly back, sipping at the ersatz brew, not even noticing any longer its loathsome taste.

"Tell me, Lise," he began casually, "what did you do before the war?"

"I was a teacher."

"A teacher. Hmm . . . What did you teach?"

"A dozen eight- and nine-year-old girls."

"Really?"

"Does that surprise you?"

Logan set down his cup and gave the question a moment's consideration before replying. "No," he said finally, "not now that I think of it. In fact, I can just picture them sitting around you in the Place du Trocadéro, faces scrubbed and smiling, looking up at you from the grass in frank admiration."

"What makes you think they would admire me?"

"Oh, I just know they would," Logan replied. "You possess an air of security, and they must surely have hung on every word you said. I have a daughter of my own, and I know she would like you."

His statement raised an obvious flicker of surprise in her normally controlled features. Logan had not intended to mention his daughter and had done so almost unconsciously.

"I guess it's my turn to surprise you," he said lightly.

"Yes, I suppose you did," she replied. "But come, it is time we got back."

They paid their bill, then walked out into the icy winter night. Only after walking a half block in silence did Lise attempt to return to the previous conversation.

"I have never thought of you as a family man," she said as they walked.

"I suppose I'm not really much of one."

"Your daughter must be very proud of you—or at least she will be when she learns of your great courage here and all the people you have helped."

"She's much too young to know what is going on. But I do hope that one day she'll find out what I did in the war, and have some reason to be proud. The Lord only knows how little else there is for her to be proud of."

"She will, Michel," said Lise with sincerity. "Someday she will look up at you with the same admiring eyes you have pictured on my students."

"I don't know . . . What does a child care about Nazis and tyranny and war?" Logan paused, questioning for the first time the validity of his motives for coming to France.

"And your wife?" Lise asked. "She is aware of what you do . . . she is proud?"

Logan did not answer. Instead he sighed deeply.

"I'm sorry . . . I only thought the wife of L'Escroc must be a proud woman."

"She knows nothing about L'Escroc," Logan blurted out finally. "She doesn't even know I'm in Paris."

"I see," replied Lise. Now it was her turn to be silent. They did not know each other well enough yet for her to probe further. At length, she sought to return the conversation to the subject of Logan's daughter, which she hoped would remove the heaviness that had descended upon them.

"But your little girl . . . you seem to think that when she is older she will not be able to understand your absence from her now. But surely when you explain—"

"Why should she? I'm not even sure I do."

Logan paused again. He had not given his family much thought in weeks. If he had hoped that by ignoring it, the problem would somehow resolve itself, he now found he was mistaken. He was just as confused about where everything stood as he was when he left Stonewycke—perhaps more so.

"I'm probably kidding myself with all this about making her proud of me," he finally added in frustration. "I think it's just a lot easier to be here doing this than back there, that's all. What's there to be proud of in that?"

"Does it take more courage to be a father than it does to be a soldier?" asked Lise pensively.

She did not actually expect an answer. But Logan stopped, then reached out and touched her arm to stop her, too. She turned back and looked at him. She could not tell if he was angry, hurt, or reprimanded by her words. She had not meant them to elicit any of those responses. The question had been merely a philosophical one, but now she wondered if she'd been wise to voice it.

A variety of reactions were surging through Logan, though anger was not one of them. His first instinct was to rebuff the whole notion. But he couldn't do that, for he had just admitted to its truth. Instead, he attempted to steer the conversation afield.

"Where did you obtain all that wisdom?" he asked.

Not one to probe where she was uninvited, Lise let him have his diversion. "No doubt from the Talmud," she answered. "My father had no sons to whom he could pass on his great learning. But that hardly mattered to him. He was just as content to pour himself into his daughters. I did not attend the yeshiva, but I know as much Talmud as any man."

They fell silent for the remainder of the walk to Lise's apartment. A light snow began to fall and they quickened their pace, arriving just at the time they were supposed to contact London. If it had been in either of their minds to ponder or further discuss any of the questions raised by their conversation, they were impeded by the sudden rush of successive events.

The transmitting that evening began on a smooth note, despite the fact that a new girl was being broken in on the London end and their messages were received with agonizing delay.

Logan paced back and forth in front of the window, pausing every now and then to peek out the blackout shade. In the frosty, darkened streets below little activity could be detected. The midnight curfew would begin in little more than an hour, and most of the cautious Parisians had retired indoors long before this, leaving only a handful of cyclists and pedestrians hurrying along to catch the last trains at eleven.

Logan glanced at his watch. He had wanted to cut off communications much sooner than this, but Lise had been confident yesterday's incident had not been aimed toward them. Besides, messages were piling up. Most of them were too urgent to wait. And with all the dangers that constantly beset them in their daily work, it seemed hardly necessary to allow something so minor to cause them to change their plans.

"How much longer?" Logan called out to Lise, who was intent on her work.

"I'm sorry it's taking so long."

"I know it's not your fault, but curfew is coming up."

Lise didn't reply immediately, for a message was just then coming through. Logan turned his attention back to the window.

Suddenly he snapped the shade closed. "Shut down! There's a van!"

Instantly Lise clicked off the machine, in the middle of the poor London trainee's painstaking reply to one of their messages. She jumped up and joined Logan at the window. Turning out the light in the room, then peering out the merest crack in the shade, they could see the detector van at the far end of the street. Rounding the corner behind it came another.

They watched, holding their breath. Had they only pinpointed the general whereabouts of the wireless sounds, or would the vans screech to a halt right in front of Lise's building?

Both vehicles stopped at the end of the street. Unless there was another wireless transmitting on this same block—an unlikely prospect—the Germans had only been able to zero in on the street. They would begin a house-to-house search.

"Let's get out of here!" said Logan, already grabbing their coats and quickly stuffing the London messages, which he hadn't had a chance to read, into his pocket, while tossing the rest into the coal stove.

"Michel, we can't leave the radio."

Logan paused and looked at the precious instrument.

Yes, it was indispensable to their work, and who could tell when London could send them a new one? But was it valuable enough to risk their lives over? He glanced out the window once more. As he had guessed, the German detection squad was now moving from building to building, and if they carried out their search with customary Nazi thoroughness, there might still be a few moments to attempt a rescue of the wireless.

"Is there a back way out of here?" he asked after a momentary pause.

"An old fire escape, up to the roof and down also."

Logan thought for a moment. "The roof might work," he said, "but we might be trapped." He paused, then went on. "No, we'd better chance it on the street. Get a box for the radio."

In less than two minutes the radio was packed into a cardboard box and the two were rushing out the door and down the hall to a large window. As he wrestled it open, the resulting squeak seemed ear-splitting in the quiet night, and Logan prayed the Nazis didn't have enough manpower to patrol every back exit while their vans crept along the front of the street.

The window opened onto the metal fire escape as Lise had indicated. Carefully they stepped out onto the metal grating, tiptoeing so as not to reveal their presence.

Slowly—very slowly—they made their way down the two flights and into the littered, darkened alley, one end of which led to the street fronting Lise's building on which the Germans were at this moment conducting their raid. Hugging the dirty brick wall, they crept in the opposite direction toward the next block.

Just as they reached the end Logan stopped abruptly and jumped back against the dark recess of the wall, shoving Lise back also.

"Gestapo," he whispered.

"We better give it up," said Lise. "If we stow the wireless in one of these garbage bins, and pretend to be a couple in love and out late, we still might get past."

"Maybe we'll have to," replied Logan, "but I'm not quite ready to give up on the radio yet."

The next instant, however, gave Logan pause to reconsider his daring. The night-call of a prowling tom cat nearly sent him into Lise's arms with panic. He grinned nervously at his reaction, and the twinkle in Lise's eyes told him he had given her a rare moment of amusement. But the serious urgency of the moment did not allow them to revel long in humor. They were trapped in an alley, with the Gestapo watching the street on the one end, and the street swarming with Germans from the two vans on the other. Even if they did stash the radio, there appeared little hope they would get by without at least being detained for questioning, during which time the alley was bound to be turned inside out and the radio discovered.

Suddenly Logan's eyes lit up.

He set the box on the ground, took out the wireless, and hid it behind a trash bin. Then he handed the empty carton to Lise. She gave him a puzzled look, but in the months of their association she had learned to accept his occasional odd behavior without question.

"Hold that box open," he said, "and stay right beside me."

Then he turned his attention to the old tom that had taken up a position on a ledge just above the trash bin, calmly observing all the strange goings-on below.

"Come here, kitty," said Logan in the loudest whisper he dared. "Come, kitty—I've got something nice for you." He attempted to give his voice a sappy inviting sound, but the cat, scrawny and mangy and as hungry as being homeless during wartime could make him, made no move except to wash his face.

"Come, Monsieur le matou," joined in Lise. Her voice too was sweet, and this time the animal looked up with some interest.

Slowly the cat stood, taking notice of the box for the first time, seemingly tempted by the unknown contents inside. Noiselessly he jumped onto a pile of trash nearby. Lise made an untimely jerk with the box and the animal froze. But before it could leap back to safety, Logan's hand shot out and grabbed it by the tail. The tom hissed and spat, while its back leg clawed Logan's wrist and its front paw whipped a vicious scratch across his cheek. But Logan did not let loose his grasp, and pulled the clawing, furious animal toward him, deposited him into the box, and snapped the lid quickly shut.

"Now what?" asked Lise, handing Logan the box, which the caged animal was beating against from inside, letting out deep pained cries.

"Now we can be on our way," said Logan. "But please, look more distraught for your poor sick *matou*, your beloved pet who has taken ill."

With bravado Logan led her out of the alley and into the street, where they were promptly stopped by the vigilant Gestapo.

"Arrêtez!" shouted one of the three standing nearby, who followed his command by running toward them, gun drawn.

Logan and Lise stopped in their tracks.

"What is in that box?" asked the man in very poor French.

"In here?" replied Logan innocently. "Why, only a sick cat we are taking to the veterinarian. We would have waited till morning, but my wife could not sleep for all the poor beast's awful cries."

"Open it up."

"Please, Monsieur Officer, it is nearly crazy since I put him into the box. I had the devil to pay just trapping it inside. You can see the scratches it gave me." Logan pointed to the blood on his cheek and held out his wrist toward the man.

"I said open it up—now!" repeated the man.

Logan cracked the lid, and with a disgusted grunt the agent bent over to peer into the box. Seeing hope of freedom, the tom lurched toward the opening. Logan's hand slipped from the lid with the animal's movement, and the cat came screaming out of its prison into the German's face. He leaped back with an angry curse, and the cat fled once more for the alley.

"Quel dommage!" exclaimed Logan, partly in apology to the startled German, and partly as if bemoaning his own ill luck. "Now I must trap the animal all over again."

"Just see that you do it before curfew," growled the angry agent, in an attempt to regain some of his lost dignity. "Fool animal-loving Frenchmen!" he muttered.

"Merci," said Logan with great sincerity. "You have a kind heart!"

He and Lise turned back into the alley after the lost cat. Once back under the cloak of darkness, Logan retrieved the wireless, set it back into the box, then waited several minutes more to allow for a plausible cat search.

"I hope these Germans are as gullible as customs officials on whom I used to see seamen pull this ruse," said Logan.

"You think they will let us stroll right by?"

"Let's hope so," answered Logan. "But why don't you go back the other way. They'll question you but eventually let you go. No sense both of us running the risk of getting caught with this thing."

"No, Michel. We are in it together."

"But we still have to get the radio across town—and before midnight."

"Perhaps not," said Lise. "Do you remember the cafe where we had dinner? The concierge there is a sympathizer."

"Do you think he will keep our *package* temporarily?"

"I think we ought to try him."

"Then let's go."

The Germans glanced up with little more than a curious interest at the couple as they came back out of the alley carrying their box. No one seemed to express much astonishment that they had found the wild cat so soon. They waved the Frenchman and woman on. They had been posted here to stop Resistance agents, not sentimental cat-lovers.

In less than ten minutes they were inside the cafe. The concierge was sweeping, preparing to close the moment the two or three of his remaining customers departed. From the look on his face he was not altogether pleased at the two new arrivals.

He listened to their highly sensitive request with even more skepticism. Sympathizer though he was, the concierge was also by necessity a very cautious man. He had a family and a decent little business. He was in sympathy, but not anxious to get involved in any underground activities. He was certainly not sympathetic enough to die for this cause. And there could be no other penalty for being caught with a wireless. In the end, however, Logan managed to convince him that his help would only be required for twelve hours. He would himself be back first thing in the morning to retrieve it.

"What could happen, after all, in such a short time? You will be asleep, and so will the Germans," said Logan.

Once the last of the customers had exited, the concierge took the box to his basement where he stowed it in a spot that he felt was safe, even should the Gestapo mount a full-scale raid of the place. Logan made a mental note of the place, for it was sure to come in handy again.

He and Lise then bade the man good night with profuse thanks, and departed. Once outside, Logan looked at his watch. He had but twenty minutes to get home. They made it back to Lise's apartment, sneaking behind the two detection vans that had progressed beyond her building and farther down the street. He retrieved his bicycle, then set off.

The frigid wind whipped across his face like fingers of ice. It had stopped snowing long ago, but the temperature must have dropped ten degrees since dinner. Logan's gloved fingers nearly froze around the handle grips, and even the exertion of pedaling twenty miles an hour did not help neutralize the cold. He tried to focus his mind on the events of the day in order to forget his discomfort.

First there had been the disquieting news about Claude's friend Louis. By now the wheels were in motion to help him, whether it was the right thing to do or not.

Suddenly the face of Alec jumped into Logan's mind. What would his father-in-law think of him helping a man who had knifed a German in the Metro? In the years of his association with Alec, Logan had often measured his own responses by how his father-in-law—a man he greatly admired—might react. But there were too many gray areas to make any clear sense of his present moral dilemma. Perhaps things would become clearer once he met Louis face-to-face. Perhaps not. It was, after all, wartime. And moral dilemmas were all the more thorny during war.

And Logan also faced the wireless problem. He had to retrieve it in the morning, but what would he do with it if he had found no new safe location from which he and Lise could operate? Her apartment could no longer be relied upon. Perhaps by the light of day the concierge would be less faint-hearted and would agree to keep it a bit longer. But the radio couldn't remain out of use for long. There were important communiques that had to be relayed to London. Logan had a pocketful of them right now. They would need responses. Without a wireless in operation, their underground activities would be seriously crippled.

The pressing needs of his present situation managed to divert Logan's mind from the wind biting into his skin. He was so absorbed in trying to sort out all the possible locations for his radio that he paid little attention to the condition of the streets. About halfway home, accelerating downhill, he rounded a corner and suddenly hit a patch of black ice. The front wheel of his bicycle twisted out of control, jerking the handlebars loose in his hands. The bicycle slid sideways out from under him, and Logan was sent sprawling up against the cement post of a street lamp.

Logan lay dazed for several moments before he could take stock of his situation. The side of his face and his shoulder were badly bruised. He forced himself to try to stand, but the left side of his body refused to cooperate. He glanced at his watch. The hands were moving steadily toward midnight.

He forced himself to his feet, ignoring the pain of his scrapes and bruises, then hobbled to where his bike lay. He stooped down to pick up the precious bicycle. A few spokes were bent, but otherwise it seemed usable. By the time he once again straddled the seat and set off again, more slowly, it was already midnight.

As soon as the opportunity presented itself, Logan turned off the main avenue he had been following and began to make his way by means of side streets, keeping to the shadows.

Three blocks from his place he had no choice but to cross a wide boulevard. It was only ten minutes past twelve. If he was lucky, he might—

"Halt!" came a sharp German voice at Logan's back.

For a split instant many thoughts flew through Logan's mind. Could he outwit the bullet that was sure to follow if he kept going and tried to make a dash for it? What was the current discipline for breakers of the curfew? If I'm lucky, perhaps only deportation to a forced labor camp in Germany, he thought glumly.

His cover was solid, his papers flawless, forgeries though they were. Might he be so lucky as to get by with a mere warning?

Suddenly his heart stopped. He still had the slips of incriminating papers in his pocket! Those wireless messages were worth a firing squad at the very least.

He was just about to make a run for it when the German shouted for him to stop a second time.

Without thinking it over, suddenly reason took over and he slammed on his brakes. There was no sense getting killed. If Skittles had taught him one thing, it was never to give up until he'd fully played out his hand.

35 / Interrogation

Logan looked about the small room for the twentieth time.

Despite the hour, he had been unable to relax enough to sleep though he was extremely tired. He had been here for hours, imprisoned in what he took to be a holding cell. It was certainly far better than the dungeonlike accommodations where they had kept Poletski downstairs.

It was not the first time he had scanned the room for some possible escape route. But since being deposited there five hours earlier, all his attempts to come up with some way out had proved equally futile.

He had been taken straight to the S.S. headquarters on the avenue Foch, and he could not miss the irony that less than a week ago he had rescued three inmates from this very place. Now *he* was the prisoner, and if he were to remain locked in this room with only a bed and chair, his stay would no doubt be a long one. There were not even sheets on the bed—only a small blanket. Someone obviously planned the accommodations to deter escape through the window, though it was covered with steel bars, or, failing that, the possibility of hanging oneself from the bare light fixture in the ceiling.

Logan was not yet ready for such extremes.

As far as he knew he was still believed to be nothing more than a common curfew breaker. Except for a cursory frisk for weapons, he had not been searched.

His messages had not been discovered, and the moment he had been left alone he set about destroying them. He tore each one into tiny bits, then, prying the window open a crack through the bars, shoved them out where the scraps floated to the ground, mingling inconspicuously with the falling snow.

Yet he could not feel completely relieved. He was worried about this long wait. Any good confidence man knows that a delay in a scam plays against the con man. The primary rule was swiftness—never give the victim the chance to think.

In this case the victim—though he laughed inwardly at the inaptness of the analogy—was the Nazis, and the longer they mulled over what to do with this curfew breaker, the more chance they might have to discover his true intentions. He would have been immensely relieved to know that the long delay was due to nothing more sinister than bureaucratic foul-up. The efficient Nazis had locked him up, then simply forgotten about him. He could thank the opening of Verdi's opera *La Traviata* for that; the cocktail party that had followed had occupied many officers, leaving head-quarters short-staffed until late into the night.

By six o'clock a.m. he had gone over every inch of the room several times, fixed his cover story firmly in his mind, and was beginning to wonder about breakfast when he heard a key in the lock.

He began pacing nervously across the room like the harried, supposedly innocent citizen he was pretending to be. But when the S.S. captain walked in, in his trim black uniform, Logan was in complete possession of himself. The German was a young man for an officer, several years Logan's junior, though his fair skin and blonde hair made him appear even younger. But for all his youthful appearance, his well-defined jaw was as firm as if it were set in granite, and his Aryan blue eyes were more reminiscent of ice than they were of the sky or the sea.

"Vous êtes, Michel Tanant?" he said in the polished French of either an educated man or a skilled con artist. Logan guessed from the captain's bearing that it was the former.

"Oui," replied Logan, then added in a frazzled voice, "Please, I've been kept here all night. I don't understand."

"You have violated the curfew."

"Oui, but—"

"Sit down!" ordered the captain.

Logan hesitated, then, complying like a whipped puppy, slumped down on the edge of the bed. The captain sat on the single chair and shuffled through a sheaf of documents that Logan recognized as his identity papers which had been confiscated upon his arrest. *Have they discovered some flaw in them?* he wondered. Even good forgeries were never perfect.

"I am Captain Neumann," said the man. "Your papers appear to be in order. I see no reason to detain you. However, there are a few questions I would like to ask you. Afterward it may be possible for you to go."

"Thank you, Captain," said Logan with immense gratitude. "I assure you that if it had not been for my accident I would have— "

"You are from Lyon?" broke in Neumann impatiently.

"Oui."

"What is your mother's name?"

"Marie."

"How many sisters has she?"

"Two."

"What are their names?"

"Why, Aunt Suzanne and Aunt Yvonne . . ."

The captain was employing a method of interrogation popular with the Germans during snap controls or at roadblocks or borders. A suspect found himself bombarded with a barrage of questions any innocent man ought to be able to answer without thought. If a suspect stumbled or faltered over any reply, he stood immediately accused.

Logan's cover had included none of the previous information, but it didn't matter. The captain would never check up on any of it. He was not even listening to the answers, only scrutinizing Logan's demeanor while responding. As Logan rattled off his answers, he did not hesitate, but answered as if such names had always been part of his life, not merely thought up that instant.

"Where do they live?"

"My aunts?"

"Yes."

"Aunt Suzanne lives in Lyon, but Aunt Yvonne married an artist and now lives in Arles—you know, following in the footsteps of Van Gogh and all that—"

"Where is your father?" interrupted Neumann, not the least bit interested in turning this interrogation into a conversation.

"He's dead."

"And your mother, Michelle . . . ?"

"It's Marie—and she's dead also."

"Buried in Lyon where your Aunt Yvonne lives?"

"No, she's the one in Arles—with the artist." Then Logan added, as in a wounded tone, "I simply don't understand the meaning of all this."

"Your mother is buried in Lyon?"

"Yes. Next to my father. But please—"

"That is all, Monsieur Tanant," said the captain crisply, rising. "You will come with me."

"But where—?"

"Quickly!" snapped the captain. Logan jumped up obediently.

They exited the tiny room. That, at least, was a small relief. Logan still had no idea what was to become of him. Neumann had left the impression that he was about to be released, but then that could be only another clever trick—raise a man's confidence so that he lets down and gets sloppy.

Logan knew he had been scrupulously careful with his responses. Perhaps too much so. There was such a fine line, and one could not always tell when or if he might have inadvertently crossed it.

He and Neumann walked side by side. Logan was quick to note that the captain did not think him a dangerous enough prisoner to draw his gun. Still, he would never be so foolish as to attempt a break in the heart of S.S. headquarters with dozens of armed soldiers close at hand. Using a surreptitious disguise was one thing. But a pitched race through these halls was quite another. He'd never make it to the end of the corridor.

Nevertheless, he would remain watchful and ever vigilant of his surroundings. One could never tell when an acceptable opportunity might arise.

They turned a corner and Logan saw the main stairway just ahead. His hopes began to rise.

Three officers were ascending and had just reached the landing. Suddenly Logan's short-lived hopes plummeted. There, at the top of the stair, was the last person Logan had ever expected to see again—Colonel Martin von Graff!

Only now Logan could plainly see it was *General*, and he wore the uniform and insignia of the S.S. rather than the Abwehr. If he recognized him, Logan was finished.

But General von Graff and his companions walked briskly past, only exchanging salutes with Neumann.

It seemed too good to be true, thought Logan, as he walked steadily on toward the door. They had met in person only that one time. Much had happened since. It was possible he had—

"Captain Neumann," came von Graff's commanding but cultured voice from behind them.

Logan felt the blood drain from his face. All the disciplined training in the world could not have prevented it. Desperately he tried to gather back his composure. There was always a way out—a bluff! He had to think fast!

Neumann turned smartly to face his superior. "Ja, mein General?" he said.

"Why do you have this man?" he asked, eyeing Logan.

"He was caught violating curfew," answered Neumann. "He was brought in last night for questioning."

"I see . . ."

Von Graff paused, apparently in thought, most likely trying to remember where he had seen the face before, and then analyzing this unexpected turn in the same way that Logan was also doing at that very instant.

"Take him to my office," von Graff finally said decisively. "I must take care of a small matter and then I will be there. I will be ten minutes at most—remain with him the entire time!"

"Ja, mein Herr!"

Logan understood enough German to know what had transpired. But he still did not know whether this was a boon or a disaster.

Von Graff continued on his way, and Neumann took his prisoner more firmly in tow back down the corridor the way they had come. Apparently there was more to this Michel Tanant than met the eye. And young Captain Neumann kept well hidden his own queasy stomach—for he had been about to release him!

"This is an unexpected surprise," said von Graff with understated irony, turning to Logan for the first time.

When he had entered the room a few moments earlier, he had gone straight up to Neumann and exchanged a few words. The captain gave his superior the particulars of Logan's arrest. Then von Graff dismissed the captain and Neumann turned briskly and left the room. Logan found it difficult to read his controlled expression.

"It is for me also," Logan replied.

The conversation was carried on in English, and Logan decided to leave it that way. Undoubtedly von Graff knew that Logan was proficient in French and there was little he could do about that. But he thought it might somehow work to his advantage if he underplayed his limited knowledge of German for the time being. In the ten minutes he had been sitting alone in silence with Neumann awaiting the general's arrival, Logan had been hastily trying to collect his wits and figure some way out of this jam he found himself in. Was his cover blown completely? Or might he possibly resurrect his old *Trinity* identity by which von Graff had known him and play out that game a little longer? Could there be some plausible reason for Trinity to be in Paris and still in league with the Nazis? If so, could he make von Graff buy it? Or had the S.S. already linked him to the underground?

"Naturally, explanations will have to be made," said von Graff.

"Naturally."

Maybe he could tell him that he had been found out by MI5 and forced to flee London. Yes . . . that could work—*if* the Trinity they had brought in to replace him had made no transmissions to Germany in the last two days. The schedule with the Abwehr when *he* had been Trinity several months ago had been one transmission a week, on Tuesdays. It was now Saturday morning. He might be in the clear. Of course all that could have changed. For all he knew MI5 might already have disposed of Trinity. When Logan had gone into the SOE they had decided to keep Trinity as a notional agent because he had been bringing in some valuable intelligence. Gunther had even begun to be slightly jealous at the Abwehr's favoring of this new recruit. Yet, in the time since he had left, Trinity could have easily played out his usefulness. In hindsight, it was foolish to have kept such a loose end active. But who could have guessed that an agent working undercover in Paris would stumble into such a coincidence?

Still, if he could just make this all work for him, he might land on his feet. He would have to feel von Graff out. If the jig *was* up, well . . . he supposed he couldn't have expected this to go on forever. Many agents were glad to last as long as he had. He tried not to think of the consequences awaiting failure. Naturally, his cyanide was in his other suit—but perhaps that was lucky too, for it would have been a dead giveaway.

If only he wasn't so tired! He hadn't slept in over twenty-four hours, and now he wished he had dozed off a bit during the last five. But he had been too keyed up. Logan knew he had to remain alert now more than ever, for he would not easily fool von Graff.

The general took in a sharp breath, the muscles tightening around his neck. Then he walked around behind his desk and sat down. At length he looked up, eyes glinting.

"Come now, Herr MacVey," he said tightly. "Are you trying to play cat and mouse with me? Do you wish to feel me out before you make any commitments?"

The man was shrewd, there was no mistaking that. He had guessed Logan's motives exactly and now there was nothing else for Logan to do but forge ahead, hoping that the story he contrived would somehow coincide with facts.

"Can you blame me, General?" said Logan. "Intelligence types aren't exactly the most trusting of individuals, and I see you are with the S.S. now—that makes it even worse."

"You have nothing to fear from us . . . if you have nothing to hide."

"Do you think that tin soldier you have out there would have believed me if I had told him I was a British subject working for the Abwehr?" asked Logan cynically. "They would have laughed me right into Fresnes Prison, and then directly before a firing squad. I figured that by sticking to my French cover, I just might get released. And then I could have continued with my original plan."

"Which is?"

"I was on my way to Berlin—to see you, actually."

"And what brought on this sudden urge for camaraderie?"

"I had to dog it out of England, that's what. MI5 raided my place and just about had a noose around my neck. But luckily I gave them the slip. That was two days ago."

"And so you decided to go to Berlin without contacting us first?"

"What else could I do? They had my wireless, and I gathered from the MI5 blokes who arrested me that Gunther was not long for this world either."

"They've captured Gunther?" Von Graff was truly surprised at this revelation.

"They didn't use names, but he's the only agent connected to me," answered Logan.

"Don't you know an interrogator's trick when you see one?" said von Graff derisively. "They tell you they have one of your comrades, and that he has been talking freely, in hopes that it will loosen your own tongue."

Logan knew the trick well, but he didn't admit that to von Graff. Instead, "Why those blighters!" said Logan, shaking his head in self-recrimination.

"I hope their ploy was unsuccessful."

"I didn't tell them a thing."

"Then continue on with your remarkable story. How did you escape?"

"You don't believe a word I'm saying, do you?"

"Time will tell, Herr MacVey. Go on."

"They let me go, thinking, I suppose, that I would lead them to some higher-ups. They had a couple of clowns on me, but I ditched them within the hour."

"And. . . ?"

"There isn't much more to say. I hired a couple of sympathizers I knew who owned a trawler, and they got me across the Channel to France."

"Where did you get these papers? Excellent forgeries, I might add."

"I still have friends in London from the old days," said Logan. "You know I did a drag in prison a few years back on a counterfeiting charge. I know a chap who has made that racket an art form."

Logan could hardly believe that the answers to von Graff's probing questions kept coming. His mind was growing so numb from fatigue that it felt as if he were running on the last fume of a very empty tank of petrol. Every now and then his eyes would lose their focus and he would have to jerk them back to attention. He tried to appear alert, but it was no use hiding his fatigue from von Graff—the general could see it plainly and was using it to his fullest advantage.

"Why the break in communications before that?" von Graff said quickly, as if hoping the sudden change in tact would catch his victim off guard.

It very nearly did. Logan was about to answer with another madeup alibi when all at once a warning went off in his head. Was it something in the general's tone, or that imperceptible squint which suddenly appeared in his eyes, as if he were watching for the answer Logan might make to this question with even more scrutiny than usual? Something from outside himself nudged him into wakefulness. His head had become so dull that he had nearly fallen into one of the oldest traps in the book—if, indeed, it was a trap. But he had no time to deliberate. He must reply immediately, or von Graff would know he was lying.

"General, really . . ." sighed Logan with a soft chuckle. "That's a rather simpleton's trick for a man of your expertise and intelligence. You know very well that I sent my usual message—that is, unless you're out of touch with the Abwehr these days."

"You seem to have an answer for everything, Herr MacVey."

"That's because there *is* an answer for everything."

"*If* your story is true."

Logan jumped up, took two quick strides to von Graff's desk and slammed his fist angrily on the polished surface.

"If you don't want to believe me, fine!" he shouted. "At this point I don't give a farthing! All I want is a bed and a few minutes sleep—then you can shoot me for all I care. I just wonder if this is how you treat all the agents who give so much for your bloody Reich!"

"It would be much simpler just to radio London," said the general calmly.

"Go ahead—by all means!" replied Logan, irate now. "I don't know why you didn't do that in the first place rather than play all these little games of yours. I just about got myself hung for you—but do I get any thanks? No, instead I'm treated like a bloody snake!"

"I have been sorely amiss, Herr MacVey," said von Graff humbly. "I apologize."

"Oh, cut the bull!" snapped Logan. "I said I was sick of your games."

"Then let me be frank with you." Von Graff's eyes caught Logan's and held them for a tense moment. The true test had come, and Logan knew it. He returned the stare, but it did not last long. Von Graff relaxed and continued. "I believe you," he said. "It would take too much nerve to make up such a tale knowing that every point can and will be verified. Nevertheless, I had to be fully convinced before I could convince my superiors."

"Okay," said Logan contritely. "My outburst may have been uncalled for—I've had a harrowing week, and I'm nearly burnt out."

"I understand," replied von Graff, "and you may consider this interview at an end. I will have Captain Neumann take you to some very comfortable quarters down the hall where you can rest while I make arrangements for a hotel for you."

"What about Berlin?"

"You have found me here. There is hardly any need to continue to Berlin, is there?"

"I suppose not," said Logan, "as long as you've got something for me to do. I don't want to sit out the war in some hotel room."

"That can be arranged. But surely you want some rest and recuperation first. And what better place for that than the City of Lights?"

"I could live with that," said Logan, smiling. "Yes, that sounds just fine."

Neumann was summoned and Logan followed him to another room, which was indeed quite finely appointed, probably serving as temporary quarters for visiting officers and the like. He was given fresh linens, a breakfast tray containing foods most Parisians had not seen in two years, and even a change of clothes. He was suddenly being given the VIP treatment. But he refused to let it go to his head, for when Neumann finally departed, Logan heard the firm turn of the outer lock on the door.

Oh well, he thought. He very nearly *had* come to the point where he no longer cared. All he wanted was some sleep. In a few hours he could face once more all the lies and deceptions. Then he would worry about Gunther's response to von Graff's unbelievable query. Then he would wonder what had become of his planned rendezvous with Louis. And then he could ponder over how he would explain all this to Henri . . . if he got the chance.

But for now, he just stretched out on the delightfully soft bed and fell instantly to sleep.

37 / Speculations _____

Sometimes Arnie Kramer longed for the clear-cut life of the front lines. When two opposing battalions meet and shoot it out, he thought, you know who are the winners and who are the losers. No matter what, you can always tell the enemy. He's the bloke on the other end of your rifle.

But in I-Corps it was never that easy.

Kramer brought his scotch and soda to his lips for another gulp, then glanced over the rim of the glass at his companion. What would Atkinson make of it all? But there was no reading that flinty eye. Arnie would just have to spell it all out and then wait for his measured, soft-spoken response. He hoped he wouldn't be too slow about it. Time was precious, and Kramer had already wasted an hour driving to the airbase and Atkinson's office.

"It was rather a giant mess to trust to the telephone," replied Kramer, taking another swallow of his drink.

"Just begin at the beginning, and give it to me," said Atkinson. "Don't leave anything out."

Kramer studied his drink a few moments more, deep in thought. Then he began.

"I've got an agent, a double, named Gunther. Some months ago his Abwehr contacts required him to expand his network and introduce them to one of his sub-agents. We set up an imaginary agent, code name Trinity, and dug up a bloke to present to the Jerrys. I opted to bring in new blood for the operation because at the time we weren't sure of Gunther's loyalty and I didn't want to risk one of our own boys. The meet came off a bit too successfully. The Abwehr was so impressed with our Trinity that they sent him off with his own wireless and a questionnaire. We've been operating the Trinity cover ever since."

"And?"

"Well," continued Kramer hesitantly. He liked Atkinson and knew he was a good man, but his reputation for ruthless perfectionism was daunting. Kramer did not like admitting a blunder to him.

He drained off the last of his drink and resumed with a deep sigh. "The fellow we brought in was good. He played the Trinity game for a while, fed the Germans some good bogus info. But I figured there was no reason for him not to go on to bigger and better things. Then, too, it became known that he could speak fluent French. Immediately the French section wanted him, and I saw no reason to keep him. Besides, I knew he wanted more action. So I had HQ bring in someone else to cover Trinity's wireless."

"What became of Trinity?"

"Well, Ray, that's the problem."

Kramer chuckled dryly, but he knew his attempt at humor wouldn't help. Major Atkinson leaned back in his chair, staring down at Arnie with fire in his eye.

"Are you trying to tell me I've got a man in occupied territory with an MI5 skeleton in his closet?" seethed Atkinson. His own code name was Mother Hen, and not without good reason. Protecting his agents was everything to the major, and seeing any of them in trouble tore him apart. And when something came up that he thought he should have known about, he made no attempt to disguise his anger.

Kramer nodded reluctantly. "And the closet door has just been thrown open."

"Talk plainly, Arnie," said Atkinson in a controlled tone despite his distress. "Who is Trinity? And how in the blazes could you have kept me blind about this?"

"Trinity was a gold mine for us," answered Kramer. "It just did not seem possible that there could ever be a conflict between the two operations."

"What if the Abwehr wanted to meet with your Trinity?"

"We'd stall them. If that wasn't possible, then we'd have Trinity imaginarily arrested by MI5, thus taking him out of commission as far as the Abwehr was concerned."

"What about my first question? Who is Trinity?"

"Logan Macintyre."

"Good Lord!" breathed Atkinson. "What kind of danger is he in?"

"That's one of the many things I'm not sure of."

Kramer took a folded paper from his coat pocket. "Gunther got this about three hours ago." He handed it over to Atkinson.

The major read the decoded words incredulously:

TRINITY ARRIVED SAFELY FRANCE STOP VERIFY CIRCUM-
STANCES RE DEPARTURE ENGLAND STOP IS YOUR PRESENT
STATUS SECURE END

"What did your agent Gunther do?" asked Atkinson.

"He feigned bad reception, which luckily with this blustery weather we've been having was perfectly believable. He told them to contact him later. They arranged to radio back in twenty-four hours. That's tomorrow evening."

"So they bought it?"

"I hope so."

"What do you propose to do now?" asked Atkinson.

"Before I make that decision, I'd like to know just what Trinity, that is, Macintyre, is up to. I don't want Gunther to give them any information that would compromise him." Kramer glanced down at his empty glass, wondering if Atkinson would break out the bottle again. "Have you been in regular contact with him? Have there been any irregularities?"

"Our most recent communication was last night as per schedule. But it was cut off prematurely."

"Then it's possible the Nazi's may have picked him up?"

"Anything is possible in the underground," said Atkinson. "We haven't heard a thing since then. To tell you the truth, I've been concerned."

"If they did pick him up," mused Kramer, "isn't it possible he invoked the Trinity cover for protection?"

"He'd never get away with it if he were caught red-handed operating a wireless." Atkinson paused, sipping his own drink, though with more disinterest than his companion. "Perhaps someone else has assumed the Trinity identity," he said at length.

"Impossible," stated Kramer firmly. "Gunther and Macintyre and I are the only ones who know about it. And Cartwright, of course, my new Trinity. No, it's got to be Macintyre himself. And I'd like to know why."

"What are you implying, Arnie?"

"Don't get me wrong, I like him. He and I were old friends. That's why I pulled him into this business in the first place. But the Germans can turn our boys just as easily as we can theirs." Though he said nothing, Kramer was thinking of his conversation with Gunther in which the German told him of his brief meeting with Logan's wife. He didn't like it. Wives only muddied an agent's existence. And he couldn't help wondering if there wasn't more to the Macintyre woman's tracking of Gunther than met the eye.

"Macintyre turned! I don't believe that for a minute." The major was incensed at the very thought. "I may have had doubts about Macintyre at first. And I wasn't even particularly nice to him. But I never doubted his loyalty. Besides, he's proved himself. The charge doesn't fit with facts. He's been in Paris four months, yet the Germans think he's only just arrived. And regardless of all that, what advantage would it be to the Germans to use the Trinity cover in this way? It just doesn't fit."

"All right," conceded Kramer. "But say he was arrested last night, and assume further that he broke under torture. What if he made promises to the Germans, compromising Gunther in the process? Their radio message could just be part of some cunning ploy."

Atkinson opened his desk drawer, took out the bottle of Scotch, and walked around to Kramer's chair and refilled his glass.

"Steady, old boy," he said, setting the bottle down and leaning on the edge of his desk. "I think you're getting a bit gun-shy about this whole business. Intrigue's the name of the game—we just have to outwit the

Nazis on this one—for Macintyre's sake."

Kramer gulped his drink. "Something's going on over there, and I don't know anything about it and *you* don't know anything about it. Doesn't that make you a bit nervous, Ray?"

Atkinson did not answer immediately. Instead, he shuffled through a stack of papers on his desk, finally removing one and handing it over to Kramer.

"Look at this, Arnie," he said. "It's a recommendation for the George Cross for Macintyre."

Kramer's thick eyebrows arched in surprise and his mouth fell open.

"It's all 'most secret' right now—the details of his activities," Atkinson went on, "but you read these reports and *then* tell me you suspect him of disloyalty or even breaking. The guy has become one of the underground's key operatives, the hub of dozens of activities. Something's going on in Paris, of that you are right. And we better give Macintyre all the support we can."

"Well," said Kramer, surprised at such high praise coming from a man like Atkinson, and yet not a little proud of his protege, as he considered Logan, "at the very least it was foolhardy of him to fall back on the Trinity cover after four months' separation."

Atkinson gave a short dry chuckle. "Now *that* does sound like Macintyre!"

"So what do you suggest we do now," asked Kramer, "in order to give him that support you are talking about?" He was quite willing to dump the decision into Atkinson's lap.

"When the Abwehr contacts Gunther," said the major without hesitation, "have him verify Macintyre's story."

"But we have no idea what his story is!"

"Yeah, you're right." Atkinson paused and thought for a moment before continuing. "Then you and I are just going to have to get inside his skin and figure out what alibi he would have given the Germans," he went on. "They must have been convinced, whatever he told them, or they wouldn't have wired Gunther. I would say if he was picked up, it was probably for something completely unrelated to his espionage activities. He's too careful to get caught in the middle of a wireless operation."

"Like picking a pocket or cheating at cards," quipped Kramer.

"Whatever . . . But afterward something must have gone sour and he saw the resurrection of his old Trinity identity as a way to cover his tracks."

"Actually," said Kramer, a sly gleam creeping into his eyes, "if we could pull this off, it could prove quite to our advantage. What a boon to have an inside man in Paris!"

"You're a crass opportunist," grunted Atkinson with disgust. "You'd be asking him to walk a dangerous tightrope. *If* we can clear him with the Germans, I want him pulled out of France at the first opportunity."

"Sure, Ray, sure."

But as he said the words, Kramer's tone was not at all convincing. The gleam was still in his eye. *I knew Logan was made for this business when I brought him in*, he thought to himself.

38 / An Elite Soirée_____

Logan was reading his third back issue of *The Signal*, France's collaborationist magazine. It was revolting fare, but since he was forced to play the part of a Nazi, it could do no harm to keep abreast of the latest propaganda.

Neumann had provided the reading material to keep Logan amused during his enforced stay at S.S. headquarters. Technically, so he was told, Logan was not a prisoner. But the room remained faithfully locked nevertheless. He had not laid eyes on von Graff since they had parted late yesterday morning. He did not know if Gunther had been contacted, but he assumed that since his status had not changed, he must still be in limbo. There was a good chance they had not been able to reach him yet, but if they had, he hoped Gunther was quick on his feet.

It was only a matter of time before the jig was up, however, if he didn't succeed in getting word to somebody on the outside. But how could he get a message to Henri? By now they probably assumed him captured and would have already begun to break up the network. The rule for a captured agent was to make every effort to give his comrades forty-eight hours to disband before breaking down. It had now been well over thirty. But even if *La Librairie* still were intact, how could he get word to them from this prison?

The real question, however, echoed in Logan's mind: Will Gunther have enough wits about him to give me the kind of support I need? Gunther had never respected Logan or been friendly toward him. But just good sense ought to tell him that more was at stake than Logan's life. In the Abwehr's eyes, Gunther was Logan's mentor. If Logan became discredited, Gunther could be blown as well.

The uncertain waiting was hardest of all to bear. If only he could be sure of his status so he would know how to play himself. Then he might formulate some plans. If he was blown, then he ought to be thinking about an escape. If by some miracle they *had* bought his story, he should be thinking more definitely how to use it to his advantage.

What wouldn't he be able to do for the Resistance effort from inside the S.S.! He grinned to himself. What a coup that would be!

Absently his eyes turned to the magazine lying in his lap. Suddenly the grin on his face faded. There on the page was a grotesque drawing of a hideous ghoul digging his fingernails into the world globe. Underneath read the caption, "Le Juif et la France." The accompanying article raved about evil Jewish global intentions, accusing the Jews of having started the war, and rallying the French people to take strong and determined action against this dangerous threat.

Logan's mind turned to the honorable Poletski. He had brought with him reports of dire atrocities committed against Polish Jews by the Germans. Thousands had disappeared without a trace. He had used a term unfamiliar to Logan, and to all civilized men—death camps. The idea was inconceivable to Logan. Surely Poletski is an alarmist, he thought at first. Yet how could a man exaggerate unless he had seen something with his own eyes to start the tale growing?

Logan shook his head. The article and the thought of Poletski reminded him what a deadly business this was. Too often he tended to think of it as a mere lark. He was glad for the sobering look at the article.

"Lord," he prayed, not caring that he hadn't offered a prayer in months, "let me make it through this. Let me have this victory. I'll do anything just to be allowed one more crack at helping to defeat these evil Nazis!"

At that moment a knock on the door interrupted him.

When Captain Neumann entered, he made no mention of communication with London. Logan could hardly ask, thus risking the appearance of being too anxious. Yet by Neumann's polite demeanor, it seemed that his cover was probably still holding up. And he also might have read a positive message in Neumann's greeting.

"Heil Hitler!" said the captain with the customary salute.

Caught off guard, Logan gaped silently for a moment until it dawned on him that he was meant to return the blasphemous greeting. Cringing inside, he forced out the words.

"Heil Hitler," he said with nominal enthusiasm, raising his arm partially in salute. He pretended to have just been awakened from a brief nap, and Neumann appeared satisfied.

Neumann addressed Logan in French, either because he knew no English or von Graff had not informed him of the "guest's" true nationality.

"The general," began Neumann, "wishes you to accompany him to a function this evening."

"A function?"

"Yes. A birthday party for a local personage." Neumann held out his arm, over which were draped several items of clothing. "The general sent this evening attire for you to wear." He laid the items over the back of a chair. "He hopes the fit is correct."

"I'm sure it will be," said Logan, strolling to the chair and fingering the fine fabric.

"I will return for you in an hour, then."

Logan nodded.

Neumann departed, locking the door obediently behind him. Logan went to the adjoining bathroom to wash, then changed into the black tuxedo.

As he stood before the mirror combing his hair, Logan was suddenly reminded of another tuxedo he had worn many years ago. At first it seemed completely incongruous that such a memory should assail him at this particular moment. But he had been playing a part then too—until the drive home, that is.

Coming home from the party in the rain that morning had been magical. He and Allison had muddied themselves in the rain and rising floodwaters, and in the process had become friends and put their incessant feuding behind them. At that moment he had seen beyond her hard veneer and had glimpsed instead into the heart of a vibrant, loving young woman. He had come to discover both vulnerability and tenderness there, and had determined to know more of that side of Allison MacNeil. Now, so far removed from everything but such sweet memories, it seemed inconceivable that they could be separated by such vast distances, distances not measured only in miles. Where had they gone wrong? What, or who, was to blame? Was it really over between them?

That morning in the pouring rain everything had seemed so right. If only they could go back.

But here he was stuck in Nazi headquarters, so up to his neck in deceit that he wondered if there would ever be a way out. With every twist he only got in deeper. What would Allison think of him going to a Nazi birthday party! Her doubts and misgivings about him certainly appeared well-founded now. No matter how much he told himself that his actions were justifiably necessary in order to counter the evil of the enemy, there were times when he could begin to understand her confusion. He got confused at times himself. What worried him most was that he did this kind of thing so well. He was, he had to admit, a born con man. He enjoyed it! Yes, he had winced at the "Heil Hitler." But he had done it, and convincingly. And tonight he would attend the party and be the best Nazi there!

Why? Because his life depended on it. But there was more to it than that, and he knew it. And there was more to it than his revulsion toward the Nazis. He would play out the charade with his best flair and style because it was a challenge. Even if this double life was confusing with all its gray areas, he still had to admit that he loved the *challenge*.

That's what he had been searching for all those years in London. That's what Allison had never been able to understand. And the real irony was that probably on that rainy day in Scotland ten years ago, Allison had been a kind of challenge too.

How about that, Allison? he thought. *Maybe you're right about me. What a chump I really am. I suppose I deserve all this Nazi company!*

By the time Neumann arrived for him, Logan was ready to throw himself into this latest ruse. He did not let his thoughts probe any deeper into his motives for now. Whether self-serving or noble, what did it matter now, anyway? He had no choice but to go through with it.

Logan was driven to a stately townhouse a few miles outside Paris in the fashionable suburb of Neuilly. The moment he entered the villa, he was immediately struck with the display of wealth all about him, a stark contrast to his four months among the deprivation and poverty of wartime Paris. What he saw could best be described as a spectacle, a grand effort to prove that "gay Paree" had survived the coming of the new regime. All the men were in full black-tie dress—no frayed and mended old models, but perfectly new and stylish suits and tuxedos. The German soldiers present were in their finest dress uniforms, the officers loaded down with decorations from this and the last war. The women were outfitted in the latest Paris fashions, bedecked with mink and jewels. The effect was dazzling, combined as it was with the light from three huge crystal chandeliers.

What drew Logan's eyes most, however, was the long refreshment table laid out with platters of roast pheasant, duck, and beef and finished off with bowls of caviar and dozens of other rich dishes—all complemented with the finest French champagne. And to think his friends in some of the poorest sections of Paris were living on bread and cheese and turnips!

"I trust you are well rested," said General von Graff, walking up suddenly behind him and greeting him.

"Very," replied Logan, "enforced though it was."

"Please, I hope you are not one to hold grudges." Von Graff paused to respond to the friendly greeting of a passerby. "Let this evening be as a way of a peace offering."

"I must say, you Germans know how to throw a soirée."

Von Graff laughed dryly as if Logan's statement had been intended as a joke. "Your host actually is a Frenchman, and the guest of honor also—Baron de Beauvoir."

Logan restrained a reaction to the name de Beauvoir. He knew it must be Jean Pierre's brother. But before he had time to think through the implications further, von Graff spoke up again.

"I shall introduce you if you wish. However, for the present I would like to keep your British origins under wraps."

"I should think it would be quite a feat for you to introduce a British convert to your friends."

"Perhaps; but if you'll indulge me this evening," said the general, adding cryptically, "It may be more advantageous to keep it quiet for now."

"Whatever you say."

"Apparently your French is quite good. So I thought I would say you are a merchant from Casablanca, Monsieur Dansette."

Logan nodded his consent, though inwardly balking at yet another identity to keep straight.

They approached a small knot of people and von Graff introduced

Logan. Common pleasantries were exchanged and soon the conversation turned into the inevitable current of war news. But Logan's attention had wandered, finally arrested by a familiar face across the room. The man at whom he found himself staring stood holding a glass of champagne and engaged in animated conversation with a uniformed German and two ladies. Except for his clerical garb, he seemed quite in keeping with the events of the evening and perfectly comfortable with this upper-class crowd. With his tall, graceful form and handsome, distinguished features, Logan could easily see him as he once must have been—the society playboy. Logan wondered what had happened to lead him into the priesthood. But his musings were suddenly interrupted.

"I see you have noticed our resident cleric," said von Graff with a cynical edge to his voice.

Logan hadn't realized he had been staring so intently nor that it had been noticeable, something he would have wished to avoid. He jerked his eyes away, berating himself for his carelessness, but making the most of his indiscretion.

"Yes," he replied. "He's rather out of place here, isn't he?"

"He is, but not because of his collar or cassock."

"How cryptic of you, General," chuckled Logan. "Why, my imagination soars with the possibilities inherent in such a statement."

"The good priest is a member of the Resistance," elaborated von Graff. However, he did not join in Logan's amusement.

"You must be jesting!" exclaimed Logan, appearing genuinely surprised with such a far-fetched statement.

"But it is true."

"Why isn't he in chains?" asked Logan. "Or do you make it a policy to invite the Resistance to your soirées?"

"It is only a matter of time before Monsignor de Beauvoir will have his prison quarters."

"De Beauvoir?"

"He is our host's brother."

"Ah . . . I see," said Logan, nodding his head. "How intriguing. Blue blood blinds the Nazis to a man's affiliations."

"Nothing of the sort!" snapped von Graff. "I'd put him in irons this instant if I could get some concrete evidence against him. He's a thorn in our flesh. And look at him! He shows up at these gatherings as if to flaunt his impervious position, and no doubt to gather what intelligence he can for his Resistance friends."

"A crafty devil . . . for a holy man," said Logan admiringly.

"Even Satan fell from grace," replied von Graff caustically, "as will this priest—sooner or later."

Logan couldn't help thinking of the old Genesis dodge he and Skittles used to run in London, and wondering how the scheme might go off in a setting like this. But to von Graff he said, "What about his brother, the baron? Is he also a patriot?"

"Baron de Beauvoir is much too pragmatic for such folly—he's making far too much money off the Germans to be able to afford patriotism. But regardless, he'd not wish to see his brother shot, if he could help it—which, believe me, he can."

"Well, General, I'm thoroughly absorbed. Could you manage an introduction?"

"Of course."

As they approached, Logan was the only one who noticed the brief flicker of consternation that passed across the priest's face when he saw him at von Graff's side. But he betrayed no other indication of his surprise at seeing his former colleague in these surroundings.

"Enchanté, Monsieur Dansette," he said graciously, extending his slim cultured hand to Logan. "How is Casablanca these days? It has been years since I was there."

"Dirty and crowded as always," replied Logan. "Paris is a refreshing breath of air by comparison."

"Yes, even despite our Teutonic guests."

Von Graff rankled at the slur, but Logan only smiled.

"You are bold, Monsignor," said Logan.

"Priests and old men can get away with anything," laughed Jean Pierre.

"But not for long, de Beauvoir," seethed von Graff. "Not for long . . ."

"Oh, General," countered the priest good-naturedly, "I hope your contact with the French will, if nothing else, serve to improve the dour German sense of humor. Or should I say *lack* of it?" He paused, took a breath, and began again in a new vein. "And your manners, too. Look, poor Monsieur Dansette, a guest to our country and to my brother's home, and he does not even have a glass of champagne in his hand. Nor, I suppose," he added, turning toward Logan, "have you partaken of the fine table my brother sets?"

"As a matter of fact I have not," replied Logan, more interested, however, in what might be in store for him at this gathering other than food. "I did only just arrive, though," he added.

"Then come along, let me be your guide."

"You need not trouble yourself, Monsignor," put in von Graff. "I will see to Monsieur Dansette's comfort."

"I insist," said Jean Pierre, taking Logan's arm. "I'm sure it has been a long enough time since Monsieur Dansette has been treated to true Parisian hospitality."

He whisked Logan away, keeping up a stream of trivial chatter until they reached the table. There was no one close by, but as he spoke he retained the light, social timber to his voice, though lowering its volume, smiling and chuckling at appropriate intervals. Logan responded in kind, as if they were still talking about the weather or the food.

"You don't know how glad I am to find you here," said Logan.

"Nor you, how *surprised* I am to find you," replied Jean Pierre. "We thought you had been arrested, and here I find you on the arm of an S.S. officer, a general no less—and looking well and fit, I might add."

"I *was* arrested," said Logan, defensiveness creeping into his disguised tone. Despite Jean Pierre's social tone, he could sense the accusation in his words.

"The Nazis have changed their style, then."

"How do you mean?"

"Wining and dining their prisoners."

"It's a long story and there is not time for it now—"

At that moment a couple strolled up to the priest's elbow.

"You must try the paté," said the priest to Logan, slicing off a slab and laying it on the plate Logan had picked up. "It's delightful. My brother employs the finest culinary staff in Europe."

"You are most kind," exaggerated Logan.

"But stay away from the caviar," rejoined Jean Pierre. "All the skill in the world cannot disguise the fact that it's not Russian. Alas, for the ravages of war!"

As the couple moved away, Logan took up the previous conversation where it had been interrupted.

"You must get a message to London for me," he said.

"How can you ask such a thing?"

"What do you mean?"

"What am I to think?" said the priest, a sadness suddenly entering his voice. "You are quite friendly with the Nazis—even a magician could not have performed such a feat in such a short time. You have had previous association with them, that is obvious. Perhaps even in the last four months."

"Jean Pierre!" Logan's voice rose dangerously. He had to clench his teeth to keep it under control. He paused until he could respond without drawing attention to himself. "You must believe me! You've *got* to send that message. I'm a dead man if you don't."

But the conversation progressed no further, for at that moment von Graff rejoined them.

"Ah," he said, "I had no idea a trip to the refreshment table could be so lengthy."

There was something odd in his tone. Did he suspect, or was it simply his natural distrust of anything out of the ordinary?

"I'm afraid," Jean Pierre answered casually, "that I have monopolized Monsieur Dansette's time with a discussion on the merits of Russian caviar over other continental varieties."

"I had no idea you were a gourmet, Monsignor," said von Graff.

"Oh, I have many talents," answered Jean Pierre airily. "But I try to keep most of them hidden."

"So I've heard."

"In fact, I was just trying to persuade our guest from Casablanca to join me at the rectory tomorrow for a truly excellent meal. Even the Pope has marveled at my delectable crepes."

"Of course I told him that would be impossible," said Logan, "under the *constraints* of my present circumstances."

"You must not be such a slave driver, General," prompted Jean Pierre.

But von Graff's attention strayed momentarily as his aide approached, appearing rather flustered.

"General, these just arrived," he said, holding out two slips of paper. "I did not think you'd want them to wait."

Logan surmised his charade was about to come to an abrupt end. He glanced about for an escape exit, even though as he did so, he realized the futility of such an effort.

In the meantime von Graff had perused the messages, and as he finished the last his color paled noticeably, though he was quick to resume his military facade.

"Bad news?" queried Jean Pierre.

"No," he replied coolly, "only rather shocking. Japan has just bombed Pearl Harbor in the Hawaiian Islands. It seems that America will now enter the war."

"Is that inevitable?" asked Logan.

"It is inevitable that America will declare war on Japan. Probably she has already done so," answered von Graff. "I have little doubt that the Führer will honor the Reich's treaty with Japan and declare war in turn on the United States."

"Mon Dieu!" breathed the priest.

"Germany has gained a formidable ally."

"Formidable enough to stand against the might of America?" countered Jean Pierre.

"Japan has not been defeated for three thousand years," replied the general, "so why not?" However, his tone lacked essential conviction, and his initial response to the telegram indicated deeper doubts. If he did not sense then, he soon would know that America's entry into the war must mean Germany's ultimate defeat.

Logan had been so absorbed in this recent development that he had nearly forgotten his own plight. But von Graff's next words brought it immediately back to mind. The ending to Logan's speculations came on a much more positive note than he had anticipated.

"By the way, Monsieur," he said to Logan, "I am going to instruct my aide to have Neumann secure a hotel room for you. He can drive you there tonight if you wish.''

''Thank you, General,'' Logan replied calmly, as if he had expected nothing else.

Yet, all the while he was shouting with exuberance inside, he knew this news was a mixed victory. He would still be under their thumb, and no doubt under surveillance, too. Had he really been set free, or had his trap only been enlarged?

39 / Luncheon at the Rectory _____

Logan jerked up in his bed, drenched with perspiration. He swung his feet out of bed, then sat there on the edge with his head resting in his trembling hands, trying to catch his breath.

It had only been a nightmare . . . nothing but a dream. But he couldn't help feeling foolish for the fright it gave him.

It had been so real! He was still breathing hard, like the man running through the city streets. He hadn't had a dream like that since he was a child.

Glancing at the bedside clock he saw it was seven a.m. He stood, walked slowly to the window, and pulled open the blackout shade. No wonder it seemed so much earlier than seven. Outside the sky was dark and brooding. The clouds were heavy laden with winter storms, and the icy blasts they held were almost palpable, even as Logan stood there in his warm hotel room.

Wakefulness gradually coming to him, he threw on the bathrobe von Graff had provided him, then called down to the front desk and asked for a pot of coffee to be brought up. The activity helped to steady him, and before long he nearly succeeded in forgetting about the unsettling interruption to his sleep.

In a few minutes the waiter came with the coffee. For the first time since arriving late last night, Logan began to consider his surroundings. The waiter, dressed in a trim hotel uniform, pushed a cart covered in white linen bearing a silver coffee service, fine china, and a silver vase containing a red rose bud. This was no cheap hotel, Logan thought to himself. He had pulled scams in places like this, but never stayed in one! The waiter bowed politely, and when Logan attempted to give him a tip, he shook his head.

"Ne vous dérangez pas," he said. "It is already taken care of."

Logan raised his eyebrows in astonishment. "Merci," he replied as the fellow left.

Logan had figured von Graff knew how to live. But this was too much. He poured out a cup of the steaming brew and unconsciously raised it to his lips for a sip.

The first taste nearly choked him. It was the real thing! He had not tasted coffee like this in months!

He sat down and gazed about him. The windows were covered with velvet drapes, the floor with a thick Persian carpet. He sat on a satin-covered

Chippendale chair. It had been so late when he came in last night that he had been too tired to notice. But now he could see that von Graff had spared nothing for his British double agent. What was that insidious Nazi up to, anyway?

Logan finished his coffee. No sense letting it go to waste. He poured himself another cup.

For the moment von Graff was the least of his problems. He still had to get in touch with London, and it seemed that his only avenue, Jean Pierre, had suddenly grown hostile toward him, or at least suspicious. Though he had good reason. After von Graff had intervened last night at the refreshment table, they never had another moment alone. Had Logan's final plea softened the priest's reticence?

There was no way of knowing. But if Jean Pierre did not believe him, and succeeded in turning the rest of *La Librairie* against him, and Logan tried to make contact with them, he could be in as much danger there as in S.S. headquarters.

What wouldn't Claude give for a chance to slit his throat as a traitor!

If he could just see Lise . . .

But immediately he shook that idea from his head. If von Graff had him under surveillance, it would be tricky trying to explain everything to her.

There had to be another way.

What an irony, he thought. He had only been superficially trained in this business, got into it almost by accident through Arnie. Now here he was in the classic jam of a spy—caught in no man's land. Mistrusted by both sides, either of which would kill him in a second if they broke his cover. Caught in a foreign land with no friend to trust him. These past four months he'd been arranging escapes for refugees. But now that he was caught in the middle, he himself had no safe house to go to.

He sipped at the coffee, and in his mind went over every detail he could recall of the last few days, trying to find an angle. What would von Graff be looking for? How would he have to change his habit patterns to keep from looking the least bit suspicious? If he chanced to see anyone he knew, he'd have to be especially on his guard. And what had Gunther told von Graff anyway?

The scenes from de Beauvoir's birthday party marched through his mind. His talk with Jean Pierre—all at once he saw it!

Jean Pierre had given him his escape route! He tried to recall his words verbatim:

". . . I was just trying to persuade our guest from Casablanca to join me in the rectory tomorrow for a truly excellent meal . . ."

That was it! Just what he was looking for. The only thing he could be accused of was accepting the kind invitation of this fascinating priest.

He instantly jumped up, forgetting all about the coffee, and prepared to dress and set out immediately.

But what was he thinking? It was still early morning. No time had been specified. How early did he dare call? He paced the room several times, trying to work it out in his mind, considering all the consequences of various actions. Finally he paused by the phone. He'd have to risk it. Calling would be easier to explain than showing up at an empty rectory.

The velo-taxi dropped Logan at the rectory door. As he walked up to the ancient oak door, he saw a black Renault sedan pull up across the street. It had followed him, none too discreetly, from the hotel. But he had covered his bases. There was nothing to worry about.

Jean Pierre welcomed him warmly. Logan found himself wondering if the priest had had a change of heart, or if the greeting was only for the benefit of the housekeeper who had led Logan to the drawing room. When she departed, the priest remained congenial, though his mood was tempered with more solemnity than was customary in the usually debonair cleric.

"I hoped you would catch my subtle cue," he said as he directed Logan to a chair, while he himself took an adjacent one.

"To be honest," replied Logan, "I didn't at first. I wondered if I'd ever see you again after our conversation last night."

"It would not have been fair of me to pass judgment under those circumstances—at least not without a full hearing of your story. I make no guarantees, however, other than listening to what you have to tell me."

"Thank you for that much," said Logan, "though I still don't know what I can say to convince you of my loyalty."

"Perhaps you ought to tell me everything from the beginning," suggested the priest.

Logan began with his MI5 work in London and proceeded to do exactly that, from his first meeting with Gunther to his ill timed encounter with von Graff after his arrest two days ago. When he was through, Jean Pierre rubbed his chin for several minutes before saying anything in reply. At length he rose and walked slowly to the window.

"I see you did not come alone," he said.

"That couldn't be helped," answered Logan. "Von Graff wouldn't trust his own mother. At least I'm out of that place. But there should be nothing incriminating about me coming here today."

"Incriminating, no . . . but you can believe von Graff will be suspicious."

"I'll just tell him I couldn't resist the thought of getting something on an underground priest."

"Just don't play it too cocky, my friend. Von Graff is nobody's fool."

"I have discovered that."

Jean Pierre continued to stare absently outside. "Look over there," he said after a moment. Logan joined him at the window. The priest cocked his head toward the corner opposite that at which the black sedan was parked. A man who would have been husky even without his thick layers of winter clothing leaned against a lamppost, puffing on a cheroot. "There's *my* shadow," he said with a coy grin.

"They have someone on you all the time?"

"In a manner of speaking," replied Jean Pierre. "They are easily gotten rid of, however, and I give them the slip whenever their presence would be . . . cumbersome."

He chuckled softly. "The Gestapo is not unlike a charging rhinoceros. Very dangerous to be sure, but not altogether smart. However, they might be smart enough to find out whether we in fact did have our meal here today, so perhaps we ought to retire to the kitchen for the sake of our cover."

"Of course," agreed Logan. But as they walked together down a corridor toward the back of the rectory, he added in a graver tone, "You may be right about the rhinoceros analogy. But don't underestimate them, Jean Pierre. They're not altogether stupid. That is exactly what they would like us to think."

The priest ushered Logan into the kitchen, where they found the housekeeper busily engaged in the process of brewing coffee for the priest and his guest.

"Ah, Madame Borrel," said Jean Pierre, "that is so kind of you. But I have promised my guest that I would prepare him one of my specialties."

"Oui, mon Père," replied the housekeeper. "But if you are planning to make crepes, we have but one egg. You're likely to end up with pancakes instead."

"We'll have to make do," said Jean Pierre. "Now, if you would like to take the morning off, I see no reason why you shouldn't."

"Merci, mon Père," Mme. Borrel answered enthusiastically, scurrying off and leaving the two men alone.

"She is a fine lady," said Jean Pierre, "and completely loyal. But it is best we take no chances." As he spoke, he took out bowls, utensils, and all the necessary ingredients, and immediately began pouring and mixing.

"You amaze me, Jean Pierre," said Logan at length.

"Anyone can make crepes."

"That's not what I meant. The way you've handled yourself—last night, and today . . . I find it remarkable."

"Because I am a priest?"

"Yes, I suppose so. All the deception and cover and evasion tactics. You couldn't have learned to be so proficient at this double life in the seminary."

"Here, take this and oil it thoroughly," said the priest, handing Logan a heavy griddle. As Logan fell to his task, Jean Pierre continued.

"No, none of what I do was learned there, believe me," he said. "Nor did I acquire it in my days before conversion in a life of crime." He paused while he cracked the single precious egg into one of the bowls. "It's a matter, I suppose, of doing what must be done."

"Why do you do it at all?" asked Logan. "It does not follow that it must be done by you. In your position, no one would blame you for staying out of the whole thing."

"Yes, I could have." His attention was momentarily diverted to the task of properly beating his egg, but Logan wondered by the intense look in Jean Pierre's eyes if he wasn't using the diversion to consider the many ramifications to his position. He hoped he wasn't trying to think of some elusive response because he still didn't trust Logan. When he finally spoke again, it was in a thoughtful tone. "Thomas Jefferson once said, 'Resistance to tyrants is obedience to God.' I have often thought about that since the war began. It is a weighty idea."

"I have never thought of it in quite those terms," said Logan. "I suppose if I was really put to it, I would have to admit that right now, with what I am doing, the last thing I feel is obedient to God."

"You doubt the morality of our methods?"

"I try not to, but sometimes I find myself doubting them. Yet it's more a personal reaction I'm speaking of than a response to our methods. Inside me, things are a little insecure."

"War brings insecurity to us all."

"Helping people escape is one thing. Being involved with killers is another. I just don't know what's right."

"The morals of the Resistance, then, are important considerations for you."

"Several years ago I tried to dedicate my life to God. Not in the way you have, I suppose—but I was sincere. I truly wanted to change. Yes, it was very important to me."

He paused and shook his head. "I don't know what happened."

"The war, Michel—it changes us . . . it changes everything."

"That may be true. But whatever it was with me happened long before the war ever came along."

Logan turned and looked intently at Jean Pierre. "Yet now I'm afraid that what has happened to me since the war began will make those changes irreversible, that somehow I will never be able to go back." He stopped and tried to assume a lighter attitude. "I'm sorry for burdening you with all this. I don't know what possessed me."

Jean Pierre tapped a floury finger against his stiff white collar. "This sometimes has a way of loosening a man's tongue. Perhaps the Gestapo ought to get rid of their whips and employ a few more priests in their interrogation rooms."

Jean Pierre began to spoon his batter onto the hot griddle while Logan watched in silence. At length he began to speak again. He did not know Jean Pierre in depth, but all at once he knew he had to talk to someone. It was perhaps more than underground business that had drawn him to seek the priest out that morning.

"Last night I had a dream," he began slowly. "Actually it was more like a nightmare. I awoke in a dreadful fright."

"Do you want to tell me about it?" Jean Pierre asked as he took two crocks of jam from a cupboard and handed them to Logan. Then he walked with the plate of crepes over to the kitchen table.

"I think I had better tell someone," sighed Logan, taking a chair and facing the priest. He had been so successful in ignoring his internal struggles that he had only at this moment realized how terribly oppressive they had become. The dream had brought it all out into the light and he could no longer push it from his mind. So as Jean Pierre dished up the crepes, Logan launched into an account of his disturbing night.

"It was rather simple, actually," Logan began, then took a thoughtful sip of the coffee his host had just poured, followed by a bite into the delicious crepe. He nodded his approval across the table. "Simple, but a little spooky too. It was too real and too bizarre all at once. I was running— at least a man was running who was meant to be me, though he bore no resemblance to me. I watched as if I were part of the audience at the cinema. But the appearance of the man changed, depending on who was chasing him. But there was always someone at his heels—von Graff was there, Gunther, Arnie, Henri, you for a moment, and even my father! That was probably the strangest part of the dream. My father died when I was ten. Before that he was in jail most of the time. I hardly knew him. I haven't thought of him more than a half-dozen times since then, and certainly not lately. And here he pops up in my dreams. I suppose Freud would have a heyday with that!

"Anyway, these people kept chasing me. Or at least they kept chasing the apparition that was supposed to be me. I was running. It wasn't like those childhood nightmares where you are terrified because you can't go any faster than a crawl. The skies were dark. I assume it was night. And we ran through city streets, narrow and close. The buildings were grimy stone and brick, like the sooty ones back in Glasgow. I was so tired. I wanted desperately to stop, but I knew I couldn't. So I just kept going. The darkness and bleakness was oppressive. I thought I would die if it kept going like that without a change.

"Suddenly my running legs broke out into the clean air. Now it *was* me that was running, but I felt light and free. The oppression of the dark city was gone. The air was clean and refreshing, the sun warm and bright. I was running on soft, pure, white sand, with a sparkling ocean immediately to my right. It was just like the grand beach of home—"

Without even realizing he had done so, Logan had used the unlikely word to describe Port Strathy, a place he hadn't felt at home in for some time. But he went right on.

"I knew I was saved at last. But for some reason I couldn't stop running. The sand stretched out forever in front of me. Soon a woman came running onto the beach from the side and she too began to chase me. All the men from the city had left the dream with the coming of the sunlight and the beach. She began to call my name. She called and called.

"Suddenly the voice broke through into my consciousness—it was Allison, my wife. I was so glad to hear her voice! But still I didn't stop. I couldn't stop. When she at last caught up to me, she took my arm and finally I stopped. But when I spun around to face her, I disappeared.

"Again I was watching the dream from the outside, rather than playing the part in it. I could see my body fade away, and my clothes fell like limp empty rags at her feet. I started to leave the dream world and drift back into consciousness. But before I did I saw Allison's face, this time close up. Huge tears were falling from her eyes as she sank down on her knees and wept over the clothes lying in the sand.

"Then I woke up."

Logan chuckled nervously. "Pretty loony, isn't it?" he said, suddenly feeling foolish again over the whole thing.

"Dreams are the only way a sane man can express his insanity," observed Jean Pierre. "Considering the kind of life you have been living these past months, I'm surprised it was as subdued as it was. I can, however, understand your consternation over it. But I don't think I would want to venture an interpretation."

Logan said nothing. He was afraid the interpretation was all too obvious. He finished his crepes. They did indeed live up to his expectations, and he was glad to concentrate on them for a while. But at length he spoke again.

"I came to France to forget myself."

"And now you are perhaps afraid you have been too successful?" The priest's intelligent, noble eyes held Logan's for a long moment. Deep within them Logan could discern a kind understanding, an empathy that Logan would not have expected from the society priest.

Finally Logan turned away and sighed deeply.

"Maybe so," he said without much conviction. "I like what I'm doing. For the first time in my life I feel I'm involved in something truly meaningful . . . worthwhile. But I was more content and sure of myself when I was cheating people at cards or swindling them out of their money. If what I am doing is a good thing, why is it so filled with confusion?"

"Perhaps because there is a greater good to be considered, Michel," said Jean Pierre after some thought.

"I don't understand."

"You said before that I have the ideal excuse for staying out of the

Resistance," Jean Pierre went on. "But the priesthood, in my opinion, should never be an excuse to be *un*involved, but rather an open door into greater involvements in the hurts of people and the world. Believe me, my clerical superiors have often urged me to take a more neutral stand. They argue that God is no respecter of persons, that His love and judgment are meted out equally to the just and the unjust. I should not take sides, therefore, but let justice come from the hand of God. They are right, of course; God *is* no respecter of persons. The Bible does say, 'Resist not evil, but turn the other cheek.' Yet justification for my position can be found in the Scriptures also; James says, 'Resist the devil and he will flee from you.' I realize each of these passages can be interpreted in many ways. But perhaps that is occasionally the reason for our confusion, as you have expressed, because God leaves it to us to hear His voice in each of our hearts. I know without a doubt that God has called me to this work we are doing. Though I am criticized for forsaking my holy calling, I know that any other path *for me* would be less than God intended. I do not judge my brothers who choose to serve the Lord or their brothers on more neutral grounds. And I do not judge you either, Michel. I only say all this because you alluded to your—what shall I call it?—your attempt to live a more godly life."

Logan nodded. "I suppose that's as good a description of it as anything."

"It is something you still desire?"

"Yes," replied Logan without deep emotion. "I always wanted to be closer to Him. But I never seemed able to fit in. I once had a pair of alligator shoes; I loved those shoes and they cost me a bundle. They hurt my feet from the first day I got them, but I wore them every day for a month until I couldn't stand it any longer and finally had to throw them out. I guess living as a Christian was a little like that for me."

"Faith is tossed aside at a much greater price than a pair of shoes."

Logan stared moodily down at his plate. He had never before considered that he had abandoned his faith until just this moment. Had he discarded it like the shoes? The whole thing had come upon him so gradually that he had not really considered it gone at all. But now he could see that perhaps he had walked away from it.

"But what does that have to do with the greater good you spoke of?" he asked, almost unintentionally trying to shift the conversation away from the personal.

"It is just this," replied Jean Pierre, "as a man with a *heart* toward God—never mind where your mind and emotions might be right now—have you considered that you may have wandered onto a different path without realizing it? Yes, what you are doing is good, and for me it is my calling, *my* greater good. Perhaps for you, there is another greater good. Something you have yet overlooked, which no doubt begins with your retrieving what you tossed aside—that is, if you truly do still desire it in your life."

"But then the question is, what do I *do*? What is *my* greater good to which *I* am called?"

"I cannot answer that for you, Michel. But I am certain it is waiting for you."

"Perhaps the priesthood?" said Logan dryly.

Jean Pierre chuckled. "That would be an irony! You the priest, me the secret agent!"

"But this all comes so naturally to me, playing the games, the cons, the masquerade. How can it be wrong?"

"There are many questions I have no answers to. I cannot say it *is* wrong. You must sort through your own confusion. It must be a signal of something, though I cannot say of what. Remember one thing, however. Certain things are natural because they come from God. Others are natural because they originate in our natural man. And these must be overcome. Do you mind if I quote you another scripture?"

"By all means," answered Logan.

" 'Do not be conformed to this world,' Paul said, 'but be transformed by the renewing of your mind, so that you may prove what is that good, and acceptable, and perfect will of God.' "

Logan whistled softly as the words struck a responsive chord in his mind, if not in his heart.

"We are meant to change," went on Jean Pierre. "We are meant to grow into an understanding of what God's will for us is by this transformation process. Perhaps you tried to wear the shoes, so to speak, without allowing the transformation to renew your heart and mind. Thus, the spiritual life you wanted never quite *fit*."

"I've never thought of it like that before," said Logan. "I'm not sure I understand it completely."

"Food for thought," said Jean Pierre. "God will give understanding in its proper season."

"And in the meantime?" sighed Logan.

"It was our Lord who wisely said that each day has troubles enough of its own to worry about."

Logan nodded. He had plenty to think of for now, and would be glad to switch mental gears for a while.

"Perhaps the first thing you could do," said Jean Pierre, "is to get von Graff to have *you* replace my shadow!" He laughed at the suggestion and Logan joined him.

"I'm glad you mentioned von Graff's name! I'd almost forgotten the most important thing of all. That's why I had to see you. You've got to get a message to London for me."

"About your latest *change* in circumstances?"

"Yes. Von Graff implied they'd been contacted and my story verified. But they have no idea what tale I spun out when I was captured."

"It would seem from your release everything has satisfactorily fallen into place."

"Maybe. They might have guessed about my having been caught and said just enough to satisfy the Germans but leaving the details vague. But there is another option."

"Which is?" said the priest.

"That they haven't found out a thing about me yet, and von Graff decided to let me go, like a piece of bait on a hook, to see what would come of it."

"Hmm," said Jean Pierre, "it wouldn't be the first time he's used a ploy like that. They are fond of these little mental cat-and-mouse games, those Germans."

"In any case, I've got to make sure they know back home what happened and what I said. Whatever my present status, von Graff won't let it go indefinitely without absolute confirmation."

"What do you want me to do?"

"Does Lise have the wireless operational again?"

"Yes, I believe so."

"In her apartment?"

"No, it's been moved."

"Have her get word to Mother Hen. Tell him I was taken, that to save my hide I resurrected *Trinity*."

"Trinity? Oh yes, your cover in England. Please, go on."

"Tell Mother Hen that I was forced to become Trinity again, and to let the word out that Trinity's cover was broken by the English last Wednesday and that they assume he escaped to France by boat on his way to Germany. Be sure they cut off all further broadcasts from the Trinity angle. If whoever they had replace me as Trinity in England tries to contact the Germans again, I'm finished. Do you have all that?"

Jean Pierre repeated everything to Logan exactly as he had heard it.

Both men were silent for several moments, deep in their own thoughts. The times were indeed perilous.

"You know," Logan said at length, with a mischievous glint in his eye, "that idea you had a while ago isn't a bad one—my being your shadow."

"Don't jest with the Gestapo, mon ami!" said Jean Pierre.

"It could be done," said Logan, rubbing his hands together in anticipation. "Just think of the possibilities!"

"Think of the dangers," rejoined Jean Pierre seriously.

"I will," said Logan, returning to a solemn tone. "In that you can trust me . . . I will undertake nothing with von Graff lightly."

"How have you found Paris, Herr MacVey?" General von Graff asked when Logan saw him later that same afternoon.

His voice contained no more guile than that of a concerned host as he sat back in his own desk chair and looked across the room at Logan.

"Perhaps you ought to ask your watchdogs that question," replied Logan, a pointed edge in his tone.

"You must forgive my little foibles."

"I thought you had confirmed my loyalty."

"But, Herr MacVey, the moment I set you free, what is the first thing you do but stretch my confidence to its limits?"

Logan wrinkled his brow, perplexed. Then slowly, as if awareness were just then dawning, he nodded in understanding.

"You mean my visit to the priest?" he said.

"What am I to think?"

"That I was bored and thought such a fascinating cleric would offer an intriguing diversion, so I decided to take him up on his invitation at his brother's party."

"A plausible explanation."

"Believe me, General, if I had anything to hide, I wouldn't have allowed my tail to have so easy a time of it."

"Why did you not confer with me first?"

"I *thought* I was a free man."

"Oh you Britishers—you have no concept of what it means to live in a police state."

Von Graff sighed. "No one is free these days," he continued after a moment. His cultured tone contained the merest hint of regret, but he resumed in a different vein. "So . . . I trust you had a pleasant diversion?"

"He's as remarkable as everyone thinks," answered Logan honestly enough.

"Did your conversation touch on political issues?"

"He didn't confide in me about his Resistance activities, if that's what you mean," answered Logan. "But it wouldn't surprise me if he did in time."

"Oh. . . ?"

"I thought you would want me to make the most of the contact, so I subtley let it be known that my true sympathies were not with the Nazis."

Von Graff leaned forward, his eyes obviously demanding an explanation.

"As a new face in town," Logan explained, "I felt I might be successful where others have failed. I let slip that I thought Pétain was possibly not acting in the best interests of the French people."

"And?"

"You know yourself, General, that these things take time. But de Beauvoir did extend me another invitation."

"And you think you can hand us the priest?"

"General, you set your sights too low." Logan shook his head as if patronizing a child. "If the priest is anything, he is only a small cog. Don't let your personal vendetta against him blind you to the overall picture. De Beauvoir is but a link. Yet lubricated properly, he could be instrumental in aiding us to pull in the entire chain."

"And you would like to do the lubricating."

"I could pull it off, and you know it."

"The idea does contain some merit."

"But no more of this watchdog business," said Logan firmly.

"Why should it bother you so, Herr MacVey?"

"Like you said, I've been spoiled. I've grown accustomed to my freedom and it makes me nervous to have a hound on my tail. But more than that, de Beauvoir is no moron. He'd sense a setup in a minute. He is already well aware of his own Gestapo shadow. Moreover, I might be able to penetrate the Resistance, but they can smell Gestapo a mile off. The minute they did, my life would be history."

"So you want, as the French say, *carte blanche*?"

"That's the only way I'll agree to it," said Logan, gambling that deep inside, the general would find it within himself to respect someone who played the game hard, like the Germans themselves did. He carried his bluff out with all the poise and just the proper dose of cockiness, just as Skittles had taught him. "You don't want a few couriers or radio operators, General," he went on, getting into the stride, "you want to pull down the structure at the top. The leadership is the heartthrob of these kinds of movements—you take away the leaders, and the rest will wither away on the vine."

Von Graff nodded his assent. The fellow knew what he was talking about, that much was certain.

"I could use my British citizenship to win their trust—and from there I know I could get to the leaders."

Von Graff rubbed his clean-shaven chin thoughtfully, considering all the aspects to Logan's daring proposal. The recent escapes had lately lowered his esteem in the eyes of his mentor and superior, Himmler, and he knew he needed to bring in some results—and soon. Here was an opportunity to cement his value to his Nazi masters. He hardly knew this MacVey, and he wasn't quite sure what to make of him. The communication from Gunther had been too vague to set him completely at ease. And MacVey himself seemed a bit too independent. But von Graff's instincts told him to take a chance with him.

Logan waited just long enough to allow von Graff to mull the whole thing over in his mind, then voiced the words that would solidify him in the general's mind as no patriot, and just the sort of man the Nazis were fond of.

"But, General," he said, "I don't intend to go a step further unless certain guarantees are made which will, shall we say, make this whole venture worth my while."

"You think you are in a position to dictate to a general of the Reich what he is about?" shouted von Graff, slamming his hand down on his desk. "If we find your proposal useful, you *shall* carry it out. Do I make myself clear?"

"Perfectly, General," replied Logan, concealing a smile. He had probed closer to the general's frustration point than he realized.

"Certainly you shall be paid," von Graff went on, calming. "But let there be no mistake—*I* shall be the one issuing the orders."

The general paused, but before he could say anything further, a knock came at his door.

He glanced up, distracted and perturbed by the untimely interruption. "Come in!" he called out.

Arnaud Soustelle stepped into the office with an apologetic yet confident look on his face. "Pardonnez-moi, Monsieur General, but your secretary is gone and I thought you would not mind if I came in unannounced."

"What is it, Soustelle?" said von Graff. "As you can see, I am with someone at the moment."

Soustelle now turned and noticed Logan for the first time. He glanced in his direction and eyed him quickly, but taking in every detail with his policeman's scrutiny.

"Oh, then again, many pardons," said the Frenchman effusively. "I will return at a more convenient time."

"This time is as convenient as any," said von Graff. "Herr MacVey is working for me."

"MacVey. . . ? An Anglais?" Soustelle's tone was heavy with speculation.

Logan stood and extended his hand in an almost extravagant effort at cordiality. "Enchanté, Monsieur Soustelle."

Soustelle took Logan's offered hand with obvious reserve, eyeing him now with deeper and more sinister perusal. The English were far from his favorite nationality at any time, but especially now. He might have been surprised to know that French collaborators were similarly at the bottom of Logan's list.

"Now, what do you want?" asked von Graff, who was either unaware or unconcerned with the unspoken tension between his two henchmen.

"This regards the assignment you have had me working on," replied Soustelle.

"The business with L'Escroc?"

Soustelle's eyebrows shot up, astonished at von Graff's candor before this Englishman. Fortunately, the general's attention was focused on Soustelle's reaction, and so Logan's own imperceptible intake of air went unnoticed. To him, at least. Soustelle, a man with certain reptilian attributes of vision, had noted Logan's reaction even as he eyed the general.

"Yes, General," replied the Frenchman, now glancing directly at Logan. His voice, as well as his look, contained something Logan could not readily identify. But the Frenchman clearly did not like to see his primary assignment treated so casually by his superior.

"Continue, Herr Soustelle," pressed von Graff abruptly.

"I have just discovered," Soustelle went on, now focusing on the general once more, "that a strong possibility exists that L'Escroc is a British agent."

"You have confirmation?"

"No confirmation. *Everything* about that man comes only from rumors and hearsay. I have a dozen people circulating about the streets of Paris in search of any more direct clue. But until today they have turned up nothing. There must be only a small handful who know his identity, and they're keeping very tight-lipped. But my source on the British angle is very reliable."

"Who might that be?"

Almost unnoticeably Logan leaned forward.

"The chauffeur of a well-known French family," Soustelle went on, "gave me the information. It appears this family has a son in the French army who was a prisoner of war in Germany until he escaped. He made it to Paris, where he was recaptured and sent to Fresnes. But while he was being transferred back to Ravensbruck, he escaped again. We believed that L'Escroc had aided in this escape, and now the chauffeur has confirmed it. He overheard his employers talking of that matter. One of them made mention of his nationality."

"You would think the fool would keep it a secret."

"Most assuredly," agreed Soustelle. "Apparently it was a fluke."

Logan remembered the incident vividly. Yes, he had blundered . . . forgotten himself in a moment of weakness—now he realized just *how* serious it had been!—when the lad he was helping mentioned a cellmate who happened to be a Glasgow acquaintance of Logan's. Luckily Logan had been wearing the disguise of an old train conductor at the time, and even if he had lapsed into English momentarily, at least he could not have been identified.

"Well, Soustelle," von Graff was saying, "this is an interesting piece of information. But does it bring you any closer to apprehending the scoundrel?"

"I think if I brought in this French family for interrogation. . . ?"

"Why do you need my permission?"

"They are not without influence."

"Haul them in!" ordered the general, "and bleed them for everything they know. See how far their influence gets them in an S.S. interrogation chamber."

The boy's family knew nothing. That much Logan knew. The whole thing had been arranged through go-betweens. He would have to try to get word out before Soustelle got to them. He shifted uncomfortably in his chair as he turned the dilemma over in his mind.

Logan's movement drew von Graff's notice.

"Do you have something on your mind, Herr MacVey?" he asked.

"L'Escroc . . ." mused Logan. "The Swindler—an interesting code name. Who is it?"

"That," replied von Graff, "is what I hoped Herr Soustelle would tell me." He cast the Frenchman a sharp look.

"I am this close!" Soustelle said, gesturing with his thumb and index finger to punctuate his words.

"That is not close enough!"

"This fellow seems to have caused quite a furor," put in Logan casually. "What has he done?"

"Our prisoners slip through our fingers like sand," answered von Graff. "And when they are gone, that name lingers in the air as if to mock us."

"Are you certain there *is* such a man?" probed Logan. "You know how underground movements love to create legends out of thin air, as a way of banding their people together."

"An interesting theory, Herr MacVey."

"Bah!" exclaimed Soustelle. "He is real. I can smell his presence in Paris. And soon I will crush him!"

"And how many more months will you need, Herr Soustelle?" said von Graff with enough emphasis to indicate his low regard for Soustelle's promises, and to point toward the Frenchman's peril in the general's eyes.

"You say he's British?" asked Logan.

"What is that to you?" snapped Soustelle.

"Nothing, of course," replied Logan. "It is none of my business. You seem to have the situation well in hand."

"What is in that conniving mind of yours, Herr MacVey?" asked von Graff.

"Really, I would not presume upon Monsieur Soustelle's territory," said Logan.

"Let me attempt to read your thoughts, Herr MacVey," said von Graff.

"There is a saying, 'It takes a thief to catch a thief.' Perhaps it could also go, 'It takes an Englishman to catch an Englishman.' "

"Perhaps," said Logan with a smile. "Notwithstanding the fact that I am a Scot and no Englishman, you have the general idea. Boche and Français and Anglais do not think alike. It might be I could assist you, Monsieur Soustelle, with whatever nationalistic insights I might possess."

"I do not require the assistance of anyone," replied Soustelle implacably.

"I will decide that," returned von Graff. "My perception is that a little assistance might be precisely what you need. But actually, Soustelle, I think you can continue as you have been doing. Interrogate the family if you wish. Herr MacVey can assist you from his sphere of influence."

"His sphere?" queried Soustelle suspiciously.

"I plan to use MacVey *inside* the Resistance itself," answered the general. "He could well make contact with L'Escroc himself."

Logan chuckled, but only he knew the true source of his amusement.

"Let's not get ahead of ourselves, General," he said. "First I have to get in. Then we can think how best to set our sights on such a prize catch."

41 / Doubts

That same afternoon, even as Logan sat in von Graff's office, Jean Pierre made his way purposefully down the rue de Varennes toward *La Librairie*. He had carried off one of his many methods of working himself free from his ever-vigilant attendant. Had his business with his four comrades been less serious, he would have been chuckling to himself at the thought of the befuddled Gestapo agent still loitering about the W.C. at the Eiffel Tower waiting for him to exit, not realizing that he was long gone.

But his business today *was* serious, and thus he found no amusement in what he had done. It had been a matter of necessity and he had already forgotten it.

As much as he was inclined to believe Tanant's story, his loyalty must lie with *La Librairie* first. He liked Michel, but how well did he really know him? The others had risked their lives one for the other; he knew where they stood. He owed them a full disclosure of what had taken place, so they could all have a say in any decision that must be made. Thus he had contacted Henri, and the impromptu meeting had been hastily arranged.

The others were all waiting when he walked into Henri's back room.

"Well, what is this news you have of our missing Monsieur Tanant?" asked Claude somewhat cynically. "Have you seen him?"

"Yes, is he safe?" said Lise, who, like the others, had heard nothing concerning Logan since he had left her three nights before and could not help but wonder if she was in any way responsible.

"Please," enjoined Henri, "at least allow the good priest to be seated. I'm sure he will tell us everything in good time."

"Thank you all for coming on such short notice," said Jean Pierre, seating himself and taking the offered cup of coffee from Henri. "Perhaps my worries are unfounded and all is exactly how it appears on the surface. But I owed you all an explanation of what I learned. If we should be in any danger, we must all know at once. If not, that should be a decision we make together."

"Worries . . . danger? What evils do such words portend, Jean Pierre?" asked Henri with grave concern in his voice.

"Our speculations concerning Michel were correct. He was picked up by the S.S. for breaking curfew on his way home last Friday night after leaving you, Lise."

"Did they imprison him?" asked Antoine.

"Yes," replied Jean Pierre, "but only for a short time."

"He is free, then?" asked Lise.

"Apparently so. But that is where the whole thing grows fuzzy. I chanced to see him at my brother's birthday celebration."

"What was he doing there?" asked Claude, his suspicious tone saying more than his words.

"That is the part which worries me," admitted Jean Pierre. "It was an extremely gala event, collaborators and Germans almost exclusively. And there who should I see, well-dressed and jovial, and in the company of a German general no less, was our own Michel Tanant."

"Mon Dieu!" exclaimed Henri. "That does not sound like him."

"I have told you all along," said Claude angrily, "that we knew nothing about this so-called *Monsieur* Tanant"—and as he said it, he spat out the word venomously—"but none of you would listen! Now he is in league with the Boche, and *La Librairie* is in danger!"

"We do not know that, Claude," put in Antoine, willing to hear arguments in Logan's favor as well as the accusations against him before passing judgment. "For myself, I want to hear the rest of Jean Pierre's story."

"I was naturally on my guard," went on the priest. "Like you, Claude, I did not like the look of it. We barely had a chance to speak last evening at the party. But the moment we were alone he began insisting that I get a message to London for him. He said he was in danger, and that the whole thing with the Germans was a facade."

"A facade, no doubt, invented on the spot the moment he saw you!" said Claude.

"Perhaps, mon ami. Perhaps. But if he *is* telling the truth, then if we do not back him up and get his message to London, it may not only mean Michel's death, it may bring yet more danger to the rest of us."

"What did you do?" asked Henri.

"In the presence of the general, I threw out an invitation for today, to see what might come of it."

"And?"

"Michel was at my door before ten."

"Alone?"

"We each had a Gestapo agent watching from a distance."

"Well, that is a good sign, that they are having him followed," said Henri. "At least if there is collusion with the Boche going on, it must not have progressed too far. They apparently do not yet trust him fully."

"Unless the tail was all part of the scheme," said Claude. "And let me guess, Jean Pierre! He told you he was 'playing along' with them, *pretending* to be sympathetic to their cause. He probably told you he was going to pretend to turn so he could infiltrate the Resistance for them and feed back information. Am I on the mark, mon père?"

Jean Pierre was silent a moment. The others all awaited his response, but his lack of a quick reply told them Claude's perception had been correct.

"What else would you have expected him to say under the circumstances?" went on Claude. "All this time he has been setting up this moment, gaining our confidence, even helping a few people to escape. But now! Now comes the moment for which he was sent into our midst—sent by the Germans! He fakes an arrest, tells us that he was captured and was 'forced' to fake a turn and that he now has to play along with them. All the while this has been his plan from the first day when he walked through this door of yours, Henri. And now that it has reached this stage, he can come and go with the Germans as he pleases, and in the meantime he has equal access through the Paris underground. A most convenient arrangement, I must say, and very cunning for the Boche to have devised!"

Claude's point seemed well taken. The others pondered his words for several moments.

"I want to know what he wanted you to tell London," said Henri at length.

"I'm afraid that only adds to the perplexity," replied Jean Pierre. "It is indeed a rather incredible tale." The priest then proceeded to tell his comrades everything Logan had said about his Trinity cover and what he had been forced to tell von Graff.

"It is too incredible *not* to believe," said Antoine.

"Bah!" shot back Claude. "You are a gullible fool! He will have us all before the Boche firing squad if we allow him back among us!"

"Claude!" said Lise, speaking now for the first time since hearing Jean Pierre's story. "Whatever your views, you have no right to say such a thing to your comrade! Your bitter protestations make me inclined to believe Michel as well—if only to spite you for your unfounded accusations!"

"You may seal your fate if you like," said Claude. "But I will trust him no more than I ever have. I will watch my flank even in my sleep. If *La Librairie* goes down, I will not go with it! Our safest course is to eliminate him, and you all know it! What can have so captivated you about this Britisher to blind your eyes, I do not know!"

"No one will be eliminated without proof," said Jean Pierre. "We will all be wary. But we cannot pass judgment too hastily."

"Jean Pierre is right," said Henri. "We have all missed one of the key ingredients to this unexpected turn of events. That is, if Michel is indeed telling the whole truth, think what benefits could be gained *for us* in having L'Escroc able to come and go inside S.S. headquarters unhindered! This may be the best thing ever to happen for the Resistance in Paris."

"Well, I'm going to transmit his message to Mother Hen just as he gave it to Jean Pierre," said Lise. "He has done much for the cause, and perhaps we owe it to him to do that much. Was that all he asked of us, Jean Pierre?"

"There was just one other thing," replied the priest. "He wanted you to meet him as soon as it could be arranged."

42 / Seeds of Vengeance_____

When Logan left von Graff's office that Monday afternoon, December 8, 1941, he was feeling more than usually pleased with himself. War had been raging in at least two corners of the world, and now all at once—with the outbreak of hostilities between Japan and the United States—it looked as if all four would now be involved. His own tiny homeland across the Channel to the west was taking a terrible beating. Yet Logan could not help feeling that he, at least, had just won a small victory. The misfortune of being caught the previous Friday night was turned suddenly around and now looked like it might prove fortuitous indeed for the fortunes of L'Escroc.

Somehow he had just managed to pull off the biggest swindle of his life since Chase Morgan. Immediately as the thought formed in his mind, he recalled his prayer while at S.S. headquarters. Could what happened have been God's way of answering that prayer for deliverance? Logan had no doubts about God's capacity to answer prayer. But over the course of the past year or two, he had never really imagined God's blessing to be on his life or what he was involved in. After all, he had not even seen Allison in . . . he didn't even know how long. He had made some halfhearted attempts to get Arnie to contact her to let her know he was okay. And since coming to France, things had been moving so fast. How could God possibly have anything to do with him anymore. The prayers he had offered arose more from desperation than from faith. And if he were following the wrong path, as Jean Pierre had suggested, then why would God help him now?

The whole thing was puzzling, and called into his mind many random images out of his past—conversations with Lady Margaret and Dorey and his in-laws, and even with Allison during their first blissful days together as young believers in a God who could be an intimate friend. It had all faded since then. God seemed once again remote. Yet he had prayed . . . and now this turn of events with von Graff.

Did God still care about him? He continued to search his mind for something that might answer the question, but he could not get that realm of his thoughts to come altogether into focus. He would have to talk to Jean Pierre again.

He turned down rue Leroux deep in thought. He should have taken a tram, but the clean, crisp winter air felt good. The sun had come out earlier, warming the icy atmosphere, and in spots melting the snow. He could take his time. He still had over two hours until his next rendezvous. That would give him plenty of time to circle around, double back, and make sure no eyes were upon him that shouldn't be.

He hoped Jean Pierre had been able to set it up with Lise as they had arranged before he left the rectory that morning. He wanted to see her, knowing it would be a far less troublesome contact to explain—if they happened to be spotted—than a meeting with Henri.

Even then, if Lise agreed to see him, the meeting in the Left Bank Cafe was to appear as nothing more than a chance encounter by two strangers. Logan had purposefully chosen a cafe in a part of Paris where he had never been before. From now on he would have to avoid those places he had frequented before. One chance word which revealed that he had been in Paris months before running into von Graff would land him into hot water with the S.S. It would be tricky; he had met a lot of people. But Paris was a huge city, and it would not be impossible. It helped that Lise had relocated since the raid near her apartment.

Logan paused at a newsstand to buy a paper. He would need it for his meeting with Lise. While glancing around, waiting for his change, he sensed he was being watched. He paused before continuing on, peering casually at the headlines, while out of the corner of his eye trying to focus on the faces off in the distance to see if his instinct had been correct.

He could see no one he recognized. Yet as he walked on, the feeling became stronger and stronger. Whoever it was behind him was good. And he was certain there was *someone* back there!

Could this be von Graff's doing again? He thought the near promise he'd managed to extract was as close to a guarantee as he was likely to get that there would be no surveillance. The possibility that the general had gone back on his word was not altogether remote. But that same instinct which told him someone was following him also told him his tail had nothing to do with von Graff.

Logan walked on another block, turning over in his mind several options for losing the unwelcome shadow. Whatever precautions he and Lise took, he still couldn't be followed to the cafe. Somehow he had to find out who was back there, and why. He at least had to know if it was friend or foe.

Lost in thought, Logan was suddenly nearly smashed into by a young girl who had lost control of her bicycle. She was already on her way down when she brushed by him. He reached out a hand, but he was too late to prevent a nasty spill. The incident came about so unexpectedly that it caught Logan's tail by surprise, and he drew a bit too close. As Logan stooped down to help the girl up, he managed to catch a brief glimpse of a furtive figure scuttling back into the shadows between two buildings. Everything happened too quickly for him to see the face or make out any details. But the size and bearing of the man bore an uncanny resemblance to someone Logan hardly knew but knew he didn't like.

Logan helped the girl to her feet, saw her safely off once again on her bicycle, then continued on himself, crossing the busy street just in front of a passing tram. Hidden momentarily by the large vehicle, Logan broke into a run and ducked into an alley way on the other side. Peering around the corner, he saw the bewildered Frenchman looking up and down the street for his quarry once the tram had passed. Then he turned in Logan's direction. Logan pulled back inside, picked his best spot, and waited.

The moment the ex-detective entered the opening of the alley Logan leaped out, grabbed him by his jacket, and yanked him into the dark recesses of the passage. It was risky business in broad daylight, but no one in Paris these days had much taste for getting involved in petty street crimes that might bring them face-to-face with their Nazi occupiers.

"Okay, Soustelle! What are you doing following me?" said Logan, as with one swift motion he slammed the Frenchman up against the wall, his nose pressed into the rough brick.

Soustelle merely growled in reply, struggling to free himself. He was larger than Logan, and probably would have made quick work of an all-out fistfight or street brawl and left Logan unconscious in a matter of seconds. But Logan was younger and lighter, and had learned a number of swift-moving tricks as part of his training.

"I will kill you for this, Anglais!" snarled Soustelle.

Logan wrenched one of the man's arms back, then swung his own arm around Soustelle's neck in a grip that would have made it impossible for the burly Frenchman to move without the risk of getting his neck broken. Thus the battle, what there was of one, was brief, leaving the former gendarme helpless and at the mercy of one he considered a puny runt half his own size.

He made a few further vain attempts to struggle free.

"C'est assez! commanded Logan. "That's enough! I don't want to break your neck, but I think you know I can from this position."

"Allez au diable!" spat Soustelle, panting.

"Not before I find out what your game is, Monsieur Soustelle," rejoined Logan. "Why are you following me?"

"You are an Anglais. That is reason enough!"

Logan jerked Soustelle's neck painfully. "Think again, Soustelle! What are you up to? And consider the consequences before you answer. I know von Graff didn't put you up to this."

Soustelle moaned, beads of sweat dripping down his brow. "What do *you* know?" he said, "and what does von Graff know!"

"You think I'm going to usurp your territory, is that it?" said Logan.

Soustelle remained doggedly silent.

"Well, perhaps I may do just that," Logan went on. "Or, we can work together. That is your choice. But if I catch you or anyone else on my tail again, you will be very sorry, Monsieur. Not only will you have to answer to me, you will also have to explain to von Graff and the S.S. just why you chose to countermand their orders. And you well know that once you have fallen into disfavor with the Germans, you will wish that I had broken your neck here and now. So what is it going to be, Soustelle?"

"I would sell my soul to the devil before I would work with an Anglais!" spat Soustelle.

"That will be a fine arrangement with me," said Logan. "I half thought you had already made such an agreement with him. In the meantime, I will do what I have to do. And I won't see you behind me again, will I?"

Logan punctuated his final words with a stiff jab upward of Soustelle's arm. The Frenchman winced in pain, but remained proudly silent, even in temporary defeat. Logan yanked once more.

"All right! All right! Have it your way!" he growled, his voice seethed with hatred.

Logan immediately slackened his hold.

"I'm going to let you go," said Logan. "I want you to turn to your right and walk down the street, and keep walking. This incident can be our little secret, but if I so much as see you look back, I will go directly to the general. Is that clear?"

Defiantly Soustelle nodded.

"You will pay for your arrogance, Monsieur MacVey!" he said. "You will live, and perhaps die, regretting this day!"

Even as he spoke, however, he began walking away from Logan and did not turn back, shuffling off down the sidewalk in mingled shame and fury. Logan watched him until he was out of sight.

His last glimpse was of the Frenchman digging his hand into his pocket, then tossing something into his mouth.

Soustelle continued down the street. His pride would not let himself show so visible a reaction to his defeat; but inside, his entire being pulsed with an indignation that quickly became a seething cauldron of hate.

He stuffed another licorice into his mouth and ground it mercilessly between his teeth, stained indelibly from the juices of his habit.

The arrogant Anglais would soon pay for his impudence!

It was not long, however, before the Frenchman began to examine his hatred with an eye toward its practical implications. This MacVey possessed the confidence of General von Graff, that much was apparent. Thus the threats in the alley were not idle. Von Graff may not have *said* it in so many words, but the implication was still there—MacVey was the darling of the S.S., and he must be placated at all costs.

"Le quel salaud!" spat Soustelle. "The dirty dog!"

But that's how it was. The French were nothing to the Germans—serfs and slaves, hated for their victory in the first war, despised for their defeat in the second!

But the British—they were different. Even Hitler admired them. And how much better an Anglais turned Nazi! Oh yes, they would do anything to keep *him* content, thinking nothing of stepping on a lowly French policeman in the process!

Yes, Soustelle told himself, I had better leave the Anglais alone—for the time being, at least. He would get around to Monsieur MacVey when the time was right. His chief objective for the present must be catching that other dog, L'Escroc. In doing that he would inflict more damage to MacVey's esteem in the eyes of the S.S. than anything else, not to mention raising his own. After that could come the real vengeance—the kind a man like Soustelle hungered after.

His footsteps soon quickened. He had another task ahead of him that afternoon which would help satiate that gnawing appetite after evil. He hailed a velo-taxi to take him across town. There lived the employers of a certain chauffeur; judicious dealing with them would bring him one step closer to his diabolical goal.

43 / Friendship Renewed _____

Logan ordered a café au lait from the garcon in the little cafe where he and Lise were to meet. Despite his run-in with Soustelle, he had arrived five minutes early and Lise was not yet there.

He sipped his warm drink, spent a few moments reading his newspaper, but before long set it aside to concentrate on his drink in what seemed a bored, detached manner. All the while, however, he remained acutely aware of each person who came and went from the small sidewalk cafe.

In about five minutes Lise entered. She took a table ten feet away from Logan, though she paid him little heed. When the garcon came, she gave him her order, while glancing causally about. Her roving eyes were arrested by the newspaper lying on Logan's table. She stood and walked over to him.

"Pardon, Monsieur," she said, "but I have not read a newspaper in two days. Would it be an imposition if I borrowed yours while I waited for my order?"

"Not in the least," replied Logan, handing her the paper. "But perhaps you would prefer more human companionship?" He smiled up at her as any Frenchman might at a pretty girl. "You are welcome to join me."

"I would not want to impose," she answered. However, the coquettish tone of her voice would tell anyone who by chance was listening that she had indeed hoped from the start for such an invitation from this handsome stranger.

"To tell the truth," said Logan, "the prospect of having coffee alone is rather a dreary one."

"In that case . . ." she said, pulling out the chair opposite Logan.

For the following fifteen minutes the conversation progressed as it might had they indeed only just met. For both it was a frustrating span of time, for each was eager to get on with what really mattered. But they played out the charade until they had completed their hot drinks and Logan could make the request anyone observing them might expect.

"Well, I must be on my way," he said, rising.

"It was very nice to meet you," Lise replied. "I'm sorry you must go so soon."

Logan paused, seeming to consider his words, then added, "Would you care to join me? I have no particular commitments at the moment."

Lise nodded with a smile, and they left the cafe together. Even von

Graff would only suspect that Logan had simply sought out some female companionship to brighten his stay in Paris. The ensuing relationship between the two should then appear quite natural.

As they began walking down the sidewalk, Logan could tell that beneath Lise's well-controlled cover, she was tense and even more reserved than usual. He waited until they had walked a good distance from the cafe and he was certain they weren't being followed, then said, "Lise, what's wrong?"

"There is much to discuss and so little time," she replied evasively.

"You too are worried about my Nazi ties?"

"We all are, Michel. How can you expect us—"

"*All?*" interrupted Logan.

"Jean Pierre told us everything."

"But I only just saw him this morning."

"He set up a meeting immediately afterward. We were all there. We discussed the situation, and what we should do about . . . you."

"And what did you decide?" asked Logan caustically.

"Come on, Michel, what did you expect us to do?" said Lise. "We had all confided in you; we thought we knew you. Now this. Jean Pierre owed it to all of us to let us share in the decision. You must know how it looks to the rest of us."

"You didn't answer my question."

"We didn't really decide anything, if that's what you mean."

"And so," asked Logan coldly, "are you not going to send the message I gave to Jean Pierre? Are you going to keep England in the dark about me and let me dangle and see what happens? Is that how you treat your comrades?"

"We risk our lives for our comrades," returned Lise sharply. "You know that! The question is whether you *are* a comrade. The underground is a dangerous business. You get killed for small mistakes. We have to take every precaution. You would do no different in our shoes."

Logan was silent. She was right, and he knew it. Still, it hurt.

"And you?" he said at length. "Do *you* trust me? Or do you think I'm Boche too?"

Now it was Lise's turn to walk along in silence. Logan held his breath, afraid to say anything further. He did not want to press, though something inside him had to know. How he hated this feeling of alienation that the war brought to everything—separation from friends, from family, even from oneself. This kind of work was lonely enough, and he had come to appreciate the feeling of camaraderie that had been developing between them. Now suddenly it was gone. Would he face the same cold reception from Henri? Jean Pierre had seemed so open, yet apparently he still doubted Logan, too. She was right—there *was* a great deal to discuss, and time was too short.

His thoughts were finally broken by her answer to his question.

"I don't know," she said. "I have to be truthful. I'm a little shaken by what Jean Pierre told us."

"But as I told him, it was all a dodge."

"A plausible enough explanation."

"A *true* explanation!" insisted Logan.

"I pray everything *is* just as you say," said Lise. "Time will clarify it all, as it has a way of doing."

"And in the meantime, I'm on my own?"

"No. I said I didn't know what to believe. That does not mean I will automatically disbelieve you. I *want* to believe you, and will do what I can for you until you give me reason to do otherwise."

"That's magnanimous of you, I must say," said Logan sarcastically.

Lise sighed. "I'm sorry. I know you want something more out of me—"

"A little trust would be nice!"

"Trust is an expensive commodity during wartime. Unfortunately—perhaps, as you say, through no fault of your own—your credibility has been damaged for a time. You will have to earn back our trust. But please, Michel, do not be offended. Try to see that you would feel just the same toward me."

"You will send my message?" asked Logan, hardly satisfied, but resigned to the way things stood.

"Yes. But you had already asked Jean Pierre to do that. Why did you want to see *me*?"

"I suppose because out of all the others, I thought you—and Henri—would be the ones most likely to believe me. I guess I had to know what you thought. And I knew it would be far less likely to raise suspicions by being seen with you—a man and a woman in Paris, you know—than with Henri. I didn't want to endanger him . . . or the group."

"Is that all?" asked Lise.

"At the time—this morning when I was with Jean Pierre—yes. But since then something's come up. I was with the general again this afternoon and I learned of some people who are in terrible danger. You've got to get word to them . . . and soon."

"Who are they?"

"Have you heard of the Gregoire family?"

"Yes, of course."

"You must get a warning to them that the Gestapo is likely to visit them soon."

"How do you know this?" asked Lise, still cautious.

"That's not important for now. If you find you can trust me, then I'll fill you in on everything too. Just answer me this: do you know a Frenchman, a collaborator, by the name of Soustelle?"

"I have heard the name. An evil man. But I have not met him."

"He is in league with von Graff. If he gets to this family before your people do, I fear for the result."

Logan and Lise had been walking toward a little park. It was too cold and icy to sit and relax, though patches of grass peeked through the snow in places, and children were tossing crusts of bread to the pigeons. Logan marveled that they had bread to spare. Maybe, he thought, they are trying to fatten up the birds for this evening's stew pot.

All at once a young man stepped into their path, hailing Lise with a friendly greeting.

"Bonjour, Paul," Lise replied. Then turning to Logan she made introductions, presenting Logan as Michel Tanant.

Logan immediately recognized the young man as Mme. Guillaume's nephew who had assisted them in transporting the two British airmen when Logan had first arrived in Paris.

"I thought it would look better," explained Lise, "if it appeared you two were just meeting for the first time."

"Yes, I suppose you're right," agreed Logan. "These last four months can't exist for me any longer. It must from now on be as if I only arrived in Paris this week. But is there some reason you set up this meeting today?"

"Henri thought that since your contact with *La Librairie* must be more limited now," said Lise, "a courier would be useful for you. Paul is willing to help, and has far fewer ties to the underground. He will raise no suspicions."

"It is nice to see you have such a high regard for my safety," said Logan, "dubious member of your clandestine entourage though I am." A trace of his former humor came through in the words.

"We have our own interests to protect," replied Lise. "And that includes our investment in you. If you are not on the up-and-up, you will be dead before you know what we know. Claude will see to that. And if you are still with us, then we owe you a great deal and we must do our best for you."

"I do wish I could talk to Henri," said Logan.

"You realize that is impossible for now. He has too much at stake. Too many lives depend on him. Now, tell me about this Soustelle."

Logan briefly recounted what he had heard in von Graff's office regarding the parents of the French soldier he had helped escape. Ever since leaving the general's office earlier, he had been pondering how he might get to them before Soustelle. Now the perfect opportunity seemed to present itself.

"Do you know where the Gregoires live?" he said to Paul.

The young man nodded

"Can you go there and warn them? Their lives may depend on your speed."

"It would be quickest to telephone them," he said.

"Never trust the telephone, Paul. The government controls the system, and I'm certain that in the case of the Gregoires, their phone is under Gestapo scrutiny by now. But you'd best dig up some kind of disguise; a delivery boy ought to do."

"Oui, Monsieur!" he said eagerly. "Just like L'Escroc, eh?"

Logan tensed. Was it possible Paul knew of L'Escroc's identity? He glanced toward Lise and noted a hint of consternation in her face as well. No, he couldn't know. It must have been but another example of how L'Escroc's reputation had seized the fancy of many patriots throughout Paris. Quickly Logan dismissed it and returned to the problem at hand.

"Be careful not to compromise yourself," he cautioned. "The situation is very dangerous. Can you handle it?"

"Oui, Monsieur!"

"All right then . . . be off!" said Logan. "You can find out how to reach me through Lise. When we meet again we will set up some kind of regular contact point. Good luck, Paul!"

The boy turned and sped off on his bicycle.

When he was out of sight, Logan glanced at Lise, as if seeking some reassurance that this obviously untried youth could perform the task given him.

"Yes, he is young," she replied, correctly reading his look. "But we have little more than the young to rely on, with so many of our men in German prisons or dead. But Paul is not as naive as he may appear. He has helped us before. I am sure we can count on him."

"I hope you're right," said Logan. "It seems he is my only lifeline at present."

But neither Logan nor Lise could know that as he sped away from them, all the experience or savvy in the world could not get Paul to the Gregoire family ahead of the villainous Frenchman.

44 / The Old Gentleman

Even while Logan and Lise were talking in the cafe, Soustelle had made all the necessary arrangements.

He and his soldiers were storming the Gregoire townhouse while Paul was still pedaling frantically across town. And by the time Paul knocked in vain on the ornate door, Soustelle was preparing to confront Monsieur Gregoire in an interrogation chamber of a small building adjacent to the S.S. headquarters where the S.D. often performed their dirty work.

Except for the actual arrest, Soustelle had decided to handle the entire matter himself. He would notify von Graff upon its successful conclusion. Thus he had ordered the S.D. agents to drag the prisoner into the chamber, then dismissed them. He was now alone with the wealthy Frenchman, who had made a fortune manufacturing perfume.

Gregoire was about seventy, with white hair and a clean-shaven face of nearly transparent skin, though it was deeply creased with wrinkles. Because of a touch of arthritis in his vertebrae, his neck jutted forward slightly, and a mild case of Parkinson's caused his head to tremble constantly on its seemingly precarious perch. The effect would have been pitiful had it not been for his proud, lively eyes and firm, determined chin. He was a man who had known little trouble in his life, having inherited an already successful business from his father. He had enjoyed a genteel existence with his wife and family, reputed to be a gentleman however tenacious he might be in the marketplace. But with the occupation of the city and the imprisonment of his only son, Gregoire had quickly learned the harsh realities of life. They were soon to become much harsher.

Soustelle strutted back and forth in front of the aged Frenchman as he sat with all the decorum he could muster under the circumstances.

"We know you are connected with the underground," said Soustelle, pausing to focus his cold gaze at his prisoner.

"That is not true!" exclaimed the proud Gregoire.

Soustelle's fleshy hand suddenly shot out, striking the older man's pale face with a savage blow. Gregoire was knocked momentarily off his seat, but caught his balance before falling to the floor, and doggedly resumed his place.

"Tell me about your son," demanded Soustelle.

"I only did what any father would do. You are a Frenchman; you should understand."

Soustelle spat on Gregoire's expensive Italian shoes.

"I understand my duty! Now tell me—who helped him escape?"

"I do not know—it was all arranged through the post."

Soustelle delivered another punishing blow, which stung the old man's ear, drawing blood.

"Lies!" snapped the Nazi henchman. "Give me names!"

"I know none to give."

"What about L'Escroc?"

Gregoire said nothing.

"You *will* talk!" said Soustelle with icy menace.

He strolled in a casual, off-hand manner to a table where his hand laid hold of a policeman's nightstick. Tapping it meaningfully in his hand, he strutted before the old man several times, a gleam of profound relish in his eyes, and, oddly enough, no licorice churning in his mouth.

"You *will* give me names," he said.

Still Gregoire remained silent.

Incensed by the man's effrontery not to be intimidated, Soustelle set to work with his club. The gentle, aged face—bloodied and purple from the Frenchman's blows—was unrecognizable within the span of but a few moments. When the old man fell to the floor, Soustelle aimed several more blows at his kidneys. But by now, even if Gregoire had known anything, he was more determined than ever not to utter a word to this evil man some would dare call his countryman.

"So be it!" spat Soustelle. "There are other methods to loosen stubborn tongues!"

Gregoire rolled over and looked up with terror at his captor.

"Yes, Gregoire," laughed Soustelle. "Your wife is in the next room. Perhaps the sound of her cries will make you talk, eh?"

"Please, no!" begged Gregoire with a pathetic whimper, all his determination to resist suddenly swallowed by panic. "Not my wife . . . she is not well."

"Then give me names! Tell me who is this L'Escroc!"

"I tell you I know nothing. Do you not think I would talk—especially now—if only I could?"

"Have it your way then."

Soustelle stalked from the room, that sinister gleam still in his eyes.

Gregoire crawled from the cold hard floor toward the door through which Soustelle had just exited.

He struggled to rise but could only get to his knees. In vain he tried the handle, but the door was locked.

Suddenly from the other side he heard a wretched scream that he knew at once to be his wife's.

"No! Dear God. . . !" he wailed, pounding a feeble fist on the door. "No. . . !"

Still the screaming went on, all but drowning out the dull thuds from Soustelle's blows.

The last sound he heard, before falling back onto the floor in blessed unconsciousness, was a horrifying laugh from Soustelle, mingled with an hysterical shriek from his dear wife.

Logan buried his face in his hands. He could not believe Lise's words. "They are dead, Michel . . ."

Despite the shakiness of his relationships with Lise and *La Librairie*, which now had to be re-forged, Logan had begun to think things would smooth out. He had already managed to forget the reality of disaster. And how much worse that disaster should strike others because of his momentary blunder. L'Escroc, indeed!

" . . . dead, Michel. Do you hear me?"

Paul had not succeeded in his mission. Logan's warning, Paul's attempt to warn them—everything had come too late. And Logan knew he was to blame.

He remembered when the Gregoires' son, now safely out of France and fighting at de Gaulle's side for Free France, had described his parents. "They are like children in wrinkled skins . . . incredibly innocent," he had said. "They are not stupid or naive! Oh no!" He had chuckled softly at the notion of his father being naive. "But they have somehow managed not to be corrupted by this cruel world of ours."

Now the picture of those dear old souls at the mercy of Soustelle and the Gestapo rose up, a stinging self-recrimination before Logan's mind. Had they been sacrificed so that his own skin might be saved? Even if such had not been his conscious intent, his over-confidence had made him careless, numbed him to realities.

"Michel," Lise's voice broke into his thoughts, "you must not blame yourself."

"Why should I not?" he asked bitterly.

"Because this is war. When you're involved in war, blame and guilt only lead to insanity. You do what you must do. You survive. If you manage to help some people one day, you cannot carry the burdens of an evil world on your shoulders the next."

Logan lifted his head so that his eyes met hers. "Then whose fault is it, Lise?" he asked. "When do people have to stop and take responsibility for their actions, even in a war?"

"You tried to save them the moment you could."

"That sounds like rather a *trusting* comment to make. What if it was all a ploy on my part to make my charade that much more believable, while all the time I was in league with Soustelle?"

Lise smiled. "I suppose that is a possibility. And a chance I must take.

But I hope I read your reaction to this news with more insight into human nature than that."

"Nevertheless, I should have done more."

"If you had done *more*—sacrifice yourself, perhaps—you might only have brought many more others into danger."

"So the lives of two old persons is a small price to pay for the safety of *La Librairie*, is that it?"

His voice was harsh, meant to bite, though not directed at Lise personally.

"I did not mean that," she replied, hurt. "Surely you know me better than that by now, whatever side you are on."

His tone softened as he reached out and took her hand.

"I'm sorry," he said. He wanted to weep, but shedding tears was one ruse he had never practiced much.

"You must forget all this," she said, trying to assume a businesslike attitude as she slipped her hand from his.

"For a moment, Lise, I thought we could go back to the way it was."

"What do you mean?"

"We were friends before," he replied. "There was trust. We could talk. In a world of lies and cover-ups and darkness, I thought we were able to understand each other . . . trust each other."

He paused, rubbing his hands across his face.

"I need that, Lise," he said. "I don't know if I can dangle out there alone anymore. Though I suppose in this kind of work, trust, attachments, caring—they are the kiss of death. Sometimes I don't know where Michel Tanant leaves off and Logan Macintyre begins."

"Don't say that name to me!"

"Can't you just for a minute forget *what* we are?"

"It's dangerous to forget."

"No, I think it's just *easier* not to forget." Logan sighed. "Lise, I have caused two innocent people to die. How can I ever forget that? That is not something the fictitious Michel Tanant did, which can be wiped out of memory like an imaginary name. *I* did it, do you understand? Me—Logan Macintyre! And *I* will never forget. When this war is long over, I will still have to deal with that fact. I will have to look into my child's eyes and remember all that happened here in France."

"Is that why you never carry a weapon and so carefully avoid violence?"

"Ha! I fear even those standards will soon be gone. Like I said, where do Michel and Logan start to be different?"

"What do you mean?"

"Today Soustelle was following me. I grabbed him and threw him up against a brick wall. I attacked him! I probably would never have been able to break his neck as I threatened. Good acting has always gotten me by—

and it'll probably be my demise, too. But what if before this is over I find myself in that same situation with a rifle in my hand? What if I *have* to kill?"

"I wish I could help you in some way, *Logan*." She spoke his real name for the first time, softly, poignantly, perhaps not even aware that that alone could be enough to help sustain him for a while.

"Thank you," was his only reply.

In her heart Lise knew that he understood. It was a great sacrifice for her to break her code by imprinting a comrade's true name into her mind with her voice.

"I wish I could help you smile again, too," she added. "But it has always been your job to bring smiles and laughter. I'm afraid I fail miserably in that area."

"Someday," said Logan, "the war will be over and we will all be able to smile and be happy again."

"Perhaps there will be happiness for others," said Lise. "But for those who survive this dark life of Nazi occupation which France has plunged itself into by its own stupidity . . . I don't know. I think we will be too changed to be happy anymore."

Logan was silent. He wished he could refute her morbid statement. But he knew he couldn't. He had said just the same thing when he had spoken of his daughter. It was a fact that lately seemed constantly haunting him. Jean Pierre had spoken of changing in a positive way. But Logan was not sure it could be so. His own depressed state over the Gregoire deaths had blinded him to the spiritual realities operating within him, and to the beauties of change. For the moment he only knew that if ever he was so lucky as to see his wife and daughter again, he would be a far different person from the one they had known before.

From his present vantage point, he could not see how such an altered Logan Macintyre would be someone they would even know . . . or love. But in one thing he was correct—he would never be the same Logan Macintyre again.

Allison felt happier than she had for months.

Nathaniel was home on leave after more than a year away. Actually he wasn't really *home*, for time did not allow for him to get all the way north to Stonewycke. But since Allison was in London, that was almost as good. He had been able to arrange a flight for Joanna to join them there, so it was going to be as near a reunion as the war-torn family had had in quite a long time.

Allison and Nathaniel had driven out to the airport in an army car to meet Joanna's plane, only to receive the news that it was an hour behind schedule. Allison didn't mind the delay, for it gave them time together as brother and sister they had seldom had, even prior to the war.

"It's funny," Allison said as they found seats on the wooden benches in the busy airport. "For so long you were always my baby brother. But now it seems we have caught up to each other."

"Ye mean I've finally caught up to *you*!" said the red-headed Nathaniel, his freckled face breaking into an unabandoned grin that was so much like his father's.

"I don't know," said Allison thoughtfully. "I may have been older, but in so many ways you were always far and away ahead of me. You always knew who you were and what was most important in life. I seem to still be struggling with the things you mastered years ago."

"But I can already tell, Ali," Nat replied, "that ye've got yer feet back on the solid foundation, as Grandma nae doobt would say."

Allison had to smile. Nat and Alec were the only members of the family to cling to the heavy Scots burr, and it was delightful to hear once again after Allison's long exposure to the southern accents.

"I hope you're right, Nat," she replied. "And I think I am close to God again, closer than ever before. Being alone, and having things go against me for a while, really forced me to examine parts of my life that I'd never looked at before. I suppose Logan and I approached our marriage like we did being Christians—a one-time decision that we thought would carry us through. I guess I'm finding out—in both areas—that there's a deeper commitment needed, something strong and enduring enough to last for years . . . forever. Being alone, and on my own, has opened my eyes to some of these things, especially to how shallow I always was. It's hardly any wonder Logan finally got tired of me."

"Ah, come on, Ali, give yersel' a break! Ye canna hae been all that muckle bad!"

"Maybe you didn't know me very well, Nat. No one did. Because I didn't even know myself."

"Weel, I'm right glad for ye noo, anyway."

"Do you remember Sarah Bramford?"

"Ay . . . a friend o' yers frae home?"

"Yes. She and I've been attending church together. It has been so good for me to have someone to talk to. She's grown a lot over the years, too. Yet there are still times of struggle when I really doubt my ability to make the kind of commitment to God I want to. And there are times when I wonder if it's not come too late. If only I had seen some of these things years ago, my marriage might have been spared."

"But ye canna give up hope, ye ken."

"All the hope in the world will be of little use if I never see Logan again."

"The Bible says that hope doesna disappoint."

Allison sighed. "You're right. But it's so discouraging to realize that in so many ways I drove Logan away without realizing what I was doing, all the time blaming him. Oh, Nat, I knew so little about what marriage was *really* meant to be, that love is serving, not receiving."

"Ye'll hae yer chance to make it right again."

"Oh, I hope so!"

"How long has it been?"

"Several months." But even as Allison spoke the words, she suddenly realized it had been a whole year, for it was now spring again, and she had last seen Logan in spring a year ago. It was 1942. In a few months they would have been married nine years. Yet she did not even know where her husband was. Each month she received the anonymous check in the mail; she assumed it meant he was all right, assuming of course that the money was indeed from him. Without realizing it she found her thoughts drifting toward their old channels: had Logan grown so cold and callous as to let their marriage disintegrate into nothing but the sending and receiving of a nameless check month after month? She could not believe he had changed that drastically.

Nat reached out and took Allison's hand in his. How large and warm they are, she thought. So much like Daddy's—comforting and reassuring. She smiled bravely at her brother. After all, this was his leave and she did not want to spoil it with her morose meditations.

"I'm surprised ye haena gone back to Stonewycke," said Nathaniel. "At least bein' oot frae under the shadow o' war would make life more tolerable."

"Then I wouldn't have been here for you!" Allison tried to laugh, but it wasn't much use. "But to tell you the truth, Nat, the shadows that are over my life would follow me wherever I went. And I suppose a part of me is afraid that if I did go, Logan might come back and think I didn't care enough to wait for him."

"But surely he'd ken ye was at home."

"Maybe. But I doubt he'd come there for me," she sighed. "He doesn't feel he belongs there."

"I'm sorry to hear that," said the young man sadly. "Why, Logan's always been family to us, e'en frae that first day we met in front o' Miss Sinclair's place."

"I believe that deep down he knows that. But there are things going on inside of him now that he's probably not clear about."

Allison still recalled vividly how confused he was that day he had left Stonewycke last spring. "But who am *I* to talk? If only I could *see* him," she went on emphatically. "I know that now I could understand him better."

"Ye can ne'er say what God will do."

"A while back I thought I might be able to find him," Allison said, going on to explain her sleuthing attempts with Billy and her eerie encounter with Gunther. "But I guess after that experience, I'm almost afraid to see Logan. Who knows *what* he might be involved in?"

"Why do you say that?" asked Nat.

"That man sounded so German," answered Allison, "and there have been so many unanswered questions—"

"What can ye be sayin', Allison?"

"I hate myself for even thinking it!"

"And ye should, too," Nat gently remonstrated. "I dinna ken Logan as weel as a wife ought to. But I ken enough to say wi' certainty that he couldna be mixed up wi' the enemy." His friendly eyes flashed momentarily with the Ramsey fire. "Allison," he went on, "if ye do naethin' else, ye must believe in him. A man needs that frae his wife, more than anythin'."

"And you still a bachelor," she teased, trying to lighten her sense of guilt. Then she added earnestly. "But such a wise bachelor!"

"I dinna ken aboot that," he replied, embarrassed at the compliment. "I think maybe I jist can give ye the man's perspective. And when ye do see Logan again, he'll ken what's in yer heart—and the one thing he'll want to be certain o' is that ye love him enough to believe in him—perhaps nae matter *what* he's been involved in."

"Love has so many aspects," mused Allison, "almost none of which a young couple getting married is aware of. I'm learning so many ways in which it's different than what I always thought it to be. You always think *love* is an emotion you feel toward another. And to now come to realize it's not that at all but rather how you behave toward others—it's quite an awakening, to say the least. And to think that in our eight years together, I never really *loved* Logan in a true sense, never really put him before myself, despite all the so-called *love* I felt for him."

"He probably never really loved you in that way either, or I doobt he'd ever hae left," said Nat. "Love, as weel's partin', is always a two-way street."

"I wonder if we'll have the chance to start again."

"I'll not stop prayin' fer ye both."

The conversation waned for a few moments, as brother and sister each lapsed into their own private musings. But time was too precious to waste on things that could wait until they were apart. Allison felt an urgency upon her to make this time together especially meaningful for them, a time of cementing the bonds that were growing between them now that they were able to relate as adults on an equal plane of relationship.

"I hope my experience hasn't soured you on the prospect of marriage, Nat," said Allison, anxious to know more about his life.

He grinned sheepishly. "Na, na," he said. "Ye couldna do that."

"But there's no one special?"

"The Lord kens best what's to come o' my future," he replied. "But He'd hae to go some to find a lady to match up wi' the women I think most highly o'—oor own mother, Lady Margaret, and e'en yersel'!"

For an instant a faraway gaze passed through his eyes. It quickly passed, however. "Oh, but there's plenty o' time fer that! War isna the time to be thinkin' o' romance. Too much can happen. I mightna live through it, ye ken."

"Nat, please!"

" 'Tis true. Everythin's uncertain in war. But if I make it through, when it's all o'er, then . . ."

"I know you'll find someone as special as you are," replied Allison, and again the two fell silent.

Allison cast a quick glance to her left, and studied her brother momentarily with admiration. He had inherited his father's tall good looks, though he was not as brawny as Alec. No doubt many girls' hearts would throb over him, but his manner was so unassuming that he would never believe they would think of him in such a way. He had much to offer a woman; he would make a grand husband someday.

At the thought a chill ran through Allison's spine as she recalled his words: *I mightna live through it, ye ken.*

She didn't want to think about such things! Not now. Not ever! He does indeed have the potential to be a good husband someday . . . and he would fulfill it, she told herself. Yes, of course war was awful. But it was unthinkable that its evil shadow could extend itself even over Stonewycke.

She glanced at Nat's face again. The boyishness was still there. But at twenty-two, there were faint hints around his eyes of the hard edges the war had forced upon him. War, as well as difficult marriages, matured men and women more rapidly than perhaps they would have wished.

"I suppose all our lives must wait till the war is over," sighed Allison.

"It seems such a waste of our youth."

"Wi' God, naethin' is wasted," replied Nat. "He always uses the tragedies to make o' us all better. Ye mind what Grandma Maggie always told us aboot her years away frae Grandpa Ian."

"I know. But to hear her tell the story, it always took on almost a romantic air. You forget how heartbreaking it was for the two of them. And maybe that's why when the heartache comes to us, we forget that it's meant for our good, for the deepening of our faith."

"Weel, we all saw that in Grandma and Grandpa. I jist hope we o' the next generations can allow the Lord the same grace to do that work in us."

"I can see that already in you, Nat," smiled Allison. "We're all so proud of you. When the 51st Highlanders so distinguished themselves at Dunkirk, you should have seen Daddy."

"Weel, we had to live up to the standard set in the Great War," replied Nat, beaming at the thought of his father's pride. "The Germans called us the 'women o' hell,' not kennin' hoo prood we was to be wearin' the kilt. It was a fine unit to be a part o' that!"

"Well, you were all from heaven as far as we're concerned," said Allison. "And where to now, Nat?"

" 'Tis all secret, ye ken."

"Secrets!" exclaimed Allison with a downcast frown. "If I hear that word one more time, I'll scream!"

Nat hesitated a moment, then appeared as if he was going to speak, but all at once a voice over the loudspeaker interrupted him.

"Flight Fifteen from Glasgow now approaching the runway."

The conversation seemed over, or at least suspended as Allison and Nat rose to walk outside to watch the landing of their mother's plane. A cold stiff wind met them and Allison had to hang on to her hat to prevent it from joining the aircraft overhead. They watched on the other side of the fence as the plane lowered its landing gear and made its approach.

"I hope Mother's flight was good," said Allison. "She does not relish the idea of flying and only did it this time for you."

"The moment I see her she'll ken hoo much I appreciate it," said Nat. "I never know when I'll be back, or if—"

He broke off suddenly, ashamed of himself for almost voicing his fears to his already burdened sister. "You both will never know how much it means to me to be able to see you now," he finally added.

Allison reached up and placed her arm around him, giving him a loving squeeze.

"Oh, Nat," she said, "forgive my selfish outburst before. I don't care where you'll be or how many secrets you have. I will be praying for you every day."

"Thank you, dear sis," he said. "You know Grandma always said that we ought to pray as specifically as possible."

"Yes . . . I remember."

"Weel, maybe I ought to give ye some help in that particular area . . ."

He paused and smiled. "I'd like ye to ken, Allison. I canna tell ye anythin' exactly. But I can say that for the next several months, I'll nae doobt be eatin' lots o' spaghetti."

"Italy?"

"Ye didna hear it frae me," he replied with a wink. "Noo, *you* hae a secret to keep! And I'm glad ye ken. I willna feel sae alone noo. The Lord will be wi' me, and I always ken that. But I think He understands my meanin'. 'Tis nice to share that kind o' thing wi' someone close to ye."

"I wish you didn't have to go, Nat," said Allison. "I wish we could go back to the time we were all just 'wee bairnies'—running on the sand, exploring the Dormin . . . Oh, I don't know! You shouldn't have to be going off to . . . who knows what!"

She looked up at him and touched his cheek with her hand. There was hardly even a stubble of beard. Yet something deep in his eyes said he was fully a man, coming of age too soon.

"It doesn't seem fair, dear, gentle Nat—"

Her voice broke down and tears rose in her eyes.

Nat bent down and gave her a kiss on the forehead. "I love ye, Allison. Ye're a dear sister. Things may be lookin' a mite dark noo. But I ken they're gaein' to improve, especially for you. Logan will come back, and the war'll be over one day, and the two o' ye will hae the kind of marriage that will match both o' yer wonderful hearts. Especially wi' all ye seem to be learnin' frae the Lord's hand. In na sae very long, we'll all be sittin' together wonderin' why we were so untrustin' and downcast during these times o' trial."

His last words were spoken with almost a distant tone, as if he were trying somehow to convince himself too of the hope of his words in the face of his coming assignment.

"And noo," he went on, "we better dry oor eyes, or Mother will wonder if we're na glad to see her."

The plane touched down, and when Joanna debarked and walked through the gate, there followed a tender reunion of a mother and the children from whom she had long been separated as poignant as such a gathering can be in a time as fearful and uncertain as wartime.

Allison's were not the only tears that flowed.

It had been a nerve-wracking five-hour train trip from Paris to Reims, only eighty miles.

Logan knew the French railway system had deteriorated drastically since 1939, no thanks to some of his own operations in recent months. But he had not expected to spend half the day traveling.

Then in Reims he had run into some difficulty contacting the local Resistance cell that had promised a vehicle to carry them the final leg of their journey, the twenty miles to Vouziers. They now had less than an hour to get there and set up their radios in time to catch the European wavelength broadcast of the BBC.

As the old bakery van jostled and bounded along the rutted dirt road through forested terrain, Logan tried to relax by reviewing the important particulars of this current assignment. But the moment he tried to concentrate, the van bounced with a horrible thud into a huge pothole.

"Can't you keep out of *some* of those holes, Claude!" he shouted over the deafening roar of the ancient engine.

"Not if you want to get there by seven!" rejoined the surly Claude sharply.

"It won't matter if we break our necks in the process, or attract a Boche escort."

"Never satisfied, Anglais!" Defiantly Claude jammed on the brakes.

Lise, who was seated between the two men, flew forward, and had her reflexes been a fraction of a second slower, she would have smacked her head into the windshield. However, her hand grabbed the dashboard in time to prevent disaster.

For the next three minutes Claude drove the van at a snail's pace, while Logan sat, fuming at his comrade, silently bemoaning the fact that Claude was the only one available to accompany him and Lise on this particularly urgent mission.

"All right!" snapped Logan at length, unable to stand it any longer. "You've had your fun, and your little joke on me. Now get moving!"

Claude neither looked at Logan nor spoke, but merely rammed his foot to the accelerator. Instantly the old van lurched forward at its former pace, though Claude kept a diligent eye on the road ahead.

Logan seriously wondered how they were going to pull this thing off under such uncooperative conditions. London had made the operation sound easy enough: During the next moon period they were to meet a Lysander at an abandoned airfield five miles southeast of the little town of Vouziers. It would deliver into their temporary care two important Gaullist agents. They were to tune into the BBC every evening at seven p.m. sharp to listen for the message: "On ne fait pas d'omelette sans casser des oeufs. You can't make an omelette without breaking eggs." When *that* came, they knew that night they must meet the plane. Their cover, while they awaited the signal, would be to appear as vacationers.

The whole thing might be plausible enough at the beginning of July. The little village of Vouziers, with the Aisne River at its back door, would have enough of an influx of tourists that three more should be able to go unnoticed. That is, if no one paused to question two men and a woman traveling in a beat-up old bakery van. And if they could somehow put a veil over Claude's foreboding features and eyes full of sinister intent.

All at once, as if the irascible driver had read Logan's unkind thoughts about the glare of his eyes, the van's wheels collided with another trench-like gouge out of the road. Logan opened his mouth to upbraid him again, thought better of it, and said nothing. Only Lise saw the look on his face, and simply shook her head and sighed with impatience at these unfortunate relations between them. In all the months they had been together, one would think Claude might have modified his prejudices. But any trust that might have developed between him and Logan had been completely negated by Logan's association with the Nazis. Back then, six months ago, his stature with them all had been on very precarious ground. . . .

Lise found herself reflecting back to the events of the previous December. Michel had been arrested just two nights prior to the bombing at Pearl Harbor. When she had gone to meet him that first time, she had indeed felt betrayed—deeply and personally, even more than she had let on to him. On her way to the Left Bank Cafe, she had fantasized that if it were true, then *she* would appoint herself his executioner. She tried to convince herself that the reason for her passionate initial reaction was that Michel had done something few had been able to accomplish since the war—he had won her trust. She had believed in him, and entrusted herself, as well as the cause she was fighting for, to him. For him to violate that was unconscionable. That was all. She forced from her mind all the other anguished and confused cries of her heart. There was only the Cause—she had no other feelings.

Of course, she could never let him know any of this. She had *wanted* to believe in him still, and tried to give him the benefit of the doubt. She would send his message to London, and would do what it might take to back his ruse with the Germans. Because of Jean Pierre she had been willing to give him a chance. But inside, her emotions balanced on the thin line between trust and deception, and it would take some time for her to refocus her feelings. And when they met in the cafe, despite her calm, even sympathetic exterior, Michel never knew that in her purse she had carried a loaded revolver. She told herself she could have, yet even now, she did not know if she *would* have been able to use it on him if he had proved a traitor.

Fortunately, she had not been given cause to find out.

When the word of the arrest and deaths of the Gregoires came to them, she had read his eyes carefully. The anguish of his invisible tears was more real than any Nazi could have put on merely to wear. She considered herself certainly that good a judge of character. She would have no use for the revolver at present, not to use on Michel Tanant, at least.

The others, however, took more time to convince. They had not seen his eyes. Claude still warily watched his flank, and seemed bent on bringing the despised Britisher face-to-face with some harm that would put an end to their mutual involvement once and for all.

A tense week had followed. Michel had so desired a meeting with Henri. But the gentle old bookseller would not risk it—protecting the operation, he said. Lise knew he was afraid to look in Michel's eyes, fearing perhaps that he might see the ugly truth of betrayal there. The strain, on both the young man and the old, was visible. The two had grown close in the months they had worked together—as close as two people could in this murderous life. And now suddenly the relationship that had been a source of sanity to both of them was gone.

A communication from Michel's London chief, Mother Hen, a week before Christmas had done much to bridge the rift and bring him back "in" for all but Claude. The communique had instructed *La Librairie* to follow Tanant's lead, doing nothing whatever to compromise his position with the Nazis. He had the complete support of British intelligence, the report read emphatically. There could be little doubt that the message was genuine. A personal note at the end had cautioned Michel to "have enough sense to know when to fold! We can get you out of France on twenty-four hours' notice if necessary."

The final re-cementing of Michel's position with *La Librairie* had come at the hand—literally!—of the boisterous Antoine. The big Frenchman had been sitting in a cafe waiting for a rendezvous with Michel. It was the end of December or the first week of January, thought Lise as she recalled it now.

Suddenly without warning the place was swarming with French police, raiding it by order of the German command in the city to gather "volunteers" for the labor camps in Germany. Antoine had been brusquely lined up against the wall with all the other likely candidates when Michel had stumbled onto the scene. Without hesitation he had stepped up to the inspector, whom he had recently met in relation to his connection with von Graff.

"What's going on here, Inspector?" he had asked with authority.

"You know how it is, Monsieur Dansette, we have quotas to meet that the Germans give us." He chuckled nervously, by all appearance reacting with some deference to Michel, according to Antoine's later recount of the incident.

"Of course," replied Michel. "I was speaking with General von Graff only yesterday about that very thing, and about resistors as well—they're more *my* line, if you understand me, Inspector," he added with a wink.

"Mais oui, Monsieur Dansette. I hear you and the general are on the trail of L'Escroc!"

"Keep it to yourself, Inspector," said Michel with a meaningful glance.

"Oui, Monsieur! You can count on me!"

Michel then gave the group lined up against the wall a casual once-over.

"You know, Inspector," he said, "that man"—he cocked his head toward Antoine "—he looks like someone I've been after. A dangerous Frenchman. He may have a clue I need. Have him taken to a back room; I'd like to question him privately."

"But of course, Monsieur!"

The inspector complied without further question.

When they were left alone in the back room, Antoine had not known whether Michel's true traitorous face had revealed itself, or if he, Antoine, had been saved from deportation to Germany.

"You're going to have to jump me and escape," said Michel as if in answer to Antoine's puzzled expression. "I know it's not a great ploy, but it's the best I could come up with on the spur of the moment."

"What do you mean . . . jump you?" asked Antoine, still confused.

"I mean knock the bloody daylights out of me, then beat it out that window!"

"You can't mean. . . ?"

"I can, and I do—make a good show of it!"

"They may not buy your explanation, and then you'd be in danger," protested Antoine. "I could only face labor camp—you could be—"

Suddenly there were sounds in the hall.

"This is no time for a debate!" said Michel. "You're going to be on your way to Germany if you don't. I'll fake some explanation. Now *do it!*" he ordered, presenting his jaw to his comrade's powerful fist.

Antoine had derived no pleasure from pummeling Michel's face that afternoon, not because he was squeamish, but because just before his fist had made contact with Michel's cheekbone, he had *known*. It was something he had caught in Michel's voice . . . in the look of his eyes . . . some intangible sense that assured Antoine's keen spy's instincts that Michel was one of them. And if that were not enough, Antoine knew that in setting him free, Michel stood in danger of losing much more than he could ever gain.

Claude, of course, had heatedly debated Antoine's whole interpretation of the day's events.

"You're just a sentimental French fool!" he blasted out. "Can't you see he arranged the whole scenario, just to win your trust, and through you, ours!"

"Perhaps that is what *you* would do, Claude," said Antoine calmly but passionately. "But L'Escroc is much too clever for such a clumsy, obvious ploy. He was just as shocked as I when he walked in and saw the French police."

"Please, this arguing must stop!" intruded Henri. He knew Claude, and knew the discussion would get them nowhere. It was not good for the organization. It was time for a firm decision on *La Librairie's* policy regarding Michel Tanant, alias L'Escroc, Englishman, leader in the French underground, and now, by accident it seemed, also a double agent in counterfeit league with the Germans. As he spoke, Henri's eyes swept around the small room, and in that moment they were as hard and intractable as Claude's. *"We must be unified!"* he said. "Thus, from this time forward, Michel Tanant will be fully accepted. I believe that events on the night of December 5th happened exactly as he represented them to us, and that he is still wholeheartedly with us. *All* of us will give him the same cooperation and loyalty as before. I am prepared to take full responsibility for this decision, so if you denounce Michel—you denounce me! If you cannot accept this, then make it known now, and be off!"

Thus *La Librairie* weathered the formidable storm of the testing of Michel Tanant's loyalties. He was restored to his place among them, though with a great deal more care now paid to secrecy. And if Claude remained bitter and surly, it was no more in evidence than it had always been.

It should have been a time of great victory for the organization, now that Michel was able to filter intelligence directly from the Nazis. But Lise remembered that their coup was not without its difficulties. Any information Michel obtained could not be used without its being passed along the underground chain and acted upon in such a way that it could not be traced back to Michel. As a result of this constriction, many choice tidbits had to be overlooked completely; any resistance knowledge of them could only have come from extremely limited sources. They were forced to create coincidental-appearing triumphs over Nazi schemes so far removed from Michel's involvement that often more time was necessary to set up the deceptions than they had.

Still, much vital intelligence passed out of S.S. headquarters into Allied hands those months, with no one the wiser, except the British War Office, whose cause—sometimes independent of the French underground altogether—was helped tremendously.

Another factor that always had to be figured into the formula of Michel's double-identity charade was the simple fact that he had to prove himself to the Nazis as well. He had to feed them enough accurate information about the Resistance to make himself useful and to validate his loyalty to the Reich.

This was understandably the most difficult aspect of the deadly game. For if his information always proved bogus or came just a day or an hour too late to do the Nazis any good, eventually their suspicions would be aroused. Many a late-night session was spent with Henri and the others, concocting scenarios that would play to von Graff, which would give the appearance of dealing deadly blows to the cause of Free France and the Resistance Movement, but which in fact would do neither, and in which never the life of a comrade was endangered. The task was not an easy one.

Michel had played the double-agent game in England as Trinity. But when he fed the Abwehr information, only inanimate objects had been endangered—a few decoy ships or planes, anti-aircraft weapons the British could do without, an airfield, an out-of-service railway, an ammo dump from which ninety-eight percent of the stores had been relocated. But now with the Resistance, playing the double-loyalty game—at one time as Michel Tanant, another as Lawrence MacVey, then as Trinity, and to certain Parisians loyal to the Reich as Monsieur Dansette—involved people. He could not sacrifice human beings. Yet that was the most valued quarry sought by the Germans, who knew the underground had nothing if it did not have its leaders. Thus he had to betray without truly betraying, and risk as little as possible to individuals, appearing to give the Nazis much, while in fact giving them nothing.

All the while, the rumors surrounding L'Escroc gradually grew, assuming the proportions of legend. Logan pretended to be moving ever closer. Soustelle's hatred of MacVey intensified, and his determination to eliminate *The Swindler* grew to a passion.

Lise had often wondered, in the months since, how Michel walked this precarious tightrope without cracking up.

As the weeks passed into months, however, she began to see the fine lines of his face etched more and more with tension. No doubt he lived in constant fear of the inevitable moment when it would all crash in upon him. He once told her about a house of cards he and a friend had constructed in a London pub. Precisely leaning cards against one another, some vertically, some horizontally, they had built a tower almost two feet tall and employing some three decks. It had taken them hours to build, but in less than a second a gust of wind from the opening door had toppled their work of art into nothingness.

He had to say no more. She knew it was exactly that fear which constantly gnawed at him day and night, that from some unforeseen corner a sudden change in the currents of his fortune would blow unsuspectingly upon him, unmasking the subtle charade he had so carefully built over himself.

His own collapse perhaps he could bear. But by now he realized that he was the single card at the bottom-center of the tower. He cherished no vaunted ideas that the Resistance depended solely upon him—it would go on long after L'Escroc was a mere memory. But too many lives were now wrapped up in his game. If he made a mistake—a shady plan, a phony betrayal, a linguistic slip-up—lives would be lost. If he played the charade too close, tipping his hand, bluffing when von Graff held the winning hand, he could lead the Gestapo right to Henri's bookstore. The Germans were said to be experimenting with drugs that *made* you talk, even against the determination of your own will. If he were captured and interrogated . . .

Yes . . . Lise could see all these things weighing heavily upon him.

When Michel had first come to Paris, she had sensed the thorough enjoyment he felt for what he was doing. She could still recall the boyish gleam in his eyes as he and the two British airmen had left Mme. Guillaume's building right into the arms of the gendarmes. He couldn't have enjoyed the ruse more!

But it was different for Michel now. Lines of anxiety had begun to crease his forehead. She could read sleepless nights in the dark hollows under his eyes. The *élan* she had rightly attributed to him was still there, but it had become a mere frame in which a different kind of picture was now taking shape.

She was both eager and afraid to see it completed. She had watched the underground life turn men into animals. Was not Claude a prime example? She hoped it didn't have to be that way. She hoped somehow Michel could escape such a fate.

Lise stole a glance at him as they bounced along the road toward Vouziers.

He was staring intently ahead, as if he expected danger, even on this sunny July afternoon on an idyllic country road. Why did he intrigue her so, and cause her stomach to do strange things when he was near? She *had* to retain her distance. She could not allow herself to become so vulnerable—it was not healthy for either of them in their present circumstances. Yet, perhaps it was too late.

Suddenly, even as her eyes were fixed upon it, Michel's face paled, and his whole body tensed.

"What's this!" he groaned.

Lise jerked her head around. Her eyes fell upon the most distressing sight imaginable.

Directly ahead of them, stretching across the dirt road, was a German checkpoint.

When Logan had reconnoitered the area two weeks ago, he had not seen so much as a bowl of sauerkraut. The only thing resembling authority in the region was a pudgy, middle-aged police inspector who, though no patriot by any stretch, collaborated with the utmost laziness. He had not even so much as asked Logan for a look at his papers, and Logan had enjoyed complete freedom to examine the town and study the airfield to insure that it still fit RAF specifications. He had even contacted the local Resistance, which consisted of an elderly farmer and his kindly wife.

Now there were Germans everywhere.

Had word of this mission somehow leaked out? Could he be approaching the final Waterloo for L'Escroc, as he had been fearing for weeks?

Claude pulled the van to a stop behind an ancient truck, his features taut but more with malice than fear.

"Claude," said Logan from where he had crouched down in the back, thinking the three of them together might appear more suspicious, "can't you try to look more like a vacationer and less like you've just slit a Boche throat?"

Claude harrumphed angrily. "You just keep out of sight and leave this to me!"

Lise shook her head and gritted her teeth against her own angry retort. Couldn't they just once lay aside their animosity? True, Claude could be unreasonable, but why did Michel antagonize him at every opportunity?

The truck coughed and sputtered on its way, and Claude pulled up into place.

"Qù est le qui se passe? What is happening?" he said, in what seemed a genuine effort to assume an appropriate attitude.

The soldier, however, had no intention of answering such a question, and instead replied with the most dreaded of German commands.

"Ausweis!"

The demand for identity papers should not have bothered these three, for everything they carried for travel and identity purposes was perfectly in order, having, in fact, been obtained through due process from the proper German departments in Paris. The anxiety rising in each stemmed more from the fact that secreted beneath a false floor in the back of the van were three wireless sets.

Claude and Lise, in the front seat, handed their papers out the window and the soldier gave them a perfunctory glance, then handed them back. Claude reached for the gear shift, but the soldier was not finished yet.

"What is in the back of the van?"

"I don't know," came Claude's unimaginative answer.

Lise immediately leaned toward the window. "We borrowed the van from my uncle in Reims," she said, "so we could tour the countryside, you know. We are on holiday from Paris."

"And that tarp . . . what is it covering?"

Lise hesitated only an instant. "My brother," she said, "he is asleep. He works all night in a factory. He was very tired."

"I must see his papers too. Wake him up."

Lise climbed in back and pretended to awaken Logan, who groggily rolled back the tarp. Lise took his papers and handed them forward.

The guard seemed to scrutinize them a moment or two longer than the others, then handed them back inside.

"Get out and open it up."

With but the faintest hint of a groan, Claude complied. Lise resumed her seat. Logan threw aside the tarp but remained where he was, praying that no one would want to search under the floor where he was sitting.

The guard opened the back of the van, poked around, shoved about a couple of boxes they had placed there as decoys, cast Logan a final wary look, and finally closed the door and waved Claude ahead.

Claude pulled the lever down into first and jerked back into motion, while his two passengers exhaled tense breaths.

In another quarter mile they entered the little village of Vouziers. There were German soldiers everywhere it seemed, although those walking the streets paid them little heed. It was hardly a comforting prospect to think of trying to complete their mission under such circumstances.

While dining in the restaurant of one of the town's two hotels, they learned the cause of the sudden German interest in the area. An army contingent had arrived the day before responding to reports of the presence of several escaped prisoners-of-war in the area. Actually, the German command in Paris had received rumors that this little out-of-the-way village had become a regular link in the underground escape route. For two days all roads had been blockaded and patrols were combing the countryside. No one could say how long they might remain, but the hotel concierge complained that it was already cutting severely into the tourist trade.

After dinner the three discussed what to do. Unfortunately, the radios they now had hidden in their rooms were only receivers brought for the specific purpose of intercepting the BBC broadcast. They had no transmitter; thus there was no way of contacting London about this hitch in their plans. They were all too worn out to consider a return to Paris only to have to turn around for another drive out to Vouziers. Therefore, they deferred their decision until morning.

By the time they awoke, however, it seemed their problem had been solved in spite of their uncertainty. Two escapees had been recaptured some time during the night, and the Germans had pulled out before dawn.

The successive days, while the weather continued fair, were peaceful ones, at least for Logan. Four days passed with no message, and he saw no reason why this excursion could not at the same time be viewed as a bit of a holiday for the beleaguered spies. Even Claude relaxed a little, though he spent most of his time in the cafes drinking too much black-market wine.

Logan and Lise took full advantage of the great weather and the lovely countryside. Leaving the van parked to conserve precious fuel, they rented bicycles at an exorbitant price and explored the banks of the Aisne River and the woods surrounding the town. Except for the tense hour every evening when he bent over his wireless listening for the BBC, Logan gave himself over completely to the holiday atmosphere of the place. At times he practically forgot his reasons for being there and the necessity for a man in his position to remain constantly vigilant.

He first spotted the youth after he and Lise returned to the hotel late one day after a picnic and swim. Lise went up to her room for a rest, while Logan tarried in the lobby exchanging pleasantries with a clerk. The coarsely dressed farm lad looked badly out of place in a hotel lobby, despite all his efforts to appear casually interested in a Paris newspaper.

The natural paranoia of his occupation, coupled with the fact that Logan thought he recognized the lad from earlier that morning, put him immediately on his guard. When he bid the clerk adieu, Logan exited the hotel, keeping his own casually camouflaged watch behind him. It seemed better to verify his suspicions sooner than later.

As he expected, the youth followed him. Logan ditched him easily, circled around the block, and came up behind the boy as he stood puzzling over which way his quarry had taken. The moment Logan firmly grabbed his arm from the rear, he nearly cried out with fright.

"Take it easy, young man," said Logan as he propelled him into a recess between two buildings where they would not attract attention. "I don't want to hurt you, but I *do* want to know why you are following me."

"They told me to be sure," panted the lad, who looked to be about sixteen years old, and completely unaccustomed to his present calling. "Who you were . . . and . . ."

"And what?" demanded Logan.

"It's . . . it's so hard to tell, and they didn't have a very good description," rambled the youth, "and they said I had to be sure. And with the Nazis here, I didn't want to—"

"All right, lad," broke in Logan, trying not to chuckle at the poor boy's discomfiture. "You haven't found a Nazi, and I doubt that I have either. Now let's see just what we *have* found. I believe we both know Monsieur Carrel."

Carrel was the farmer and resister Logan had met briefly on his last visit to Vouziers.

The boy nodded his head vigorously. "Oui!" he said, much relieved. "You are Monsieur Tanant, non?"

"I am," replied Logan. "Now, why did Monsieur Carrel send you after me?"

"My father knew you were returning during the moon period," said the young Carrel. "But you had both agreed not to contact each other unless it was an emergency. So he sent me into town every day to see if you had arrived."

"We've been here four days already."

"I did not look so hard when the Germans were here," admitted the boy sheepishly. "And you were perhaps out in the country often?"

"Oui, that's true," said Logan. "So what does your father want?"

The boy glanced fearfully this way and that before speaking. "He has what the Boche were looking for."

"An escapee?"

"Oui."

"And he'd like some help getting him out?"

"Very much so, I think."

The first thing Logan noticed on stepping into the Carrel home was the warm, earthy atmosphere. He had been too rushed and disoriented the first time to pay much attention. But now, in a calmer frame of mind, he realized that he had not been in a place like this since the last time he was in Port Strathy and had visited Jesse Cameron's cottage. Madame Carrel was busy kneading bread in the kitchen area, while a young girl of about ten or eleven was thrusting a log into the cookstove fire. In the corner by the stove a calico cat was lapping milk from a bowl.

Mme. Carrel greeted Logan with a ready warmth, no matter that it was wartime and the enemy had occupied her country. She was, and would always be, a simple, open-hearted farm wife, and might well have greeted General von Graff in the same manner.

"Come this way please, Monsieur Tanant," said her husband.

Logan regretted being led away from the friendly kitchen. Yet it remained in view, for the rest of the large central room—consisting of a dining and sitting area—was merely an extension of the kitchen.

Now for the first time Logan's eyes fell on the figure sitting toward the back of the room in a large rocking chair with his feet propped up, facing the brick hearth. The fellow's back was to Logan and his first impression of the man was of a brilliant shock of red hair.

"Monsieur le Lieutenant," said Carrel to his other guest in faltering English, "I have brought a visitor."

"Wonderful!" said the man, also in his native tongue, turning in his chair. "Forgive me for na risin'."

Logan had stepped forward to shake his countryman's hand—for from the accent he knew immediately Carrel's guest was a Scot—but before the fellow had finished speaking and fully turned, Logan stopped and gasped.

"Nathaniel!" he exclaimed.

"The Lord be praised!" said Nat, now making a concerted effort to stand. "Confound this leg," he muttered.

But Logan had reached him in an instant, and, bending over the chair, gave his brother-in-law an exuberant embrace. How good it felt to be so close to someone from home—to family!

"I see you two know each other," said Carrel, this time in French, grinning at the happy scene. Briefly Logan translated his words. Then, almost in unison, both men exclaimed—one in English, one in French:

"Indeed we do!"

"Then I'll leave you to yourselves, while I finish up my chores."

Carrel went outside and Logan pulled a stool up next to Nat.

"What in the world are you doing here?" he asked.

"I was jist goin' to ask ye the very same thing!" said Nat.

"It's a long story, Nat," replied Logan. Suddenly he felt very uncomfortable, and his smile faded. He looked away, pretending interest in the fire.

"Listen here, Logan," said Nat. "Ye dinna hae to be that way wi' *me*! I'm Allison's baby brother, remember . . . the wee tyke who worships the ground Logan Macintyre walks on!"

Logan smiled and faced Nat again. "I'm sorry," he said. "So much has happened . . ."

"But never so much that we'd stop bein' brothers," replied Nat. "And ye ken, Logan, that no matter what, that's hoo I'm always goin' to think o' ye."

Logan laid his hand on Nat's shoulder. "Thank you," he said, not without a great deal of emotion in his voice.

"Noo," continued Nat in a lighter tone, "let me get my story over wi' so I can hear yers—which'll nae doobt be the more interestin' tale."

Logan nodded his agreement with the plan, though he wasn't so sure he wanted to get into his own story. But Nat was talking.

"I was transferred frae the 51st Highlanders after Dunkirk and got into a commando unit. Dinna ask me why I did it—I suppose on account o' my C.O.'s sayin' I'd be good at it. But he'll nae doobt change his mind when he hears hoo this assignment went. I was off trainin' Partisans in Italy— quite a trick wi'oot kennin' a word o' Italian! But we managed pretty weel, and I think we had a good outfit. That was, what, about three months ago— just after seein' Allison and Mother in London. As I was sayin', it went weel enough, until this new fellow joined us. 'Twas my fault, 'cause I liked him and wasna so careful as I should hae been. The bloke wound up betrayin' the whole lot o' us to the Germans. They had me in San Remo prison for a while; then they were plannin' to transfer me to Buchenwald. On the train I kept lookin' for me chance to escape. But we got to Germany before that chance came. Then the train was derailed, and in the mayhem, five o' us slipped away. We've been on the run for a month, though by the time we got here, we was doon to three. We ran into a German patrol aboot a week ago, and all took off in separate directions. That's when I took this bullet in the leg. I dinna ken what's become o' the other two—an American pilot frae Texas and a lad frae British intelligence."

"I heard the Boche caught two escapees about four days ago," put in Logan.

" 'Tis a shame," said Nat. "They were good lads. I suppose they'll jist hae to start o'er again."

"How bad is your leg, Nat?"

"It'd feel a lot better if that bullet weren't still floatin' around in there—"

Nat winced in pain, even as he said the words. When the spasm passed, he went on with a wan laugh—

"But I had more pain when I was a lad o' ten and got a fishhook caught in my shoulder!"

"What does the doctor say . . . or have you seen one?"

"Carrel doesna trust the local fellow, but Mme. Carrel has been keepin' it clean. I can walk, wi' a crutch we made—that is, if ye hae plenty o' time to wait for me."

He paused, then said, "And what aboot yersel', Logan?—Though I think I can guess at some o' it."

"Well," said Logan, deciding that some story must be given. "For openers, I suppose you ought to use my code name, especially when there's anyone about. My comrades in the underground have never even heard the name Logan Macintyre. So when you hear the name Michel Tanant, it's me they're talking about."

"Then I'm right—ye're wi' Intelligence."

Logan nodded.

"There's really not much more I ought to tell than that," he continued. "I got into it almost by accident, recruited by a friend for one simple assignment that only lasted an hour or two. They needed someone and I happened to fit the bill. But it was at a time when I was floundering—you know, Allison and I weren't doing too well, I hated my job. So when the chance to get more deeply involved came along, I took it . . . and here I am."

"How long hae ye been in France?" Nat asked.

"Quite a while, I suppose," replied Logan, then paused reflectively. "Longer than I ever expected to be, that's for sure."

He stopped again, reticent to talk about himself. "I don't know, Nat," he went on at length. "Suddenly none of it seems so important. Right now, you don't know how *good* it is to see you! I've felt so lost lately, but seeing you—"

He stopped and shook his head slowly. "I'm sorry," he said. "I never used to be this downcast."

"I imagine we've all hae to do a fast job o' growin' up in these last few years," said Nat. "I'm sure it's been no easier for ye than me."

"What I'd really like to know is, how is . . . everyone back home?"

"Ye're meanin' Allison, o' coorse?"

"Yes."

"Why didna ye tell her aboot what ye was doin'?"

"You know how it is—security . . ." Even as he spoke, Logan could see by Nat's pointed look that he would never accept that pat answer.

"All right," he continued resignedly. "I didn't tell her because I wanted her to believe in me—just in *me*. It seemed, to me at least, that the only way I could live down my past was knowing at least one person—Allison—trusted me completely, even without knowing every detail. I suppose maybe I was wrong. But that's how I felt then."

"She's only human, ye ken."

Logan nodded.

" 'Twas a lot o' pressure ye put on her, Logan. And she felt it more'n she let ye see."

"I know that . . . now. I put so much on her. I tried to validate my whole existence through her. I'm surprised *she* didn't walk out on me first. She would have had every right."

"Are ye, Logan? Are ye truly surprised?"

Logan hesitated. "No, I suppose I'm really not. Allison was always strong . . . never a quitter."

"I saw her jist afore I left on this assignment," said Nat.

"What did she say?"

"That she loved ye."

"I never doubted that."

"She's changin', Logan. Changin' wi' the kind o' changes God makes—as I think maybe ye are yersel'."

"I only hope it hasn't come too late," sighed Logan.

"Allison said the exact same thing."

"Did she?"

It was such a small thing—the two of them making the same statement. Is it foolish to place a hope in it? Logan wondered. Have I come to the place that I can let myself hope again, let myself believe that I might somehow fit once more into a life with Allison? Part of him yearned to be able to answer *yes*. That same part of him longed for her, and for all the things in his existence she represented—all the things he had repudiated in his own mind the day he left Stonewycke.

It had all come upon him again suddenly the moment he laid eyes on Nat. How desperately he wanted to be part of that life again! Yet at the same time he was afraid he had already gone beyond the point of no return.

"I don't know anymore, Nat," Logan said after a long pause. "I'm not afraid to tell you the whole thing confuses me more than a little. I'm so—"

He stopped again, suddenly feeling uncomfortable pouring out his innermost feelings to the younger brother he had always striven to impress with his maturity and worldly wisdom. *Anyhow*, he reasoned to himself as he tried to bring his emotions back under control, it's not right of me to burden him. He's got enough troubles of his own right now.

But Nat had little concern for his own problems, for he knew the Lord was in control of them. Instead, his focus remained zeroed in on the struggles of his brother-in-law.

"Ye dinna hae to be afraid," he said sincerely, reading in Logan's eyes what his pride could not express, "when ye belong to God."

"Who said I was afraid?" asked Logan defensively.

"I can tell."

"How did you know?"

"I've battled enough fear mysel' lately to be able to recognize it in another—it's ne'er far frae ye when ye're crouched doon on the battlefield. But I hae a feelin' yers is a more difficult kind o' confrontation because the source o' yer fear comes frae within' yersel'. But ye dinna hae to fight alone, ye ken that, dinna ye, Logan?"

"I want to know—" he replied, before his voice broke off suddenly. Tears rose to the surface of his eyes, and his voice became strangled.

He jumped up, turned away, and strode to the stone hearth, keeping his back to Nat.

"Listen," he went on after a moment, "it's too bad this war doesn't leave us the luxury of mulling over the complexities of life. In the meantime, we've got too many more urgent things to talk about than all my woes."

"*I* dinna agree, Logan," countered Nat with resignation in his tone, looking and sounding more like the battle-worn soldier he was.

"Well, I don't want to talk about it now," said Logan, "or I'm liable to turn into a blubbering fool."

"There's nothin' wrong wi' a few tears if they bring healin' to yer heart."

"You sound just like Lady Margaret."

" 'Tis nae wonder. Her blood runs through me, and she gave o' her great wisdom to all o' us. And the blood runs through *you* o' one frae whom she learned a great deal o' what she told the rest o' us. So I ken ye understand what I'm sayin'."

"In this case, however," said Logan stubbornly, "there's *everything* wrong with that particular bit of wisdom about tears and healing. It's different out here. There's no healing to be had on the front lines, Nat."

"The front lines o' life are exactly where healin' must begin," urged Nat. "When everythin's easy and there's nae tryin' o' yer faith, life takes nae inner strength. When it's all easy, ye can manage yersel'. But when things are tough, when ye *are* on the front lines, that's when yer true need shows itsel'. Ye're right—it's different here. But here ye need God *more*, not less!"

"Out here control is life—and that's one thing I can't lose, Nat: control . . . of myself."

He turned to face Nat, almost as if in unconscious challenge.

But Nat had learned something else from his great-grandmother, and that was when to leave off and allow the Spirit to perform its surgical work inside the heart of another.

The tense moment passed.

Logan immediately regretted the severity of his response. He hadn't meant to direct it toward dear Nat at all. Somehow he sensed that his brother-in-law understood. When Logan spoke again, it was in a lighter tone, as if announcing his intention to forget all that had gone before. But Nat's brow remained creased for some time, with a deep ache for his brother-in-law.

"Now," said Logan, "why don't we begin talking about how we're going to get you out of France?"

In the days that followed as they met together and began to formulate a plan, the conversation never again touched upon such personal ground. It would take a still greater tragedy than his own personal need to bring the full thrust of Nat's words, and their deeper implications, back into Logan's troubled mind.

49 / Aborted Shortcut_____

Two more nights passed without word from the BBC. But on the third evening after Logan's visit with Nat, the message finally came through:

"On ne fait pas d'omelette sans casser des oeufs."

They could expect the Lysander sometime tonight between ten p.m. and three a.m.

Logan ate dinner at the hotel with Claude and Lise, and somehow the three managed to pass the time until the hour when they would at last embark upon this long-awaited mission. Since the Carrel farm lay in the opposite direction from the airfield, they decided that Claude and Lise should go directly to the field, just in case the plane was early. Logan would retrieve Nat from the farm and take him with him to rendezvous with the others, in hopes that he could get him on the plane and safely on his way back to England.

It was nine o' clock when Logan arrived at the farm.

"Are you ready to go, Nat?"

"It's tonight, then?"

Logan nodded, and Nat flashed a grin through his pale features. Pulling himself painfully up from the chair, with Logan's assistance he hobbled to the corner where his pack lay ready and waiting.

"It is still amazin' to me," he said, "hoo my arrival in Vouziers could hae been timed so perfectly—jist in time to catch a plane ride back home."

He attempted a soft laugh, but it only ended in a painful cough. The festering wound was clearly taking its toll on his body's strength.

As they stepped out of the house, Carrel's son René volunteered to go along, and Logan gladly accepted the offer. An extra pair of hands might come in handy with Nat if they ran into any problems.

They climbed into the van and set out for the airfield, a seven mile jaunt from the farm. A full moon shone on a clear summer's night, perfectly conducive for a Lysander landing. Logan was glad they had the boy along, for without the luxury of the van's headlamps, due to the blackout, he would have been hard put to find his way on the unfamiliar roads, even in the moonlight.

After ten minutes Logan said, "I thought it was only about seven kilometers from your place to the airfield," worried that he had not yet seen any familiar landmarks indicating they were approaching their destination.

"Perhaps as the crow flies," said the lad. "But the road veers quite a bit to the north before it meets the airport road that you probably took out of town."

"I must have misread my map," said Logan. "We don't have time for delays!" It was not quite nine-thirty, but Logan was worried that he was cutting it too close. Though the plane could be several hours later, he didn't want to take any chances of Nat's not getting on board. "Is there a shorter way?" he asked after a moment's thought.

"There is an old dirt road up ahead," replied René, "not much more than a path, actually. It cuts through the woods and is very rough. But before the war it was not unknown for a young man to take his sweetheart down it in whatever vehicle he could get."

"Is it wide enough for the van?"

"Oh, oui! You should have seen some of the trucks that got through!"

"How much will it save us?"

"I don't know exactly—three or four kilometers perhaps. It's maybe three kilometers through the woods, and the airfield can't be but another kilometer or two beyond that. But the road, I would guess, is eight or nine kilometers still to go."

"We'll chance it! Where is the turnoff?"

"It should be coming up . . . there it is!"

His hand shot out the open window. Logan braked, and swung the van hard to the right and into the densely wooded area.

The road was exactly as René had described it—perhaps worse. It was soon obvious to Logan that they would probably save no time at all. But by the time the realization came they had gone too far to turn back. He therefore continued to push hard, determined to save every minute possible. He knew he had no one to blame for his poor decision other than himself.

The old van bumped and rattled along, now in nearly pitch darkness on account of the forest. Occasionally Logan heard muffled gasps from Nat. Still he drove on, squinting to see the road in the scant rays of moonlight that reached the ground.

Suddenly the sound he dreaded most to hear, next to the report of a Gestapo pistol, came unmistakably through to his ear—the sickening hiss of a tire breathing its last. He slammed on the brakes with disgust. He would now have to pay twenty minutes for the ten he had hoped to save! He climbed out of the van and walked around to the back to get the spare. With incredulity a moment later he opened the tool compartment to see nothing but emptiness!

With tires as old and threadbare as the van's, it seemed incredible that anyone would have driven it without a spare, even despite rubber rationing. But what was most disturbing of all was that he had not checked out this detail in advance. *How stupid of me!* he thought.

Sulkily, he informed his companions of their plight.

"It can't be more than two or three kilometers to go," offered René hopefully.

Logan climbed back in, seemed to debate with himself for a moment, then started the engine.

"There's no sense worrying about this wheel now," he muttered. "We may as well just see if we can push it through!"

He shifted down into first and lurched forward.

Now the ruts and potholes and deeply worn tracks of the road were next to impossible to negotiate, steering a tire with no rubber. In less than two hundred yards Logan was sweating freely with the effort of trying to control the wheel, which behaved as if it had a mind of its own. In the darkness he could not even see the rock, much less try to avoid it. Suddenly Logan's arms were wrenched from the steering wheel and the van careened into the ditch at the side of the road.

"It's my fault," groaned Logan. "I'm sorry, mates." Glancing at his watch, he saw they would never make it by ten. At least they had not yet heard the sounds of approaching aircraft.

Slowly Logan opened the door and got out. The night was still and quiet. Had there not been a war on, René's observation was probably most apt—this *would* be a romantic place. But what was he to do now?

"Let's strike oot on foot," said Nat cheerfully.

"How could you possibly make it?" asked Logan.

"I got this far, didna I? Dinna forget, that plane's my ticket home. I'll make it, I tell ye!"

"If you're up to it."

" 'Tisna but a wee bit o' a walk," said Nat encouragingly. "Wi' the two o' ye to help me, we'll get there."

"Let's just pray that the plane doesn't set down at ten and want to be back in the sky by five after."

"Aye!"

The going was painfully slow, but they moved doggedly ahead. In eleven or twelve minutes they had covered about a kilometer and the forest had begun to thin somewhat, offering more light for their path as they advanced. Nat was braced between Logan and René, and Logan was heartened with their progress when suddenly he stopped and signalled them both to be quiet.

"Did you hear that?" he whispered.

The others shook their heads. They were, however, not inclined to argue when Logan silently led them off the path into the deeper cover of the pine wood. Crouching down behind an old tree stump, with held breath they waited to see what would come of whatever sound Logan had heard.

"Monsieur," breathed René.

Logan kept his eyes toward the road, but indicated silence by raising his finger to his mouth.

"Monsieur," repeated René in a scarcely audible whisper, handing something to Logan.

"What's this?" said Logan as he took the object. As soon as his hands closed around it, he knew the answer to his own question.

"My father saw that you carried no weapon," explained René, "so he gave this to me. But I do not know how to use it."

"Well, I doubt we'll have need of it," replied Logan, reluctantly jamming the Webley revolver into his belt. "Let's go . . . I think my imagination is too active tonight."

They arose from their hiding place, inched their way forward back to the widened path, and continued on their way. In another ten minutes they had cleared the woods. The ground appeared to level out before them and the road widened perceptibly. The going had been rough for poor Nat, but now Logan hoisted him a little more strongly upon his shoulder and whispered whatever encouragement he could think of to keep his spirits up. In the distance he was sure he could make out the vague shapes of buildings.

The airfield!

"Come on, Nat!" he said, "we're almost there!"

Suddenly the disaster every agent fears struck without warning.

As if springing up from the earth itself, two German soldiers loomed up before them, blocking their way. The next instant a flash of brilliant light blinded Logan's eyes, accompanied by the sharp commands of German voices. Instantly Logan knew that all the wit in the world would not avail him this time, for he could never explain away the weapon in his belt, much less his limping, red-headed companion who carried no papers, making for a deserted airport in the middle of the night.

50 / Tragedy

Lise looked toward the road for the tenth time in the last half hour.

Since Logan had the van and she and Claude only bicycles, she had fully anticipated Logan to arrive at the airfield at nearly the same time as they, despite his detour to the farm. But she and Claude had already been there thirty minutes and still there had been no sign of the van.

She strode over to the runway where Claude was busy clearing away scattered brush and rock from the airstrip.

He glanced up as she approached. "We should have come out here days ago to do this," he grunted.

"Michel didn't want to draw unnecessary attention, either to us or to this place." She bent over, picked up a branch and flung it away. "It's not so bad, and we still have time." She could hardly believe the condition of the landing surface was Claude's only concern. "Aren't you worried?" she finally asked.

"Yes, I'm worried," he answered coldly. "We are going to have a job of it signaling the plane with only two of us."

"Claude!" exclaimed Lise angrily. "Don't you care what happens to Michel? What if he's lying dead in some ditch!"

"It is one less pair of Anglais boots to lick."

"He has never lorded it over any of us—especially you!"

"I'm going to pace off the lamp positions," he said, ignoring Lise's words. "It's nearly ten."

"You plan to do nothing about Michel?"

"I am going to do what *has* to be done, what we came here to do."

"And what makes you think we can go ahead and signal the plane without knowing what trouble there may be out there?"

"The stupid Anglais is probably just lost."

Lise grabbed up a large rock from the ground and hefted it in her hands with fire in her dark eyes. Even Claude might have felt some trepidation at that moment had there been daylight to reveal the flash from those angry orbs. But it was dark, and an instant later she heaved the rock in the air and well away from him.

"I'm going out to look for Michel," she said resolutely.

"Don't be foolish. You have no idea where he might be."

"If something happened he would try to make it here however he could—even on foot if necessary. If the road was blocked, he would go out across country, maybe through the woods. Nothing would stop him except a German patrol."

"And there are none in this area. *He* said that, remember?"

"Things can change. The Germans know this airfield is here, too. They have maps. Who knows but that they might keep it under watch? Michel may have missed something. I just know I don't like the delay."

She turned and walked off, intent on skirting the circumference of the old airport.

"You could never hope to find him out there!" called Claude after her. "It's a foolhardy attempt."

"*You* are the fool, Claude," she spat back as she wheeled around. "You revel in killing your Germans, but when the war is over, what will it all be for? Friends? Country? Ideals? You don't care about any of that. It's all for hatred. And when the last Boche is dead, what will you have gained in return? They will be dead, but you will still be carrying your hatred with you. I do not intend to turn out that way. I won't!"

She turned again and started off, but Claude threw down the armload of branches he held and called out for her to stop.

"Pace off the lamp positions," he ordered. "I'll look for your Anglais." He grabbed up the rucksack that held his Sten sub-machine gun and stalked away. But before he had gone ten paces, he stopped and turned back momentarily to face Lise. "But you are wrong. You *will* end up like me—all of you will if you want to survive. There is no other way."

Then he tramped off into the night, not realizing the stark contradiction between his present action and his words of hopelessness.

Lise watched him as he disappeared into the field that surrounded the airstrip on all sides. Was it possible that her words had actually penetrated? He didn't *have* to go. Had she just witnessed a genuine act of selflessness on the part of the seemingly unfeeling Frenchman? Maybe Claude *was* human, after all.

She shook her head at the unlikely notion. He had probably done it just to shut her up!

With a sigh, Lise returned to the task at hand. They might not have need of the lights, but they had to be ready nonetheless. She tilted her eyes up toward the star-studded sky, then back to the woods that fringed the fields in the distance. It would be just like the Germans, she thought, to keep a patrol out there—invisible, just inside the trees, waiting, watching, trying to lure the Resistance into using what appeared to be nothing but a long-forgotten and abandoned strip of concrete.

Please, she silently cried in her heart—*please, let everything turn out all right!*

"Your weapons!" ordered one of the soldiers.

Logan took the small pistol out of his belt and threw it into the dirt.

The soldier pointed his rifle at Nat and René. "Weapons!" he repeated.

"They're not armed," said Logan in his inept German.

Keeping his rifle roving between the three and his eyes glaring at them for any sudden movements, the soldier nodded to his partner.

Logan squinted into the spotlight still pointed directly into his face to see if he could determine anything about their plight, but he could see nothing. A moment later he felt hands frisking him. The second soldier then moved on to Nat and René. When he was satisfied that they had been armed only with the handgun, he stepped back with his rifle.

"What are you doing here?" demanded the first soldier.

The question seemed oddly inappropriate to Logan. Why not just haul them into Vouziers, or to their commanding officer and let Intelligence handle the questioning? But something about these two seemed peculiar . . . hesitant.

If he could just stall them somehow, thought Logan. The longer he could keep them from taking action, the more time he had to figure out something.

"My name is Michel Tanant," said Logan. "From Paris. I have travel papers."

"And do you have papers for that?" The soldier cocked his head toward the Webley. "I've seen no such weapons except what we've confiscated from the underground."

"This is all a mistake," Logan went on, hardly thinking about what he said, just trying to buy some time. "We found it along the road. We were coming to turn it in."

The young soldier smiled. Not a cruel smile, but rather one displaying profound amusement at the audacious attempt at such a ridiculous lie. The two soldiers exchanged meaningful looks from which Logan was at last able to guess what was troubling these two.

Could they be lost? he thought to himself.

Here they were, with three prisoners of war, and yet with no idea how to get them back to their unit.

"And your friend there?" asked the Nazi, indicating Nat. "He's just out for a stroll in these deserted woods, with a bad wound like he's got?"

"He's my brother-in-law," replied Logan, the truth spilling out without his even pausing to think about it. "Yes, you're right, he's wounded. Got into a scuffle with a Resistance agent. I was trying to get him into town, but our van broke down and we lost our way."

"Why are you not on the main road?"

"Because if those Free France maniacs get hold of us, they'll slit our throats. You know how they are. It's just lucky we ran into you two! Can you help us into—"

But before he could say anything further, the blinding light which the German had trained on his face was suddenly extinguished, seemingly from the sharp blast of rifle that echoed through the night.

Logan dropped to the ground. More gunfire exploded all around him. Voices shouted out in a multitude of languages. In the confusion he could understand none of it.

He scrambled around, trying to locate his gun where it had fallen. "Nat!" he called. "Nat . . . where are you?"

The only answer that met his ears was more gunfire, this time from close by. The two Germans were firing, but not at him, it seemed. More volleys sounded, this time from farther away, toward the airfield.

Logan heard a scream. It sounded like René, but he could not be sure. He still had heard nothing from Nat, but then Nat was already weak and was probably trying to conserve his strength.

More gunshots, explosive bursts of fire lighting the night, followed by blackness. Another scream of pain, followed by the throaty cursing of a German voice.

Out of the corner of his eye, Logan suddenly saw a figure spring forward. It was Nat, lurching toward one of the German soldiers who had the sights of his gun leveled directly at Logan's head. He hardly heard the quick succession of shots that followed.

Indistinctly aware of the danger he was in, Logan rolled, his fingers closing around the Webley as he did so. Another bullet whizzed within a fraction of an inch from his head. Another quickly followed, spraying dirt at his shoulder. He spun around, trying to make out Nat's form, and while dirt and grass were still spattering up into Logan's face from a third shot, he fired the revolver almost blindly in the direction of the other soldier. Even as he squeezed the trigger, something in his confused brain expected his wild shot to be followed immediately by a fatal slug from one of the Nazis which would end this sudden nightmare.

But no shot came. Everything suddenly fell silent.

Logan pulled himself to his knees, gripping the pistol in one hand and rubbing the dirt from his eyes with the other.

As his vision cleared and the moonlight brought the battlefield into focus at his feet, his whole body convulsed with the sight that met his eyes.

Three bodies bloodied the ground around him.

51 / The Landing

I should never have made Claude go, thought Lise frantically to herself. Now they were *all* separated, perhaps *all* in danger. What was worse: Lise was now stuck at the airfield alone. She did not dare leave it to search on her own, lest they return and find *her* missing.

What could have happened to Michel . . . to Claude? Was it merely some silly miscommunication they would all laugh about later? Something inside told her otherwise.

Lise paced back and forth, every now and then glancing up into the sky. At least the plane had not yet come. She was concerned for Michel's friend. Who could tell when another chance like this would come for him to get out of France so easily? His wound would make any other route impossible, even fatal.

All at once Lise heard sounds. Instinctively she glanced up into the sky again. But she realized immediately it was not the sounds of aircraft she heard. They came from far away, carried to her ears probably by a trick of the breeze.

They were short, sharp blasts—the unmistakable sounds of gunfire.

Lise scanned the fields in the direction Claude had gone, her heart trembling within her. More shots penetrated the night air. She could see occasional flashes of gunfire off in the distance, perhaps a kilometer away, at the edge of the woods.

Without even thinking her actions through, Lise started running toward the sounds, dreading what she might find. She could hear more gunfire, and shouting.

Several more shots; then all fell silent.

Lise stopped. What if the gunfire had nothing to do with her comrades? To continue on, if what she had seen and heard was indeed from a German patrol, might only attract Boche attention toward the airfield.

But what if Michel and Claude were hurt or in danger, and needed her?

She glanced back toward the airfield, then again at the now silent darkness ahead of her.

Slowly she decided to inch ahead. If she heard anything from the airfield, she would turn immediately and hasten back to it. In the meantime, remaining as cautious, quiet, and out of sight as she was able, she *had* to try to find out what had prompted the gunfire. If her comrades were wounded or dead, the plane would mean little to her now.

Slowly she made her way forward through the uncut grass, crouching now and then to keep out of sight. Minutes passed. Still she saw and heard nothing. Still she seemed no nearer her destination.

Then in the distance came the sound she had been half-dreading. Faintly overhead came the distant whine of the single-engine aircraft.

Logan crouched on the ground, numb. Gradually he awoke from his stupor, his hands shaking. About a foot away lay the revolver where it had slipped from his fingers.

Suddenly he remembered. A young German soldier lay dead, probably less than ten feet away. He could not make out whatever expression had been fixed on his face when Logan's reckless bullet had snuffed out his life. Logan could not see past the circle of blood in his chest. He turned around, lurched, and was sick.

A moment later he felt a gentle hand on his shoulder. He started half to his feet, turned, and nearly shrank away. He looked up into René's stricken face. The boy had tears streaming down his dirty cheeks. Logan couldn't cry. The devastation wracking his brain was too tormenting for weeping to wash away.

There were other bodies nearby, but Logan was afraid to look at them. He knew one was Nat's.

Less than two minutes had passed since the first rounds had been fired. He didn't want to face more death. But he had to. Nat was there.

He forced himself up to his feet, then to his brother-in-law's prostrate form. He laid a hand on the lad's chest. Was there a faint movement he felt? Nat slowly opened his eyes.

"Logan," he whispered weakly, "ye're all right, then?"

"Nat. . . !" cried Logan, but whatever other words he felt in his heart caught in his throat.

He tore off his jacket and pressed it against the wound in Nat's abdomen. Then he slumped down beside the wasted form, staring blankly ahead.

Some flickering remnant of who he was, or who he was supposed to be, kept trying to force its way into his dulled consciousness. He had to *do* something! The shots might have alerted the rest of some German patrol; they had to get moving!

"Your comrade is coming around," called René into the blur of Logan's mind.

"What?"

"Your other comrade," said the youth. "It was he who surprised our captors, off there in the field."

Logan gently laid down Nat's head and went in the direction the boy pointed. Claude had a deep gash on his head, whether from the gunfire or from striking a nearby rock as he had dived for cover Logan couldn't immediately tell. But he would survive, with only another ragged, ugly scar to add to his morbid collection. Logan reached a hand out to help him as he tried to rise, but Claude shook him away.

"I can manage," he growled. "What happened to the Boche?"

"You killed one," replied Logan. "I owe you my life."

"Save your thanks for someone who needs it! And the other?"

"I killed him," said Logan.

"You, Anglais?" exclaimed Claude in derisive disbelief. "I didn't think you had the guts!"

Logan did not reply.

"We'd better get out of here!" said Claude.

Still Logan just stared blankly forward. How could Claude think so clearly after all that had just happened? But then, this wasn't Claude's *first* killing. Did it get easier? Would he one day be able to gun down his enemy without a thought? Such a prospect was even more fearsome than the act of killing itself.

What finally forced Logan back into action, mechanical though it might have been, was the thought of Nat. He was still alive! If they could just make it to the airstrip and get him aboard the Lysander! He had to get Nat home—home to Stonewycke, to his mother, to Allison.

They walked back, and with Logan and René carrying Nat, and Claude stumbling ahead, they managed to get on the move again. Whatever their difficulties had been before, they were multiplied tenfold now. Though Nat should never have been moved, Logan knew whatever chance he had at all depended on that plane. Fortunately, by this time Nat was beyond pain.

"Faster," urged Claude, starting to outdistance them. "It's not far."

But the words were barely out of his mouth when they heard the sound of the plane. In another moment it came into sight in the light of the moon, though it carried no lights of its own. The little Lysander buzzed once over the airstrip, the pilot probably checking his coordinates to assure himself that this dark area was indeed the right field. It circled once more, dipping low enough to make out whatever figures might be below, if there were any.

By this time Lise was sprinting back toward the runway. Suddenly Logan's numbed mind snapped back into action. That plane represented Nat's only hope! It might circle one more time, but then it would take the lack of activity as a sign that the mission had been scrubbed. They had to signal the pilot.

"René," said Logan hurriedly, "run on ahead to the field and help Lise signal the plane."

"There may be a Boche patrol out there, fool!" said Claude. "We must let the plane go!"

"I don't care if the entire Wehrmacht is out there!" cried Logan "Go, René—now! You too, Claude."

Perhaps in his weakened condition Claude had no more heart to argue.

Perhaps the thought of Logan in the hands of the Boche again wasn't such a bad idea after all. Whatever the case, he trotted off as quickly as he could.

By now Lise was almost back to the strip, but she still did not know if it would be safe to light the lamps.

Logan picked up Nat, carrying him in both arms, and, staggering under the weight, continued on one slow step at a time.

"Logan," Nat breathed, his voice barely audible, thin and pale. "We've got to stop . . . the pain—"

"It's not far, Nat! Can you hear the plane?"

"I'm na goin' to make the plane—Logan—got to rest—"

"No," said Logan. "We'll make it!"

He quickened his pace only to stumble over an exposed root. He crumpled to his knees, easing Nat as gently to the ground as he could. Immediately he got his arms around Nat's shoulders and under his knees and tried again to stand, though his own strength was all but spent.

"Please, Logan . . . rest . . ."

"You're almost home, Nat. Just a bit farther."

"I'm on my way home, Logan, but na to Stonewycke."

"You can't die, Nat! Hang on!"

"I love ye, Logan! But let me go. 'Tis all right, ye ken . . . I dinna mind sae much as long as I ken ye and dear Allison will be together again."

"We will be, I promise."

"Ye was always a big brother to me—I'm glad it's you that's wi' me noo . . . at the end." He winced sharply in pain, but struggled to go on speaking: "Do ye remember when the old Austin was stalled and ye—?"

But young Nathaniel MacNeil said no more. In the arms of his sister's husband, he calmly slipped away into that rest he longed for, with the smile of a happy memory of their first meeting on his lips.

The moment Claude and René had arrived, Lise had left them to greet the plane and its delivery of the two Gaullist agents. Then she shot off to help Logan in whatever way she might.

Before she had run twenty yards into the darkness, she heard the bitter groan of Logan's voice in the distance, crying his brother-in-law's name. Logan's heartfelt agony and self-recrimination was too keen to accept the reality before him. Neither could he even begin to comprehend the peace on Nat's dying face.

When Lise approached she found Logan hunched over Nat, his body shaking in a convulsion of weeping.

52 / Duplicity

Now it was no longer a game to Logan Macintyre. No more jocular cons. The whole thing had soured, and the business turned dirty.

Lise had seen it coming. Perhaps he had sensed it, too. Now all his reasons for being where he was had faded into reality, and a hollow emptiness settled over both Logan Macintyre and Michel Tanant.

He had always mastered the art of distancing himself from death. Claude and Antoine and others in the underground had done the killing. Nat and Alec and two soldiers in a Vouziers wood faced the bloody battlefields of the war. But now Logan *himself* had tasted the guilt of blood on his own hands. Days later the thought of what he had done turned his stomach. True, he had grabbed the gun and fired out of the sheer instinct for preservation of life—both his and Nat's. But such reasoning could not quell the self-reproach in his heart. It would never erase the horrible picture of the blood-spattered German soldier lying at his feet.

Nor would he ever be able to forget the awful helplessness of holding his dying brother-in-law in his arms.

Lise tried to convince him it wasn't his fault. And of course, it wasn't. But Nat's death had been a truly heroic one—a wounded man, throwing himself at an enemy soldier, saving the life of his brother-in-law, his hero, by taking the fatal bullet in his own chest.

What had he ever done himself that could compare in heroism? Nothing! His life was marked by duplicity and falsehood. His own wife didn't even know where he was, and with her brother dead at his feet, all he could do was load the battered body onto the plane and watch it soar back into the night sky for England.

The facts may not have indicted him. But he could not escape the feeling of culpability. That night in the Vouziers wood had been a night of death, and Logan would never be the same again.

Logan gazed around the crowded cafe where he had just met Paul and passed some messages on to him for Henri. Paul was gone now, and Logan too should be on his way. He had to meet with von Graff in half an hour, and that surely was reason enough to linger. He watched absently as a group of drunken patriots sang *La Marseillaise* in celebration of Bastille Day.

Allons, enfants de la patrie!
Hark! hark! what myriads bid you rise!

273

> Yours children, wives, and grandsires hoary,
> Behold their tears and hear their cries!

But Logan's patriotic fervor could not be nudged. In the past year he had been in France, he had become as much a Frenchman as any Scot could hope to become. He should feel a pride in thus having united himself with his country's ancient ally. With what pride would not the grand dame of Scottish legend, Mary Queen of Scots, look down on him for his efforts to help the kinsmen of her mother! Now, like so many noble Scotsmen of past times, he had even killed for the glorious cause.

But there was no joy in the heart of Logan Macintyre today. And as he sat listening to the rousing song, all he could think was that those poor blokes were likely to end up in front of a firing squad for their efforts.

Wearily Logan rose. He could not prolong his meeting any longer.

Von Graff wore an unhappy expression, one that seemed to mark his aristocratic features more and more of late.

"You were gone from Paris a whole week!" he stormed.

"My girl wanted a holiday," Logan replied stoically.

"Yet you did not see fit to inform me?"

"I didn't see that it was your business."

"Everything you do is my business!"

Logan shrugged.

Von Graff rose ominously from his chair.

"Anyway," Logan went on defiantly, "I thought we agreed that I would have no watchdogs."

"And *I* kept our bargain," said the general, sitting back in his chair more composed. "*This* is how I found out."

He held up a document which Logan assumed was his application for travel papers.

He eyed it indifferently.

Von Graff laid down the application, and after studying Logan's expression for a moment, spoke again.

"What's wrong with you, Herr MacVey?" he said in a more sympathetic tone than he had yet used. "Are you growing weary of the double game—mixed loyalties—betraying your own countrymen—all of that? It happens, believe me . . . only too often."

Logan followed von Graff's lead. After all, it was more than half true.

"I think the week in Reims helped," he replied. "Sometimes it's just nice to forget about everything. I guess that's why I went without saying anything."

"There was Resistance activity some forty kilometers from Reims last week."

"Oh?"

"Is that all you have to say?"

"I try not to blow up trains when I'm on holiday."

"It was not a train."

"What then?"

"Nothing was blown up at all, Herr MacVey. I thought you might already know that important fact."

Logan lifted up his eyes to squarely meet von Graff's. "After all these months," he said, "I think I'd be somewhat immune from these tiresome cross-examinations."

"No one is immune," replied von Graff. "Even I must face them."

"You, General?"

"When the Jewish section chief, Herr Eichmann, visited Paris recently, I was hard-pressed to make as good an account of my months here as I would have liked."

"Had you up against the wall, did he?"

"I hoped I might be able to report more significant arrests."

"But at least you didn't have as many *significant* escapes," said Logan optimistically. "You must admit I've done that much for you."

"Perhaps. But the escapes *do* go on, and L'Escroc remains unapprehended."

"L'Escroc has been lying low lately."

"True, but by now I had hoped to see more results from your operations."

"I've set you up with several ideal opportunities," parried Logan. "Can I be blamed if your strong-arm boys haven't kept up their end?"

"All right, MacVey, no blame is laid," conceded the general. "But tomorrow night we may all have a chance to reprieve ourselves."

"A new assault against Free France, eh?"

"Not exactly. A new thrust which Hitler apparently feels is equally important to the subduing of resistant regimes: there is to be a raid on Parisian Jews. Some thirty thousand are scheduled for arrest."

"Thirty thousand Jews!" exclaimed Logan in unmasked shock.

"It's all part of Herr Eichmann's Final Solution. It should come as no surprise really. Berlin's racial loyalties, shall we say, are well known. It would come as no surprise to me if this is merely the beginning."

"Such an action will play havoc with the terms of the Armistice," said Logan. "The Führer will lose much support."

"The Armistice is a sham and always has been. Even Pétain knows that. As far as the Führer's popularity goes—I doubt it will suffer much. He's never been popular with the Jews anyway."

Herr von Graff attempted a chuckle, but even he was capable of realizing how inept humor seemed at that moment. "Besides," he went on, "the French police will conduct the raid—no German soldiers will be involved at all."

"So why are you telling me all this?"

"I want you on your toes," replied von Graff. "An event of this magnitude is likely to bring the underground out in droves—especially its leaders. We could make quite a score in addition to the Jewish scenario—perhaps even L'Escroc will show his face."

"Shall I dangle this information about today, and see if I get any bites . . . stir up the pot, so to speak?" Logan knew he would have to warn the underground of the raid; he hoped with von Graff's affirmative answer to be able to protect his Trinity cover at the same time.

"We prefer the utmost security," replied von Graff. "However, we know there has already been some leaking. Not enough to endanger the scheme, however."

"No mass exodus of Jews?"

"Where would they go? Most are marked well enough by their foreign accents and identification papers. All the railroad stations and exits from the city are being stringently watched. And the punishment for getting picked up with false papers is far worse than the prospect of a labor camp."

"That's where they will be sent, then?"

"That is my assumption. What else would they do with them?"

"But I cannot imagine facilities large enough for such an army of prisoners."

"No matter. What happens to them after the raid is not our concern, now is it?"

53 / Vouziers Once More _____

The fine summer day gleaming over the Vouziers countryside went unnoticed by Arnaud Soustelle.

He had not come here on holiday as Trinity had claimed so convincingly to General von Graff. The general was a fool, for some idiotic reason mesmerized by the smooth-talking Anglais.

Soustelle, however, was neither mesmerized nor convinced. He did not like his influence being usurped and was determined to rectify the situation. He had argued stoutly against the chances of such a coincidence occurring. But von Graff insisted on believing his double agent. Perhaps von Graff has come to the point of being forced to support MacVey, thought Soustelle. If Trinity turns out to be counterfeit, it will reflect very poorly on the S.S. General who recruited him, especially at the very time his fortunes were sagging on other fronts. Nonetheless, Soustelle was going to bring down Trinity, even if it meant taking von Graff with him.

"Stay away from him, Soustelle," von Graff had warned. "Don't let that calm exterior deceive you. MacVey is nobody's patsy!"

"Bah!" replied the Frenchman. "You think I fear such a snail!"

"I doubt you have the senses to fear him," answered the general. "I'm simply telling you that if you insist on carrying on this petty little rivalry, I cannot help it if you bring trouble upon your own head."

"I will do what suits me, and even you cannot stop me, General!" sneered Soustelle.

Von Graff smiled. "Do not tempt me, Soustelle," he said, evidently pleased at the thought of Soustelle crossing the line and going a step too far.

Soustelle said nothing further, only turned and left the general's office, more resolute than ever.

Thus it was, now knowing the content of the conversation between the general and the Anglais, that Soustelle had taken the next early morning express to Reims—a quicker ride than Logan had enjoyed. Working a couple of local connections, he had been led to a certain bakery which, hardly a surprise to Soustelle, turned out to be a cog in the Resistance network. Three agents had been arrested and interrogated. No telling what gems would be dragged from those three before they were finally shot, thought Soustelle with grim pleasure. He had walked away from the interrogation proceedings, leaving the rest of the questioning in the hands of

277

the local Gestapo chief the moment the first important bit of information had been obtained. A bakery van had been taken to Vouziers.

The pieces were fitting together nicely. MacVey goes to Reims, supposedly on holiday. Then, what do you know? A Resistance van departs to Vouziers, only a few kilometers from the underground operation that had taken place in the area. Soustelle wanted to know: who was driving that van? He could have hung around Reims until the information was forced out of one of the captured agents. But that could take days. Vouziers was a small enough village; it would be a simple matter to circulate a description of MacVey about.

Soustelle glanced at his watch as he bounced along the back road in a commandeered Gestapo automobile. He'd drive back to Paris after he had finished in Vouziers; he'd be there some time tonight.

"Ha! ha!" he said almost merrily. "Before tomorrow I will have Trinity in irons!"

He had already decided to gather his evidence and grab Trinity before saying a word to von Graff. He would handle the whole thing on his own, except perhaps for a few well-placed Gestapo agents to make sure he didn't slip away from him. But he wouldn't chance the stupidity of others to foul his coup. Besides, if he nabbed MacVey himself, it would give him time to rough up that pretty face a little before having to turn him in. Above all, he didn't want to allow that Anglais-loving Nazi von Graff to take the glory for himself of exposing Trinity for the traitor Soustelle knew him to be.

Soustelle popped a licorice drop into his mouth, revelling in fantasies of his great victory.

He turned into the town. His first stop would be the French police inspector. He happened to know him from his own days as a gendarme— a fat, lazy excuse for authority. But he could be easily bought.

It was after ten p.m. when Soustelle arrived back in Paris from his successful foray to Vouziers. The drive had been wearing, but he wasn't about to pause in the hunt, not when he was so close.

Lawrence MacVey had indeed been to Vouziers, not only in the company of a woman but also with a sinister-looking man, so he had gathered from a number of interviews. As far as the ex-policeman was concerned, *that* was plenty to accuse him of his double game. But he was prepared should von Graff insist on even more evidence. There were a couple of low-lifes in the town whom he had paid handsomely to swear they had seen MacVey in the vicinity of the abandoned airport where a British plane was reported to have landed at the time when MacVey had been around. Soustelle knew the Anglais was guilty, no matter what the softbellied general said. If he had to manufacture a few facts to support it, then so be it.

Unfortunately his successes had come to an abrupt end the moment he entered Paris. He'd driven directly to MacVey's apartment, but the scoundrel wasn't there. Then had begun several more hours of wearisome detective work in an attempt to track the traitor down, but to little avail. He'd gone to the cafe he knew to be a favorite with Trinity. He'd rousted several persons out of bed for questioning. He had canvassed the neighborhood. He came back to the apartment, picked the lock, gave the place a thorough search, but saw that the British agent was extremely careful—the rooms were spotlessly clean, except for a book of matches from one of the many Left Bank cafes. He tried that cafe, hung around till it closed, questioned the employees, but learning nothing more than what he had already been told: MacVey had been seen two or three times in the company of the same woman.

At length, before departing to follow a new tack, Soustelle called in a couple of S.D. agents particularly loyal to him, whose silence he knew he could trust. He picked them up, drove them to the apartment, stationed them across the street to watch the building, then ran inside and up the stairs one more time himself. In several moments he emerged back onto the street, crossing it slowly to his cronies.

"Still no sign of him," he said. "He must be beyond worrying about curfew. It's almost two a.m."

"What do you want us to do if he comes, Herr Soustelle?" asked one of the men.

"Make sure he stays inside. Don't apprehend him unless he tries to leave again. If he goes in, lay low and wait for me. This traitor is mine! If he tries to go out again, nab him. But don't hurt so much as a hair of his head. That pleasure, too, will be mine!"

"You will be back soon?"

"I don't know. You just watch the building and wait. I have one other lead to try."

With that Soustelle turned away and walked down the street quickly into the Paris night. This Trinity, whoever he really was, had proved more slippery than he had anticipated. But if he was not home yet, there could be but one other place he was spending the night. It now seemed this woman with whom he had been seen so often might be his only lead. He knew well enough where to find her. He should have gone straight there in the first place! Where else could the fool MacVey be?

Lise had left Logan and returned to her apartment just before midnight. She and Logan and Antoine had spent the entire day spreading the alarm about the coming roundup of Jews, as quickly yet discreetly as possible, so as not to endanger Logan's cover.

She would still be about that business had not Michel insisted she return to the safety of her home. There was no telling what might befall a Jewish girl on the streets that night.

She lay down on her bed, not intending to sleep. She had not even changed her clothes. She had worked hard knocking on doors, passing along secret messages, warning of the raid. She only hoped no Nazi agents had seen their activities. It wouldn't take much for them to put two and two together, she thought. Her association with Michel was well known. Yet there was a time to cast caution to the wind. And tonight, with thousands of Jewish lives in the balance, seemed like just such a time.

Reflecting on the day's events, Lise fell into a deep sleep.

Some hours later, she was suddenly awakened by a sharp sound. She started up, glanced quickly about, and tried to collect her wits.

It was still dark. All was quiet. It must still be the middle of the night.

She had been dreaming vaguely of gendarmes pounding on Jewish doors, dragging them off to violent deaths. Slowly she lay back down, breathing heavily and perspiring freely.

There came the pounding again! This time it was no dream! Someone was beating on *her* door, and the angry yells that accompanied it did not sound friendly. Even with all her precautions, was *she* going to be raided and hauled off to Germany?

Shaking with fear, she jerked up again and leaped from her bed. Flight would be foolish. She would have to confront them, whoever it was.

She threw a bathrobe over her clothes as a precaution, so as not to look like she had been out, then crept to the front room. Desperately she tried to shake off the remnants of sleep and organize her mind. The knock was not one of the prearranged Resistance signals. It could be no friend. Even as she realized it could be only the Gestapo or the French police, she tried to gain confidence thinking how Michel, with his bravado, would handle the situation. "There's always an angle," he would say.

She switched on a light, then turned the deadbolt and opened the door, squinting sleepily.

"What is it?" she said in a thick, sluggish voice not too difficult to assume at that hour.

"You are Claire Giraud?"

"Yes, I am," she answered. The name was an alias she had used to rent the apartment.

The man who spoke seemed vaguely familiar to her, a Frenchman to be sure, judging by his lack of accent. He was a large, barrel-chested man with a strange odor hanging about him that she could not immediately place. He was not Gestapo, but there was something about him . . .

Then she remembered. Arnaud Soustelle.

"You are acquainted with Michel Tanant?" he demanded rather than asked.

"I—" She rubbed her eyes groggily. "It's so late. What is going on?"

"Do not play games with me, Mademoiselle! I know you are his woman!"

"Is he all right?" she asked. It would have been futile to deny knowing him.

"Quit stalling!" barked Soustelle. "Tell me where he is!"

"I don't know. Has there been an accident?"

Without answering, Soustelle shoved her aside and stalked into the apartment. Roughly pulling apart drapes, throwing aside bedcovers, and flinging open closet doors, he made a hasty search of the three small rooms. Then he turned on Lise again.

"The man is an enemy agent!" he spat. "Though I have few doubts that piece of information is news to you! And he will be captured . . . tonight! If you do not want to join him, you better tell me where to find him!"

"An agent? What can you mean?"

"Bah! You are a fool for protecting him!"

"I can't believe it. He told me—"

"Where is he?" yelled Soustelle, losing his grip on what little patience he still possessed.

"I—I assume he is at home in bed, where every sane person ought to be at such an hour."

"Tanant is neither at home in bed, nor is he a sane man for attempting his dirty double-cross."

"This is all such a shock," said Lise in a trembly voice. She ran a frustrated hand through her hair. "I just don't know anything."

"You *must* know that Tanant is not his real name!"

"I thought he was—"

"Thought he was what?" interrupted Soustelle.

"He told me he was from Lyon," said Lise, praying it was the same story Michel had told the Germans. "He said he was a bookseller."

Soustelle eyed her thoughtfully for a moment.

"I wonder . . ." he mused. Then in a sudden, lightning-quick move, he grabbed Lise by the arm and spun her around so that the arm twisted up painfully behind her back. The act caught her completely by surprise and she gasped in genuine pain.

"I could force the information from you, you know!"

"P—please," sputtered Lise. "We've gone out a few times—I know nothing *about* him. A few cafes, that's all. You must believe me."

"Which cafes?" She gave him two names, neither of which she or Michel had ever been to.

"Who are his friends?"

"I know none of them."

Soustelle gave her arm a cruel jerk.

"Don't you think I would tell you? It was always just he and I—alone. I thought maybe he was married, and so kept our relationship very discreet. Please! I am telling the truth." Real tears flowed from her eyes. But the act did not seem to move Soustelle.

The Frenchman ruminated a moment over her words, then loosened his grip. But before letting go completely, he gave her a harsh shove and she crumpled to the floor.

"You are lying!" he sneered. "I can smell the deceit in every word! And do not think you will escape! I will be back when I have time, and will take more thorough steps to extract the information from you!"

Soustelle spun around and stomped away. Lise remained a moment longer where she sat on the floor, still stunned that he had left without arresting her.

But there was no time to spend enjoying her momentary triumph.

She had to warn Michel!

Yet, how could she? She had no more idea where he was than Soustelle did! But she had to do something!

In a sudden moment of resolve, Lise jumped from the floor, grabbed her coat and put it on in place of the robe, paused another minute to take her revolver out of hiding, dropped it into her handbag, and flew for the door. If she couldn't locate Michel to warn him, she at least had to keep an eye on Soustelle. If Michel had been found out, everything could tumble down. She had to keep the Frenchman away from him!

As she exited her building, Lise caught a fading glimpse of Soustelle's black Renault rounding a corner in the distance. She jumped on her bicycle and hurried in pursuit in that direction. It was going to be difficult keeping him in sight. She would have to stay in the shadows and watch her every move. Not only was it well beyond curfew, but of all nights, this was not a safe one for a Jew to be abroad in the streets of Paris.

55 / "La Grande Rafle"

At three a.m., July 16, 1942, nine thousand French policemen were dispatched to conduct the Great Raid.

Truckloads of police roared onto the rue Vieille du Temple and other Jewish districts of Paris. They poured through the narrow streets and stormed the buildings, where, inside, their terrified, helpless victims crouched in dread.

Thousands had been able to heed the warnings tirelessly spread by the underground, but many simply had not the means or the strength or the capacity to believe that such a horror was possible.

Many men fled, leaving wives and children behind, believing they would be spared as they had always been in the past. But the gendarmes beat down doors and dragged them out—not only the men they could find, but women and children also. One frenzied Jewess, clutching her infant child in her arms, leaped from her upper-story window, carrying them both to their deaths on the street below rather than face what she now realized must be their only alternative.

It was a new reign of terror in Paris, and somehow as Logan trudged down a darkened back street with Antoine, he could not find much solace in reminding himself of the thousands that had been saved. Later, when he saw the statistics on von Graff's desk, he would know the bold facts: almost thirteen thousand Jews would be arrested before this Nazi operation was over, with over four thousand of that number children.

But on that sultry summer night, his eyes saw what no statistics could tell. Hundreds of human beings were prodded like cattle down the street before him, some with suitcases or hastily assembled bundles of their meager belongings.

At one point as Logan watched from the shadows, a woman struggling with three children and two clumsy bundles, shuffled past. One of the children stumbled over a loose brick in the sidewalk, and, skinning his hands and knees, cried out to his mother. Instinctively Logan began to step forward to help, but Antoine grabbed his arm and yanked him back.

"Don't be foolish," hissed the Frenchman.

Logan wrenched his arm from Antoine's grasp, but it was too late. A gendarme had grabbed up the child and shoved him toward his mother.

"Keep moving!" he shouted, jabbing each of them in the back with the butt of his rifle.

The sad parade continued past. Neither Logan nor Antoine moved, for they both realized they could do no more. Why they even stayed, watching the procession well beyond the curfew as it was, they could not tell. Perhaps their utter feeling of emotional helplessness had made their legs unable to move also. Perhaps because something deep inside them hoped that the impression of such a sight into the hearts and minds of sane men might prevent it from ever happening again.

In another few minutes an aged rabbi hobbled by, a prayer shawl peeking out from beneath his drab coat, his white sidelocks dripping with perspiration from the intense strain of this late night ordeal. Sewed to the front of his coat was the yellow star all French Jews had recently been forced to wear. But above the star, he had defiantly pinned his Croix de Guerre and Legion d'Honneur medals—a hero of France marching in disgrace, herded aboard a truck like a sheep to the slaughter.

Logan watched, feeling the shame any sensitive man must certainly feel at such a sight. But before he had a chance to reflect on the plight of the old rabbi further, at his side Logan heard a strangled cry. He looked around and saw that Antoine's face was twisted with agony from the sight. Tears coursed down his cheeks.

"Mon Dieu!" he breathed, his hands clenched into fists at his side.

The old Jew heard Antoine's words and paused, looking directly at the two Resistance men. His penetrating gaze, to their surprise, was not one that spoke of defeat, but rather was filled with pride, and even displayed a courageous attempt to comfort his countrymen.

"Hear, O Israel, the Lord our God, the Lord is One" was all he could say before he shuffled off with his people.

Antoine started forward out of the shadows. Now it was Logan's turn to restrain his friend.

"What are you doing?" asked Logan.

"Going with my people," replied Antoine.

"Your people?"

"That's right . . . I qualify as one of them," he returned bitterly.

"What?" said Logan in alarm.

"I have a great-grandfather, though always it was hidden because we were good Catholics."

"Antoine, I can understand this must be hard for you. But you cannot do what you are thinking."

The Frenchman's sole response was to take another step forward.

"We need you, Antoine!" Logan called desperately.

He turned his large, shaggy head around. "I think perhaps now is a time when they need me more," he said. "Who knows, maybe I can do some good there." He turned back around and stepped out in line with the slow procession.

Logan said nothing further.

Perhaps Antoine was right. What might not the vibrant, passionate patriot be able to accomplish among these Jews just now to hearten them, perhaps even somehow to help deliver them? He watched as Antoine picked up two struggling children in his strong arms. No, Logan could not stop him, despite the emptiness he felt inside at the loss of his friend.

As soon as this group was past and no more gendarmes were in sight, Logan turned and walked out of his hiding place and in the opposite direction into the night.

Antoine seemed to have found his way—his special path, as had Jean Pierre. Logan wondered if he would ever find his. Tonight he had helped to save many lives, yet he could still not feel the satisfaction that should have come had what he was doing been right—truly *right*—for him. He had even ceased to have that tingling sense of exhilaration he had always experienced before. He was like a dead man—no past, no present, no future, no sense of who he was or who he ought to be.

But his thoughts were interrupted, as they often were these days, the next instant. At the end of the street he spotted a gendarme. Quickly he sprang into the cover of a dark building. His heart pounded and his body pulsed with the overpowering instinct of survival. No matter what his head tried to tell him, his emotions were *not* dead. Something was keeping him from complete despair, stubbornly stirring the embers of life inside him. He *wanted* to live. *Is it possible*, he wondered, the thought flashing through his brain in the very moment of his fear, *that even though I have gone my own way, God has kept His tether tenaciously around me—this far from home, this far from my past life? Is God still there, still loving me as I felt ten years ago?*

Back then life had seemed simple enough. He was a one-dimensional being. Now it had all grown so complicated. His wife . . . his daughter . . . this horrible war! Back then it had been relatively easy to say *yes* to God. But through the years it had proved more and more difficult to bring God into the daily struggles of life. And now. . . ? Now suddenly it seemed that so much time had passed . . . and gradually his life with God had evaporated as if it were only a distant memory. He felt as if he were a prisoner of events, herded along just like the poor Jews he had tried to save. He too was being prodded and pushed by circumstances and times and people outside his control, toward an unknown and fearsome future. For him, as for the Jews, there seemed to be no way out. What could he do to change it? People depended on him. He had cut the bonds to the past.

Yet . . . was he truly being pushed against his will? No. He was not like the Jews. *They* were victims; he was not. He had created his own prison—his own death camp. He could not blame the war, he could not blame Allison, he could not blame God. He knew there was only one person to blame.

The gendarme passed.

Logan had several more blocks to go before he was out of the Jewish district. His need to be especially vigilant forced his probing thoughts once more into abeyance. For the moment he must concentrate on getting home, where he would then be safe to explore the paths of his frustrated mind. By now, however, he had learned that self-examination could sometimes be no less perilous than walking the dangerous streets of Nazi-occupied Paris.

Once he had distanced himself from the Jewish sections of the city, Logan encountered no obstacles as he made his way through the deep, moonless, quiet night. Everything around him was still, even peaceful. There was, however, an eerie aspect with which the tall stone buildings were clothed. The city itself seemed to take on a sinister feel when Logan reminded himself of the awful and cruel upheaval to so many lives occurring only a kilometer or two away.

But in less than fifteen minutes Logan turned onto his own street. Soon he would be safely home, where he could rest his weary body and tormented mind.

Breathlessly Lise stopped short at the end of the street.

She had managed to catch up with Soustelle after leaving her place, but in the dark, both staying with him and avoiding his detection was not easy. It did not take long for her to realize that he was heading directly for Michel's. She would literally have had to fly in order to outdistance the ill-intentioned Frenchman and warn Michel before his arrival, even taking paths his auto could not traverse. So she contented herself to follow as closely as she dared. She only hoped some way help would present itself. Now she was almost to Michel's apartment.

Soustelle braked his Renault and stepped out. Lise could proceed no farther because her prey had not gone directly to the building. Instead, he had crossed the street and was now conferring with two agents—either Gestapo or S.D., she couldn't tell from where she stood—who had been hiding in the shadows directly across from the building. Soustelle was not in this alone; the suspicions must be more widespread than she thought if they had the whole place under surveillance!

Lise waited where she was and watched.

After his brief conversation with his comrades, the French detective turned toward the building. Michel cannot possibly have returned by now! she thought. In desperation she had phoned him ten minutes ago, nearly losing Soustelle as she had paused at a phone booth. But by then she had been sure of his destination and decided to risk the delay. In any case, there had been no answer. What was Soustelle up to? Did he plan to wait for Michel inside the building?

While she was puzzling over what to do, suddenly Lise saw Logan approaching from the opposite end of the street. He was already closer to the building than she, unaware of the two agents watching opposite, who had ducked out of sight at his approach. Lise couldn't call out a warning now without alerting the enemy too, and there was no telling how many agents Soustelle had posted about the place.

She had to warn Michel of the trap awaiting him!

While the watching agents were hidden, Lise, now on foot, darted across to the same side of the street as the apartment, edged her way closer, trying to keep out of view. By now Logan had already entered the building.

Lise hastily scrambled her way around a corner and to an alleyway she knew. There was only one thing for her to do now—she had to try to get to Michel *inside* the building, and before Soustelle got his hands on him. If only she wasn't already too late!

Once out of sight from the front, Lise tore down the alley and to a side entrance to the building she and Michel had used several times. Once inside she quietly ran along the corridor to the main staircase, turned, and sneaked hurriedly up the stairs toward Michel's apartment.

Logan's senses were keenly enough honed that he should have sensed his danger, even if his eyes did not *see* it.

But it was four in the morning, and he had been on his feet for twenty-four hours. All he could think of was a hot bath and a few hours sleep.

He turned in to his building, unconscious of all the eyes upon him, and trudged up the stairs to his second floor flat.

He unlocked his door, pushed it open, and entered.

Suddenly his dull senses sprang to life. A faint whiff of something lingered in the thick, dark air . . . a strange odor he had noticed on one or two other occasions. Where had he been when he had detected it before? Hadn't it been when he and von Graff—

But the moment Logan remembered, and thus recognized his danger, it was too late.

Licorice!

In the very instant of the realization, suddenly the large hands of Arnaud Soustelle grabbed him from behind, wrapping a vise-grip around his shoulders and neck.

"So, Anglais!" he growled menacingly. "We meet again! But this time it is I who seem to have the advantage."

Logan struggled to free himself, but he was no match for the overpowering bulk and street-trained skill of the Frenchman. Soustelle laughed scornfully at the attempt, then threw him crashing up against an adjacent wall, twisting Logan's arm up mercilessly behind him. The moment Logan felt the cold steel of a blade against his throat, he ceased his writhing to get loose.

"I would like to save you for the Gestapo," rasped Soustelle, panting from the effort of his attack on Logan, "but it would grieve me not the least to slit your throat here and now!"

"What do you have against me?" asked Logan, his voice choking from one of Soustelle's muscular arms.

"Nothing I do not share against all Englishmen!" replied Soustelle, hatred oozing from his tone.

"I thought we were on the same side, Soustelle!" said Logan, though all his instincts told him the charade was over.

"I know all about you, MacVey, or Tanant, or Trinity, or whatever your name might be."

"I don't know what you're talking about."

"It's all over, don't you understand? I know you are a British agent!"

"Even von Graff knows that! Why do you think I'm so useful to him?"

"You are through playing games with me!" sneered Soustelle. "It's over, I tell you. You're *still* a British agent, through and through. And I think I can also prove that you are L'Escroc."

"That's absurd, Soustelle! Wait till I tell von Graff that you—"

The Frenchman pressed the knife against Logan's skin. "Shut up, you miserable Anglais! You may swindle the stupid Germans, but the game is up with me. Perhaps you would like to confess now, and save us the trouble of interrogation, eh?"

Even as he spoke, Soustelle began to drag Logan toward the door of the apartment and onto the landing. Once there, he didn't much care whether the Anglais went voluntarily or if he had to kick him tumbling down the stairs. He had him now!

"So, how did von Graff find out?" asked Logan, trying to buy time.

"Von Graff, bah!" spat Soustelle as he kicked open the apartment door and began dragging Logan toward the head of the stairway about ten feet away. "As far as that witless Nazi is concerned, you are still his little pet!"

"Well, I'm impressed, Soustelle," taunted Logan. "I never thought you had it in you."

"Why you filthy—!" Soustelle raised his knife ominously into the air. "I'll kill you now—"

All at once a shot rang through the quiet corridor.

The first thought that raced through Logan's bewildered brain was that the Frenchman must have an accomplice. Then the heavy body of his attacker slumped, and he felt the grip of his arms loosen before the ponderous heft of the ex-detective collapsed lifelessly to the floor.

The next instant, before he had a chance to collect his wits, the door below burst open and the building was filled with shouting German voices.

"The shot came from upstairs!"

"Follow me!"

"Two of you, around back!"

Logan had no time to think. He could only react as the sounds of booted feet clamored onto the stairs and toward him.

He ran hastily back into his apartment, pausing only long enough to bolt the door. Then he turned, ran to his window, and climbed out onto the fire escape.

He could hear shouts and attempts to break in the door as he scrambled down, leaping to the hard cobbles only a moment before the Gestapo agents reached the alley.

Meanwhile, upstairs two other agents bent over Soustelle's body, one pressing two fingers against the dead man's carotid artery. He looked up and shook his head.

"What was the fool up to anyway?" he said, "coming in here by himself?"

"He probably didn't think the suspect would resist," answered the other.

"More likely he overestimated his own skill."

"Wouldn't be the first time."

"And now he has a bullet in his back for his foolhardy independence."

"What was he after, anyway?"

"He said nothing to me. Just wanted us to watch the building."

"I'll find a telephone; you see how the others are doing."

While both men exited and walked back into the street, a slim figure stirred from a dark recessed corner of the upper corridor.

Still trembling, she rose, dropped the warm revolver into her handbag, and crept from her hiding place. She stole to the landing, stepped over the massive body, and tiptoed down the stairway, now deathly silent.

She tried not to think of what had just happened. Like Logan, before this moment she had never killed. But though she felt the same revulsion at taking another's life, Lise experienced no tormenting self-recrimination.

There would be no regrets for her. She had done what she had done for a worthy cause. And she had saved the life of the man she now knew she cared more about than anyone she had ever met.

57 / Outbursts

At six a.m. Logan stormed into von Graff's office.

Even at that early hour, the general was in, awaiting preliminary reports on the progression of the raid.

"I'll tell him you are here, Herr Dansette—" said his secretary, who had also been pressed into early service.

But Logan did not give her the chance. He rushed past her desk and burst into the inner room where the general sat. The moment he had fled his apartment, he had realized there would be but one way to save his neck and keep his position with the Nazis secure. He had to take a strong initiative, act as the aggressor, and never give von Graff the opportunity to form any conclusions of his own.

"What is the meaning of this, MacVey?" said the general, not a little taken aback by the rash intrusion, not to mention Logan's wild and disheveled appearance.

"I am the one to be asking *that* question, General!" Logan shot back.

"I'm afraid I do not understand you."

"I've had it with you, von Graff!" shouted Logan.

"Please, calm yourself," replied the general, a little alarmed. He rose from his desk and hurriedly closed the door to his office. "What can be so wrong to have upset you like this?"

"We had a deal, and you reneged!" exclaimed Logan, turning on the general with a look of vengeance.

"Sit down and collect yourself," ordered the general calmly. "I don't know what you are talking about, but I'm sure we can—"

"I told you what would happen if you had me followed—and I was nearly killed!"

"Sit down," repeated the general. He then took his own seat, glad to have his desk to serve as a barrier between himself and this wild man.

Logan complied with his order, but he remained on the edge of his chair, still fuming.

"But it looks as if the only one dead is Soustelle," continued von Graff calmly.

So, thought Logan to himself, the general knows everything already. It was indeed a good thing he had played this little rant-and-rave routine rather than trying to play dumb.

"He's dead, then?"

"Come now, MacVey . . . are you trying to tell me you *didn't* know?"

"I thought as much, but couldn't be sure."

"The word that came to me two hours ago was that *you* killed him."

"*Me!* That's ridiculous!"

"Tell me what happened."

"I'm not even sure myself," answered Logan, making an apparent effort to control his ire. "Soustelle attacked me at the door to my place, pulled a knife on me, started making all kinds of wild accusations. Then suddenly a shot fired out of nowhere and Soustelle fell. I figured someone in the Resistance may have seen us and was trying to get me, or maybe both of us."

"So, did you see who fired the shot?"

"Are you kidding? I got out of there!"

"You ran, MacVey?" said the general with a smile. "Hardly sounds like the daring courage of a double agent."

"For all I knew a second shot meant for me would follow on the heels of the first. And in two seconds the place was crawling with blokes— Gestapo or Resistance, who knows? I didn't wait to find out!"

"What's important is that you are still alive."

"No!" exploded Logan, playing his hand out to the full. "What's important is that you went back on your word. You knew Soustelle well enough, didn't you?"

"I knew about his crazy suspicions," admitted von Graff. "But I warned him not to follow you. What more could I do?"

"You could have warned *me!*"

"You were not to be reached—and by the way, what were you doing out at such an hour?"

"You told me to keep my eyes and ears open last night. I just hope this little fiasco hasn't jeopardized my place in the Resistance."

"Might it?"

"Soustelle had a knife to my throat," said Logan, "and the killer may have seen that. Since that's hardly the act of a compatriot, perhaps my cover is still intact."

"Good," said von Graff optimistically. "I would hate for an otherwise successful day to be spoiled."

"Then the raid turned out well?" Logan only barely managed to keep the distress from his voice.

"It's too soon to tell for certain. Many have escaped, of that I am sure. But the successes I mentioned come from a slightly different quarter than the raid itself."

"Oh?"

"Three underground safe houses were raided last night."

"And everyone taken?"

"Yes. Besides the Jews they were harboring, we arrested eight Resistants—probably not the big fish I should like, but arrests are arrests. It'll make my report look good, and who knows what our interrogators will get out of them. We may get a lead on L'Escroc!"

"Very good!" was all Logan could force himself to say. Inside his heart ached, wondering who had been arrested, fearing for his friends.

La Librairie met later that same afternoon.

For security reasons they made use of the offices of Dr. Jacques Tournoux, a sympathizer who offered his rooms on occasion when the group needed greater precaution. It did not arouse suspicion for an unusual mix of men and women to come and go from a doctor's office.

The doctor ushered each one of them in turn from the reception areas and to a private room on the second floor. Then he left them alone. Logan arrived late, for he had taken extra pains to insure he was not followed. The only others present were Henri, Lise, and Claude.

"Where's Jean Pierre?" asked Logan, a gnawing fear suddenly coming into his mind.

"He's been arrested," answered Henri bleakly.

"Who else?"

"We have heard nothing from Antoine."

"He's been arrested as well," said Logan. "That is, he voluntarily went with the Jews. He thought he could help them—I don't know, maybe he can."

"Then we are all that is left."

"I'll get Jean Pierre out," declared Logan flatly.

"But," said Henri, his cherubic face grim and taut, "we must prepare for the worst."

"Jean Pierre will never talk!" exclaimed Lise.

"Nevertheless, we must all relocate and change our names."

"Whether L'Escroc does it, or Trinity," said Logan, "I'm going to get him out tonight."

A silence enveloped the group for several moments as they tried to absorb the stunning blow that had struck them. Such things were to be expected. But it was made all the more difficult when it happened to good men like the faithful Antoine and dear Jean Pierre. Both had provided a kind of stability to *La Librairie* that only the spirits of those remaining could bear witness to.

Claude at last broke the silence. "At least we have lost a dangerous enemy," he announced. "Arnaud Soustelle was killed this morning."

Then he leveled his dark gaze on Logan. "But perhaps you were planning to tell us all about that, Anglais?"

"Funny, Claude," rejoined Logan. "I was going to ask you the same question."

"Ha! I only wish it *had* been my bullet to cut him down!"

"What happened, Michel?" asked Henri.

Logan proceeded to tell about his run-in with Soustelle. "I never saw who did the shooting," he finished. "I'm still not sure whether the slug was meant for him or me."

"But he admitted he knew all about you," said Claude.

"Yes," sighed Logan, "but I'm sure he hadn't told anyone. I think the scoundrel was afraid to blow the whistle until he had positive proof. Von Graff has too much invested in me to be easily convinced. I've already seen him and cleared myself."

"Very convenient!" mumbled Claude darkly.

"Quiet, Claude!" snapped Henri. "There will be none of that—not now!"

Claude slumped back in his chair and said nothing more.

"I wonder who did it," mused Henri, "and why? Of course a man like Soustelle would have no dearth of enemies—"

"Who cares!" cut in Lise, with more emotion than seemed necessary. "The vermin is dead—another enemy is destroyed! Who cares why or how? We are rid of him, that's all that matters!"

For a moment no one said anything, unable to respond to the uncharacteristic outburst. Then Henri's concern showed through.

"Lise . . . what is it? Are you all right?"

"No! I'm not—I will never be right again!"

With the words she jumped up and fled the room.

Logan and Henri exchanged puzzled glances; then Logan rose and went after her. She had only gone to the end of the hall, where she now stood in a small windowed alcove of the bay window overlooking the pleasant street where Dr. Tournoux's office was located.

Lise was gazing out, though she hardly even noticed the lovely summer scene below. When she heard the footsteps approaching behind her, she did not turn. But she knew it was Michel. As much as she longed to be near him, she was also afraid to face him.

She had already decided not to tell him what she had done. She was a killer now. She knew how distasteful violence was to him, despite what had occurred in Vouziers. He could not help but look on her differently now. If she had secretly hoped for love, she knew now it could never come about between them.

Neither could she tell him what had happened in order to win his gratitude. Her very act of supreme loyalty might well win his love, or else foster a sense of obligation that might be confused with love.

But she could not have his love that way—she could not have it anyway. That was clear now.

Perhaps it might have been possible with Michel Tanant. But never with Logan Macintyre, the man that still dwelt within him—the man who, in what seemed an altogether foreign world, another lifetime from this, had a child, a wife.

She could not turn and face him. She could not look into those eyes so filled with vitality and sensitivity.

"Lise . . . what's troubling you?" he asked quietly.

"Nothing." Her voice was as thin and empty as her lame response.

"You're concerned about Jean Pierre?"

"Yes . . . that's it."

He sat down on the window seat next to where she stood.

"He'll be fine," he assured her. "I'm going to see to it."

"I believe you, Michel," she said. "I believe you can do anything you set your mind to."

He shook his head in weary denial.

"It's not true. It never was. Maybe I was lucky. But no—it wasn't even that. For some reason, God seems to have been with me. I still can't figure why He bothers. I suppose it won't be long before He realizes I'm a lost cause."

"No, Michel. *That's* what is not true. God must not give up because He sees your heart. It is a good heart. It is only a little mixed up right now. But you are a good man." She sat down, and finally faced him.

"A little mixed up—that is an understatement." He rubbed his hands despairingly across his face.

Lise looked at him intently. "Someday . . ." she began, then without thinking she reached out and gently touched his cheek.

He laid his hand over hers.

"Oh, Michel," she murmured, "what is to become of us?"

They looked deeply into each other's eyes for what seemed an eternity. Then suddenly Logan squeezed his eyes shut and turned away from her gaze.

"Michel," said Lise quietly, "you know how I feel . . . you know that I—"

He lurched to his feet, as if not wanting to hear what she was about to say, and yet something inside wanting to say the same thing himself.

"Blast this war—this life!" he exclaimed.

"I'm sorry, Michel. I shouldn't have—"

"It's not your fault." But now it was he who could not look at her.

"Don't you see, Lise," he went on after a moment. "I feel the same way. In another time, another place, we might have . . . you must know what I mean. You and I . . . it's there, Lise. We both know it. But this isn't the real world. This is only a moment of time . . . when our paths chanced to cross, and—"

He stopped, searching for the right words, but knowing there were none.

"This war!" he exclaimed in a moment. "It has robbed me of everything! I've given my identity for it. I've lied for it. Dear Lord, I've even killed for it! There's only one thing I have left, though I'm hardly even sure of that anymore. Oh, Lise! Allison is the only part of who I *really* am that still exists. Sometimes it would be easy to lose myself completely in Michel Tanant, and never go back—"

Now he turned to face her again.

"—so very easy, Lise! But I can't. She is my wife, and if I destroy that, then I've destroyed *everything*!"

"Do you love her, Michel?"

Logan thought for a minute or two.

"Yes . . . yes, I do," he finally replied. "Of course I do."

Even as he spoke Logan realized that Allison was his lifeline, the source of stability which God had provided to see him through this time.

"There has never been a question of loving her," he added. "The problem was inside me—my discontentment was with myself. But never with her. Yes, I love her . . . more than anything."

Though he thought he had left England to run away from her, Logan saw that all the time he had carried her with him, not as some chain of guilt around his neck, but rather as a precious link to who he was. Not only as Logan Macintyre instead of all the other fictional selves that had made their claim upon him. It went even deeper than that. His very personhood had its roots in her love for him. Everything he was as a man, even as a man of God, was wrapped up intrinsically in their relationship. Everything Logan wanted in life was there . . . with her—he knew that now.

Lise was a gentle, beautiful island in the crazy, dark, unreal world of horrors where he finally realized he did not belong. To reach out to her now, in the wrong way, whatever immediate comfort it might provide, would mean sacrificing all he truly was, for a mirage.

Though at this very moment it all seemed hopeless, somehow Logan Macintyre would rise from all the mire of his double life and deceit. And when he did, he wanted only Allison to be there reaching out to him.

59 / A Family Parting

Allison looked out the window at the busy London street below. Somehow the flow of this place never ceased. A woman walking her dog, children bouncing a ball, a boy selling newspapers—no doubt each one had felt the stab of pain and loss inflicted by the insanity of war.

Yet each continued on with life, as Allison also had done.

Dear Nat was gone . . . for eternity. Her brother Ian and her father were thousands of miles away, and Logan too was gone—perhaps forever.

Still Allison managed to survive. She knew now, more than ever before, about the sustaining hand of God. He had indeed enabled her to weather the heartbreaking separations of the last year. But sometimes she could not help wondering what use it was. Why go on trying to be strong?

She did not have to look far for answers. First of all, there was the indefatigable Ramsey blood that flowed in her veins. God may have given her the ability, but her heritage had set the example. She could not break down even if she wanted to. The instinct to survive, and to conquer, was too deeply ingrained.

But there were even stronger reasons, found in the persons of her child and her husband. Her daughter depended on her. Not that Allison any longer thought she had to put on some false front to live up to her name for the child's sake. The season for facades in Allison's life was long past. She had wept sufficient tears in the company of her daughter to attest to that. Yet a child, especially one without a father, needed the security of her mother. Allison could not withdraw into herself no matter how often she wanted to turn away from *everything*. Allison also had a remote feeling that Logan needed her as well. It would sound ridiculous had she dared voice that feeling to anyone. After all, he had left her, disappeared without a trace, cut himself off without a single visible regret or thought of her.

But deep inside she knew that was not true. Somewhere Logan was suffering in his own way. In his pain and confusion he had, she was sure, convinced himself that the only answer was to banish himself from those closest to him, those who could help. He had probably convinced himself they were all better off without him.

But strong within her woman's heart beat the sense that he *wasn't* gone forever, and that something would happen . . . and soon. Was it instinct, or mere wishful thinking? She couldn't tell. But she knew right now she had to do what he had always wanted her to do—trust him. She had to keep loving him, trusting him in spite of everything shouting out that he wasn't worth it, and believe with all her strength that the dark tunnel of their separation would soon be past.

Yes, she thought, Logan needs me. She was sure of it. But she knew now it was not in the way she had always thought he needed her. He didn't need her abilities, her sense of responsibility, her money, her family name.

Logan needed *her*—the person she was. He needed her love, unconditionally and selflessly.

That had been her mistake when they were together. She had given him everything but the one thing most vital to a marriage—the commitment of her very self. She had said the words, but never until recently had she realized how much she was holding back. Now that her eyes were open, however, she had to believe that even if Logan chose never to see her again, he would still be able to feel that love. That was what he needed most to receive, and what she needed most to be able to give—the knowledge that even across the miles of separation, love was reaching out between them.

Sounds at the front door slowly nudged Allison from her thoughts. She looked up just as the door opened. It was her mother, preceded by her cheerful, bouncing namesake.

"Hello, sweetheart!" smiled Allison as her daughter bounded into her arms.

"Mama!" exclaimed the girl, "Grandma buyed me flower!" She held out her hand, and now Allison saw she was clutching a pink lily, still pretty, though a bit wilted from constant handling.

"It's beautiful, honey," said Allison.

"I bought a whole bouquet," put in Joanna as she laid her bundles on a table. "I hope you don't mind."

"Of course not, Mother. We could use some brightening up around here."

"I thought so, too." Joanna went to the kitchen for a vase.

In a moment she returned with a crystal vase. Allison fleetingly recalled receiving it for a wedding gift, though it had hardly seen much use since.

"This should be perfect," said Joanna. She unwrapped the bouquet and began arranging it in the bowl. "The last of the summer blooms will be blossoming at Stonewycke. Dorey's nursery will have some lovely ones, probably for another month or so. He was always able to coax life out of his flowers clear into October and beyond."

"Are you homesick, Mother?"

"I suppose I might be." Joanna looked up wistfully. "September is when the heather blooms on the hills," she added.

"I'm keeping you here, aren't I?"

"I needed to be away for a time," replied Joanna. "Even the happy memories were bringing tears to my eyes. With May in America and you here, the place had almost become like I found it that first time I walked up the hill to the foreboding old place, as an uninvited housebreaker!" She paused, recalling the passing of the years with a melancholy fondness. "Yes," she went on with a sigh, "I needed to be away. But now . . . perhaps it *is* time."

"I've been so happy to have you with me, Mother," said Allison. "But I don't want to keep you. I'll be fine whenever you are ready to go back."

"I know you will be."

Joanna left the flowers and walked to the sofa to sit with her daughter and granddaughter. She took Allison's hands in hers.

"Dear Allison . . ." She smiled, though tears had begun to fill her eyes. "I have no worries about you. Not anymore—except of course the usual motherly ones. I know those things that are most important have come together for you in your heart. Still . . . if I returned to Stonewycke, I would so like you to come with me."

"Oh, Mother," sighed Allison. "I miss home, too! But you know why I must stay. And lately, I've been feeling much more strongly that I'll see Logan soon. I know it sounds silly, but—"

"I understand," answered Joanna. "They say a breakthrough in the war could come any time."

"You miss Daddy too, I know."

Joanna smiled. "Perhaps both our men will be home soon."

"We can pray so."

"Sure you won't reconsider about coming with me? It will be so empty having that huge place all to myself."

"Go to Grandma's house!" piped up the enthusiastic voice of the child nestled between the two women.

"You'd like to go, wouldn't you, pumpkin?" said Allison, giving her a tender squeeze.

"We are all country girls at heart," said Joanna.

Allison was quiet for a moment as an idea began to take shape in her mind.

"You know, Mother," she said at length, "I've been keeping pretty occupied here with my job and the volunteer work. The pace of activity has been good for me. I have to stay here, for a while longer at least, until I know something about Logan. But I was thinking, perhaps, that you and . . ."

She let her look and knowing nod complete the thought for her.

"Jo loves Stonewycke," Allison went on. "And I have been concerned with keeping her here with the renewed bombing. Now that we are attacking Germany, they say it can only get worse. There've been attacks on rail lines, army depots, and even a few near London again. What do you think? Would you like to take her to Stonewycke?"

"I can't think of a more delightful prospect! But are you sure?"

"I think it's the perfect solution. What could possibly happen to her there?"

Allison paused and glanced down at her daughter, who was clapping excitedly. "Look at her! She can't wait—Stonewycke is in her blood, too."

"So, the decision is made!" exclaimed Joanna with a laugh.

The following days were spent making preparations for the trip. The nurse, Hannah, had to make arrangements of her own for the lengthy absence. Though she would be returning to London as soon as a suitable nurse could be hired in Port Strathy, it was possible she could be away a month or six weeks. Therefore, it was a week before the train tickets could be purchased.

At last the day of departure arrived. Allison tried her best to be stoic. This had been her idea, after all. But as the time neared, she began to anticipate the loneliness that was bound to surround her once these two dearly loved companions were gone. The temptation to change her mind might have grown overpowering except for the joyful glow on her mother's face. The prospect of returning to Stonewycke, and having her three-year-old granddaughter with her besides, set her spirit positively shining. Just watching her mother was a healing balm to Allison's grieving heart.

It was the best answer for now. And who could tell? Before very long both Allison *and* Logan might be able to join them!

The morning of their departure came, and Allison sat in her room dressing her daughter for the trip. They had chosen her pretty heather-colored frock in honor of the return to Scotland. Allison tied the sash at the back into a bow, then spun the giggling child about in admiration.

"You look absolutely lovely in that color!" exclaimed Allison. "It was Lady Margaret's best color too. She always loved the heather, and its mysterious shades suited her perfectly."

She turned pensive a moment, then smiled again at her daughter. "A wee Scottish lassie ye are, my bairn!" she said.

They both giggled together. "Come, let me brush your hair."

Allison boosted her up onto her knee and began brushing the silky amber locks.

"Will you come to Grandma's soon, Mama?" asked the girl, as she snuggled close to her mother.

"Oh yes, I will," answered Allison. "I couldn't be away from you for too long."

"Daddy too?"

"We must keep praying for Daddy. I know he wants to, dear. We must give him time."

"Daddy know I love him?" she asked pensively.

Tears struggled to rise in Allison's eyes. "Yes, dear," she said softly. "Daddy knows that. And you keep loving him with all your heart. He needs that from us now more than anything."

"Will he get hurt like Uncle Nat?"

A knot suddenly tightened Allison's throat.

"We must trust God, my wee bairn," Allison replied in a trembly voice. "Whatever God does is because He loves us and wants the best for us—even sometimes being apart from those we love. But that doesn't mean forever. It was the best thing for Uncle Nat to be with Jesus. Just think how happy he is right now!"

She wrapped her arms around her daughter and hugged her tight. "Jesus is with Daddy, honey! Daddy will be back with us soon, just like you and I will be apart only a short time. We'll see each other again before you know it. I promise!"

Allison shook off the sorrow trying to envelop her at the thought of parting with her daughter. She wanted this day to be a happy one.

"I've got a special present for you, honey!" she said.

"Oh, goody—what, Mama?"

Allison opened a drawer in her dressing table and took out a small velvet-covered box.

"This has been in Mama's family for a long, long time," she said. "Long before you or I, or even Grandma was born."

"Ooooh!" exclaimed the wide-eyed child.

"Many years ago, when your great-great grandmother, Lady Margaret, was a girl, Great-great Grandpa Dorey gave this to her," continued Allison. "They were in love, and were going to be married. He wanted to give her something special. And this was it."

She opened the box and lifted out a delicate gold locket.

"Before Lady Margaret died, she gave it to me. It's always been very special to me ever since. Now, I'd like you to keep it for me a little while—so *you* have something special to remember me while we're apart."

Tenderly she placed the chain of the locket around her daughter's neck.

"Will you take good care of it, and think of me a lot?"

"Yes, Mama." She put her arms around her mother's neck and planted a wet kiss on her mouth. "Thank you, Mama!"

"I will pray for you every day," said Allison in a husky voice, filled with emotion.

"Me too, Mama. I pray for you, too."

"Thank you, dear. I love you."

When the train chugged slowly away two hours later, Allison did not try to hide her tears. Suddenly everyone she loved was gone from her, and she could not help but doubt her decision.

But she was being selfish again, she chided herself as she walked out of the station. This was the best thing, and it would do no good to get melancholy over it and start feeling sorry for herself. Certainly she would be lonely. But what she had told her mother was true; she had much to keep her occupied here in London.

Back out on the street, the sounds of aircraft winging overhead reminded her that this was wartime and her services to the needs of the country were vital. It reminded her, too, that London was never completely safe these days. Her daughter would be better off at Stonewycke, far removed from harm.

She was glad they weren't flying. At least the trains were safe enough.

Shaking off thoughts of war, bombs, and explosions, Allison turned and hailed a cab.

As the train slowly pulled out of London on its northern journey, Joanna's thoughts were not far divergent from her daughter's.

Her anticipation of being home again was tempered with ever-present reflections on the war. Sometimes she felt she could not bear another single moment of it. And she prayed she would not have to bear another loss as a result of the fighting! How could she? Yet she knew the answer. Her Father in heaven had always upheld her, and would continue to do so whatever further blow this nightmare of world war might send their way.

Oddly enough, one of the most difficult aspects of the ordeal of Nathaniel's death had been the brevity of Alec's furlough for the funeral. After so many months apart, the time should have been a joyous one. But more than the tragedy of their son's death had marred it. Alec had tried to put on a brave show, but Joanna knew him too well; plainly, the years of war were wearing away at him.

In an unguarded moment he had shared with her about the bloody battle of Tobruk that June, just weeks prior to the funeral. Rommel had captured the stronghold and the 8th Army was pushed back all the way to El Alamein, after sustaining fifty thousand casualties.

"Fifty thousand men, Joanna!" he had exclaimed. "I still canna believe it. All I could think when I saw the dead an' wounded was that all those lives were lost fer nothin'. Even if we hae hung on to the city—what was it all fer? 'Tis hard oot there t' keep sight o' a madman in Berlin. There are some o' oor troops who actually tend t' admire Rommel an' his Afrika Korps. 'Tis crazy . . . senseless! When I heard aboot Nat, I wanted to hate, to find some revenge. But I couldna—it jist wasna there!"

"You couldn't, Alec," said Joanna, "because such feelings are foreign to your nature—foreign to the Spirit of God within you."

"Then why am I oot there at all? Am I not bein' a mite hypocritical?"

"Perhaps it's *because* of who you are. If there were no men like you on the battlefield, I'd hate to think of the kind of insanity it would become. Aren't good men needed everywhere, even in the most ungodly of settings? Maybe *especially* there!"

Alec sighed and shook his head. " 'Tisna sae easy to understand—when ye're oot there in it every day."

"I don't know what to say, Alec. I suppose there will always be lingering doubts."

"Ah, Joanna—it wouldna be sae hard if ye were wi' me."

He put his arm around her and drew her close. "Fer all yer retirin' ways, my dear wee wifie, ye are strong an' wise beyond my ken. I knew it that first day I met ye. Ye were all green about the gills watchin' old Nathaniel's cow give birth, but ye stuck it oot."

"Probably more from stubbornness than wisdom or strength," said Joanna. "I was not about to let an ill-tempered veterinarian get the better of me!"

"Despite mud an' manure on yer fine city dress!"

"Oh, the smell of that byre!" laughed Joanna.

Alec threw his head back and roared.

It had been one of the few times during their brief time together that Joanna had seen that side of her husband surface. And now Joanna tried to keep that pleasant memory of Alec in her mind.

Oh, Alec, she thought while gazing out the train window watching the concrete of the city as it began to give way to the more open spaces of the countryside, *one day we will laugh again!*

Though three years of war, with its sorrows and separations, might do its best to sap them of their very lives, Joanna clutched her Father's promises firmly in the depths of her heart: "Weeping may endure for a night, but joy cometh in the morning."

Still, she did at times wonder what tomorrow would hold for her and her family. She did not question the future as one might who had no hope. She did not look ahead in fear, but rather in a kind of anticipation. Despite its grief and pain, each day held promise for Joanna. To her belonged the uncommon privilege of being aware of God's purposeful moving in the lives of men and women, not measured in mere weeks, months, or even years, but rather in the very generations of her predecessors.

For some fifteen years, since she suddenly awoke to the realization that her grandmother Lady Margaret would eventually die and the legacy of her life be gone, Joanna had been keeping a careful chronicle of the Ramsey clan. It had begun with the memories of Lady Margaret's life, as the older woman passed the details of her story on to her beloved granddaughter. But the more the two women shared and talked, the more intrigued Joanna became to record for her posterity the saga that involved others of the family as well, even stretching back into times long past to the very beginnings of Stonewycke. As it grew, her writings were not simply a recounting of events—births, deaths, marriages—but rather an attempt to trace spiritual and emotional journeys as well, telling tales of growth and development, heartaches and joys, that could never be measured by years, by statistics, by money. And every moment Joanna recorded from the past helped give her hope for the future.

She gazed down at the child, now sound asleep, nestled in the crook of her arm. This little one was part of that future. What would the coming years hold for her? If she did not someday become the literal heir, she was certainly bound to inherit the tradition handed down through the generations of women who helped keep alive the family bond with the ancient estate of Stonewycke. This child, in less than four years, already had an attachment to the land with its rugged seascapes, hills of scraggly heather, moors of barren heath, and lush green pasturelands. She would carry on for the austere Atlanta, for dear Lady Margaret, and even for Eleanor, Joanna's own mother, who had never even set eyes upon the heather hills. Yes, and for Joanna too, and Allison.

Was it too much to place the burden of such a legacy on a woman? Especially on a child, scarcely more than a baby?

It had nearly destroyed Allison. Yet, whenever it seemed the spiritual traditions were about to be swallowed up in the passage of time and in new generations, God had always stepped in faithfully. He had miraculously brought Joanna herself to Scotland. He had restored Margaret and Ian to their rightful places despite their advancing years. He had brought Allison into the fullness of her mother's and father's faith. And now, after ten years of God's refining fires in Allison's life, that faith was becoming deep enough for others—especially this little daughter—to be able to draw from.

Joanna recalled Lady Margaret's prophetic words of many years ago, spoken on the day Allison had given her heart to the Lord: "I do not doubt that as the history of Stonewycke continues down through the years, Allison, you will play a pivotal role in it. And as you look back, it may be that this moment when we three generations of Duncan women can join in oneness with our Lord will prove an important crossroads."

God was faithful.

If for nothing else, the Ramsey clan could proudly claim they mirrored that one abiding truth. And as the Stonewycke legacy would carry on despite death, despite separation from loved ones, despite turmoil and war and loss, so would the eternal legacy of God's unfailing love continue on throughout all eternity.

That thought alone was enough to make Joanna content. And soon she would be home, a bonus she could only at that moment appreciate. Grief and loneliness had forced her away for a season. But now she could anticipate her return with true Ramsey/Duncan zeal. Of course, the presence of her little granddaughter would help immensely!

When the conductor ambled by a while later announcing dinner in an hour, Joanna could hardly believe they had been traveling for nearly two hours. All signs of the city were well behind them now. The hues of autumn clung to the Middlesex countryside. Off in the distance she could see a lovely picturesque little stone bridge, its sides, about waist high, arching over a bubbling burn. Beyond it, in a crook made by the sides of two adjoining grass-covered rises in the terrain, sat a cozy-looking little thatch-roofed cottage, constructed out of the same stone as the bridge. Out of the chimney a thin wisp of smoke curled skyward. Inside, no doubt, thought Joanna as she watched the pleasant scene pass, a homely farm woman is kneading out her ration of flour into a fragrant loaf of hearty bread.

Yes, Joanna was truly a country girl, although when she had first come to Scotland thirty-one years ago, she had hardly been able to tell one end of a cow from the other. But now the thought of the earthy sights and sounds and smells of Port Strathy warmed her heart as it could only to one who truly belonged there heart and soul.

All at once a horribly discordant sight intruded upon the pleasant scene. Ugly lengths of chain-link fencing stretched out in the midst of the rolling countryside. The ten-foot-high fence was topped with three or four rows of barbed wire. There was no sign identifying the installation, but it needed none. Joanna recognized the fenced area as one of the revolting by-products of war—an ammunition dump, most likely.

Joanna sighed. What a contrast! A storage dump for ammunition to kill thousands sitting just across the tracks from such an idyllic country scene of peace.

Joanna was just vaguely aware of the sounds of aircraft whining over the monotonous clatter of the train when she was distracted from the unpleasant scene by a friendly voice in the aisle to her left.

"Lady MacNeil! What a nice surprise!"

Joanna turned with a reciprocal smile on her face, when she saw who it was that had greeted her.

"Why, Olivia!" she said to Allison's old school chum, Olivia Fairgate, "this *is* delightful!" She knew Olivia was married now, but could not for the life of her recall the girl's married name. "It's been a long time . . . I forget how you young people grow up."

"Yes, we do. Why, I've got four children now."

"My goodness!" exclaimed Joanna. "But you are traveling alone now?"

"Oh no! Everyone's two cars over. I was just seeing about having some formula warmed for the twins."

"Twins! . . . I didn't know."

"Two months old tomorrow—what a handful!"

She began rummaging through her purse, but then stopped. "I was going to show you a photo," she said. "But why don't you come and see the real thing—or things, I should say?" She giggled at her unintentional joke.

"I'd love to," answered Joanna, realizing that it would feel good to stand. "I need to stretch my legs a bit."

She turned to the nurse. "Hannah, you don't mind, do you?"

"Not at all, mum."

Gently Joanna eased her granddaughter out of her arms and into the lap of the nurse. Still asleep, the child snuggled into the nurse's arms and sighed contentedly.

"I should only be a few minutes," said Joanna; then she walked away with Olivia, both chatting, filling in the gaps of the years since they had seen each other.

"Was that Allison's daughter you were holding?" asked Olivia. At Joanna's nod, she added, "What a precious child. We really ought to get together more often. My little James is just about her age."

They made their way through the next car, and on to the one beyond it. Joanna had little trouble picking out Olivia's brood—in that particular corner of the railway car, all the activity for the entire train seemed concentrated. A four-year-old lad was sitting on his knees, backward on his seat, straining to see everything that was going on. Next to him, an older boy of about seven was occupied with a book, though only about a minute out of every three was spent reading. Above the clacking of the train's wheels along the tracks could be heard the unmistakable infant cries of two hungry babies. A frazzled nurse looked up with pleading eyes as the two women drew near.

In all the mayhem of the moment, Joanna no longer noticed the drone of approaching aircraft, now much louder than before.

"Hey, Mother," called out the seven-year-old as Olivia walked up, "look at those airplanes! They're coming right toward us!"

But before Olivia could reply, suddenly an ear-splitting explosion burst through the air, forcing their part of the world into chaos and upheaval. There was but an instant for Joanna's sensations to register her shock and terror. She did not even have time to think about Hannah and her granddaughter two cars away.

The train jerked violently, knocking her from her feet and into unconsciousness.

Joanna awoke with an audible gasp. All around her were the white, antiseptic sights and smells of a hospital room.

She struggled to rise, but a firm hand settled her back into place. She opened her mouth, but no words would come. Her bedclothes seemed drenched in perspiration. In her groggy state, scenes from her long, traumatic sleep assaulted her mind—wild, terrifying bursts of deafening explosions, blinding flashes of light. And always the screams, especially the one childish scream she could never seem to reach.

Now she was being wheeled along a corridor. Voices spoke softly above her, but she could see no faces. Was this but a horrifying nightmare?

But more flashes of memory continued to penetrate her consciousness. The nightmare *had* been real! Snatches of the scene came back to her. Scenes that would forever haunt her, in sleep and in waking, from that awful day.

Suddenly she remembered an earlier waking. How could she have forgotten? A porter, his uniform smattered with blood and torn in many places, was leaning over her.

"Are ye wakin', mum?" he asked compassionately.

"My granddaughter . . ." was all Joanna could say. "My baby . . ."

" 'Tis many youngsters in this car, mum, but none dead. We'll find her."

"No . . . not this car . . . two ahead . . ."

Suddenly the man's tender expression became stricken with pain.

"Two cars ahead, ye say?"

But Joanna, clutching at the man and ignoring the pain from injuries she would later discover, tried to pull herself up.

"I have to get to her!"

"But, mum—"

Paying no heed to the man's entreaties, Joanna staggered to her feet, then attempted to run, stumbling along and climbing through the debris to make her way through the appalling disaster. All the while the kindly man hurried after her.

Somehow she managed to get free of what was left of the railway car and into the open air. She ran along the dirt where already the injured and dead were being dragged out and tended to.

Suddenly she stopped. The porter who had been close on her heels came up sharply at her side.

Several cars, one on its side and half blown apart, were engulfed in uncontrollable flames.

She started to run toward the blaze, screaming, "No!" But the porter grabbed her firmly.

" 'Tis no use, mum," he said wearily. "Them cars ahead o' yers took a direct hit."

With the fatal words of the porter still ringing in her ears, mingled with the incoherent voices of nurses and doctors, and the blurry whiteness of an unfamiliar ceiling spinning around above her, Joanna lapsed again into unconsciousness, and remembered no more.

Sarah Bramford came the moment she had received Allison's call. She had been out of town, however, and could not be reached for nearly twenty-four hours after the accident.

The moment she walked in, Allison's appalling appearance told more than any words could. Where she sat in the brassy light of the hospital's waiting room, with dark hollow eyes and pale skin, she appeared so lost, like a stranger in some bizarre foreign land where all was against her. She had often complained about her dreadful pallor, calling it the Duncan curse. But the look on her face went far beyond any familial inheritance.

Sarah rushed immediately to her side and threw her arms around her friend.

Allison said nothing, but burst into fresh tears.

Both women held each other tight and wept; then Sarah finally managed to speak through her tears.

"Your mother . . . is she—?"

Allison nodded. "She'll be fine," she replied haltingly. "A mild concussion, a broken arm, some broken ribs—"

"Oh my!" exclaimed Sarah, "the poor woman!"

"She's just come out of surgery and is asleep—oh, Lord! I don't know what I would have done had I lost her, too!"

Gently Sarah stroked Allison's head, her own tears of heart-wrenching compassion flowing without restraint.

"Oh, Sarah!" sobbed Allison, "what am I going to do!"

Thirty minutes later some calm had been restored to Allison's grief-stricken heart. She looked at Sarah, still with that empty, wasted expression of loss on her face. But she had to talk; it seemed the only way to accept the reality of what had happened.

"The bombers were apparently after some military installation on the other side of the tracks," she said, her voice cracked and tentative. "But some of the bombs came in low, and . . . hit the train—"

She stopped and could not go on for several minutes.

"My little Joanna was in one of them," she sobbed. "Mother had left for a few minutes . . . to visit Olivia in another car—"

"Olivia Fairgate?"

"Yes, she was on the train . . . she and her children. But they're all fine. Their car wasn't . . . they didn't get a direct hit—"

The words caught on Allison's lips. "Oh, Sarah!" she moaned, then was silent for several minutes.

"You don't have to tell me now, dear."

"No . . . it's all right . . . I've got to get it said . . ."

"Tell me whatever you want to," said Sarah tenderly.

"It took them hours to account for everyone. Some went to nearby farms for first aid . . . the Army came out to help, but of course they had their own casualties. . . . But now they know—I just heard it—over two hundred injured . . . sixty-three dead. . . ."

Again the two friends fell silent. Sarah waited, silently ministering the tender sympathy of true compassion.

"God knew what He was doing when He gave you to me for a friend," said Allison, speaking at last. "Thank you, Sarah."

"Let's go get something to eat," said Sarah brightly. "When's the last time you had a good meal?"

"I honestly don't remember," answered Allison. "I haven't been hungry."

"Come on," urged Sarah, rising. "You must have something."

"Well, maybe I could use a change of scenery."

Arm-in-arm they left the tiny, comfortless room, found the stairs, and eventually located the dining room. The tea proved adequate, but everything else was bland and tasteless. Allison toyed with a bowl of soup until it was cold besides. The tea was soothing, however, and when Sarah poured out a second cup, Allison accepted it gratefully.

"I should probably get back upstairs," she said, "in case Mother wakes up."

"I'm surprised she's here in London," commented Sarah.

"There were no adequate facilities in the rural area where the bombing took place," said Allison. "So they brought most of the casualties back to the city."

They both concentrated on their tea for a few moments.

Then Sarah reached across the table and gently placed her hand on Allison's.

"Why don't you come stay with me while your mother is in the hospital?" she said. "Even after she is released, you would both be welcome. You know I have scads of room."

"Thank you, Sarah," Allison replied. She proceeded to stare into her cup a moment. "But I . . . I . . . feel I should stay at the flat. I can't leave. If Logan should come, I *must* be there."

"But we can leave word for him."

"No, I have to *be* there. I don't know how this will affect all we might have had. I don't even know if I'll ever see him again. But I just know I have to stay there."

"Of one thing we can be sure," said Sarah quietly. "God doesn't *cause* such tragedies, but He can *use* them in ways we in the midst of our grief can never imagine."

Allison smiled, for the first time in many hours.

"You have grown so much, Sarah. I can't tell you how much it means to me to have you right now. I don't have much to cling to, and I'm so thankful to God that I *do* have you."

Over the next days and weeks, Allison did manage to endure the emptiness of her grief. Sarah stayed with her in the Shoreditch flat until Joanna was released from the hospital nine days after the accident. After that, Allison's loneliest moments were relieved in eager service to her mother. By the time Joanna was ready to return north, Allison too seemed back on her feet emotionally, at least enough to go on with life.

God had, and would, continue to use her grief. He was calling her to a higher level of faith, a new plane of trust in Him.

She had heard about such things many times from her great-grandparents. Her own mother and father had told her that the pain of loss and separation was the very thing which had cemented the young love shared by Maggie and Ian into an eternal legacy of love. She had heard, she had read—so many times, in fact, that the truths had little impact for her personally.

In her spirit now, however, she began to discern that the truth of those words was what her own life now desperately required if she was to grow through this time and be strong again.

Now was the time when her trust in God, her love for Logan, and her belief in God's ultimate goodness in the face of black circumstances all around must be stretched to humanly impossible limits. Now was the time when she would have to decide to what extent she was willing to give God her trust. Daily she opened her New Testament to read the words at once so painful and yet so full of hope:

"We rejoice in our sufferings, because we know that suffering produces patience, and patience produces strength of character, and strength of character produces hope. And hope will never disappoint us, because God has poured out his love into our hearts by the Holy Spirit. . . . Consider it joy when you face trials, because you know that the testing of your faith develops perseverance, which must finish its work, so that you may be mature and complete, and lacking in nothing."

To allow this process to work its maturing and strengthening in her heart, she needed to depend upon God more than she ever had in her young life.

"Father," she prayed one evening in the quiet of her room, "following your ways has never been easy for me. Please—help me, dear Lord! I want to trust you, I want to believe this is all for the good! I want to believe that that scripture is true, and that you are working it out in my life. Help me, even if not to *believe* it completely, at least help me to *want* to believe it! Help me somehow to trust you in spite of my own unbelief. I want to trust you, Lord, but I am weak on my own! And more than anything, please, dear Lord, keep your loving hand on Logan. He needs you, too. Let these separate paths we are on help us both to see the light of your Spirit illuminating the way before us.''

They called this rattletrap *The Berlin to Paris Express*.

Some express! The word was more likely a euphemism for simply making it a thousand kilometers without encountering a bomb! The phrase could certainly have nothing whatever to do with speed! Thus concluded Jason Channing with a disgruntled smirk.

He wondered about the necessity of his current decision to travel to Paris. If for no other reason, he was going because the Führer had encouraged him to see the city—how did he phrase it?—under the "guardianship" of the Third Reich. Hitler may have been a maniac in many ways, but he did possess a tenderness for the arts. Probably it was his way of deflecting attention from his common birth, and perhaps relieving the sting from the memory of being twice rejected by the Academy of Fine Arts in Vienna. The struggling young artist had turned instead to surviving as a street painter in the Austrian capital, and now, thirty-four years later, fancied himself a connoisseur of things fine and cultured. He carried with him such a bloated impression of his own skill that several years ago he had gone on a campaign to round up and destroy what he considered forgeries of his own early work. As if any of them were good enough to forge! And now in his vision for the Reich—purified, as it was, from the stains of both Jews and forgeries—he perceived Paris as the crowning glory.

Besides, the Führer was not a man to be refused; even Jason Channing had the sense to recognize that.

Hitler's major goal with Paris had been to see that the cinema, the theater, and other arts should continue to thrive. The world would see that the Reich did not ultimately bring destruction, but culture.

Well, thought Channing, perhaps the tyrant has succeeded. Even in the midst of the war, France led the world, even America, in publishing. The stage still attracted some of Europe's biggest names. The Louvre was still the world's greatest art gallery and the Left Bank still attracted many up-and-coming new artists. Parisian night life seemed to be flourishing. Jews were *verboten*, of course, from participating in any of this. But who needed their money? There were enough other Parisian artisans and German financiers to keep the creative hub of the world bursting with the appearance of health and happiness. The peasants had no bread, but the Führer saw to it that they had art in abundance.

Channing was no sentimentalist like the Führer. He would never have made this ghastly train ride just to see some ridiculous pictures on canvas, or to hear Karajan conduct *Tristan and Isolde*, although he would no doubt be willing enough to take advantage of some of the other diversions Paris offered a man of the world.

Most of all, however, he had endless business deals to cement. "Thank God for the war!" he was known to have said on occasion. He was scoring a bundle. He may have been black-listed from American industry and unwelcome in certain parts of Britain, but who cared? Germany had proved a veritable gold mine. After the crash of '29, he had taken a chance with his remaining bankroll and invested in aircraft. His associates all called him crazy, but Channing's greed smelled another war in the not-so-distant future. If everyone else back then chose to ignore Germany's steady buildup of armaments, Channing was not one to be duped by soothing words. He knew what was going on, and where the world was headed.

It had been rough at first, until the government contracts began pouring in near the end of the thirties. Now he couldn't produce enough *Messerschmitts* or *Hurricanes*, not to mention his growing contracts with the Japanese.

Because of the war, Channing was now a millionaire in just about any currency he chose.

And since he wasn't a patriot, it caused him no particular qualms that the fortunes of the Third Reich were steadily plummeting. All along he'd known the arrangement would end one day. He made sure not to invest too much of his own money in the factories, at the same time funneling the cash profits in his own direction. When the end came he wanted to make sure he would be able to beat a hasty retreat to some nice neutral spot like Morocco, out of sight of the Germans, out of sight of the Americans and English, and live like a king while setting up some new ventures.

And the Third Reich did seem to be plummeting. Last month the Eighth Army had squashed Rommel at El Alamein in Egypt, a major victory for the British, insuring Allied protection of the Suez Canal. And only a few days ago, on November 8, of this pivotal year of 1942, the British and the Americans had launched their long-awaited invasion of North Africa. Churchill had recently declared, "This is not the end. It is not even the beginning of the end. But it is, perhaps, the end of the beginning."

Why couldn't the pompous snob come right out and say it? thought Channing. The Reich was doomed. Not only in the south but in the east too. There they were slowly crumbling before the rallied might of the great Russian bear.

But to Channing none of the world's political fortunes mattered. He had his wealth secreted away in the safety of a Swiss bank. No matter which way the war went, he would come up smelling like a rose.

So much for the business end of this visit to the City of Lights.

He was also looking forward to seeing his old acquaintance, Martin von Graff, now a general in the S.S. For beyond business and finances, there was a still more vital thrust to Channing's existence: power. It was his reason for being, what kept him driven with the passion of men thirty years his junior.

To the end of possessing power over men and situations and circumstances, Jason Channing had over the years developed a finely honed network of international "eyes and ears." He had in his clutches more dirt on more well-placed personalities than he could ever use in one lifetime. But even if it went unused, the mere fact of its possession was what really mattered. You never knew when it would come in handy to expedite a deal, or encourage a man of influence to close his eyes at the proper time. To know more about another than he knew you knew gave Channing a hidden measure of control. And with control came power!

One of the focal points toward which he had directed his spying activities was none other than his old nemesis, Stonewycke. By now Channing's vendetta was not limited merely to that feisty snip of a girl who had laughed in his face thirty-one years ago, and then run off to marry a ridiculous, manure-sloshing animal doctor. That affront he would *never* forgive! He would carry out his revenge on anyone associated with the place. Of course, the pressing demands of the war had limited his diligence in this area. But he had instructed his people at least to keep a watch for any unusual behavior.

And what could be more unusual than a nervous young woman slipping out in the dead of night to rendezvous with a sinister German at a deserted pub near the Thames shipyards? The daughter, no less! To have something on her might even be better than a direct hit. Parents were so sentimental! That was the perfect way to really make them hurt—get to their children!

Yes, sir! You just never knew what was going to turn up! The noble *Lady* Joanna MacNeil's own daughter meeting with Germans!

Channing *had* to know what it was all about! This was fraught with cunning possibilities!

Thus he directed his antennae toward that little part of the globe. He kept a man watching the girl—what was her name? Allison. But he'd come up consistently empty. He'd stuck a man immediately on the kraut, too. That was more promising.

The name was Gunther. His code name, at least—in reality his informant identified him as one Rolf Pingel. Not that his real name mattered. He was a double agent, ostensibly working for British intelligence. However, the man was a slippery fellow; even Channing was not sure which side of the fence he really called home. Probably *both* sides. "I like the guy already!" Channing laughed to himself.

Channing put his best man on Gunther. But even at that they had a beast of a time keeping up with him. They lost his track several times, but then caught a whiff of him again as he boarded a plane for Lisbon. Suddenly things began to look up. For in Lisbon, who should he meet but Martin von Graff, just before von Graff switched his lot to the S.S.

From the submarine off the northern coast of Scotland—where Channing himself had returned with his dredging equipment some time later—and now to his association with a spy who had links to the MacNeil daughter, the name of Martin von Graff seemed to keep bearing in on the fortunes of Stonewycke, and Channing's schemes.

What might the general possibly know? Channing never could come up with any details on the Lisbon meeting—both men were prime intriguers and knew how to keep quiet. And Channing didn't want to risk spooking any potential leads, so he adopted a wait-and-see posture. Then other priorities occupied his attentions for a while—after all, he still did have a business to operate. The Führer demanded his presence in Berlin for some time, and he could not think of refusing the man whose war was so nicely lining his pocketbook.

But the incident with the Macintyre girl did not cease to churn about in the recesses of his warped brain. He'd followed the society pages enough—and kept his subscription to an Aberdeen paper open for just such a purpose—to keep limited track of the whole brood of them, including that ne'er-do-well husband of hers. He had been troublesome during the whole episode with that fool Ross Sprague. Luckily, it had all turned out satisfactorily in the end. Channing would get to the bottom of this new development at the first opportunity, and then use whatever information he gained to bring down that whole arrogant family.

Getting the Ramsey treasure wasn't enough. It hadn't even bothered them that it had been found and lost again so quickly. Confound those people! What could you do against idiots who didn't even care about money? They were impenetrable, like that spy Gunther! And for all the good that big heavy box had done him, he might as well have left it at the bottom of the drink. It certainly hadn't improved his fortunes much!

Oh, he had been able to gloat for a time in that small victory. But without her to *know* he had won, it was a hollow triumph, indeed. And from a monetary standpoint, it was no easy thing turning a profit from a cache of thousand-year-old relics. He'd no doubt have more luck fencing the stuff after the war.

In the meantime, there they sat in their castle on that blasted hill covered with ridiculous and useless heather. They acted as if they were as impregnable as their feudal ancestors. But this German connection—it could be their Waterloo. And even if it meant nothing, he might still be able to parlay it to his own advantage.

First, he'd pump von Graff. The general no longer had any loyalties to the Abwehr. He might be more willing to divulge some of their more minor secrets. Such as, who was this Gunther? What was his connection to MI5? Who were some of his contacts? And what could he possibly have to do with young Allison Macintyre? Was there any chance her husband was involved somehow?

If the general was reluctant to talk, Channing could always utilize his close relationship with the Führer to loosen him up.

The train whistle sounded a shrill note. Channing caught a glimpse of the Marne outside. He would soon be in Paris.

63 / A Visit With Henri

A gusty autumn wind accompanied Logan as he walked down the rue de Varennes. He remembered the first time he had made his way down this very street, so confident, so untried. Lise had said that first day they had talked, "You are so naive! But you will learn your lessons soon enough."

Three months ago in Vouziers he had passed through the graduate school of his brutal underground education. Had it really been that long? It hardly seemed possible! Already three months since he had snuffed out the life of that German, and held his dying brother-in-law in his arms.

After such a hideous experience, how had he managed to continue?

He'd been given the opportunity to go back to London. Atkinson had offered.

But Logan held on. Perhaps it was wrong of him to do so. He knew a part of him had lost heart, and thus the danger of becoming sloppy was even more possible. Not only did it place him in more danger, it endangered the lives of others as well. Now Logan knew beyond a doubt that he did not belong here.

Yet something else kept him. It had to do with his conversation with Atkinson before he came to Paris.

"You lack discipline," the major had said. "And you lack staying power. According to your record, the only thing you've ever done that's lasted longer than a year is to get married—and now it appears as if that is failing also. . . ."

A year ago Logan had bought into France's cause. To abandon it now that it had soured for him would be in the act of the old Logan Macintyre— the man who thought nothing of walking out on a marriage the moment it failed to suit his fancy. If I am going to learn the kind of commitment necessary for a marriage, he thought, what better place to start than right here and now? If he ever did make it out of France, and Allison would still have him, she would deserve some assurance. Maybe he needed that, too— needed to know that he had it in him to weather it when life got rough.

So here he was walking again down the rue de Varennes, still in France, still playing his double and triple roles, still helping escapees get safely to Britain. Sometimes he seemed merely to be going through the motions. But he was trying to be faithful to the commitments he had made, yet now looking forward to the day when it would end.

How long would he need to remain to prove his commitment? Logan

320

didn't know. But he had been praying about it. He had been spending a lot more time in prayer these days. And he felt an assurance that God would direct him, that somehow the Lord would let him know when the time was right.

Logan arrived at the bookstore, opening the door to the familiar clang of the overhead bell. He had been looking forward to this meeting with Henri—there had been too few since he had become Trinity again. He liked the man, and enjoyed their time together whenever circumstances would allow. He had gradually established himself at several bookstores around Paris, so an occasional visit to *La Librairie* would not be suspicious.

An old gentleman was browsing among the stacks. When Henri entered from the back, both men deliberately down-played their greetings.

"Ah, Monsieur Tanant," said the shopkeeper politely, "I have the books you ordered in back. I'll be but a moment; they are still packed."

"Merci," replied Logan. "Can I be of assistance?"

"If it is no trouble—the boxes are rather cumbersome."

They retreated to the back room where, though keeping their voices subdued, they were able to greet one another properly.

"How good it is to see you, Michel!" said Henri, giving Logan an affectionate embrace.

"Likewise, Henri."

Still in his reflective mood, Logan recalled the day Henri had promised him a peaceful cup of real coffee when the war ended. He longed for the fulfillment of that invitation now more than ever.

Before they could continue, the customer from the front called to Henri.

"Help yourself to some coffee," said Henri as he ducked out through the curtained doorway.

Logan took a cup from the rack on the wall and poured the coffee. He had just settled himself on one of the crates when he heard the bell sound. He hoped it wasn't a new visitor. But in a moment Henri reappeared.

"We are alone now, mon ami," he said, "so we must use the precious time judiciously. Though I would rather chat," he added with a laugh. "At the very least, I must know—are you well, Michel?" The question held in it more than the mere exchange of pleasantries.

"Yes, Henri," Logan replied in the earnest tone that was becoming more characteristic of his speech lately. "We survive . . . we must. Have you heard the latest news, that the Boche have moved in to occupy all of France?"

"Oui. Their way of retaliating for the invasion of North Africa. Let them have it. It won't be theirs for long!"

"True, Henri," said Logan, thoughtfully sipping his coffee. "But even if the war lasts only another year or two, they can—and will—make those final years ones of living hell for us. Already the execution posters have become a more frequent sight. Arrests are increasing, and I recently heard a rumor that a French militia is to be formed—blokes that will make Arnaud Soustelle look like an angel. These Frenchmen will be able to spy on and ferret out their countrymen like no German ever could. And if they can't, then the new Family Hostage Law will—"

"Inhuman!" exclaimed Henri bitterly. "Executing male relatives and condemning females to hard labor if so-called terrorists do not surrender themselves. I do not like to even consider the possibilities for betrayal this brings to the entire underground movement. But, Michel, what are you getting at?"

"Just because the Boche seem to be losing the war at the moment," replied Logan, "we cannot think we can just relax. It can only make everything worse—bring out the latent beast in our enemy."

"Latent!" spat Henri. "Ha! it has always been visible enough."

"Well," sighed Logan, "I suppose it makes little difference. It will not alter what we must do—except that we must be all the more careful."

"Oui."

The conversation lagged a few moments as the two men drank their coffee and pondered their unpredictable futures.

"We can only be thankful, Michel," said Henri at length, "that our families are safely away from here. I feel for those who will have to make such a choice."

He set down his cup. "But we must get to business—perhaps we can shave a few months off this war."

"Even a few days might be worth our efforts."

"I have the report from Claude that London wanted on the drop sites," Henri went on.

"Good. I'll get that to Lise immediately."

"Now . . ." Henri hesitated a moment before beginning again with more resolution in his voice. "I have a task for L'Escroc."

"I thought we had put him to rest."

"We may have our chance to get Jean Pierre," said Henri.

Logan leaned back. He remembered his confident declaration about freeing the priest on the night when he had been arrested. But his words had turned out to be impotent thus far. The S.S. were not about to let their prize slip easily through their fingers. Logan had worked on von Graff as much as he dared to learn anything that would help them get to him, but to no avail. The general was especially tight-lipped about his captive. Trinity got nowhere. And L'Escroc had had no luck either.

Jean Pierre was being kept in solitary confinement under special guard. He'd been locked in Cherche-Midi for about a month, and Logan hadn't been able to get near him, using any personality or disguise—though he had made some gallant, and as it turned out, humorous efforts.

He did manage to learn that Jean Pierre had not broken under interrogation and, to his relief, that the Nazis were exercising restraint in their handling of this particular prisoner, whether out of respect for his priestly collar or because of the influence of his brother, no one knew. Logan remained constantly on the alert for some breakdown in the general's guard, but when his only opportunity came, he missed it. He knew a transfer would have been the perfect moment, but when they moved him to Fresnes, it had been cloaked in such secrecy that Logan did not learn of the action until after the fact.

As time passed, Logan's interest did not so much flag, but the desperation of the situation seemed to lessen. This, coupled with the fact that they had tried without result, gradually lowered the priority in their minds of making an all-out escape effort. Jean Pierre would not be shot, and he was not going to talk. Moreover, the Germans seemed to be satisfying themselves with the mere victory of having him under lock and key. At this point it seemed the risks of rescuing their comrade outweighed the risks of capture and certain death. For whatever leniency they demonstrated toward the priest would certainly never carry over to anyone caught trying to spring him.

There was more to it than that, however. Logan knew it would take nerve to walk into Fresnes and extract their prize catch. Risk was one thing, and he had always been willing to take certain risks. But with his mind more and more on getting back home, on Allison, on his *real* life, he wasn't sure he had what it took to put it all on the line many more times. He did not think it had as much to do with courage as it did with that *élan* Lise had once spoken of.

Logan looked up toward Henri. He had to listen to the proposal.

"They are going to transfer him again," Henri began.

"How did you manage to learn that?"

"Straight from von Graff's desk," grinned Henri. "Sometimes a janitor is more effective than a double agent, eh?"

"I have no argument there," said Logan.

"We have people in high *and* low places," Henri went on.

"And sometimes equally effective! But are you sure it's reliable? We were so blind last time—could this be some sort of trap?"

"That is always a possibility."

Henri sighed, then reached for the coffeepot and refilled their cups. "Perhaps it is wrong of me to take this so personally, but Jean Pierre is a special man and a dear friend. I cannot bear to see him in *their* hands."

"I'm sorry, Henri. I suppose all these months have finally dulled my sensitivities. Though the very thought of it appalls me, too."

"You are troubled, mon ami. Might it help to talk about it? I have not Jean Pierre's wisdom, but I am able to listen."

"Time is too pressing," hedged Logan.

"I think it is a necessary risk."

"Like rescuing Jean Pierre?"

"Perhaps."

Henri paused, then said softly, "Sometimes, Michel, all the secrecy drowns us. But we each have our own personal breaking point."

"I don't think I'm quite there . . . yet," replied Logan, then stopped. He took a scrap of paper from his pocket and handed it to Henri.

Henri studied it a moment, then looked up at Logan. "Congratulations!" he said. "But you do not seem overjoyed."

Logan took the paper and glanced at it again. It was from London, Atkinson in particular. It read:

HAVE YOUR CAPTAIN'S PIPS IN DRAWER STOP PROMOTION JUST CAME THRU TODAY STOP KEEP UP THE GOOD WORK END

"No . . ." said Logan slowly. "I'm not overjoyed, though I know I should be. Here I never thought I'd get into action at all, and now suddenly I'm a captain! But I guess what really matters to me has changed recently."

"Perhaps you just need a furlough—you have been under much pressure."

"If I went now, Trinity would be blown. There is no way I could go to London and cover my tracks."

"Trinity cannot go on forever. Maybe it would be best for you to eliminate him before the Boche do. Drop out of sight and leave von Graff forever wondering who you were and where you have gone. A satisfying final move, it seems to me."

"Except not being able to see his face when he *knew*—that would be a great sacrifice."

"Ah, oui! That would indeed be the *pièce de resistance*!"

"I've thought of the possibility," said Logan, "of simply disappearing. And no doubt it will have to come to that in the end. I'm trying to be attuned to the right moment to fold."

He paused and sipped his coffee, now lukewarm. "You see, Henri, there is another reason why I must stay, and it's in that wire. I have to prove something to the man who wrote it. Even more, I've got to prove something to myself. I cannot leave France until I'm certain my work here is finished. I can't walk out on it like I've done with so many other things in my life. I can't retreat when the going gets rough. I've got to see it out. Yet at the same time, I'm not sure I'm up to something as big as Jean Pierre's escape."

"You will do fine, mon ami. I am certain. And you will not be alone. You will be one of many, and together . . . you will do it!"

64 / Springing the Priest

Logan caught a brief glimpse of his reflection in the window as the train sped through a short tunnel.

The image that stared back at him was momentarily startling; the disguise was certainly effective. His hair, topped with a black wool beret, was streaked with gray, as was his moustache. Wire-rimmed spectacles outlined deep-set eyes, created with the judicious application of makeup and not a few sleepless nights. He wore an ill-fitting and frayed dark suit that might possibly have been in style twenty years ago. He appeared in every way as the venerable educator to which his papers bore witness, off for a month of sabbatical.

To his left, in the seat across the aisle, sat young Paul Guillaume, who appeared absorbed in this morning's edition of *Le Matin*. Logan, however, could detect his discomfiture regardless of his extravagant attempt to mask it.

Who could blame the lad? Besides the dozen or so German soldiers scattered throughout the car, there were three extremely vigilant S.S. soldiers. There was a sufficient show of German force to daunt anyone, especially a young underground agent barely dry behind the ears. Logan had anticipated the heavy German presence; after all, the trains to and from Paris were jammed with soldiers going back to the Fatherland on leaves, or returning to their assignments.

The S.S. were different, of course. They were the ones to worry about, for it was the S.S. who were guarding Jean Pierre. It had been good to see the priest after so long, even if they had only two seconds to exchange covert glances and establish recognition.

The three months in Fresnes showed clearly on his debonair features. Logan thought his hair seemed slightly grayer and his skin was pale and sagging, especially around the eyes, which had become cavernous hollows. But despite all that, a brief smile had flickered briefly across his face as he beheld Logan's outfit. Three months had not broken his spirit. That fact was all the more evident in the time since the train had pulled out of Paris. The suave cleric had spent a good part of the time in animated conversation with his guards. They had no idea that the coy priest was more interested in distracting them than in pleasant conversation.

Logan wondered if he had understood, or even received, the cryptic message he had managed to get to him. It merely read: *"W.C. five minutes to Coulommiers."*

He had no doubts, however, in Jean Pierre's ability to carry out his performance in this life-and-death scenario, if he *had* received the note. But his own part had begun to unravel the moment he had boarded in Paris. His contact in the railroad had given his word that the S.S. and their prisoner would be in car number 7, that abutting the baggage car. How he could be sure of that Logan did not know, but he had had little choice but to accept his guarantee. When the boarding was complete, however, the S.S. wound up two cars away, and Logan had to improvise some way to get Jean Pierre through to the next car.

They had rigged up a false wall in the water closet of that particular car. All Jean Pierre had to do was step inside, where even the S.S. might give him a few moments of privacy. A few seconds later he would step on to the outside platform of the car, and thence into the adjoining baggage car, where he would be as good as a free man.

Simple enough. But the timing had to be precise. He had to start for the W.C. no sooner than five minutes before the train made its brief stop at Coulommiers. They would have about three minutes to get Jean Pierre out of the bathroom and off the train before the guards would get suspicious. Once he made it to the baggage compartment, there would be a crate awaiting him that would be unloaded with all the other cargo scheduled for the little village located seventy kilometers east of Paris.

Logan hoped that by the time the Gestapo were alerted, there would be so much confusion that the simple crate would go unnoticed until Jean Pierre could be removed. There were risks everywhere; Logan fully realized that. But then, every escape plan carried with it the imminent risk of failure. It was part of this business.

But in this present instance, Logan had tried his best to cover every angle: he and Paul would oversee the car; there were two men in the baggage compartment, and he had two other men stationed at the depot in Coulommiers. Besides these, a conductor and a coalman were patriots who would be willing to run interference in a pinch. Each man was under strict instructions that if the thing went sour, they were to scatter everyone on his own; one agent alone was harder to track down than a hoard of eight.

That final injunction against disaster had been fairly routine, not given out of some sense of premonition. But now Logan wondered. He didn't like starting out on the wrong foot. It wasn't as if the switched cars were an insurmountable barrier—he had already thought of a remedy. But it just did not set well.

He glanced at his watch. Fifteen minutes until Coulommiers.

He rose and made his way slowly down the aisle, taking awkward, careless steps, playing his role of absent-minded bookworm to the hilt.

He reached the water closet and entered. Now came the risky part. To jam the door's lock effectively, he would have to do so from outside. Most of the passengers would all be facing the other direction. But if someone chanced by, or some stray eyes fell his way, his innocent little act of sabotage would be undone.

Logan grabbed a small piece of the waxed onion-skin they tried to pass off as toilet paper, crumpled it into a tiny wad, reopened the door a crack, threw the lock shut, then removed a small tool from his pocket. With it he proceeded to stuff the wad of paper into the lock mechanism from the inside, as well as a small piece into the keyhole on the outside of the door.

So far so good. No one had come by.

Now he walked back out into the aisle, pulled the door to him and closed it with a quick jerk, which made more noise than he was comfortable with. But the lock had engaged! Just a few seconds more! Another tiny wad of paper jammed into the lock! He tried the door. It was shut fast!

The job was done. The door would not budge. Whoever tried to make use of this W.C.—including Jean Pierre—would have to go on to the one in the next car. He hoped Jean Pierre picked up the improvisation in the plan!

Slowly Logan turned and ambled the few steps toward the rear of the car, opened the door, stepped onto the landing outside, crossed into the next car—number 7—and continued through it, past the W.C. in which they had installed the false wall, and outside onto the landing. There he paused. Jean Pierre would soon be following right in his footsteps, through car 6, where he would try the disabled W.C. door, on into car 7—no doubt by this time with his guards growing touchy—and into the bogus bathroom there. The plan was admittedly thin, but it was all he had.

Logan waited. In a few moments, even over the racket of the train clacking down the tracks, he should hear Jean Pierre enter the tiny stall on the other side of the wall. From where he stood between the cars, his visibility was limited, but the station could not be much farther. Yet the cold November wind stung through the thin fabric of his cheap suit, and the minutes dragged by.

At last he heard the sound of the door opening, followed by sounds from inside.

All at once Logan realized a minor flaw in his carefully thoughtout plan. He had devised no way to insure that it was in reality Jean Pierre in the W.C. If he opened the false door at the wrong time, it would prove not only highly embarrassing, but would also destroy the rescue. Furthermore, what if his attendant guard took it in his head to get some fresh air while waiting and joined Logan on the platform?

Well . . . so far there was no sign of a guard. Logan decided to try one of the signals they had used to indicate friendly callers at safe houses. Two long, followed by three short knocks. If it was Jean Pierre, he would surely catch the signal and make himself known.

Logan knocked, and waited but a moment until he heard another of their codes in response—very light, to be sure, but recognizable.

Quickly Logan opened the false door, Jean Pierre stared at him, a bit incredulous. But he wasted no precious time with talk. He hurried out onto the landing. Logan quickly refastened the door; then they hastened into the baggage car, just as the engine sounded its whistle and began to slow for Coulommiers.

"You shouldn't have done this," Jean Pierre said, speaking for the first time.

"This is not the place to argue," replied Logan. "Besides, you are practically free now. Get in here." He lifted the lid to a large wooden crate.

Realizing the futility of a protest at such a point, the priest obeyed. While his two men closed and re-nailed the top, Logan tore off his professor's garb and hitched on a worn pair of overalls and wool coat to look the part of a freight loader.

The instant the train stopped, Logan pushed open the baggage door about a foot. He quickly scanned the depot area. His two other men were not immediately visible; perhaps they were still inside. Then he saw Paul step off the train from the door to car 7. But the lad froze the instant his feet touched the ground. Logan snapped his gaze to his left.

Gestapo! He could see them inside the depot; several appeared to be searching those inside. They would have his own men there in custody within moments and be heading for the loading dock.

Logan groaned inwardly. They had walked into a trap!

Paul caught his eyes for a brief moment and Logan answered his questioning look with a sharp jerk of his head. Paul got the message—they were all going to have to clear out as best they could. Paul headed in the opposite direction.

Don't break into a run! Logan silently cried, as if Paul might be able to hear his thoughts.

But he couldn't tarry watching Paul. There were others whose safety he also had to worry about. He turned back into the baggage car and closed its door.

"Gestapo!" he said. "Let's get the priest out and then we'll have to make a run for it through the rear door and hope to get away from the station through those fields."

In a moment they were outside crowded on the small platform between cars. The first man jumped from the train toward the depot. The Gestapo were still inside and his disguise was good. He walked straight toward them.

What are you doing? Logan wanted to yell after him. But he soon knew well enough. The man had always been a devil-may-care sort, and this was his way of insuring the escape of his comrades. If anything went wrong, he would figure out some way to detain the Gestapo.

But there was no time to waste! His other companion stepped off the train platform in the other direction, and hurried off to the right and into the large field that bordered the station.

Jean Pierre was next, but his cassock caught on a broken metal fitting as he made his leap. The fabric tore, but not in time. It threw off his landing and his foot twisted painfully under him. Logan jumped down and straight to where his friend lay on the ground next to the track.

"Come on, I'll lift you," he said, grabbing Jean Pierre under his arms and shoulders.

"No!" said the priest. "I will slow you down. I'll try to follow, but you must go."

"But—"

"Now it's *you* who must do as I say. You have no time to argue," countered Jean Pierre. "It is important you get away. I will be all right, but they will kill you. Your danger is far greater."

"I won't leave you."

"You must, Michel! I will always appreciate what you have tried to do here, but the game is up."

"No! We can still make it!"

"*You* can still make it! But not with a crippled escapee hobbling behind you. Now go! Don't despair, Michel! I am content. God has me where He wants me, and He will use this time—that is what matters. I will not be harmed, of that I am certain. Now go! Hurry!"

Logan hesitated, then dropped to the ground and embraced Jean Pierre.

"I am so sorry," he said as the sting of tears filled his eyes. Jean Pierre kissed his cheek tenderly. "Go with God, my dear son."

"Au revoir!" said Logan, meaning the words in the depth of their literal sense—*Until we meet again!*

Suddenly shouts and the sounds of Gestapo boots broke from the depot area. In the distance Logan could see one of his comrades three-quarters of the way across the field and beating his way for the woods that lay about half a kilometer from the tracks. In the other direction, walking casually along a country road as if he hadn't a care in the world, was the man whose escape had taken him through the depot and under the very noses of the Boche. He saw no sign of Paul.

Logan jumped up and headed for the field.

"Au revoir, mon ami!" came Jean Pierre's voice behind him.

Logan could not even turn to take one last look at his friend. But somehow, perhaps it was in the sound of the priest's voice, Logan was certain they *would* meet again.

Each of Logan's companions had taken off in separate directions, and Logan too shot off on his own. He hoped the men in the depot, as well as Paul, hadn't been taken. But now all he could think of was making it to those woods! One of his companions, several hundred yards to the south, had just made it to the protection of the trees, and now Logan saw that the other had veered off the road he had been strolling along and was heading for cover as well.

Suddenly a barrage of Gestapo gunfire erupted behind him. Logan flew toward the woods, all but certain that the next shot would end his frenzied retreat.

Miraculously, he was still alive when he reached the leaves of the overhanging trees forty seconds later. He stopped for a moment to glance behind him. The shooting had stopped, but he could see a half dozen S.S. soldiers starting out across the field toward him. Behind them, two or three others appeared to be helping a black-robed figure to his feet.

Logan turned back into the forest, and though tears and sweat mingled in his eyes to blur his vision, raced away as fast as he could run.

"A glass of schnapps, mein Herr?"

"Thank you, General. The offerings of your hospitality have certainly changed since our last meeting on the submarine."

Von Graff took a bottle and two crystal glasses from the antique liquor cabinet behind him and poured out two generous measures.

"I hope you are finding Paris pleasant, Herr Channing," he said as he handed a glass to his guest and then resumed his place.

Both men were seated comfortably in tapestry chairs in von Graff's office. Channing brought his glass to his lips and sipped the strong liquor. He had already been in Paris two days—he hadn't wanted to appear over-zealous in looking up von Graff. He was glad he had waited, for von Graff had changed from those days when he had commanded a Reich U-boat. He seemed more deliberate now, with perhaps a cunning edge. He would take careful handling. But nonetheless, Channing was certain he *could* be handled. Time and power had made him both vain and greedy for still more power—or at least to hang on to what he had. Power was what drove him—one of those twisted human thirsts for which there is no quenching.

"Paris is an entertaining city," replied Channing broadly. "I really must consider opening a branch office here. The Führer may have his cultural center, but there is no reason for not developing the industrial potential of the Rhine and the rest of France."

"How is the Führer these days?"

"Optimistic."

"Aren't we all?" Von Graff's question carried with it a definite probing quality.

"Are we, General?" countered Channing. "It's not an easy mentality to maintain these days, what with Churchill prattling on about the end of the beginning and the turning of the hinge of fate, or whatever he calls it."

"So you agree that the Reich is doomed, Herr Channing?"

"I prefer to remain a neutral spectator in these matters."

"But a man who hobnobs with Adolph Hitler can hardly be considered *neutral*, especially—God forbid!—should the war turn against us."

"I've never been one to back myself into corners," replied Channing. "It's a smart man who keeps his options open, wouldn't you agree?"

An ironic smile flickered across von Graff's face. "As a general in the

S.S.," he said, "I am hardly the man to talk to about keeping out of corners. I, too, have a duty to remain optimistic."

"But supposing Germany did lose the war?"

"Such a statement could be construed as seditious."

"Do you think the Führer sent me here to trap you, General?"

"It might be an interesting possibility."

"Come, General," said Channing, leaning forward confidentially, "can't we talk off the record for a moment? Surely you have given the question some thought. Or at least you must have considered your own future. The war cannot last forever."

"Am I mistaken, Herr Channing, or are you not building up to some kind of proposition?"

The man is definitely shrewd, thought Channing. *He could be useful in more ways than one.*

"Channing Global Enterprises is growing rapidly, General," replied Channing, "and after the war I am going to want some good men in the operation. To be quite honest, I've had my eye on you since that first time we worked together—remember?"

"You commandeered a German U-boat for some urgent mission off the coast of Scotland," said von Graff. "Your contact's boat, as I recall, sank and he was lost."

"Well, no matter. It all turned out successfully in the end. But that is neither here nor there." Channing leaned back and drank from his glass. "I sensed even then that you were a man I could use."

"*Use?*" repeated von Graff, his eyebrows arched with deep implications.

"In my company," returned Channing quickly. "You'd have no argument against a thirty-thousand-dollar-a-year job after the war—twelve thousand pounds, a hundred fifty thousand marks—I'll pay you in whatever currency you like. Of course, your mark may not be worth much by then," added Channing almost as an aside.

"But if our cause is doomed, as you so subtly imply," said von Graff, "I may well be occupied less pleasantly after the war."

"I never took you for the bullet-in-the-head type, General."

"It might be better than the other options, like rotting in some British or American prison."

Channing did not respond immediately, but instead nursed his drink. Then he continued. "No one need be caught in the debris and wreckage of a falling Reich. I plan on protecting my own."

"Your family?"

"I have only a six-year-old daughter who is quite safe somewhere in America. I was thinking more in terms of my friends."

"I see . . ." The general drew out the word with deliberate extravagance. "And you are offering me your *friendship*?"

"For a price, of course."

"Of course."

At that moment the intercom on von Graff's desk buzzed. He rose, went to it, and flipped the switch.

"Herr MacVey is here to see you, General," came the voice of his secretary.

"Have him wait," said von Graff. "I'm with someone."

He paused, and was about to flip down the switch when he changed his mind and added, "On second thought," he said, "send him in."

He then turned off the intercom and said to Channing, "I hope you don't mind the interruption. I think you might find it a stimulating interlude. I have the feeling my caller is your kind of man."

Von Graff strode to the door just as Logan was about to reach for the handle.

"Good afternoon, Herr MacVey," said the general. "Do come in."

"Good afternoon, General," replied Logan. "Have I caught you at a bad time?"

"Not at all. I have someone here I'd like you to meet."

Von Graff directed Logan to the sitting area of his office. "Jason Channing, please meet Lawrence MacVey . . ."

Von Graff had not the vaguest idea of what hornet's nest he was stirring into life with his seemingly benign introduction. The two men shook hands, neither betraying even the faintest hint of recognition.

Logan knew the name *Jason Channing* instantly. Joanna's stories about first coming to Stonewycke were well-recounted family lore. Though he had never seen the man's face and could not be positive this was the same Channing, his inner ears perked up and the rest of the interview took on heightened significance. Joanna's Channing would be somewhere in his late sixties, maybe seventy by now. This man *looked* younger, and extremely fit . . . but he *could* be about the right age. Such were Logan's thoughts in the brief seconds following von Graff's introduction.

On Channing's part, his keen eye had recognized the face before him the moment Logan walked in, even if the name that fell from the general's lips was an unfamiliar one. He had seen photos of the new young graft into the Stonewycke line, and would not easily forget the man Ross Sprague had shadowed for him ten years ago. He would especially not forget a man who had almost gotten the better of him. He wondered if this Macintyre knew him or had heard of him. It was doubtful. Best keep his own counsel for the time being; no telling how a chance meeting like this could be of use in his machinations against the Scottish family he had come to despise.

"Charmed," said Channing, offering his hand.

"The pleasure is all mine, Herr—what was it . . . Channing?—" said Logan brightly, shaking his hand firmly.

"Herr MacVey is one of my agents," went on von Graff, oblivious to the stirrings within his guests, "who is aiding us in the capture of a desperate French criminal."

"Desperate criminal?" said Logan, a bit perplexed.

"L'Escroc," said von Graff, and turning toward Channing, explained further, "an underground leader in the Resistance." Then to Logan again he said, "Surely you have not already forgotten him?"

"We haven't heard from him in so long, I thought perhaps he was no longer a threat."

"We have reason to believe he came out of hiding last night. That is why I had you called."

"So," said Logan, "who have you lost this time?"

"An attempt was made to rescue an old friend of yours, the priest, de Beauvoir."

"I'm sorry you lost such a prize."

"You misunderstood me, Herr MacVey. We lost no one—the attempt was foiled."

"My congratulations, General," replied Logan brightly. "But that doesn't sound like the work of L'Escroc."

"Perhaps it is presumptuous of me to ask," put in Channing, "but who is this fellow? He sounds intriguing."

"*L'Escroc* . . . the name means *The Swindler*," answered von Graff. "He is a low-life British agent whom the ignorant people have turned into a folk hero."

"I thought you said he was French?"

"French . . . British—who knows? One time he is reported to be one, the next another. One rumor came in that he was Hungarian. But the most reliable word is that he is indeed British. Unfortunately, we can't seem to get our hands on him to learn his identity for certain."

"We don't even have a reliable description," added Logan, playing his part so thoroughly that the humor of his words hardly fazed him.

"But after last night's fiasco, we're closer than ever," said von Graff. "We captured two of his compatriots—men who worked with him and know him."

Logan masked his surprise and dismay. He had arrived in Paris only a few hours ago, after a grueling night trying to elude the Gestapo. He had fallen asleep in his room; when he awoke, the desk clerk gave him the message from von Graff to come by his office. He had not taken the time to make contacts that would sort out the aftermath of the ill-fated rescue, for the others would no doubt have had to stay away from the city longer than he. Thus he had seen no one since they all separated at the depot. He had assumed—*hoped*—that all had made it.

Perhaps, had he known more of how things had ultimately turned out he might have delayed this meeting with the general. But there should be nothing to fear: none of the men working with him yesterday knew him as anything but a bespectacled old man. And none knew the name Michel Tanant . . . no one, that is, except—"

But just as the thought crossed his mind, the voice of von Graff intruded into his reflection as if he had read his very thoughts, "And these two *will* talk," the general continued, "before we shoot them."

"What makes you think," said Logan, revealing no hint of strain from the sense that all at once everything was closing in on him, "that you haven't got L'Escroc himself?"

"Our police described one of the men who escaped—a gray-haired old man who ran like a youth!"

Von Graff's eyes narrowed and his mouth tightened. "That was him— I know it! He is too smart to be caught so easily. Besides, of the two we captured, one is a boy and the other doesn't fit the vague description we do have of the so-called swindler."

Poor Paul! thought Logan. *I should never have left him alone!*

But in his anguish over the lad, Logan momentarily forgot his own imminent danger. For Paul knew Michel Tanant. And from his capture and the events of the previous day, the Germans could well trace Logan's underground identity. Indeed, Paul knew plenty—enough to convince von Graff that Logan's true allegiance lay to the west, not the east.

Logan realized that as of now he would have but a matter of days, perhaps only hours, to get permanently underground and out of von Graff's clutches for good. The jig was now assuredly up. But he had to know still one more thing before he began to beat his retreat.

"What of de Beauvoir?" he asked.

"He'll be questioned when he is released from the infirmary," replied von Graff. "He broke his ankle in the attempt."

"And then shot with the others?"

"You appear uncharacteristically concerned over the man's fate, Herr MacVey."

"He was a likeable chap," replied Logan without flinching. "It would seem such a waste."

"Well, rest easy. Baron de Beauvoir still calls the shots where the priest is concerned." He chuckled. "No pun intended."

It was a small comfort that at least Jean Pierre might still make it. He would have to take some immediate action to see what could be done about freeing the others. Only one thing was positively clear in his mind—he would never enter this building again. His stint as a Nazi was up.

When Logan left von Graff's office a few minutes later, he had all but forgotten about Jason Channing in the wake of the news of his friends. Before he had stepped onto the avenue Foch, he already had the beginnings of a plan in his mind for another rescue attempt. When reason prevailed some time later, however, after a serious talk with Henri, he saw that the time for his involvement in such things had passed.

"We will get them out, Michel," his friend had assured him. "But the game has now changed. L'Escroc is dead and must never resurface. Neither can Michel Tanant or Trinity. Until we have Paul safely back, and learn from him what the Boche know, we must take every precaution. Your life is in danger."

"But I must—"

"No, Michel! You must *not*. The season of your valiant service to our cause is past. It is time you began preparations to return to England."

"But, Henri," protested Logan, "there is still—"

Henri calmed him with his silencing hand. "Please, my friend," he said, "do not make this more difficult for either of us. In your heart you knew this time was coming. And now, as leader of *La Librairie*, I tell you, it *has* come. You have done all you could do. You have fulfilled your mission."

66 / Channing's Realization _____

Jason Channing dined with friends that evening at *Shéhérazade*.

He had by no means forgotten his encounter with Logan Macintyre. Though the remainder of the afternoon had been occupied with various appointments and business matters, Macintyre remained on the edges of his consciousness the whole time. Without Channing's even being aware of it, his intuitive, suspicious nature had been probing, doubting, wondering. He had a sixth sense about these sorts of things. And he could detect the faint smell of deception in progress, though he hadn't even taken the time to examine the precise reasons for his uneasiness.

As conversation lagged, however, he found himself giving it fuller consideration. He had said nothing to von Graff about his knowledge of MacVey's true identity. On the surface it did not seem to have any bearing on matters with the general. Von Graff undoubtedly knew MacVey to be an assumed name; no one in the spy business used his real name. So Channing knew Macintyre's family—what of it? von Graff would say.

But the strongest reason for his silence was simply that Channing had not yet figured out how best to use what he knew. He would not divulge information prematurely. And in this present case, he was still not sure he grasped fully the complexities of what was going on.

What *was* going on? That was the question. Something smelled wrong. He hadn't liked the look in Macintyre's eye. His responses to von Graff were . . . he couldn't quite put his finger on it.

For years he had been on the prowl for some bit of slander to use against the Stonewycke brood. On the surface it would seem he had been dealt the very cards to bring down their spotless name—one of their own number a German spy! The scandal could cause an uproar in Scotland and bring down the high and mighty Joanna once and for all.

That had always been the problem—they were all so confounded above reproach. He'd thought he had them when that Macintyre married into the family ten years ago. But no—the whole matter was treated openly as a matter of public record. Imagine, an elite family of the British nobility admitting a confidence man into their number, a common swindler becoming one of the family; the facts of his past, even his run-ins with the authorities, couldn't be used against them!

There is no justice, mused Channing to himself.

Now, it seemed as if he finally had something really good. He had

337

stumbled upon a major discovery, one even more powerful if Macintyre didn't realize who Channing was—which was certainly possible.

But Channing had grown wary over the years. Those infernal MacNeils had a way of coming out on top, and he had learned to show more caution than usual where they were concerned. Their son-in-law a Nazi! What a find! It was enough to disgrace any British family. Yet those people were such oddballs—it probably wouldn't bother them. They'd accepted him as a swindler, why not as a Nazi?

And still there was that something stirring in his gut which said things were not what they seemed.

Channing brought his glass to his lips. Again his train of thought shifted back to the encounter in von Graff's office. There was something there, something he could use. He knew it.

Some indefinable peculiarity of MacVey's interaction with the general had set his subconscious to work. Was Macintyre completely on the up-and-up? He had shown a bit too much concern for the captured priest—even von Graff had noted that.

But no, there was something else. Was he too eager, too cocky, too unflinching?

They had talked about the rescue of the priest, the captures. But what was it they had mentioned before that? A fellow they were after, a British agent whom no one could even describe?

L'Escroc, that's what they had called him. The Swindler . . .

Channing leaned back, the word spinning with gathered momentum in his brain. L'Escroc . . . British agent . . . master of disguises . . .

Suddenly Channing set his glass to the table with a thud.

The Swindler! Of course!

A swindler and a con man had married into the highbrow Stonewycke clan. And now that same man was swindling the Germans! It is almost too fantastic to believe, thought Channing, an evil smile of mingled esteem and scorn spreading over his cunning lips.

Macintyre playing a double game! He could almost admire the man. If it weren't for his in-laws, he might try to find a place for *him* at Channing Enterprises after the war! But as it was, this was his key to bringing down the whole lot of them!

Of course, he could never prove any of it to von Graff. The man had obviously bought Macintyre's act hook, line, and sinker. And all he had to go on himself was his intuition and his ability to read people's motives, sometimes even better than they knew them themselves. But he had learned over the years to trust that intuition. It had served him well. And this present discovery would make up for that one glaring time when his perceptions had failed him, when he had sought to make an innocent young lady his own, and been rebuffed for his efforts.

Yes, his revenge would come at last! And would be all the sweeter in having taken so long to bear fruit.

67 / End of the Charade_____

They met in the back room of a cafe belonging to one of Claude's friends. It was now too dangerous to go to *La Librairie*.

Claude sat on a bench against a grimy wall cleaning and oiling a rifle. Henri was seated at a plain wooden table with an untouched glass of wine in front of him. Logan paced the floor in front of him. There were only three of them; the war had brought many changes.

Logan didn't know why he was so agitated. He wasn't nervous. He didn't think he was afraid. Yet he was unable to sit still. Perhaps it was because he knew he had something to do, but everything was taking too much time.

The air in the small, dimly lit room was pungent with the odor of cigarette smoke and cheap wine, and jovial voices drifting in from the cafe. It served to remind each person present how isolated he was from a normal existence—now more than ever.

Logan paused in his pacing and looked at Claude. "Why did you bring that thing in here?" he asked peevishly. "It's bad enough that the place is crawling with Germans tonight."

"It's a pretty specimen, non?" returned Claude, purposefully ignoring the thrust of Logan's remark. "A friend found it in the sewer and made it a special gift to me." Claude almost let a smile slip across his scarred countenance. "Those criminals in the old days did not know that when they dumped their incriminating weapons, they would be arming the people for a revolution."

" 'Divisés d'interêts, et pour le crime unis.' 'Divided by interests, and united by crime.' " quoted Henri dryly.

"Bah!" spat Claude. "Even your de Gaulle has called the French people to revolution. That is the one good thing that will emerge from this war— a new France!"

"The *old* France was not so bad."

"What do old men know?"

Henri merely grunted, apparently deciding that his time was best occupied with his wine. Then he looked up at Logan.

"Please, mon ami," he said, "sit down. You are making us nervous."

"It's just that I had come here prepared to say my final goodbyes."

"I know," replied Henri. "But the delay could not be helped. Your new identification papers are not yet ready. And as I told you, Lise got

339

word to me that she could not come. She was being watched and thought the danger to you would be too great."

"I know," said Logan, at last taking a chair. "And Paul?" he said after a pause. "Have you heard anything?"

"Whether he has talked? No, we have not heard. He is young and untried."

"I hate to think of what they might do to him!"

"Then do not think of it," said Henri. "You must trust us, that we will get him out. In the meantime, while we are making preparations for that, you must bide your time. You must remain until the new papers are ready, otherwise you will never get out of France. The rest of us have done what we can to protect ourselves."

"Besides," put in Claude flatly, "you and Lise were the only ones he could betray."

"Do not fool yourself, Claude," said Henri. "When one is in danger, all are in danger."

"Philosophies!" muttered Claude as he cocked the rifle several times to work in the oil.

The room fell silent. This would be one of their last times together, yet the gathering lacked essential warmth. It would have been better, thought Logan, if Claude hadn't come. But no, it was as much his fault as the Frenchman's. He had been tense and short-tempered too. Mostly he was angry with himself for bringing about this catastrophe. He had played it too close—not just with the Jean Pierre rescue, but the whole Trinity business. He had started out too sure of himself, overconfident. Then when the reality of the dangers involved had gradually become clear, he was in so deep it seemed it could only end one way. He should have taken Henri's advice and pulled out before it came to this.

But he hadn't. He had been waiting for God to show him. Was this now God's answer?

Even if by some miracle they got Paul out before he talked, he could not go on. Only last night he'd remembered that Paul not only knew a great deal about his operations in the French underground, he also knew Logan's real name from that blunder he had made months ago when talking to the Scottish flyer they had helped escape. Too many threads were coming unraveled. In a way it was a relief. It would be over soon—it almost didn't matter *how* it ended, only that he would be able to go back to a somewhat normal existence. Henri was right—he knew that now. His days as Michel Tanant were past.

But now that the die had been cast, it only added to his present tension to prolong the inevitable. It had been two days since Paul's arrest. Logan had not been back to his room. He had already contacted Atkinson, but the major's reply had been far from encouraging. A plane could not be spared; could he make it out over the Pyrenees? They'd keep trying on the aircraft, but just in case, he ought to get things rolling on the other option. Things had changed; the war was heating up. It wasn't as easy as it used to be.

The prospect of still *another* identity to cope with, as well as weeks of travel through the south, now also occupied by the Nazis, was not an appealing one. It was nearly impossible to find guides willing to risk the Pyrenees crossing now that there were heavier German patrols guarding the frontier. Some were charging as much as 100,000 francs for the job, and Logan feared he would have to resort to his old shady life to garner that kind of money.

Well, maybe Atkinson will still find a way to dredge up a plane, thought Logan. But in the meantime, the uncertain waiting was hardest of all. Before he realized it, his thoughts had him pacing once more.

"I thought we'd have more to discuss," said Logan, jamming his hands into his pockets and glancing around. "Maybe it wasn't as necessary as I thought to get together."

He paused. "I wanted to make sure I had a chance to say goodbye," he went on. "But then Lise isn't here, and the papers aren't ready."

"We will meet again in two days at this time," said Henri. "You may see her then. I know that is what you are waiting for."

Logan nodded. "The papers?"

"Hopefully by then as well, my friend," replied Henri. "You have decided to travel south?"

"I must not remain any longer than absolutely necessary," replied Logan. "If Lise doesn't bring a message from London guaranteeing a plane, then I'll leave as soon as I get the papers. I have a couple contacts in Lyon and Marseilles. Maybe by the time I get that far, London will have come up with something. But it will be best for me to keep moving."

"Forty-eight hours, then," said Henri, rising and putting a hand on Logan's shoulder. Logan nodded, and they left the room, Henri to exit through the cafe, Logan to follow the corridor in the opposite direction and out through the rear door into the narrow alley.

Claude remained seated where he was several minutes more, a cynical gaze in his eye. Slowly he raised the rifle to his shoulder and took imaginary aim down its barrel. Gently he squeezed the trigger till the hammer released and clicked down upon the empty chamber with a resounding metallic echo that reverberated through the small darkened room.

The following morning, while Logan finalized plans for leaving the city within a day or two, Channing again walked into von Graff's office. The general was in high spirits and broke out his best bottle of cognac.

"Never mind the hour, Herr Channing," he said buoyantly. "I am in the mood to celebrate!"

"What . . . has the Reich taken Stalingrad or repelled the Allies from the shore of Tripoli?" quipped Channing as he took the offered cognac, not in the least squeamish about a shot or two of good brandy at ten in the morning.

"Better, much better!" replied the general. Von Graff sat back and savored his drink a moment.

"I can't imagine."

"I've got L'Escroc!"

"You've captured him?" said Channing in surprise, suddenly solemn. If von Graff saw anything unusual in Channing's strong reaction to something he had heard about only in passing, he made no mention of it.

"Not exactly in my hands . . . but it is only a matter of time now," answered the general. "One of our prisoners has talked. It seems this fellow—a mere boy, really—acted as a courier for L'Escroc, picking up and leaving messages at a certain mail drop. I've sent a unit to watch the spot, and have every reason to believe it will lead us directly to L'Escroc himself, or at least someone high up in his network."

"It would seem congratulations are in order," said Channing, wondering to himself where this latest bit of information fit into his own schemes.

"And now I know for certain that he *is* indeed a British agent: I've learned his true identity! It seems his name is Logan Macintyre, a Scotsman. I can have my contacts in Britain get me a physical description. I anticipate having him within the week!"

"What good will a mere description do you?" said Channing. "The man will surely take precautions. And Paris is a city of several million."

"We will find him," insisted von Graff, "if I have to track him for months!"

"If he knows one of his operative has been captured, he will no doubt try to leave the city."

"Are you trying to spoil my celebration, Herr Channing?" said von Graff with a frown. "Besides, precautions take time. According to this

Guillaume, he did not contact L'Escroc on a daily basis. Thus he may not even know of the boy's arrest—we have kept it quiet.''

"Precautions take time, but so does tracking down a swindler when you have nothing to go on. And how can you be certain the lad is telling the truth?''

"Herr Channing, have you ever had your teeth filed down, one by one? Or had a spiked belt gradually tightened around your chest? Such methods do not foster a lying spirit.''

"All of which does nothing to satisfy my question: Even with the information you possess, how do you intend to locate this L'Escroc, this Macintyre, especially when in all likelihood he will be out of Paris for good inside the week?''

"All of a sudden, mein Herr, your interest strikes me as something more than causal. You seem to have something on your mind.''

"What would you say, General, if I were to tell you that I came here this morning with none other than your L'Escroc on my mind? What would you say were I to tell you that I could deliver him to you with ease, and save you days, even weeks, of grief?''

Von Graff's eyes glinted as he carefully set down his drink. He knew that Jason Channing possessed resources and contacts beyond imagination. Was it possible he had known of L'Escroc all along?

"I would say that I am intrigued,'' answered von Graff coyly.

"I had certain suspicions which you have just confirmed,'' replied Channing. "My personal gut feeling in matters of this kind is something I have learned to rely on. Still it is beneficial to have supporting evidence. And I assure you that I am just as keen as you to see this swindler in irons. However, I think I may have a more effective means to that end.''

"Do you plan on making this a guessing game?'' asked the general caustically. "You implied that you knew what would put this Macintyre into our hands. Do you intend to drop hints and then dangle me along like one of your lackeys?'' Von Graff had never really trusted Channing, and now he definitely did not like this little game of his, or the tone in his voice, for that matter.

"Not at all,'' answered Channing. "I am merely reluctant to proceed further because I don't know how you will respond to what I have to say.''

"Come now, Channing, we are not children!''

Channing cleared his throat and raised an eyebrow, as if to say, *So be it*. Then he spoke:

"Have it your way, General. You want your L'Escroc, alias Logan Macintyre? Well, he is none other than your own Lawrence MacVey!''

Channing's words hit von Graff like a thunderbolt. "That's impossible!'' he declared. "He has worked with me almost a year, providing valuable information . . .''

But though his first words were ones of denial, his voice quickly lost its vigor and faded into a stunned silence. Almost immediately he knew it was true. He had been standing at his desk and now sank back into his chair—for one of the first times in his life utterly daunted. He did not need to ponder the implications of the situation long to realize what it meant for him. He had stuck his neck out for MacVey, while all along the vermin was slowly slipping a noose around it. Unless he delivered MacVey's head on a platter, his own career as a German commander would come to an abrupt end. He had no delusions. Himmler was hardly the forgiving sort.

"I'll kill him!" seethed von Graff, all his patrician refinement swallowed in animal hatred.

"You have to catch him first," Channing reminded him.

"What do you know of this matter?"

"I have had dealings in the past with Macintyre, and with people very close to him. I recognized him the moment you introduced us the other day, but it took some time to fit all the pieces together."

"But you said nothing."

"I had my reasons. I had to be sure. Believe me, I want to get my hands on him as much as you do, General."

Gradually von Graff began to pull his wits back around him. Channing was wrong—no one wanted MacVey worse than he! If he was going to succeed, he had to think straight. He was a soldier. He had fought in two wars. He was trained to use his head. It was the only way to remain effective. He had to keep control.

Von Graff straightened in his chair, pulled his shoulders back, and focused on Channing.

"What did you have in mind, Herr Channing?" he said slowly, deliberately.

"We may have both grossly underestimated this Macintyre," began Channing. "I thought he was nothing but a third-rate con man, and you thought he was someone you could control. Well, perhaps we were both wrong . . ."

Von Graff shifted uneasily in his chair, but said nothing. Channing continued.

"He follows no patterns, and it's no use trying to second-guess him. What he lacks in finesse he makes up for in sheer audacity. He is L'Escroc— The Swindler—and he won't easily fall for tricks from others. If he is still in the city at all, you may be sure he will not return to any of the places where you might think to look for him. Neither will he look like the MacVey you know. He has probably already adopted one of his many disguises. And he will certainly never walk into one of your snap controls. He knows his man has been arrested, and so is probably already making arrangements to leave the country, even as we talk."

"You make it sound rather hopeless," said von Graff cynically.

"All these preparations will take time, even for L'Escroc."

"So what do *you* propose, Channing?" Von Graff's voice rose as he spoke, on the bare edge of control.

"We would be fools to go after him," replied Channing smugly. "He's too cagey. But he does possess one weakness, which might bring him *to us!*"

Channing smiled, his cunning eyes flashing triumphantly. "He has a family—"

"Of course!" exclaimed von Graff. "It's inspired! But can we do it? Is there time, before he returns and whisks them to safety?"

"I have a man on his wife at this very moment."

"You already knew . . . I'm afraid I don't—"

"As I said, I have other interests in his family. I've had a tail on her for some time, even before Macintyre stumbled across my path. One call and I can have her here in twenty-four hours."

"Then what are we waiting for!" exclaimed von Graff, jumping up and pulling a telephone toward him. "We'll call—now!"

"There is still the matter of how to contact Macintyre once we have our prize and the snare is set."

"No problem! We'll be able to get a message to him!" said von Graff eagerly. "Just grab the girl and leave the rest to me!"

He rubbed his hands together in anticipation. This *was* an inspiration! Small wonder that Channing was such a successful businessman! After all this time, L'Escroc had been under his nose all along! Well, now he would walk right into his arms. This would be better than just putting a bullet through him, though he'd enjoy that pleasure too. But in addition he would have the man's wife to use as leverage. What information might not he be able to drag out of the traitor! It would more than exonerate von Graff in the eyes of Herr Himmler! And when L'Escroc had spilled his guts, *then*— and not before—he would put a bullet through his heart . . . with his wife looking on! Ah, the revenge would be sweet! It would almost make it worth having been temporarily played for a fool!

The general was practically drooling with evil anticipation as he lifted the receiver to ring the switchboard.

"Get my radio man in here," he said. "We have to contact London immediately."

It was five in the afternoon when Logan again made his way into the alley and through the back door of the cafe. He'd been wearing the disguise of a French beggar all day and the beard itched terribly. He hoped good news would be awaiting him.

Claude was sitting silently in the same chair as before, the rifle across his lap, looking as if he hadn't moved in forty-eight hours. Logan merely nodded, then shook Henri's hand where he stood on the other side of the small room.

In answer to Logan's unspoken question, he held up a handful of papers in front of him, smiling broadly.

"Yes, Michel, they are here. I have your papers!" he said.

Logan sighed deeply. "It is a sad day, Henri," he said in reply after a moment. "A sad day in which to bid friends farewell. Sad . . . but necessary."

"Yes, Michel. You must go."

Unconsciously Logan glanced toward the door.

"She will be here, my friend," said Henri. "I spoke with her around noon. She knows you leave Paris tonight."

"Then there is still no word of an airplane?"

"Not as of then."

A noise at the door forced the two men into sudden silence. They did not move for a long moment. Then came a soft knock—

"It's me . . . Lise," whispered a voice.

Logan strode to the door, unlocked and opened it just wide enough to let her in, then shut and bolted it again.

She looked at each man, but there was no friendly greeting in return to the probing warmth of anticipated farewell in Logan's eyes.

"I take it there has been no message?" he said.

"Not the one you have hoped for," answered Lise solemnly.

"Then you *have* been contacted?"

"Not by London!"

"What are you telling us, Lise?" asked Henri.

"It looks as if Paul has talked," she said bluntly.

"Poor boy!" sighed Henri.

"Are you certain?" said Logan.

"I went to my mail drop before coming here," she replied. "Paul uses it sometimes. I had hoped perhaps—"

"I had forgotten about the mail drops," groaned Henri.

"I picked up the messages—actually there was only one—and started to leave," Lise went on. "Then I realized I was being followed."

"Followed?" said Logan. "You mean no attempt was made to arrest you?"

"I know what you are thinking," she replied. "They hoped that whoever picked up the mail would lead them to the whole nest. But I lost them."

"Are you certain?" put in Claude sharply.

Lise ignored his question. "The odd thing," she added, "is that this message is addressed to *Logan Macintyre*."

Slowly Logan reached for the small paper Lise now held out to him. He stared at it a long while before he finally tore open the envelope. He quickly scanned the message.

"Dear Lord!" he breathed as he sank into a chair, handing the folded paper to Henri.

Henri looked at the words, shook his head, then read them aloud:

"Greetings, Logan Macintyre—alias L'Escroc, alias Trinity, alias Lawrence MacVey! Yes, mein Herr, we know who you are! We know all about you. And we also know that within twelve hours you will freely *unarmed and alone* walk through the doors of S.S. headquarters and voluntarily give yourself up. How do we know this? Because we have at this very moment in our possession something you will desperately want. We have your wife, Herr Macintyre! If you do not believe us, her signature at the close of this note is all the proof we will provide. You have but a matter of hours to decide. At five a.m. of the morning following the date of this communique, she will be shot as a spy if you have not made your appearance."

So, thought Logan, *the nightmare has come full circle*. It hardly seemed possible that Allison could be dragged into this world which had so occupied him these many months. But he knew even before he saw her handwriting that von Graff was not bluffing. His gambler's instincts had not dulled over the years; he had always been good at sniffing out the false show of a worthless hand. This was not one. Von Graff held the cards.

And now, at last, Logan had his answer. He had been praying for guidance about what to do. Now he knew. There would be no storming of the gates, no escape plans, no daring rescues, no more deceptions. It had to end—here and now. *Help me, Lord*, he said silently, *to have the courage to trust you now, rather than trying to do it by myself.*

Resolutely Logan stood up.

"What are you doing?" said Lise.

"I am going to the avenue Foch."

"Michel! They will kill you!" she almost shrieked. "And probably never let her go even if you do give yourself up."

"We must try to get her out," interjected Henri. "I have other people we could use. You would not have to—"

"No, Henri," said Logan. "I can't do it that way. The time has come for me to lay down my arms. The fight is no longer mine, but the Lord's. He will protect and deliver her."

"You speak of ancient myths when the Nazis are holding your wife!" spat Claude. "You have lost your senses!"

Logan looked around at his friends. How could he make them understand all that was going on within him?

"The power of God is greater than a division of Nazis," he replied. "I cannot explain it. I only know that I must do what I must do. You may each be called differently. But right now, at this moment, this is my destiny. I *must* go."

He turned toward the door, but Claude's voice intervened from his dark corner.

"So, Anglais, it has come to this! You intend to walk straight into the arms of the S.S.?" It was a challenge, not a question.

"I have no choice."

"*Here* is your choice!" shouted Claude, wielding his rifle in the air in a defiant fashion. Then, with a quick motion, he tossed it across the room to Logan.

On reflex, Logan caught the weapon, just as he had Major Atkinson's gun that day so long ago in England. For a moment he held the rifle in his two hands, staring down at it; then he glanced back toward Claude. But for an instant he did not see the Frenchman, or indeed any of his present surroundings. Many images raced through his mind—but not the images of a crook named Lombardi, or even of a dead German soldier in a blood-stained French wood. He saw instead images of a man who had spent his life hiding behind one role, one charade, one con game after another. A man who had been careening along his own path for years, grasping at the only way he knew, a way of self-sufficiency and independence—afraid to let it go, afraid of what might happen if he relinquished control of his life, afraid of the path that had beckoned to him more than ten years ago . . . fearful of the way God might want him to follow.

Suddenly Logan realized that his way of life—having to trust solely in his own strength—had become an awful burden, dragging him down like a giant millstone. As a Christian he suddenly saw that it hadn't had to be that way, that he could have chosen to trust in God, but he had not *wanted* to see that path. He had *wanted* to go his own way, to be his own man. It had been easier to blame everything on externals—on Allison, on the marriage, on his lousy jobs, on his prison record. On anything but his own blind self-reliance!

He looked down again at the gun. It suddenly seemed to represent the solution the old headstrong, stand-on-his-own-feet, bold Logan Macintyre would have chosen—storm the citadel of the enemy, if not with might like a man such as Claude, then with cunning and with plans of his own devising.

But the charade was over. He could no longer be somebody unreal, some imaginary Trinity or Tanant or Dansette—no more L'Escroc, no more *swindler*. Storming the complexities of life with his own pitiful *self* was over. He had to be Logan Macintyre again. The time had come to allow God to take command!

He tossed the rifle back to Claude.

"No, Claude," he said. "That is not the way. Neither is L'Escroc. Not this time. This time I will put my fate in God's hands, not my own."

"Bah! You are more of a fool than I thought! You speak the pious words of a child!"

"You may speak more of the truth than you know," replied Logan. "Perhaps a child is what I should have been all along," he added with a thin smile.

"You are an idiot! You think you will go in there and sacrifice yourself to satisfy some . . . some insane urge inside your twisted brain! You will do nothing but betray us all!"

Logan turned beseeching eyes toward Henri. "You understand . . . don't you, Henri?"

The old bookseller nodded. "I understand, mon ami. I would perhaps do the same were I in your shoes."

"Never!" shouted Claude. In an instant he leaped up and took aim at Logan's head down the long barrel of his rifle. The others now realized that while he had been shadowed by the dim light in the corner of the room, he had slipped shells into the chamber.

"Think, Claude!" pleaded Henri, knowing the angry Frenchman well enough to realize that his distorted emotions were taut and that he might do anything. "One shot will have half the Wehrmacht on you."

"What do I care? We are as good as betrayed anyway!"

Quickly Lise stepped in front of Logan. Henri, scrambling from his chair, joined her.

"Then kill us all," she defied.

"Why shouldn't I?" he returned.

"Because then you would be no better than the murdering Nazis you have fought so hard against," argued Henri. "What could your life mean if you were just like them?"

They stood thus for several seconds that seemed to each as an eon, the tension palpable. Then with an angry curse Claude threw down the rifle and stalked toward the door. There he paused and turned, glaring.

"You are *all* fools!" he spat hatefully. "I am done with you!"

When he was gone, Logan looked down for a moment at the gun where it lay on the floor, sighed, then turned with a heavy smile of thanks to his friends.

"I cannot promise anything," he said, "but I will do my best not to talk. I wish I could give you more assurance for all you have done for me. But this is something I must do, come of it what may. The Lord has many ways to deliver His people."

"We need no more assurance, Michel," said Henri. "We have no fear."

After speaking quietly together for a few final moments, Logan placed his arms around the old bookseller in a warm embrace.

"I doubt I will see you again, mon ami," he said, tears standing in his eyes. "But I will never forget you. Please do what you can for Allison if you have the chance. Adieu, dear friend."

"No, Michel," replied Henri, "not *adieu*, but *au revoir* . . . something tells me we will yet again look upon each other's faces."

Tenderly he kissed Logan's cheek.

Logan turned to Lise. They exchanged poignant gazes. War had thrown them together, forcing upon them forbidden desires and painful sacrifices. But out of it each had grown, and out of the rubble of what could never be had blossomed a friendship that would remain forever in the memory of both, though they would never lay eyes upon each other again.

"*Adieu*," Lise said to him, and Logan knew she had chosen the word purposefully.

"Adieu, Lise."

Logan exhaled a deep breath, took one last loving look at his two friends, then turned toward the door.

The small room was icy cold.

Allison shivered and drew the coarse wool blanket more tightly about her shoulders. She glanced at the barred window. It was dark out, but she had no idea what time it was—probably nine or ten at night.

What a fool she had been! She realized that now.

But it all seemed so different yesterday when the two men had stopped her as she walked home from work. "We can take you to your husband," one of them said. She hadn't even paused to think it over rationally, hadn't thought to ask for an explanation or some kind of identification. She still did not suspect foul play when she had mentioned that she should notify her mother and they insisted there was no time, a slight sinister edge creeping into the second man's voice.

Stupidly, irrationally, thinking only of seeing Logan rather than the dangers of wartime, she got into the car with them.

It was too late for sensible thinking once they drew guns and hustled her aboard a private plane. They'd landed once in Lisbon, but she had remained inside the plane the whole time, dozing occasionally, cold, hungry. And now here she was in France—she had seen the Arc de Triomphe from the car window on the way from the airport.

She had been kidnapped, that much was clear, and put in this room, or prison cell, she couldn't quite tell. Until two hours ago she had had no idea why, or if it had anything to do with Logan or if she would in fact see him.

Then she had had visitors.

The door had opened and Allison shot up from the bunk where she had been lying. Two men entered. One appeared to be in his late forties, very refined looking, dressed in a trim black uniform, obviously a German officer, though Allison didn't know enough about their insignias to tell his rank. The other man was considerably older, probably in his sixties, though vigorous enough. He was handsome for a man of his age; dressed in an expensive blue surge suit. He also appeared quite distinguished, though with an entirely different air than the German officer.

The officer stepped forward and held out his hand graciously. "I am General von Graff, Frau Macintyre," he said politely in well-cultivated English. "I trust you are doing well."

"What do you expect me to say, General?" she answered petulantly. "I am hungry and cold. I have been forcibly taken from my home and locked up like a common criminal with no idea—"

"Forgive me for these accommodations. I wish we could provide something more fitting your station."

"They said I would see my husband."

"That is yet to be seen," answered von Graff.

"But I thought—"

"It is entirely up to your husband, Mrs. Macintyre," put in the other man, whose accent now further identified him as an American.

"What is this all about?" asked Allison. "I don't understand."

"Perhaps I might introduce myself," went on the older man. He held out his hand as if he were trying to mimic the general's earlier gesture. "Jason Channing, at your service!"

Allison's brow suddenly creased. She immediately recognized the name, but her perplexity stemmed from the fact that it came so unexpectedly, almost as if she were meeting some historical figure from the distant past.

"You are familiar with my name?" he asked in an almost jovial tone, clearly enjoying the moment so richly satisfying to his vengeful nature. This might not quite settle the old score, but it would certainly help him at least sleep nights with a smile on his face!

All at once in her mind's eye Allison saw her mother, young and untried, standing in a meadow of Port Strathy, facing an influential, debonair man of the world, a man who had flattered her with empty words, a man who had lied and cheated and had tried to bring destruction upon the whole town. In the vision of her imagination—just as her father had described to her many times—she could see her then shy, retiring mother pull back her shoulders and denounce that man before all the residents of Port Strathy.

And now here he was again, with that same arrogant look upon his face that Joanna had so aptly described to her family. Allison wondered that she hadn't recognized him just from that smirk on his face even though she had never seen him before. *How could he be mixed up in all this mystery involving Logan?* she wondered. Was he still, after all these years, striking out against the family of the woman who refused him? One look into his eyes gave her all the answer she needed.

But Allison was not to be cowed. In her veins flowed the blood of Lady Atlanta and Lady Margaret, the same blood that had given her mother courage in her moment of crisis. Allison stuck out her chin, every inch of her small but hardy frame emanating that feisty Duncan stock.

"Channing . . ." She appeared to muse over the name. "Yes . . . it does sound vaguely familiar, though I must say it warranted hardly more than a passing mention."

Channing's eyes sparked at the barb like steel against steel. But he was too proud to show that the wound had penetrated. He, too, was suddenly thrust back in memory to that same Strathy meadow facing the only person who had ever dared refuse him—a frail, worthless, bumpkin of a woman at that! This ridiculous girl was just like her mother—haughty in the face of superiority, fearless even when facing imprisonment or death! But her arrogance would only make his vengeance all the sweeter!

"Have your moment, my dear," he said coldly. "It will be your last."

"What do you want with me?"

"For myself," replied Channing, "it is just a bit of sport. But for the general here, your presence is of purely utilitarian value."

"It is nothing personal, Frau Macintyre," put in von Graff, "for *me*, that is," he added, casting a quick glance toward Channing. "You were simply an extremely convenient way to obtain what I really am after."

"And that is. . . ?" said Allison.

"Your husband, actually."

Allison closed her eyes as the full reality of her circumstances finally dawned upon her. She was being used as bait! But she tried not to show the faltering of her courage, though when she spoke again, her voice was weaker than before. "I'm afraid I still don't understand . . ."

"You need not understand anything further, mein Frau. But Herr Channing was anxious to meet you. He insisted that you know something of the situation."

Von Graff clicked his heels together and bowed slightly. "We will take our leave now," he said. "It is entirely possible that you might also be free to go as soon as your husband graces us with his presence."

Von Graff turned smartly and opened the door. Channing lingered a moment.

"It has truly been a pleasure, Mrs. Macintyre," he said with a smile. "You are every inch your mother's daughter, and I must say that makes the satisfaction of meeting you all the sweeter."

Then he turned and followed von Graff out.

That had been at least two hours ago, maybe four, for all Allison could tell. In anguish she had spent those hours praying that there might be some way to warn Logan. For no matter how long they had been apart, she knew he would turn himself in immediately upon learning these men had her. Knowing he was safe, she could endure this place. If only she could warn him somehow!

71 / Together at Last

Slowly Logan made his way down the darkened avenue Foch.

He had been along here many times in the past months as a supposed German informant. But never in the middle of the night.

After leaving his friends he had returned to his room. He knew it was being watched, just as he knew he had been followed ever since. But none of that mattered now.

He had needed a little time alone, to think, to collect himself for the ordeal that was sure to come. Time to solidify his commitment, both to Allison and the Lord, and to gather strength through prayer for the path he had chosen to walk—a path he had little doubt would lead to his ultimate death. When he left a few hours later he knew he was ready, for the first time in his life, to face the final consequence of war. He was at last ready to lay down his life, in quite a literal sense, for his wife. He was finally a man at peace—with himself and with his God.

On a more practical level, he had wanted to pay his final bill as well, and to scour his room to make sure all traces of any connection to *La Librairie* or any of its people were utterly gone. That done, he glanced around one more time. His personal effects, of which there were few, hardly mattered now either. He made sure he was dressed warmly, bundled up in his overcoat, then turned and headed out into the night.

There would be only one more stop—at the cafe where he spent so much time while in Paris. There was time for a good hot meal. Who can tell? he thought grimly. It would probably be his last.

When he finally began the long walk down the avenue Foch, it was just after ten p.m.

Thirty minutes later, he stood before the somber outer walls of the S.S. garrison. He walked toward the guardhouse, where two uniformed men were stationed. As he approached, they poised themselves with rifles ready.

"Logan Macintyre to see General von Graff," said Logan simply.

"Ah yes, Herr Macintyre," replied one of the men, relaxing his weapon. "We were told to expect you. I will call and tell him you are here."

Even as he spoke, the other guard walked around behind Logan and began binding his hands.

Logan said nothing further, and made no resistance to his captors.

When Channing and von Graff left her, Allison lay back down and tried to sleep. The bed—a thin mattress over a wooden bunk—wasn't much. But she was too exhausted to care. Within moments she was sound asleep.

Suddenly Allison started awake. She had no idea how much time had passed. It was still the dead of night. Sounds outside the door had roused her. She sat up.

The door opened, and light blazed in from the single bulb in the corridor outside. Allison squinted as she looked toward the door. A German soldier stepped in, followed by a man dressed in civilian clothes, and another soldier who held a drawn pistol.

Suddenly Allison's face came aglow and seemed to lighten the darkened cell where she sat.

"Logan!" she cried, jumping up. "It *is* you!"

"Oh, Ali," he said softly, "I am so sorry it has to be this way!"

Tears of joy streaming down her face, Allison rushed forward, but instantly the two guards closed ranks around Logan. She stopped, and for the first time beheld her husband's appearance.

She could tell at once that he had changed, yet not in the way she had always feared. He had not hardened, but rather—in spite of the visible strain and the toll of the past year—seemed softer, at peace. It was as if a mask had been removed and she was at last seeing into the depths of the real man—the man she had always known was there but which had remained hidden below the surface. She felt that she was seeing *into* him, as she had always wanted to be able to do. What she saw on his face made her glad and ache all at once. There was love, and yet pain and sadness in his eyes. Something had happened to him since leaving London, and she saw that the changes had not come easily.

Logan turned to one of the guards. "Neumann," he said, "can't you give us some time alone?"

Neumann hesitated, glanced from Logan to Allison, not so much assessing their potential capacity to escape, but rather with a kind of pity. Then he looked at the other guard.

"Warten für mich draussen," he said. The guard about-faced and left the room. Then to Logan, Neumann said, "Five minutes, Herr Macintyre; that is all." And he too was gone.

Allison and Logan stood still a moment longer, gazing upon each other, then as if of one mind each took a step. Allison opened her arms to embrace her husband, then saw that his hands were manacled together. She fell into fresh weeping and threw her arms around him, resting her head on his shoulder.

"I'm so sorry for getting you into this, Ali," he said tenderly.

"Oh, Logan . . . dear Logan!" she sobbed through her tears. "I'm just so happy to see you!"

He took a half-step backward, then raised his bound hands and cupped her chin then—that sweet, soft, determined chin!

"Logan . . . I want you to know—"

"Ali," he interrupted, "there's so little time, and I must tell you something—I may not have another chance."

He paused, as if he thought she would protest. But he too saw a change in his young wife.

"Ali," he went on, "I was a selfish fool. I know that now. I had everything so wrong, so turned around. Lady Margaret tried to show me, and Dorey, and even your parents. But I wouldn't listen. I don't know why. I guess I was so stubborn I had to learn the hard way—"

"Logan, please! Don't—"

"Hear me out, Allison. It's all true. I didn't have the slightest inkling what love meant, that it goes beyond happiness and feelings. The kind of love that makes a marriage work is so much different than anything I ever thought. But God is showing me, Ali. He's finally opened my eyes to see that the commitment we made to each other goes beyond all that."

He paused and smiled at her. "I know it's too late now, but . . . as poorly as I'm explaining this, I had to try to make you understand. I never was much good at expressing what was on my heart—I suppose I never really knew my heart before. But, Ali . . . will you forgive me?"

"Oh, Logan, we both had so much to learn," Allison replied. "So much of it was my own fault too. But you know I forgive you."

"I wish we could have the last nine years back, Ali," he said. "I want nothing more than the chance to try to do it right . . . but these five minutes might be the only second chance we have—"

"Logan, no! Don't say it!"

He motioned to the bed. "Let's sit down."

"We must be strong," he said as they sat together on the edge. "But then you never had a problem with that. I suppose it's me I'm worried about. I can be strong too . . . if you'll help me, if I know you'll be all right after I'm gone—"

"Logan, please! There *must* be some way out of this!" cried Allison.

"Oh, if only there were, my darling," sighed Logan. "But you know what they do with captured spies."

"Spies?"

"I've been part of the French underground all this time, acting as a German double agent. They just discovered my identity a few days ago. They grabbed you so they could lure me out of hiding. But having seen you again, and knowing that you still love me, I think I can now face death calmly."

Allison threw her arms again around Logan, her tears flowing freely.

"And our daughter—" Logan went on. "I wanted so much to have the chance to be the right kind of father to her. Please at least tell her that, as miserable a fellow as her father was for a while, he loved her, and . . . Allison, what's wrong?" As Logan spoke, Allison suddenly let out an anguished sob, pressing a hand against her mouth.

"Oh, I wasn't going to tell you now," she wept. "I didn't want to add even more to your grief, but . . . but . . ."

Again she broke out in a mournful cry.

"Please, Ali, share your pain with me. Whatever it is, I've got to know."

"Oh, Logan, it's not just *my* pain!" she sobbed.

"What is it?"

"Oh, Logan, little Joanna—she's . . . she's dead, Logan! She was with Mother; there was a bombing . . . the train was half destroyed! I'm so sorry to have to tell you!"

Logan was silent a moment. Then he said, "And Joanna . . . ?"

"She had to be hospitalized," replied Allison, trying to calm herself. "But nothing serious. She's all right."

"Oh, Ali . . . if only I could have been more to the two of you!"

He wanted desperately to take her in his arms, but his hands were cuffed. He wrenched at them in frustration.

Allison held him in her arms instead as much to comfort herself as him. Neither spoke for several moments. Never before had they been closer than during these several silent seconds that passed. But their unity did not stem so much from their shared grief—though that had perhaps given focus to it—but rather from the mutual turning of their hearts at last to the God whose desire had always been to bring them together as one. Each was praying for the strength of the other for the trials they knew were coming.

Soon their quiet was interrupted by a sharp tap on the door.

"Two minutes," called Neumann.

Logan shook his head toward the door with a sigh. "I must tell you something else," he said. "I haven't even given you a chance to talk, but I think I know now what you might have said to me, and that will have to be enough."

"This war seems so unfair," said Allison.

"We're in God's hands, Ali. Lady Margaret would say nothing happens by accident."

She smiled. "I love you, Logan. And you're right—I can just see her saying that very thing."

"I love you, my dear Ali—more than ever!"

He paused, with another sigh, then continued almost begrudgingly. "Oh, how I hate to spend our last moments on *business*. But even if my fate is sealed—"

"Logan, I won't accept that! There must be some way!"

"If only there were! But please . . . listen to me. I must know that you're going to be safe. That's all I have right now. I'm pretty sure von Graff will let you go. I dropped some hints to him that you knew more about the underground operation than you do, so he'll cut you loose, hoping you will lead him to my associates. There's no way to eliminate the danger.

Just be careful, and warn the others that you are probably being followed. But it's the only way I can be sure you'll get home safely. Now, go to the hotel on—"

"No, Logan! I don't want to go! It's all too complicated! Let me stay here and die with you!"

"Allison, please. Don't you see? I've failed as a husband. My own foolish life has gotten me into this mess. I have nothing left but to try to save you, and to die with honor. That's all that can now give meaning to a past life that has been anything but heroic. I have to know that I have not given my life in vain, that you will live on and maybe remember me once in a while as a man in the end you could be proud of."

"Oh, Logan . . . I *am* so proud of you!" But Allison could say no more through her quiet weeping.

"Now, in the morning go to the Hotel de Luxe on the rue Saint Yves. Do you have that?"

Allison nodded, but Logan was not sure. Her mind hardly seemed focused on the details. The Lord would have to bring it all back to her—there was no time to say it all more than once.

"The rue Saint Yves. Remember . . . it's important. Hotel de Luxe. There's an old woman out front who sells flowers. Buy a bouquet from her, then go to the little park on the corner and sit on a bench. You should arrive by ten a.m. A friend of mine will contact you—he'll know you by the flowers. You'll know him when he uses the name *L'Oiselet*. He will get you out of France."

"Let me stay with you, Logan," Allison pleaded. "I've waited so long for us to be together."

"Dear . . ." He kissed her gently. "Don't you see? The only way I can face what's ahead is to know you are safe. If you remained here, they could use you as leverage. They might torture you to get information out of me. I could stand anything but that. I knew that risk when I turned myself in. But I had to see you. And I had to hope that my gamble with von Graff would pay off and that he would release you. I know they're going to kill me in the end, but if your life were in the balance too, I might betray friends and cause much suffering. With you safe, I can be strong . . . and keep silent."

"Logan! I can't . . . I can't face life without you!" sobbed Allison.

"You will, dear Ali. God will give you strength. He is with me, and He will be with you. You can trust me to Him without fear."

All at once the door burst open and the guards clattered into the room. Neumann held the door while the other marched abruptly up to Logan, grabbed him by the arm, and jerked him to his feet.

"I love you, Ali!" he called hurriedly as they yanked him away. "Be strong . . . the Lord will watch over me!"

"I love you, Logan!" cried Allison through tears of agony. "I will always love you!"

She watched helplessly as he disappeared from sight and the heavy door was thrown shut and bolted after him.

Thirty minutes later, Allison's tears of anguish had spent themselves. She took several deep breaths in an attempt to regain her control, then slowly sat up. She *would* be strong! She would honor his memory by carrying out his last wish. She would remember all he had told her, and would do as he said. He deserved that much from her. She would be brave and strong . . . for *his* sake! Could she do anything less for such a courageous husband? If he were to die with honor, then she would honor him in life. She would not even let the Germans follow her! She would do her best to protect his friends!

Allison sank to her knees beside the bed.

"Oh, Lord," she prayed quietly. "Give me the courage to be strong. Help me to trust you . . . and to trust Logan to you. Give him grace to endure, Lord. Protect him in your love."

The woman appeared so old and frail, it seemed a miracle that the biting November wind did not whisk here away. She glanced up at Allison, and her wrinkled, brittle face cracked into a toothless grin. Even if Allison had not been instructed to purchase a bouquet from her, she would have done so merely from pity. She took a coin from her purse and bought a bunch of brown and orange mums.

"Merci beaucoup!" said the old flower-lady, nodding profusely.

"De rien, je vous en prie," Allison replied, trying to recall some of her French from school. But *thank you* and *you're welcome* were about the extent of it.

As she continued on her way, she noticed the man in the black jacket. He had followed her last night from S.S. headquarters, and there had been another man standing in front of the hotel. Logan had been right—they were keeping an eye on her. She had made a few vain attempts last night to lose the man. This morning, feeling gradually braver, she determined to do better.

Did they really think she would lead them to the underground? General von Graff had been most gracious about releasing her, even offering to call a hotel. She told him she preferred to stay in a hotel she had used before the war. He made a vague noncommittal reference to her returning to London, but she said she wanted to be near her husband. He said he understood, and she would be welcome in Paris as long as was necessary, pretending that their "little difficulty" with Logan would soon be resolved. She knew he was lying, but said nothing.

As she walked away from the front of the Hotel de Luxe, Allison tried to think of what she might do so as to be alone when she reached the park. Above all, she did not want to endanger any of Logan's friends. Her one possible advantage would be that the man shadowing her would never expect any sudden moves. If she acted quickly, the element of surprise would be on her side.

But what could she do? She knew nothing about this sort of thing.

Ahead she spotted several shops, a cafe, and another hotel. As she approached, she stopped to look in one of the store windows. Yes, the man was still behind her, about half a block away. She could see his reflection.

She turned and continued on. On the other side of the hotel stood a small motion picture theater. That might be a possibility. Back in London, such places always had rear exits. And it was open—a matinee was playing! Without thinking further, she ducked inside, bought a ticket, and hastened into the darkened auditorium.

Now came the moment she had to act quickly. By the time the man behind her bought a ticket, got inside, and became accustomed to the dim light, she would be long gone!

She ran down the right aisle, spotted at the far end the emergency exit, and without a hesitation tried the door handle.

It opened! She stepped through it, closed it quickly behind her, and suddenly found herself in an outside alley that ran behind the hotel. She ran to the end, glanced up and down the street, turned to her left, ran the half-block to the next intersection, turned left again and ran all the way to the next cross-street, where she crossed the wide boulevard and turned up the street to the right. At last she paused to catch her breath.

If that man can find me now, she thought, he deserves to know where I'm going!

Nearly an hour later, Allison, by many circuitous routes, finally arrived at the park Logan had told her about. It was thirty minutes past the appointed time and she hoped she was not too late. The day was a chilly one, but the park was still filled with people. The sun was shining brightly, and that was apparently enough to entice the Parisians out-of-doors. She had not seen her German tail since the theater, but still strolled about for a while, trying to make it appear that she was here for no specific reason, just in case any unwanted eyes *were* still upon her. She was certain Logan would not lead her into danger. She had the distinct impression, as she recalled his words, that he knew exactly what he was doing in setting up this meeting.

She found a bench and sat down, idly watching some children playing ball, trying very hard not to glance about.

In five minutes an old gentleman ambled up and seated himself on the bench that backed Allison's. Before long he began reading a book—Allison could not see his activity, for she still sat facing the opposite direction, but she heard him leafing through the pages. Then she heard his soft voice. At first she thought possibly he was mumbling or reading to himself. Then she heard:

"Madame Macintyre—do not turn or speak."

The urge to do just those two things was nearly overwhelming. But Allison managed to complacently keep her gaze on the children.

"I know you by the flowers," the man went on in English, though with a heavy French accent. "You will know me by the name L'Oiselet. Listen closely. In a few moments lay down your flowers and freshen your lipstick. Then rise, leave the flowers behind you, and walk on."

That was all. The only other sound from the gentleman was that of another page being turned.

Allison followed his instructions, squelching the dozen questions that immediately rose to her mind. She laid the flowers down, took up her purse, added some fresh color to her lips, and, looking in the mirror of her compact, also gave her hair a quick pat. When she had satisfactorily given the impression of a woman fixing her face, she rose and started off. It was hardly the kind of meeting she had expected. She was leaving knowing no more than when she had come.

She had gone about fifty paces when she heard a child's voice calling after her.

"Mademoiselle! Voici vos fleurs!"

Allison turned and a little boy ran up to her waving the bouquet in the air.

"Merci," said Allison with a smile, taking the flowers. She turned and began on her way again. She felt rather than saw the paper wrapped around the stems of the flowers.

Fighting the urge to grab the paper and read the note she was certain would be there, she continued on. She couldn't relax yet. It was entirely possible von Graff had put two or three men on her.

Allison walked straight to her hotel, climbed the stairs to her room, and, once inside, tore the paper off the bouquet. The message read:

"Spend afternoon shopping, with a casual stop at the bookstore *La Librairie*, 124 rue de Varennes, 3 p.m."

What the Germans would think of her shopping while her husband lay in prison a condemned man, Allison could hardly imagine.

Her follower, who had managed to get back on the trail when she returned to her hotel for a rest, would report that she had spent the afternoon distracting herself in the shops, a perfumer's, a dress boutique, two or three bookstores, making a few idle purchases, not appearing to enjoy herself overly much.

At a few minutes before three she wandered onto the rue de Varennes and entered her third bookstore of the day. Her shadow paused outside across the street. The man behind the cluttered counter appeared about sixty years of age with a pleasant, friendly face. When he spoke, she realized it was the same man from the park, though she had not had so much as a glimpse of him then.

"Bonjour, Madame," he said. "I see they are following you."

"I tried to be discreet," said Allison. "I gathered that to be the intent of your message."

"He appears none too suspicious or concerned," said Henri. "Michel has taught you well, eh?"

"Michel?"

"Your husband . . . oh, but I forget! I ought to get used to his real name—the pseudonym is of little use now."

"He said you were a friend of his."

"And I am honored to be counted as such," Henri replied warmly, though a sadness crept into his eyes. "Come, let us browse among the books over here."

He led her to a shelf toward the back of the store. "Your Boche might get suspicious if I took you into the back, so this will have to do."

Suddenly Allison tensed. All at once she became aware that they were not alone in the small shop, and yet the man spoke freely and seemed to take not the slightest notice. A woman stood leaning against the wall between the high bookcases. When Allison came into view, she stood straight and faced her and Henri as they approached.

"Ah, Lise," the old man said in a subdued tone, "she has come!"

He turned to Allison, motioning her to speak softly. "Madame Macintyre, may I present another of your husband's friends from our small band? This is Lise, and I myself am called Henri. We are glad to have you visit us, though we wish it could be under more pleasant circumstances."

"Bonjour, Madame Macintyre," said Lise, stepping forward and offering her hand.

"I am happy to meet you, Lise," said Allison, accepting the handshake. As their eyes met, the peculiar sensation pulsed through her that the sad, intense, beautiful eyes of the French woman were assessing her merit. She returned the look steadily, until Lise's lips twitched into a half smile, and released her hand, apparently satisfied with what she saw. Allison returned the smile.

"Time is short," said Henri, snapping Allison out of her momentary reverie, "for how long can one be expected to stand in a bookstore? Now, Madame, of primary importance—which Michel was most concerned with—is that papers are being printed for you and arrangements are being made to smuggle you out of the city and back to your home. After that—"

"What about my husband?" Allison cut in abruptly.

Henri shook his head regretfully. "Dear Michel," he sighed. "We want nothing more than to help him, but he is under even closer guard than another of our number, Jean Pierre."

"But you can't just let them kill him!"

"Don't you think we would get him out if we could?" rejoined Lise sharply. "But there is no possible way! We've already discussed everything!" Then she glanced away and appeared embarrassed at her outburst. "I'm sorry," she said, "I did not mean . . ."

"We are all very upset by the situation," said Henri.

But Lise would not accept Henri's attempt to give her a reprieve. "If my English is better," she said, "I am perhaps able to explain that nothing is more important to us than helping Michel."

"Your English is fine," said Allison. "I suppose since you are all strangers to me, it is hard to realize you can be as concerned for Logan as I am. I also apologize."

"Your husband is a remarkable man," said Lise. "He has sacrificed much for our cause, taken many risks. He is very brave, and has rescued countless Frenchmen and Britons and Americans from the Boche. But now that he comes to face the ultimate sacrifice, we must stand helplessly by. It makes our hearts . . . je ne sais pas quoi—" She stopped short, searching for the correct way to express her thoughts. "It is difficult," she added at length.

"He made us swear that we would attempt nothing until you were safe," added Henri.

"Surely you don't always just sit by when one of your people is in danger?"

"No, of course not. Michel was one of the boldest in planning rescues and carrying them out. But you must understand the dangers. Just recently an effort to gain back one of our dear friends failed. Not only is our beloved priest still in prison, he is being guarded more closely than ever. Two others are dead, a young boy has been tortured, and all has led to the imprisonment of your husband. You see, the consequences for failure are severe. It is entirely possible that to leave Michel to rely on his own wits with the Germans he is already well-acquainted with will be the safest course of action in the long run. To try a frontal assault to break him out would only get some of our own people killed; it would probably endanger him far worse."

"What could be worse than a firing squad?" said Allison, starting to cry.

"I'm simply saying, my dear Madame Macintyre, that I cannot risk your life and the lives of others who depend on me. I would gladly risk my own life for him . . . I'm sure Lise would, as well. But until you are safe, and until I know more how my life might be used to gain his release, I see nothing that I can do."

"I am as safe as anyone in Paris," said Allison determinedly. "Thus you have kept your word to Logan."

"Not until we have seen you safely *out* of Paris."

"Time enough for that later," replied Allison. "But I will not leave without him!"

"I think," smiled Henri, "that you are maybe as remarkable as your husband."

"No, Monsieur," replied Allison, "just *very* stubborn. It's a family trait." She returned Henri's smile, wiped away her tears, and took a deep breath. "Logan told me, just before they took him away, that I had to trust God for him. I suppose I have to learn to trust the instincts of his friends, too. But if you're waiting for him to bring his wits and silver tongue to his own aid, I have to tell you, he sounded resigned to martyrdom. I don't think he's going to lift a finger on his own behalf. I think he's made peace with himself, with God, and now with me . . . and is ready to die."

Just then the doorbell rang. Henri hurried away, in case the newcomer was an unwelcome patron. His familiar greeting told the two women all was well, but they remained where they were.

"Did you know Logan well?" Allison asked Lise, following a moment of silence.

"We worked together for over a year," answered Lise. "Henri and I and several others. A few are now in prison. One is a Jew who was taken to a camp in Germany."

"How horrible!"

"War is ugly."

"I would so like to understand what it was like for him here," said Allison earnestly. "If only to grasp more fully the changes that took place in him."

Lise smiled, apparently lost in thought for several moments. It was not a particularly warm or cheerful smile, yet Allison oddly sensed there was something in this melancholy woman she could trust.

"Madame Macintyre," said Lise, the smile fading from her lips, but lingering as a new warmth came into her eyes, "I thought many times that Michel's wife must be a very lucky woman. I am now beginning to see why Michel always held you in such high regard, and spoke of you as fondly as he did. Seeing you helps me understand much about the man I grew to care for."

"It sounds like the two of you were . . . close."

"Yes, Madame Macintyre. I would not be truthful to say otherwise. Your husband—Logan—was a close and dear friend. Before he came I had grown bitter from the war. He helped me in many ways to . . . to be a *person* again. He will always be special to me. But you need have no fear. No one could ever replace you for him. He was an open-hearted man who loved all those he met. But toward the end, I could tell he longed for you terribly. He had many friends, but only one Allison."

"Thank you, Lise," said Allison softly. "You don't know how much your kind words mean to me. But now I think it is time for me to go. I will be back. I hope we may have the opportunity to talk again."

"I will look forward to it," replied Lise.

74 / Incommunicado _____

The walls told the story.

Logan passed the long hours trying to make sense out of the poignant statements, some legible, some merely undecipherable scratchings, etched into the plaster around him with a nail or sharp rock. The prison graffiti told of courage and bitterness and fears, the final pre-death messages of those who had gone before him in the dungeon-like cells of Fresnes Prison.

Some spent the final moments of their lives making clear to anyone who cared their political stands.

Death to Pétain! one had scratched boldly. *Long live de Gaulle!* wrote another, and *Long live the Red Army!*

Others seized the moment to decry their bitter disappointments: *Jean Aubrac—betrayed by a friend!* mourned a Frenchman condemned to the firing squad. And, *Marie Bonnard—I hope my little Suzanne is well*, lamented a patriotic mother; an unidentified cynic simply said: *I don't mind dying; it's a rotten world, anyway.*

An American flyer took the opportunity to calculate the pay he was saving by sitting in prison. And below his computations was an especially odd inscription: *Sgt. Helmut Mölders, to be shot for aiding and abetting the enemy—but my only enemy is the Führer!* "An interesting point of view for a German sergeant to hold," murmured Logan. Yet he realized at the same time that in a sense Germany too was an occupied country, with many inside its borders also struggling to regain their freedom in different ways.

Some of the inscriptions attempted to lend hope to future sufferers. One, quoting World War I poet Rupert Brooke, especially touched Logan in his melancholy moments: *If I should die, think only this of me: that there's some corner of a foreign field that is forever England.* It was signed, *Lt. Bruce Dexter, Flight Officer, RAF—condemned to die, March 10, 1941.*

A priest had painstakingly etched the Lord's Prayer into the wall, and Logan read the words over and over, grateful for some piece of the Scriptures to sustain him. How he wished he could remember more than mere fragments of an occasional verse here and there! But he used the long, silent hours trying to force back into his mind the bits he was able to recall.

I ought to leave something behind too, Logan thought. A man contemplating death can hardly avoid the urge to pass along some "final message" as a statement of his own enduring personhood. But as yet nothing had come to him. So he passed day after day—he soon lost count—in the cold, filthy cell, the only break from his solitary confinement coming when they dragged him out for interrogation.

"I am Captain Logan Macintyre, service number GSDQ 985617," he would say doggedly, over and over, revealing nothing more, despite their brutal questioning. He would never betray his friends. He was ready to die. But when the moment came, he would die alone. He would take no one down with him.

Von Graff himself officiated at the sessions on frequent occasions, though two brawny S.S. sergeants were called upon to perform the actual beatings and other tortures at which they had become highly skilled.

"Who is your commanding officer?" demanded the general.

"I am Captain Logan Mac—"

A swift clubbing from one of the sergeants was his only reward for such determined stubbornness.

"Who is your Paris contact?"

"I am Logan—" But another vicious thrust drew blood from his eye.

"Your hometown, I believe, is Glasgow. What is your address?"

"Logan Macintyre, service number—"

This time an ironlike fist to the midsection doubled Logan's body and he crumpled to the floor in semi-consciousness.

"Come now, Herr Macintyre, why do you put yourself through this? We already have names—Lise Giraud, Jacques Nicolet, Jacques Tournoux, L'Oiselet—Why suffer these needless daily ordeals? You have only to give one word of confirmation."

"I know none of these you speak of," gasped Logan in a faint whisper.

Von Graff grabbed him by the scruff of the neck and, with the help of one of the men, yanked him back up into his chair. Then he angrily took him by the throat and shook him violently. "You're running out of time, you idiot!" he cried. "Don't you care that I am a general in the S.S.? Talk before I give the order to have you shot!"

"I doubt anything I say will change your plans, General," replied Logan, gaining back his breath.

"And you care nothing for life?" shrieked von Graff. "Talk, I tell you . . . save yourself!"

"I care for life, General . . . but I am also prepared to die."

"Bah! You are a stupid fool!" yelled the general, striking Logan's cheek with the back of his hand. "You *will* tell me what I want to know. And then you *will* be shot for your insolence!"

Von Graff turned to leave, saying to his henchmen as he walked away, "Give him some more motivation, then return him to his cell."

An hour later they dumped Logan in a heap on the hard, comfortless stone floor of his tiny cell.

He tried to muster up some pride in himself for not talking, even if only pride enough to give him strength to endure another day's beating in silence.

How easy it would have been just to say the names . . . Henri Renouvin, Major Rayburn Atkinson, Gunther. Thank goodness he didn't know Lise's real name! Of course, maybe Henri wasn't Henri either. No doubt they had both changed their names by now, anyway. Henri could hardly leave his bookstore, but Lise would be long gone from her apartment. Poor Henri! thought Logan. What if he has to abandon his dear books to the underground?

So many times his friends were right on the tip of his swollen tongue— names, places, addresses, plans, code words. They would understand if he talked . . . how much could a man bear? They would have changed everything! Why shouldn't he tell what he knew? They would all be safe by now. . . .

But then in the midst of his thoughts of capitulating, he would catch a hazy image of someone's face, and he would remember—he loved them, and he *could* die for them!

So instead of pride, his feelings turned to mere thankfulness.

He had made it through another day. Maybe by tomorrow the general would finally give up and the execution squad would come for him and he wouldn't have to face it again. Yet it seemed that every day, when the booted feet of death made their daily ritual march down the outside corridor at five a.m., they always stopped at some other poor bloke's cell. He wondered if the men they took instead of him had been tortured to the extent that they looked upon a bullet through the heart as a welcome relief, or as a terrifying moment of eternal doubt.

He was glad that he was at last prepared to die. He hoped when the boots stopped at his door, he would be able to walk out into that open yard with head held high.

Many times in the dark, solemn hours his mind had turned to old Dorey Duncan. How close he felt now to Allison's dear old great-grandfather! Logan had spent enough time in other jails in his past. But now he thought of Dorey, perhaps because, like him, he did not deserve to be here. He wondered what Lord Duncan had thought about during his months of imprisonment. He had never spoken much about that time. But he must have thought of Maggie, from whom he had been so cruelly separated. He knew that Dorey's time in prison had ended in something close to insanity, thinking he had lost her forever. Logan could see how this existence could foster insanity. Yet he had enough to hang on to keep his brain somewhat intact. He knew how it would all end. He didn't have the anxiety of uncertainty. He knew Allison was all right and that she loved him. And Logan finally had his relationship with God to sustain him as well.

He had told Allison that she could entrust him to God without fear, and now he himself must cling desperately to the truth of those words.

He gave his spiritual state before his Maker a great deal of thought in those quiet moments. But he couldn't shake one nagging fear. Eleven years ago, he had turned to God another time when he lay dying. He had felt so sincere back then. Yet the years that followed only served to reveal how shallow his commitment had really been. He had given himself to God in becoming a Christian in much the same way he had given himself to Allison in marriage—with surface emotions and mere mental assent to the truth of the Christian gospel. He had said "I believe," yet had held back his deepest self. He had never confronted the surgeon's scalpel in God's hand and willingly said, "Remake me according to *your* pattern . . . cause my character to reflect the image of your Son." In short, Logan now realized that though he *had* prayed the prayer of belief, he had never truly given his heart—totally and unreservedly—to the Lord. He had given a piece of himself, but not all. He had misunderstood the Christian life just as he had misunderstood the basic nature of marriage, by never grasping the foundational necessity of total, sacrificial commitment. Thus after eleven years, both as a Christian and as a husband, he was still essentially the same Logan Macintyre. The transformation of his character to reflect his Maker—the fundamental essence of spirituality—had still not begun.

He was afraid, therefore, that as he now sat in prison, his thoughts of renewed commitment toward Allison and toward the Lord might be but another last-ditch effort to reprieve himself. Whether the rest of his life was a matter of weeks, days, or possibly even hours, he wanted, even in that short time, to make what beginning he could to surrender his *whole* being to the transforming might of God's love. No more bits and pieces of his personality, no more convenient commitment, no more halfhearted prayers, no more keeping his own image of himself intact. He had played so many roles, worn so many masks, been called by so many names. It was finally time to lay them all down in order to become the man he had *really* been meant to be all along. No more running from one unreal identity to the next. The time had come to become the Logan Macintyre of God's perfect design.

Again his thoughts turned to Dorey. It had been years since he had recalled that day just before the old family patriarch had died. He'd called Logan into his room, and Logan remembered thinking it odd that he should be thus singled out. Dorey had, of course, spoken with every member of the family of that day, but at the time he hadn't even *been* a member of the family. Lord Duncan lay on his bed, the life slipping slowly from his worn-out physical frame and into the new body awaiting him.

"Did I even tell you how much you remind me of myself when I was a lad?" he had asked in a weak, yet still determined voice.

Logan shook his head.

"I could laugh at life," Dorey went on, "and I was such an expert at running from it when necessary. But you're starting out on a better foot than I—you've seen your need for God while you're yet young. You'll likely be just fine, lad."

He paused and let out a long sigh, which revealed that there was more on his mind than he had let on.

"But . . ." he continued in a moment, struggling to voice his concerns in a way the young Logan could grasp, "maybe because we're so alike, I fear more for the pitfalls of life that you may face. I'm ending my life, and you're just starting yours, and . . . Oh, but perhaps it's wrong of me to be so gloomy."

"I respect what you have to say, sir," said Logan.

"I guess what concerns me, lad, is that I think we are both adept at finding the easy way of life," Dorey continued. "I did it with a joke, a dance, and a glass of ale. You had your schemes and gambling tables. And I wouldn't for a moment suggest that God would ever want to take away that twinkle in your eye and your love for a good time. Yet sometimes the way God lays out for us is not an easy one. But it will always be the best one."

"I know that now, Lord Duncan," Logan had affirmed confidently, "now that I'm a Christian."

"I pray it is so," the old man had replied in a retrospective tone. "But *becoming* a Christian is only the beginning of the road, not the end of it. That step is but a door that opens into a new way of life. It's easy to walk through the door and then stop. Many people do just that, continuing in their natural ways, thinking that they have taken some miracle cure with the step of salvation, and that's all there is to it. I ran from God before I knew Him. But there are some who run from Him *after* they know Him. We all have our ways of avoiding what God wants to do with us, inside our hearts."

"Are you saying you are afraid I'm not sincere in my decision?" asked Logan.

"If only sincerity were all we needed!" Dorey replied. "My father used to say, 'The road to nowhere is well-paved with good intentions.' " He chuckled softly at the memory from so long ago. " 'Tis a long road ahead of you, lad. You'll be needing *daily* refills on that sincerity to make it last, especially on those uphill runs when the going gets hard."

How right he had been!

But at the time Logan had accepted his words with the cocky confidence of a new believer. He had, despite Dorey's warning, assumed that his initial decision would propel him along. When its power had waned, he had taken it as an indication that he had gone as far as possible with his life as a Christian. It had been easy to rely on his own power. Yet it wasn't sufficient to keep the dissatisfaction from gradually creeping in—with his jobs, his marriage, his home . . . and with himself. Without even realizing it, he had started to run again, just like Dorey said—a Christian running from God. His very life of intrigue, which contained so many ready-made identities, served him with a wealth of hiding places. His real self *never* had to surface if he so chose.

But that was yesterday.

Finally his eyes were opened to the true nature of his need. His time might indeed be short. Nothing could change that now. The consequences of the life he had chosen were his to face, and his alone. But from now on he could make the decision to follow God's way rather than his own, even if the arena for such a change had to be lived out solely in his own attitudes from within a tiny prison cell. Dorey had said there would be no easy way.

So if the execution squad came for him tomorrow, he knew with assurance that they would not be taking out the same man that had been deposited in this cell so many days ago. They would not be blindfolding Michel Tanant, or Trinity, or L'Escroc, or Lawrence MacVey—poor von Graff would be robbed of his moment of victory. For the man who would go to his death was a new man. Not born again, for that had happened eleven years ago. But a man at last aware enough of his own weakness to surrender his *whole* heart to the One who had called his name back then on the road to Stonewycke. Now he could pray, with whole worlds of deeper meaning and firmer intent, the same prayer he prayed then: "Help me, Lord, to become a *true* man."

Logan glanced at the grimy, stained wall of his prison cell. He found a rusty old nail that had fallen into a crack in the floor, probably left by some other chronicler of the past. He reached up and pressed its point into the ancient plaster, recalling to mind an old hymn.

"I am Logan Macintyre," he wrote. "I was lost, but now am found. I was blind, but now I see. I was dead . . . but at last I am ready to live!"

75 / The Approaching Sound of Heavy Boots____

For two men who had seen their designs so successfully concluded, von Graff and Channing appeared particularly glum.

"I'm afraid," said von Graff dolefully, "if a man doesn't talk in two weeks, the chances are slim that he ever will."

"Time always works for the victim," offered Channing, puffing grimly on the Cuban cigar von Graff had provided. "I never thought he had it in him."

"You yourself said we had underestimated Macintyre."

"The scoundrel! You'd think he really was one of *them*!"

"What do you mean?"

"Nothing," Channing replied. Yet he could not get out of his mind how the infernal Duncan clan always managed to get the upper hand. And now, even in the death of the blasted woman's son-in-law, they were about to do it again! Just knowing he had failed to thoroughly *break* the principled fool was enough to twist this at least half into a victory for *them*!

"I dare not torture him further," said von Graff. "It would take all the meaning out of the firing squad. A man has to be in his right mind as he stares down the barrels of those rifles, knowing he's only moments away from eternity. It's that look of terror in his eyes that is the ultimate triumph."

"You don't fool me, General," chided Channing. "You don't want to torture him further because you are still sentimental about your protege."

"Ha!" Von Graff savagely ground his half-finished Havana into an ashtray. "I'm only afraid he'll drop dead under the whip and cudgels and deprive us at the last of watching him shot."

"Yes, I suppose you're right. We must have that, at least." Channing studied the burning end of his cigar a moment. "And how much longer must we wait?" he asked.

"I was still hoping his wife would provide us with something," answered von Graff.

"She's still in Paris?"

"Yes. I've had men on her constantly. And I must say her movements are a bit strange for a woman about to become a widow. But nothing suspicious. And certainly nothing of any use to us. Apparently she was telling the truth, and does, in fact, know nothing about her husband's activities."

"Then why is she still here?"

"Probably waiting to take the body home—who knows?"

"You're going to give her the body?"

"I thought you suggested that earlier—something to do with your old feud with her family?"

"Ah, yes! How considerate of you."

"The point is, the girl will be of no use once her husband is executed. Perhaps we've played them both to the limit, and it's now time to have done with them."

"That would be my vote," said Channing with something akin to glee.

"Then let's pull the Macintyre woman back in, and proceed with her husband's execution."

"Yes! Yes!" agreed Channing enthusiastically.

Von Graff leaned over to switch on his intercom. "Please send in Captain Neumann," he said to his secretary.

In another five minutes a brisk knock came and von Graff told his aide to enter.

"Captain Neumann," he said, "will you inform Fresnes that they are to prepare the prisoner Macintyre for execution at Montrouge."

He turned to Channing. "How does seven a.m. tomorrow morning sound?"

Channing nodded with a lusty puff of smoke billowing through his lips.

"He is to face the firing squad?" said Neumann.

"Is there some problem?" asked von Graff sourly.

Neumann snapped to an even smarter attention than he had already been assuming. "Nein, mein General!" he rejoined obediently. "I shall make all the arrangements, sir."

At six-thirty the following morning the winter sky showed no signs of the approaching dawn. The five persons exiting the S.S. headquarters, however, paid little attention to the portents of the sky. The two S.S. officers at the lead of the group walked with precise military gait. They paused when they reached the S.S. staff car parked at the curb. The lieutenant stepped forward and climbed in behind the wheel, while Captain Neumann opened the rear door for the three others of the small entourage.

Channing climbed into the back seat first, followed by Allison. Von Graff slid in beside her. Neumann briskly shut the door, then opened his front passenger door. Before climbing in, he glanced momentarily over the roof of the automobile, as if scanning the area for something, probably just the first hints of coming daylight and an end to this assignment. Then he, too, ducked into the car.

The automobile proceeded east on the avenue Foch, then south down the avenue Marceau, crossing the Seine at the Place de L'Alma. The dark streets were quiet; the City of Lights had not yet come to life on that chilly Sunday morning. It was a ten-minute drive over the uncongested streets to

Fort Montrouge. The black of the sky had begun turning gray with the first light of dawn, and a mild drizzle had begun to fall as the car turned into the old fort.

The stone walls of the fortress had seen more glorious days; now age and disuse coupled with infamy to tarnish its reputation, for here the Third Reich performed many of its grim executions. Allison gave a shudder as they drove through the gates. To her left stood the execution post, with its two deadly shot-riddled scars in the wood, one at eye-level for bullets to the head, and one lower down for bullets to the heart.

Dear God, she prayed silently, *be very near to us now!*

The car slowed to a halt and soon the car doors were opened. Allison was ordered to get out. Von Graff and Channing stood next to her, the rain beginning to fall more earnestly now, but hardly dampening the spirit of their triumph.

In another moment her concentration was distracted from the morbid sight as two "Black Marias" rumbled through the gates, just moments after she and von Graff and Channing had stepped out of their vehicle. The two vans stopped next to the execution site some fifty feet from them.

Out of the back of one of the vans clambered eight armed German soldiers. They jogged to the execution post where the prisoner would be tied, then turned and paced off their positions. They then stood attending to their rifles. At the same time the driver of the second van had emerged; now he walked around to the back, opened the wide door, and reached inside to haul out his passenger.

Allison could not hold back a gasp as Logan was dragged out and forced to stand beside the van. When he had been nearly dying from the gunshot wound he had received eleven years ago, he had not looked so dreadful. Even in the dim pre-dawn light, she could see that during the two weeks of his imprisonment he had lost a great deal of weight. His hollowed eyes were ringed with dark circles, or perhaps bruises, Allison could not tell. A definite wound, festering and dirty, crossed the side of his cheek. Dried blood was evident from a wound on his arm, and he walked with a painful and unsteady limp. The injured arm hung limp by his side.

Allison glared at von Graff, her eyes dark and searing.

"How can you do this to fellow human beings?" she demanded. "You must be an animal!"

Von Graff's eyebrows raised and his jaws tightened, but he made her no reply. Her words were perhaps too disquieting to one who had always considered himself a cultivated man. This war was indeed turning men into beasts, but he could not pause to consider the implications of her statement just now.

Logan paused, perhaps hearing a familiar voice through the hazy morning. A look of distress passed across his sallow face when he saw Allison. He jerked his eyes to von Graff.

"Why did you bring her here?" he demanded sharply, though his voice was so weak it lacked force.

"I would not want to deprive a wife a last moment with her husband," replied the general.

But Logan had turned his attention back to Allison and was slowly limping toward her. The guards made no move to stop him.

"Be brave, Ali," he said. "It is not really so bad—I will die with honor. God is with me."

At last, prompted by a jerk from von Graff's head, one of the guards grabbed Logan's arm and pulled him roughly away.

"Logan . . . have faith!" called Allison. "I love you!"

The guard jerked him forward, but he called over his shoulder, "I have always loved you, Ali—"

His words were cut short by a sharp blow to the back that sent him to his knees. Allison stifled a scream, her eyes at last filling with tears. Painfully she watched as the guard yanked Logan back to his feet and slammed his back up against the firing post. While the guard was securing him, von Graff turned to his companions.

"Herr Channing," he said, "why don't you and Frau Macintyre retire to that guardhouse over there where you will have a clear view and remain dry at the same time. This cursed rain is becoming annoying. I will join you momentarily."

"Capital idea, General," said Channing.

Von Graff left them and strode to where Logan was now tied securely to the post.

Logan spoke first.

"Von Graff, I don't care what you do to me, but you have no reason to harm my wife. Let her go back to England. She knows nothing of all this."

"I cannot promise anything," replied the general. "You should know by now that I am not my own man."

"She knows nothing, I tell you."

"After watching her these past two weeks, I am inclined to believe you. She is a woman with peculiar shopping habits, and with a tendency toward odd associations. But one day with her confirms that she is no spy. She is of little use to us. I assume she will go unharmed."

He paused, then held out the blindfold to Logan.

Logan shook his head.

"The stoic to the end?"

"No stoic, General. Just a man who is finally prepared to face life as it comes to him, without trying to hide behind any masks. Life . . . *and* death."

"An admirable point of view, for anyone but a man facing a firing squad."

Logan did not reply.

"I want you to know, Macintyre," von Graff continued, "that despite this unfortunate end to our relationship, I have nothing personal against you. Actually, I have a great deal of regard for you. You played well, Macintyre." He paused and sighed. "But, alas, we were both always fully aware of the rules of the game."

"I know now, General, that this was no mere game," said Logan.

"Dying men always have their 'revelations.' But tell me, Macintyre, now that it is over, and you are about to die an ignominious death which no one will ever know about—tell me, do you have any regrets?"

All was silent for a moment about them. Thirty feet away the execution squad stood resolutely at attention. Not a sound could be heard throughout the semi-deserted compound.

"Regrets, General?" said Logan at length. "Sure I regret that I lived my life so long for myself. Regrets, perhaps—but no doubts. For I know that my life is not now given without meaning. I am laying it down for my wife and for my God. And there are few causes worthier to die for than helping rid the world of your kind of evil."

Von Graff smiled, thinking back to their first conversation aboard the sub in the North Sea. "You are a fanatic, after all, Herr Macintyre. As much as I admire you, I have to admit to some disappointment."

"I apologize for nothing, General."

"I would hardly expect it."

"One last thing, General," said Logan.

"Yes?"

"Though it may not matter to you, I bear you no malice. As God forgives you, so do I."

"You waste your last words on such sentimentalities."

"Perhaps someday they will mean something to you."

Von Graff shrugged, then turned to go. Almost as if an afterthought had just occurred to him, he paused and looked back.

"You will want a word with the priest now I assume," he said.

"Priest?"

"The priest you requested."

"Yes, certainly, but I—" replied Logan, puzzled. He had asked for no such thing. But by now von Graff was fifteen steps from him and walking briskly away.

The general had nearly reached the guardhouse when a new figure stepped out of one of the "Black Marias." He was tall and walked with a practiced poise, marred only by a slight limp, his black cassock trailing out behind him. A thick graying beard and moustache covered his face, and wire-rimmed spectacles perched on his finely chiseled nose.

He approached close to Logan and laid one hand on his shoulder. In the other, Logan saw he clutched a missal and a rosary.

The priest looked deep into Logan's eyes.

"God be with you, my son," he said.

"And with you, Father," replied Logan, his eyes opening wide in dawning awareness.

"Take courage, my son . . . this is your final performance."

Logan's dulled senses suddenly sprang fully alert as he recognized the voice of the only priest in France he had ever known.

Inside the guardhouse, Channing had taken up an advantageous position in front of the window. At the moment, however, his gaze was fixed on Allison, who had retreated a safe distance away.

"Come closer, my dear," he said in a smug voice. "This is your husband's moment of honor—probably the only one he has had in his crooked and dishonest life."

"My husband is worth a hundred of you, Mr. Channing!" declared Allison proudly.

"You might cause me to enjoy this less," sneered Channing, "if you made some attempt at contrition. But then, I forget whose daughter you are."

"A daughter whose father is a true man alongside snakes like you!"

Channing stepped toward her, grabbed her arm, and forcefully drew her nearer the window.

"You *will* watch your husband die!" he growled. "Then we will see what comes of your Scotch stoicism! I'll see you on your knees before this day is through, and then your mother will know to whom the final victory belongs!"

Allison watched as the priest approached Logan. Then von Graff entered the guardhouse, distracting her attention.

"It won't be long now," he said. "Blast this rain keeping us from a clearer view."

"It will be clear enough, won't it, my sweet?" taunted Channing.

Allison stuck out her chin and straightened her shoulders, but said nothing.

"You're just like that cursed mother of yours," muttered Channing. "We'll see what good that stubborn pride does you now!"

But before Allison had the chance to utter the biting reply that sprang to her lips, the dreaded command filtered into the guardroom from outside in the yard:

Ready!

Eight rifles were instantly readied at shoulder level.

Aim!

All at once Allison saw from the corner of her eye that Channing's gaze was fixed, not on the window nor the proceedings outside at all, but on her. He cared nothing about Logan—alive *or* dead. The true focus of his

malicious revenge was centered only on her, and the family she represented.
Fire!

Instantly a salvo of shots rang through the morning air.

Logan's body slumped over on the post, kept from falling by the ropes that bound him.

A piercing scream escaped from Allison's lips.

"Logan!" she cried, making for the guardhouse door.

But Channing grabbed her arm and kept her from running out into the compound.

"Not so fast, my haughty little heiress!" he said with self-important satisfaction. "Stay here with us to complete my celebration!" He wrenched her backward and threw her against the far wall of the small room, where she fell on the floor.

Channing looked outside again to see several men removing Logan from the post to take him away.

"Well, General," said Channing, "it would appear that we have done it!" His voice was jubilant.

"So it would appear," replied von Graff in a subdued tone, his eyes casting some doubt on the extent of his triumph.

They turned away from the window toward the middle of the room.

"I took the liberty of making some small preparations for this great moment," said Channing as they approached a small table. On it stood a bottle and two crystal glasses. "It deserved at least a minor ceremonial remembrance. Will you join me in some champagne, General?"

"Of course, Herr Channing."

Channing uncorked the bottle and poured out two generous measures of the bubbling liquid.

He took one of the glasses, then handed the other to von Graff.

"May I propose a toast?" he said.

Von Graff nodded, as if to say, "The moment of victory is all yours."

Both men raised their glasses as Channing spoke: "To the now-departed L'Escroc. We have outswindled the Swindler!"

Behind them an unexpected but familiar voice broke through the morning air:

"Ah, L'Escroc . . . it was indeed one of my finest roles!"

Spinning around in shock, Channing's glass fell to the floor with a shattering crash. Logan stood before them in the doorway. Allison jumped up from the floor.

"Logan!" she cried.

She ran to him and threw her arms around his wet and bruised body.

"So sorry to disappoint you, General, Mr. Channing," said Logan, "but my comrades asked me to break in on your little victory party. We are—I'm sure you can understand—in somewhat of a hurry to be away from this dreary place."

He paused long enough to bend over and kiss Allison lightly, keeping his eye on his prey.

"I was almost afraid something had gone wrong," she said.

"The only thing that might have gone wrong is that I could have died of a heart attack standing there in front of those guns!" said Logan. "Why didn't you let me know?"

"We couldn't get word to you," said Allison.

"So," seethed Channing with mingled wrath and chagrin, "you knew of this all along! Now I understand your blasted calm!"

"Yes, Mr. Channing," replied Allison. "And your recapturing me was just a decoy, with which you cooperated very nicely. You see, I had no heart to rob you of your one imaginary moment of success. But that, I am afraid, is all you will have."

"Ha!" laughed Channing with scorn. "Do you actually think you can hurt me with your ridiculous little productions! Jason Channing cares nothing for such trivia! I am the ultimate victor. For I still possess the legendary Stonewycke treasure!"

A look of astonishment passed over both Logan and Allison's faces at the words.

"Ha! ha! ha!" gloated Channing with perverse glee. "Surprised? Ha! ha! That idiot Sprague was worth all I paid him, and more, though the fool was so stupid he couldn't even keep himself alive! You just tell your mother, little Miss Stonewycke, that I have her grandmother's priceless Pict box, and that she'll never lay eyes on it. Ha! ha! ha!"

As Channing spoke, already von Graff was thinking of self-preservation. He had inched his way toward a corner of the room, where a rifle sat propped against a wall.

"Not so fast, Monsieur General!" came a voice from the doorway. They turned to see a German soldier standing with rifle poised on von Graff.

Von Graff squinted in sheer confusion. Not only was the man with the drop on him too old, but he was uncommonly small. Yet the gun in his hands discouraged argument.

"You really ought to get to know your soldiers better," said Logan to von Graff. "Perhaps then you could tell good *Frenchmen* from Boche!"

Von Graff jerked his head around toward the window. Outside, the eight supposed soldiers of the execution squad now held their weapons on the four or five real members of von Graff's S.S. detail. The new prisoners were being prodded toward the guardroom.

"Good work, my dear," said Henri to Allison. "Your elaborate plan appears to have come off with scarcely a hitch."

"Her plan?" repeated an astonished Logan.

"Mais Oui, Michel," said Henri with a twinkle in his eye. "Did you think all the savvy for intrigue in the family was yours? She refused to let us sit still for your imprisonment. "What you once told me is true: "*The Lord has many ways to deliver His people.*"

Logan laughed. "Ah, me fair lass. Ye done yer man prood!"

"Come," said Henri, "it is time to be off!"

Clinging closely to one another, Allison supported Logan's weary frame as they retreated out into the compound. Allison glanced back for one last glimpse of Channing. Unlike the defeated general, Channing's eyes yet glowed with the embers of red-hot fire—sufficient even for a man of seventy to give proof that he would be back again.

As Logan emerged again into the open air, his eyes caught and held those of one of the captive German prisoners. Neumann returned his stare only momentarily, but long enough to say, "I wish you well, L'Escroc Macintyre." And perhaps also in his eyes was the parting request, *Pray for me sometimes, when I am brought to your mind.*

But this meeting of minds lasted only an instant, and then was past. Henri tarried at the guardhouse until the contingent of Germans was locked securely inside with Channing and von Graff. Then he turned and trotted to where Logan and Jean Pierre were enjoying a more thorough and warm reunion.

"It's not much of a story," laughed the priest in response to Logan's wondering inquiries.

"I couldn't believe my ears when I heard your voice!"

"My brother took great pity on me," went on Jean Pierre, "after my injury. So you see, your rescue attempt on the train *was* a success! He interceded on my behalf, and here I am! Perhaps there is hope for him, after all."

"I never dreamed all of us would be together again except in eternity," said Logan.

"I told you we would meet again," laughed Jean Pierre.

"As did Henri," added Logan. He paused and glanced around, suddenly aware that someone was missing.

"Where is Lise?" he asked.

"She realized this was not her moment, Michel," said Henri. "But she asked me to tell you that she wishes you Godspeed."

"Tell her the same when you see her, Henri. Tell her I will pray for her. And give her my thanks."

"I will, mon ami," said the bookseller. "Now . . . let us be off! That"— he cocked his head toward the locked guardroom—"won't hold them for long."

They ran toward the van they intended to use. Henri paused long enough to spray a round of bullets into the tires of the staff car and the other van.

Then the group of a dozen resistors scrambled into the remaining van. Henri slipped in behind the wheel, ground the vehicle into gear, spun it around, and sped through the gates.

Logan sat back against the jarring wall of the careening vehicle. His body was ready to collapse from the onrush of unexpected events, yet despite the fatigue, his mind remained keen.

"The telephone," he said all at once, not knowing who other than Allison at his side could even hear him above the engine. "We should have cut the line to the guardroom."

"Rotten oversight!" said Henri from the front. "And we are headed right past the main prison. They're sure to be waiting for us."

He slammed his foot on the brake in order to negotiate a u-turn and head in the opposite direction.

"Wait!" cried Logan. "Keep going! The last thing they'll expect is for us to drive right past their backyard. They'll figure us to be going south, away from the city, not back past the prison!"

Henri laughed as he pressed his foot back on the accelerator. "L'Escroc lives!" he cried. "We will dare it! Right past Fresnes!"

"We must breed a new L'Escroc to take your place," said Jean Pierre.

"Monsieur L'Oiselet was not doing so bad a job before L'Escroc came," said Logan. "And I have a feeling he will continue long after L'Escroc is but a passing memory."

In another five minutes the prison came into view. Almost immediately the speeding van encountered several German vehicles roaring past them, all storming westward to Montrouge.

A great cheer went up inside the van.

"Our ploy will give us but a momentary advantage," cautioned Henri. "We still have two stops to make. They will discover their error and overtake us before we know it."

Before long the van drifted to a stop. The larger part of the group jumped out the back. Logan had not even noticed that they had changed out of their German uniforms, under which they had been wearing their normal French attire. "There's a farmhouse just over that field," explained Henri to Logan. "They'll put our people up and get them safely back to the city."

One by one the men ran around to Logan's side of the vehicle, each shaking his hand warmly. He thanked them all, not without deep emotion. Then within moments they had retreated into the wood and the van pulled onto the road again. It now carried only Henri, Jean Pierre, Allison and Logan.

"Next stop for you two . . . England!" shouted Jean Pierre. "And in case I do not have the opportunity to say it later," he added, "God's blessings be upon you! I will think of you often, and when I do, be assured that prayers of grateful remembrance will pass my lips!"

"Oh, Jean Pierre," said Allison, "thank you! Thank you for helping take care of my Logan all this time. And you too, dear Henri! Thank you both so much for delivering him back safely to me! I will never forget you, dear friends!"

"Where are we going?" asked Logan.

"To an airstrip," answered Allison before either of the Frenchmen could respond. "Actually, Henri says it's hardly more than a smooth meadow."

"But where? I never knew about any airstrip out here."

"It's rough, mon ami," said Henri. "But all we could manage. It's about thirty kilometers from here."

"A plane is waiting for us," added Allison.

Logan smiled.

"So, Mother Hen came through, after all!"

He glanced over at Allison. "You are really something!" he said. "How did you manage all this? Is it true, what Henri said back there, that this was *your* plan?" His pride was evident even as he asked the question.

"I didn't do much really," she answered. "I just kept prodding, and trying to figure something out, and asking Henri and Lise questions, until finally the whole thing started to unfold. Jean Pierre's release was a big help, too!"

"Do not let her fool you, Michel," put in Henri. "She lived up to every inch of your reputation!"

"I'm only sorry you had to stay behind bars so long! But we had to wait till word reached us they were moving you."

"Are you kidding? It was worth every gray hair it may have caused to see von Graff's and Channing's faces! What a grand story it will make to tell your mother!"

"There was just one moment, when the guns went off, when for an instant I wondered if everything *had* come off. Those men firing the guns looked *so* German! I wasn't sure our plan had succeeded until I saw you in the doorway. You were so brave—though I never doubted you would be."

" 'Twas naethin', me lass!" grinned Logan, then closed his eyes and let his head rest on Allison's shoulder. "I'm just glad to be alive—and with the woman I love."

They drove on in relative silence for about ten or fifteen more minutes, Henri keeping to a conservative speed so as not to attract unwanted attention. Suddenly he groaned.

"I think we have company," he said. From the rearview mirror he saw four vehicles bearing down upon them from behind, including what looked like a Gestapo staff car. They were about half a mile back.

"Hang on!" he cried, and pressed the accelerator to the floor. The van surged forward.

Gradually he lengthened the distance between them. Ahead lay the meadow.

"Here we go!" said Henri. "Grab whatever you can!"

He turned the steering wheel and the van careened off the pavement, smashing through a rickety wooden fence, and hardly slackening speed as they flew over the grass toward where the Lysander sat in the middle of the field, looking incongruous amidst stacks of hay from last year's harvest.

The pilot saw them coming, realized they were being chased, and ignited his engines. The propellers of the small plane whirred into motion.

A barrage of shots pinged off the sides of the van.

The distance was still too great for the bullets to hurt them unless they happened to hit either a window or a tire. The retiring bookseller at the wheel did not falter but kept his nerves steady as the van bounced and crashed over the uneven ground.

"How will you two get away?" shouted Logan. "We can't just leave you here!"

"Not to worry!" replied Jean Pierre. "There's a road we'll catch on the other side of the meadow. All we'll need is a hundred-meter lead. After a bend in the road, we'll jump, the van will crash over a high embankment, and we'll escape through the woods. When the Germans round the corner, all they'll see is the van tumbling down over the side. By the time they've gone down to investigate and find no bodies, we'll be halfway back to Paris. There's a friendly farmhouse only about a kilometer from there through the forest. So you see, it's all been arranged."

Logan looked up. He could hear the Lysander's roaring engines. Henri sped onto the runway, maintaining top speed until the very last moment. Then suddenly he slammed the van to a screeching halt.

In less than an instant he and Jean Pierre were outside and opening the doors to help Logan and Allison out.

Explosive bursts of gunfire sounded behind them.

"Hurry, mates!" yelled the pilot from the small plane. "If we take one of them slugs in the tank, we're all goners!"

"Come with us!" said Logan.

"We can still be of use here," said Henri.

"Look at him!" laughed Jean Pierre. "We couldn't drag L'Oiselet out of France!"

In the distance, the German cars were wheeling recklessly across the meadow toward them. Out of every window leaned soldiers firing wildly.

"Go, dear friends!" said Henri.

"You too!" replied Logan. "Drive like the wind, Henri! I want to see you two after the war!"

Logan took several more seconds to throw his arms first around the bookseller, then around the priest—companions and friends he would never forget. With tears in her eyes, Allison gave them each a hurried hug.

Then, leaning on Allison for support, and hobbling as rapidly as Logan was able, they raced to the plane, while Henri and Jean Pierre scrambled back into the black van.

Hands reached down from the fuselage door, grabbed hold of Logan's shoulders to hoist him inside. The plane was already moving when Allison jumped onto the small stairway and climbed up. The pilot closed the doors and thrust forward the controls and the plane taxied across the meadow.

Behind them sharp reports of gunfire vainly tried to stop the takeoff, but already the Lysander had picked up speed and was nearly out of range.

Logan pulled himself up to a window just as he felt the plane lift off the ground. Already the van with Henri and Jean Pierre was speeding toward the opposite side of the field and into a wood. The German cars had stopped momentarily, with soldiers pouring out to draw better aim on the ascending British plane.

Then Logan saw two figures emerge from the staff car.

He could not see the expressions on the faces of the general and the businessman as they watched their precious quarry wing out of firing range. But he could well imagine their fury and bitter dismay.

Then just as suddenly as they had stopped, the four vehicles filled again, and sped off across the meadow.

Logan slumped back in his seat, realizing all at once how weary he was. Gently Allison took his hand.

He glanced toward her, smiled, and let out a long breath. She too exhaled a long sigh of relief, as if to say, "Whew . . . we made it!"

"We'll soon be home, Logan," she said after a few moments.

"Home to Stonewycke," he murmured drowsily. "I can hardly believe it." He closed his eyes, and with visions of the beloved estate floating dreamily in his mind, he was soon fast asleep.

Atkinson wore a particularly smug look on his face—almost an expression of fatherly pride.

But it was I, thought Kramer with his own vain grin plastered firmly on his countenance, *who saw Macintyre's potential right from the beginning*. Though he had to admit, if only for honesty's sake, that it was the major who had stuck up for Macintyre when the cards were down.

Not that he wouldn't have himself, of course. But someone had to play the devil's advocate.

Thus Kramer had wrangled the privilege of joining Atkinson to receive their Captain Logan Macintyre who had arrived from France a week ago. He had spent the ensuing days in a hospital recuperating from his brutal torture by the Nazis, but was now fit enough to be debriefed and to consider a lengthy leave.

"This is the best part of the job," commented Atkinson.

"Seeing one of your chicks safely home, eh, Mother Hen?"

"Exactly!" smiled the major. Then his eye grew momentarily introspective. "It doesn't happen often enough," he mused. "I pray they will all be coming home soon."

"It won't be long, what with the way our boys are beating the tar out of those Nazis now!"

"I wish I could be as optimistic as you," said Atkinson. "But I think the Nazis have a few more tricks up their sleeve yet. I think we're looking at years rather than months, Arnie."

Kramer's eyes gleamed and he leaned forward. "How would you like to put some money on that, Ray?"

Before Atkinson could respond, a knock at the door interrupted them.

Logan did look fit. At least better than he had a week ago when he had climbed out of the Lysander, taking his first step on British soil in over a year. As Logan now stood framed in the doorway, Atkinson suddenly realized it was the first time he had seen Macintyre in uniform. It made him look quite different. And though he wore the uniform of his country with a glow of pride, it looked rather incongruous on him.

But Atkinson could see that the changes in Logan went deeper than a mere uniform. He no longer wore that look of defensiveness about him. Whatever else had happened in France, there was no doubt in the major's view that Logan Macintyre had found himself.

"Good morning, Captain Macintyre."

"Good morning, sir," replied Logan, shaking Atkinson's extended hand, then turning to Kramer. "And to you also, Major Kramer."

Kramer stepped buoyantly up to Logan.

"Forget that *Major* business!" He grabbed Logan's hand and shook it vigorously, while slapping Logan's shoulder with his free hand. "We're all proud of you, Logan!"

Atkinson picked up a small box from his desk and held it out.

"This is for you, son."

Logan opened the box and gazed down on the sparkling George Cross inside. He was too surprised, and humbled, to speak.

"You earned it, Logan," said Atkinson.

"Thank you, sir," replied Logan. Atkinson's words meant as much as the medal itself.

"It's all got to be kept unofficial for now," added Atkinson. "Security and all that, you know."

"But after the war," put in Kramer, "you'll be a hero of Britain. Of France, too, for that matter!" Then a coy grin erupted on his broad face. "Why, you'd probably be able to win a seat in Parliament!"

Logan smiled at the outrageous idea.

"All I want to do now is go home and live a normal life for a while."

"You shall have that, my boy," said Atkinson.

"But the war isn't over yet," said Kramer. "We can still use you."

Logan knew the demands of war would continue to be felt for some time. Yet at the same time, the mere thought of returning to the kind of existence he had led in France made him cringe.

Atkinson noted the faint shadow that had passed momentarily across Logan's face. "I do have something in mind for you," he said. "*After* a long time of recuperation. It's an extremely vital job in the intelligence effort, and one which I think you'll be perfectly suited for with your first-hand experience. Of course it would be up to you. I think you've earned some say in your next assignment."

"What did you have in mind, sir?"

"We desperately need instructors in our training program, Logan, and I think you'd have a great deal to offer the chaps just starting out. What do you say?"

Logan grinned, both relieved and honored.

"Thank you, sir," he said. "I gladly accept the offer."

Notwithstanding Arnie's crestfallen face, they all shook hands warmly before Logan set about making his report of his time in France.

When he left an hour later, it was with a sense that his sacrifices over the last year, the emotional and physical pain he had undergone, had not been wasted. He had served his country, if not with great distinction, yet with integrity and virtue. He knew at last he could stand with pride alongside his Stonewycke ancestor, old Digory MacNab.

Never had the somber gray walls of Stonewycke, with snow now piled up against them, seemed more like home to Logan as they did that Christmas of 1942. How good it was to be back! He knew now—in a deeper way than ever—what it meant to be part of something greater than himself—a cause, a family, a faith. He knew they were worth the sacrifice of commitment, the surrendering of his whole self.

He stood by the crackling blaze in the hearth of the family room, watching as Allison strung the last bit of tinsel on the tree.

It was a somber holiday season. There had been great suffering and deep griefs. Alec was still in Africa. Ian had managed to obtain a furlough, but would not be home until the first week in January. May's presence—home from her studies in the States to announce her engagement to a young American law student—added a spark of gaiety to the festivities. Yet the joy pervading the small gathering at Stonewycke that Christmas Eve could not help but be of a rather quiet kind.

Logan saw the contrast most visibly on Allison's face. The outward show of Christmas happiness could not keep an occasional tear from trickling down her cheek. He walked over and placed an arm around her waist. Despite the trembling of her lips, she smiled up at him.

"She always used to grab at the tinsel," she said, "because it was so sparkling and pretty."

"I suppose this time of year will always be the most difficult." Logan knew she spoke of their daughter.

"Last year, in London, it was just the two of us, you were gone. It was such a sad, bleak time. But we decorated the tree, and . . . oh, Logan, if only I'd known it would be our last Christmas together!" Allison stifled a sob.

Logan gently stroked her hair while holding her tenderly.

"I have thought often of the gospel story and of Mary since then," Allison finally went on. "The moment her son was born was a time of joy mixed with sorrows too. Losing our daughter has helped me understand maybe a little of what she felt in her heart. What does it say in *Luke*? 'Yea, a sword shall pierce through thy own soul also.' She knew the true meaning of bittersweet joy. I am so happy that you are alive, Logan, and that we are at last together. Yet I cannot help feeling sad also."

"I know," said Logan gently. "There is something about Christmas that always brings out the extremes of feeling, the happiness that *is*, the memories of what *was*."

"Will it always be so?"

"Right now our wounds are still raw and tender. But one day, Ali, we will be able to lift up each precious memory of our dear little Joanna, and those visions of her will be to us the pure joy that God intended. God doesn't mind a little sorrow for a season. But we mustn't allow our grief to force us to abandon those memories."

"It's just so hard, especially when I remember her smiling, happy face."

"I know, dear," replied Logan. "But you have to remember, we do not live in this world only. She *is* alive. God has chosen us for a great honor. For those who have lost a son or daughter can feel, in ways we cannot know except through such loss, part of the enormity of what God did in allowing *His* Son to die. Even in our sadness, and in your mother's grief over Nat, we are able to partake in the divine grief of the universe—the shedding of God's blood for the sins of mankind. It is a privilege to know that kind of heartache, and then be able to give it up to His care."

"You're right, Logan. Where did you get such wisdom?"

Logan laughed lightly. "I don't know. I guess sorrow has a way of forcing people into greater understanding of things they can't see when life is perfectly smooth. I don't think God is as concerned with giving happy endings to our lives as He is forcing us into greater depths of laying down of self. For of course, that's where true joy originates—not from surface happiness, but from giving ourselves up to Him. I suppose if there's anything I've learned from this past year, it's that. *Begun* to learn, I should say! I'm still such an infant, Allison, in trying to see from a new perspective."

"Oh, Logan, I *am* thankful for what God is doing in our lives. But the growth can be so painful."

"It usually is. Progress never comes without a struggle."

"And I am thankful for *you*, Logan!"

At that moment Joanna came in carrying a tray of refreshments.

"I made some wassail for us to toast the season," she said, setting the tray on a table and pouring portions of the punch into four glasses.

"Where's May?" asked Logan.

"In the kitchen putting the finishing touches on some scones. She'll be here in a minute."

While they were waiting, Joanna walked toward the large window and stood looking out into the black night. Behind her the warm fire crackled cheerily, oblivious to the stormy winter night outside. Tiny white flakes of powdery snow swirled and danced against the darkened pane, collecting against the bottom corners of the windows. When she turned back toward the others, her face wore the same mixture of emotion Allison and Logan had been feeling.

"You know," she said softly, "I haven't felt much of a holiday spirit this year. It's not been an easy time for any of us, these last months. But just now, as I was thinking, I remembered my first meal in this place. I suppose the fire reminded me of it, though it was in the old banquet hall. That was the day I first knew that Dorey was my grandfather."

Joanna paused, and sighed deeply. Clearly the memory was filled with feelings of many kinds.

"Poor Dorey and Maggie were separated for over forty years," Joanna went on. "Our heartaches can't begin to compare with theirs. Yet look what kind of people they became in the end! Who wouldn't want to radiate love like they each did? Yet the price is high. Suffering is often the price we have to pay for true joy . . . true compassion. They paid the price, and their characters reflected the result. I want God to do that kind of work in my heart too, yet I resist and complain just to be separated from my dear husband for a year or two. Yes, I've lost a son, yet not really lost him—only given him back to God for a while."

She stopped. Allison went to her.

"Oh, Mother," she said, "you seem so strong to us. When I think of Lady Margaret's faith, I think immediately of you, too."

"Thank you, dear," said Joanna, wiping a solitary tear from her eye. "You are a daughter to be proud of.—God, help us all to give ourselves to your work in our hearts!" The mother and daughter embraced warmly, while Logan silently looked on, his own tears rising.

All at once the door leading toward the kitchen burst open.

In walked May, a bright smile on her spunky twenty-year-old face. "The scones are ready!" she announced as she bore the wooden tray to the table. "Complete with fresh butter from the Cunningham farm, churned today, and the berry jam Mrs. Galbreath sent up from town!"

"Ah, May!" said Logan, "how glad we three are that you could come home to join us! What would Christmas be without scones . . . and at least one carefree face among us? Right, ladies?" he added, with a grin toward Allison and Joanna.

They laughed.

"Come," said Joanna, "it is time to remember what the season is about."

They each took their glasses and lifted them toward one another.

"To those," said Logan, "whom we love who cannot be with us."

"May the Lord bless them, one and all," added May, "and give them peace."

"Help us to remember them in prayer," said Allison.

"And," added Joanna, "may the new year see us together again! Thank you, Lord, for the birth of your Son!"

The new year was not to bring the kind of reunion Joanna had hoped for. The war was to rage on for nearly three more years.

There were, however, major Allied advances throughout 1943. By mid year the Allies controlled the Mediterranean and most of the major sea routes. Alec was able to spend a week in Scotland during the summer before being sent to a new assignment. Ian, now twenty-five, had to continue to postpone his university studies.

In September, Italy surrendered unconditionally, and in the following year, June of 1944, the long-awaited invasion of Europe finally took place. Many of Logan's trainees played a vital role in preparing the way for the advance of troops which followed the landing. On August 24 the first Allies reached Paris, and the next day Charles de Gaulle drove through the city in an open car, to the wild cheering of thousands of Parisians. In the months that followed a million arrests were made in France of Nazi collaborators, with tens of thousands of summary executions. It would be many years before real peace would be restored to the torn nation.

The "thousand year Reich" finally collapsed in May of 1945, with Japan capitulating a few months later in the wake of the world's first nuclear explosion on a massive scale.

Thus the glories of victory continued to be mingled with the ongoing horrors of war. But the millions of returning soldiers did not need newspaper accounts of the destruction of Hiroshima to remind them that the world was forever changed. They were changed men. Some were emotionally destroyed, some had allowed the experience to broaden them. Relationships had been forged which would never be forgotten. War had caused both strengths and weaknesses to surface. Most had grown, all had changed, and they well knew that the world they now faced was changed, too.

In Britain, the old ways, long slowly fading, were now all but gone. Though she had, almost single-handedly, kept back facism from taking over Europe in 1940, Britain would never again be the economic and military powerhouse she had been in the pre-war years. New alignments of power would soon emerge, which would change the political and military landscape of the twentieth century forever.

The post-war years would bring these new times, with their accompanying stresses, to the northern Scottish estate of Stonewycke as well. Though the soldiers returned, they did not bring with them a return to the world of the 1920's. A new era had dawned.

A stiff sea breeze bent the purple heads of heather.

The sky shone blue and vivid, the air felt crisp and clean. The fishermen predicted a storm to blow in tomorrow, but today the shore and hills and fields were bright and welcome. The world was at peace.

Alec had arrived home the day before. For good! He had spent the evening getting reacquainted with his family and swapping tales with Logan. Now this morning one of the first things he had wanted to do was get out for a long walk with Joanna.

So today they would delight in the sunshine. And if the storm did come, they would enjoy it also. They were together again at their bonny Scottish home; a few drops of rain could not dampen their joy.

Alec clasped Joanna's hand tightly as they crested the final hill on their way back to the ancient family home. Both waking and sleeping, during those long, lonely years in the desert and on other assignments, this very picture had dominated his dreams—his dear wife, the glorious hills of purple, the gray stone walls. He had held on to his loves of family and wife and home and country with such a passion that they were able to sustain him, though it sometimes seemed he could not bear to wake to the grim smell of heat and sand and battle.

"We'll have to cancel our picnic tomorrow if it rains," said Joanna, slightly out of breath after the climb.

"They're sayin' 'twill be a braw storm," Alec replied, glancing toward the sea.

"Why, Alec MacNeil!" laughed Joanna, "I do believe you're actually looking forward to it!"

He laughed with her. "After the Sahara, ye'll ne'er catch me complainin' aboot a wee drap o' rain again!"

They paused to take in the view. The Strathy Valley spread out in lovely panorama before them. Though the summer was just past, like most of Scotland it remained a lush green, accented by the gently waving fields of golden grain, ripening for the soon-coming harvest. The little town of Port Strathy lay about two miles distant at the ocean's edge, from which the shoreline spread out, curving slowly toward the jutting point of land in the hazy distance.

"I never tire of coming here," said Joanna wistfully. "Just seeing the land, the valley, the little farms . . . it keeps me aware of our heritage. I don't know exactly, but something in me doesn't ever want to forget the past, the roots, those who came before. The legacy they left us is too important to let slip away as new generations come along."

"Which is why ye're so devoted t' that journal o' yers," said Alec. "Ye probably added three or four hundred pages since I left fer the war."

Joanna laughed. "Not quite that much, dear! But those long, lonely nights around here did give me plenty of time to work on it. I finished writing about my coming to Scotland, and meeting you, and all that happened then. Now I'm in the midst of trying to put everything Lady Margaret told me through the years into some kind of order. I'm rewriting her childhood from all the stories she gave me."

"And ye still hae t' tell aboot Dorey's comin', an' their sad partin'."

"Yes, not to mention all the years since, and the new generations. Our Ian's at Oxford now. May's engaged to her lawyer and planning to live in America. And Nat, now with the Lord, has left a legacy in the gentle spirit that will always be part of the ongoing heritage of the family. And Allison! Remember when I was so worried about her?"

"Aye, do I!"

"Her struggles before and during the war have caused such a growth and maturing in her. I see her really coming of age as the next heiress of Maggie's legacy. How could I have ever doubted the Lord's power to work in her life? And of course, who could forget her Logan!"

"Who indeed! What a blessed character o' the Lord's creation! I think he'll always hae that foxy twinkle in his eye!"

"Oh, Alec, we *are* fortunate! God has been so good to us! And what stories there are still to tell about this family and this estate!"

"But tell me noo honestly, do ye think anyone's gaein' t' read all ye're writin' besides yer lovin' husband?"

"Oh, Alec," exclaimed Joanna, "it hardly matters! Some stories just have to be told. Even if nobody reads them, they're still important . . . to me! But of course, I'm writing it for the children . . . and their children— for future generations, so that they'll remember the legacy of their ancestors. We mustn't forget our roots, Alec!"

"An' speakin' o' oor children an' their husbands, an' the stories they hae t' tell, look who's comin' yon across the way."

The warm breeze bringing the scent of ocean spray to the land had also beckoned to Allison and Logan; they had taken their way on horseback in the opposite direction from Allison's parents. They had ridden south, across the desolate heath known as Braenock Ridge, down into the valley, through several meadows to the bank of the Lindow, then back across the valley, down through the ravine separating it from Stonewycke, up the other side, and were now walking their two horses across a wide moor toward the little summit on which Alec and Joanna stood observing them. Allison held both reins, listening to Logan who, as he walked, read from a letter received only that morning from Henri.

> . . . life is so changed, mon ami, from the dark days of the Nazis. Our nation remains in much turmoil, but I have faith that what was always good in France has not been destroyed by the war and will emerge again. As for me, I am happy. My dear wife and children are with me once more, people are once again starting to think about reading, and as they do they are buying books. L'Escroc and L'Oiselet will now live only in memory. But rest assured, Logan, whom I will always think of as *Michel*, that my fondest memories of the war are of those times spent with you. As for the others, Antoine returned unharmed to France, Jean Pierre is still . . . well, he is still himself! Always with a cause, with people to help. Now *he* is trying to keep his brother from death because of his assistance to the Nazis! How the fortunes of time change the political landscape! Lise has gone to Israel. A new cause has ignited her passion, and now her dedication is bent on helping the many Jews released from concentration camps—including her sister—find new hope in Israel. I had a letter from her only last week. I can tell she is, if not yet quite *content*, at least happy for now. Claude I have lost track of. The last I was able to find out, he was in some difficulty with the authorities, some problem with the Russians, I believe. And you, my dear Michel—my apologies again! I must be growing old, I forget so quickly! —I almost forgot to congratulate you on your receiving of the *Croix de Guerre*. Now two medals, one from each country! You are indeed a hero of France, as I said you would be! . . . God be with you, mon ami!

Logan sighed deeply.

"You loved them, didn't you?" said Allison softly.

He nodded. "I guess I would have to say I didn't feel a great affection for Claude," he replied reflectively. "Yet even with him there was, I don't know, another kind of bond, even in the midst of the conflict. You don't go through a war with people, putting your life on the line for them, without attachments forming that will always be with you."

"I knew them only for days," returned Allison. "But I can almost feel a little of it with you."

"But that was then," said Logan. "Now it is time to look to the future . . . to our life truly *together* at last."

"Logan." Allison looked up at him after a moment, her eyes filled with gratefulness. "Thank you for not deserting me. I hardly gave you much of myself. I hope I now know better."

"It is *I* who owe *you* thanks! I was so blind, Allison, so caught up in my own self. I'm so thankful you stuck by me."

"Marriage is such a precious, yet fragile thing," Allison mused. "God has been good to us, Logan. We could have thrown away all we had if He hadn't somehow managed to get through to us."

Logan took his horse's rein, then slipped his arm around Allison's shoulder. Together they walked on up the hill.

"Ho, Alec . . . Joanna!" called out Logan as they approached; "watching for the storm coming in?"

"We'll hae nae talk o' storms today, laddie!" said Alec, reaching out his hand and giving Logan's a vigorous shake. "The wee wifie here winna hae me spoilin' tomorrow's plans wi' talk o' rain. Aye, but it's good to see ye, man! Ye're lookin' as well in the sunlight as ye did last night!"

"And you, Alec! The war hasn't changed you at all."

"Ah, ye should ken better than that!" replied Alec. "Ye may be a smooth talkin' enough city man t' beguile my daughter. But ye canna lie to a cagey auld vet like me! Why, man, jist one look at all this gray on top o' my head'll tell ye I'm no the same man I was in '40! Why, I turned sixty last year, and didna e'en hae me wife wi' me t' feel sorry fer me!"

Logan threw his head back and laughed heartily.

"One thing that hasn't changed is your sense of humor! And you know what the Bible says about gray—it is the sign of wisdom and honor."

"Amen to that!" laughed Joanna.

Silence fell for a moment as each of the four gazed upon the scene spread out before them. There they stood for several minutes more, the one couple arm-in-arm representing the generational link to the roots of the past, the other—holding hands as if still newly in love, as indeed they were—the symbol of the generations of the future.

Then, as if with one accord, they turned and began to make their way together down the hill, toward the ancient family home known as Stonewycke.

Epilogue / London, 1969 _____

When the Honorable Logan Macintyre exited Number Ten Downing Street that chill spring morning, he had every reason to be in good spirits. A pat on the back from the Prime Minister was no small thing.

However, though he wouldn't refuse the praise, he knew that yesterday's session of the Commons merely represented the result of his doing his job as Minister of Economic Affairs. Morton Giddings represented a block of votes Labour needed, and Logan had simply steered them in the right direction.

"Only last week," the Prime Minister had said, unable to keep from gloating, "Giddings said he'd never go our way."

"I suppose a great deal can happen in a week," Logan replied modestly.

"Not with Giddings! He's the biggest diehard we have."

Prime Minister Wilson leaned forward and winked. "Come now, tell me—how did you pull it off, old boy?"

"You really don't want to know, Harold."

"You know I'll find out sooner or later. Surely you of all people didn't pull something shady, did you, Logan?" The Prime Minister grinned conspiratorially.

"It was completely on the up-and-up, I assure you!"

"Never doubted you for a minute—all you need to do is turn on that Scottish charm of yours, do a little song-and-dance with that silver tongue you were endowed with, and things always seem to happen."

He paused. "But I have a feeling it took more than that with Giddings," he added at length.

"Well," Logan answered after another moment's hesitation, "you know how Giddings is constantly bragging about his prowess at cribbage. . . ?"

"Indeed!" exclaimed Wilson with a knowing look. "He bores everyone to distraction and has cleaned out more than a few new boys—"

Suddenly he stopped as realization dawned on him.

"Logan, you *didn't*!"

Logan smiled sheepishly.

"You played for his votes?" pressed the Prime Minister.

Logan nodded.

Wilson laughed outright. "You rascal," he said through his mirth. "And he wasn't aware of your—ah, how shall I phrase it?—your *expertise* with a deck of cards?"

"It's a matter of public record, isn't it? But you know I haven't gambled for years. Gave it up after the war. This was just an innocent game of cribbage."

Wilson continued to chuckle. "Giddings was never very good at doing his homework. I must say this is one of the most ingenious ways you've ever thought of—and you've had some gems!—to cajole your colleagues into voting your way on something you believed in. Come, old boy, this calls for a bit of a celebration."

Yes, Logan was satisfied with himself, and satisfied too with the path his life had followed since the war. Parliamentary wheeling and dealing was a most fulfilling use both of the talents God had given him and his personality, which enjoyed people and activity—especially when worthwhile causes lay in the balance. He had found his place in life during the past twenty years, and in it had gained the respect of his peers—as a man, a statesman, a humanitarian, and a Christian. Those who knew him, as well as those who knew *of* him, saw clearly a man who gave himself for others, not only out of Christian duty—though he was an outspoken national figure for the practical living out of the Christian faith—but also out of plain ethics and morality as a human being. He was a man who honored goodness and desired to see it operating between men—for the sake of goodness itself, and for the sake of God. Yet, being in the national spotlight had in no way dimmed the twinkle in his eye nor the love of an old-fashioned good time. There were still moments when he thought about a reckless scheme—for a worthwhile enterprise, of course!—just in memory of the good old days!

Logan was about to hail a cab, but then decided the day was too beautiful to waste. Besides, it was only a short walk to his office. He pressed down his hat against a gust of wind that persisted in spite of the sunny blue sky. He neared a newspaper vendor and dug a coin from his pocket and tossed it to the boy, who caught it deftly.

"Mornin', Mr. Macintyre!" said the lad above the din of traffic. " 'Ere's yer paper."

"Thanks, Joe."

"An' don't ferget yer change, sir."

"Not a bit of it, Joe!"

"Thank 'ee kindly, sir!" said Joe, grinning at the tip. "An' by-the-by, me mum ain't soon goin' t' ferget what you did fer me in that business with the constable last week. An' neither am I."

The youth had run afoul of the law for supposed possession of marijuana. When Logan, who had been buying *The Times* from him for two years, heard of it, he took the matter in hand, interceded on the boy's behalf, and eventually discovered that Joe had been mistaken for a vendor a couple blocks away whose newsstand was being used for small-time drug deals.

Logan had expected no thanks, however. It was the most natural thing for him to do. He well remembered what it was like for a boy trying to live on the streets.

"Well," Joe continued, "she—me mum, that is—she wanted to invite ye t' dinner, but I said as how an important man like yersel'—"

"I'd love to come!" interrupted Logan. "You know my office number—you just call me and let me know when."

"I sure will, Mr. Macintyre! Me mum'll be pleased pink when I tells her!"

Logan tucked the folded newspaper under his arm and continued on. In another ten minutes he reached his office. His secretary, Agnes Stillwell, middle-aged, efficient, and devoted, greeted him warmly.

"You've several messages here, Mr. Macintyre."

She picked up a pad and followed him into his private office.

"James Callaghan in the Home office called and wants to meet with you before this afternoon's session," she began.

"Fine. Go ahead and set up a time with him. Anything else?"

She briskly flipped a page of her pad. "Your wife called to remind you about your dinner guests from Aberdeen tonight. And Alexander Hart of the BBC wanted to know if Monday would be convenient for the interview—"

"Oh, I forgot all about that! How does Monday look?"

"I think we can clear the afternoon."

Logan grinned. "I'd be lost without you, Aggie!"

It was difficult for Mrs. Stillwell to continue to look efficient while beaming under her boss's praise, but somehow she managed.

"And then there's this last message from a Hannah Whitley," she added, straightening her glasses self-consciously.

"Hannah Whitley . . ." Logan repeated thoughtfully. "Who's she?"

"I don't know, sir. She had a most down-to-earth sound . . . almost like a domestic or something. I can't imagine what she wanted."

"I don't think I've ever heard the name," said Logan. "What was the message?"

"Rather odd, really," Mrs. Stillwell replied. "She said she needed to speak with you and wanted to know when you would be in. I asked her to leave her number and said you would return her call if she wished. She seemed reluctant, but finally consented. Here's the number."

"Doesn't sound too odd," remarked Logan, taking the slip of paper his secretary handed him.

"I suppose it was mostly in her tone."

"Well, let's see." Logan pulled his phone across the desk toward him, glanced at the paper, and dialed the number. After a silent pause, he hung up. "Now that *is* odd," he said. "The number is out of service. Didn't she just call?"

"I wonder if I could have copied it down wrong. I'm terribly sorry."

"Impossible, Aggie. But don't worry about it." He carelessly tossed the paper into the "incoming" basket on his desk. "If it's important, I've no doubt the matter will catch up with us another time."